SURRENDER TO PASSION

"Are you sure you want to do this, love?" Dan asked softly.

Her voice was constricted by desire as she replied, "Yes, I want to experience everything with you."

"You will, Rachel, tonight and forever."

Tonight there would be no turning back. They would delve into the magic that enchanted and united them. They would be anchored together in heart and flesh.

Rachel was nervous but Dan was so gentle and stirring that she responded to every kiss and caress, every unspoken promise of what was to come. Suddenly she knew why she had never felt this way before. Love made the difference. She loved Captain Daniel Slade! She could only pray that this special and powerful bond between them was strong enough to survive the secrets that lay ahead . . .

JANELLE TAYLOR

PROMISE ME FOREVER

ZEBRA BOOKS
KENSINGTON PUBLISHING CORP.

ZEBRA BOOKS

are published by

Kensington Publishing Corp.
475 Park Avenue South
New York, NY 10016

First Zebra Books paperback edition: May, 1992

Printed in the United States of America

DEDICATIONS AND ACKNOWLEDGMENTS

To Carin Cohen Ritter, the best editor and adviser an author can have.

To Michael Taylor, the best husband and research assistant an author can have.

To Randall Floyd, who gave me the idea for this "Black Widow" plot from one of his "Southern Mysteries" articles in an Augusta newspaper.

To Sonia V. Migliore de Helfer, professor at Augusta College, for her translations into Spanish.

To Linda Pritchard, who furnished me with many maps of historical Augusta, including an 1875 one with all the names of the original streets, businesses, sites, and residents of that time period.

To the wonderful ladies in the Athens Welcome Center and Athens/Clarke Historical Foundation, who provided me with 1875 data and period maps on Athens, my hometown.

To the ever-patient and helpful staffs of the Augusta–Richmond County Library and Evans/Gibbs Library for research assistance on all settings and topics used. My adopted towns of residence.

To the nice ladies in the Savannah Welcome Center, the staffs of historical sites, and friendly residents of the lovely and gracious Savannah—one of my favorite Old South towns.

To my Readers, with hopes you won't think mistakes are made when I use the original names and locations of streets, sites, monuments, etc. All of these are accurate for 1875 in Athens, Augusta, and Savannah. I would also like to remind a few worried readers that characters' unfavorable opinions of certain people and places do not reflect those of this author.

Chapter 1

"You sure it's legal to buries Mr. Phillip in secret, Miss Rachel? Mercy, this be the third husband you done laid to rest in less than three years. All that nasty tawk about you is bound to start all over again."

"It can't be helped, Lula Mae," Rachel informed the housekeeper. "I don't want trouble with the law or for more gossip to start and delay me before I can get away to take care of important business. This happened so fast. I need time to think and plan. You and Burke will have to keep silent until I figure out how to report this."

"You going to sells them gun and bullets cumpnies, soaz you'll have money to leaves here afore the law comes chasing you again? What abouts that shipping cumpny here?"

"I'm not going to get rid of any of them right now; I can't, but I need to check over the two out-of-town companies immediately. I'll tell Phillip's three partners he's away on business. I doubt they'll become suspicious for a while. Later, I want to sell everything and leave Savannah. I can't breathe anymore without creating gossip and dangerous suspicions."

"How you gonna hide this under the covers that long?"

"If my claim he's out of town doesn't work, I don't know yet. But I'll find a way; I must!"

Lula Mae clucked her tongue like a mother hen. "I kin jest hears them mean tongues wagging 'bout the Black Widder and her new prey. My bones are aquivering in fear. This time, Miss Rachel, they'll arrest you for sure, even if they don't find nary proof you be guilty."

"I'll check the house from bottom to top to make sure there isn't any proof I caused Phillip's death. The law didn't find any evidence against me the other times, and they won't find any this time. But before I get tangled up in another investigation, I need answers to some big questions. I have to go to Augusta and Athens to see George and Harry."

"What questions you need be answered, Miss Rachel?"

"Nothing for you to worry about, my dear friend. When I get things settled, I'm gone from Savannah, probably from Georgia. Of course you'll come with me, Lula Mae; I couldn't do without you." Rachel released a long, heavy sigh. She was so weary and scared. "The law has tried its damnedest to get me for three murders; I know how this fourth death will look to them and to the townfolk. This time they'll be determined to slam a prison door behind me. I can't make any mistakes, Lula Mae, so I'm going to handle this slowly and carefully."

Lula Mae patted the young woman's shoulder. "You was too smarts for 'em those other times."

"That isn't how I would describe it, but clever wits help when you're under attack. For certain, the minute this news is out, Earl Starger will be slithering around like the snake he is. That man could really harm me. He's the one who needs killing. If he doesn't leave me alone, I might oblige him," Rachel murmured, too exhausted and dazed to be aware of how what she was saying might sound to another person. She needed to get away from here so she could think clearly and make plans. She prayed for her husband's troubled soul and for herself. "Good-bye, Phillip. If you'd been more careful, this wouldn't have happened. It was too soon for you to die."

"Spring's the most awfullest time to go adying."

"No time is any better or worse than another, Lula Mae," she responded, though the spring of 1875 looked as if it was going to be the hardest time of her life, if she survived it. "I'll get back to the house. Burke will finish up here. He sent Jim and Henry on errands so they wouldn't be involved in this. I don't want them getting scared and making a slip to someone. Burke will make certain this grave isn't noticeable."

"Come along, Miss Rachel; I always takes good care of you after these things happen. You jest git weak as a kitten fresh from its ma when it's over. Let's git you in the house to rest up a spell whilst I tend my chores."

Rachel Anne Fleming Barlow Newman McCandless followed the trusted housekeeper to the lovely Georgian house. At twenty-one, Rachel was alone again. She envisioned what loomed ahead. The Savannah authorities would be all over her and their home as soon as she released this shocking news. She would tell the truth, but would she be believed, when even *she* suspected there was more to Phillip's sudden and painful death than the cholera she was blaming? She recalled his last words, the strange and frightening mutterings only she had heard. The smartest and safest thing for her to do was investigate what Phillip had told her before she went to the law.

At the front steps of the slate-blue wooden house with its rust-red trim, Rachel halted and instructed: "When Burke finishes with the burial, Lula Mae, bring him to me."

* * *

None of the three people saw the man who watched their actions and listened to their words. The tall, black-haired figure remained concealed behind a large live oak. His blue eyes, as dark and stormy as a violent ocean, exposed the mixture of anguish and fury he was experiencing. What Dan had learned about this sinister woman since docking last night and what he had just witnessed raced through his mind as he formed a grim opinion of his brother's wife. No, he corrected in bitterness, his brother's widow.

When he and his first mate had visited a local tavern late last night, Dan hadn't revealed who he was to the chatty bartender, a man who delighted in talking about the notorious and beautiful woman Phillip McCandless had married. He and his best friend had pretended they were sailors who were seeking work on Phillip's ships and wanted to know everything about him before signing on with his Savannah firm. They had acted intrigued and appreciative.

Dan squeezed some facts from all the enlightening rumors: at eighteen, Rachel Fleming had come to town and wed a rich older man; a month later Barlow's son died from a suspicious fall; two months later, her first husband was dead under curious circumstances. The police had investigated her as the cause of both deaths, but couldn't prove the men had been murdered. Gossip had begun, and the townspeople started calling her the Black Widow. She had waited only two months before preying on a rich but young man, then buried him in four months, a result of another dubious fall. That incident had evoked a second investigation—a longer and more persistent one—and had induced more gossip. Still, the authorities failed to find enough evidence to even arrest her.

Following her second husband's death, a local newspaper had carried a front-page article headlined "Beautiful Black Widow: She Mates and She Kills!" To protect itself from a lawsuit, it hadn't used names or dates and had called the story a "fiction"; but everyone had known it referred to Rachel, and had believed it, including the bartender. The insidious vixen had then been cautious enough to sit in her golden web for a year before stalking her next victim. She had entangled his brother, who was dead now after spending eight months in her silky arms. Her motive for burying Phillip secretly escaped him, for she couldn't claim her inheritance until she reported his death. All of her victims had been wealthy, and she was the only heir each time. Or so she believed. No one—including a desperate Phillip—knew for certain that Dan was still alive.

Dan wanted to storm the house to drag the treacherous female to the law. Yet something halted him from taking swift and rash action. This clever female had gotten away with killing two previous husbands and, if he didn't handle this matter with cunning, she might get away with Phillip's death. He couldn't permit that outrage.

The hazy contents of Phillip's last letter haunted him; it had been an urgent cry for help that had reached Dan too late. But he would see that justice was done. The information Rachel sought in Augusta and Athens must hold clues to her motives. Before he exposed this vixen's foul deed, he wanted those answers, too, as evidence. He would return to town, take care of his cargo, seek more information about her, then come back later to meet his sister-in-law to study her for himself. This time, that little predator would pay, with or without the law's help. . . .

"You sure we should burn all the eveedence, Miss Rachel?" the housekeeper asked. "How you gonna prove your story then?"

Rachel glanced at Lula Mae and Burke. All three people were dressed in old clothes and gloves to prevent contact with the items they must handle. If they were contaminated with cholera as Phillip's symptoms suggested, the disease could be spread by touch. "It has to be done for our protection, Lula Mae. I want everything Phillip touched last night and this morning burned or sterilized."

"I opened every winder, but it won't be doing much good until we git rid of this mess." Lula Mae looked at the rumpled bed with its stained and smelly covers.

"Mr. Phillip shore wuz pow'ful sick las' night," Burke remarked. "Ah'll see too it dese covers are burned good. We don't wants no mo sickness here."

Rachel met the black plantation manager's woeful gaze and replied, "Yes he was, Burke. Maybe a doctor could have saved him. I feel guilty about how he suffered and the attention he needed and never received."

"No, ma'am, he wuz too far gown down the heaven road, Miz Rachel. A man cain't be called back onest he's awalkin' it with angels. Folk 'round here gonna be pow'ful scared whenst they hears 'bout dis sickness."

"That's why I want it handled quickly and quietly, Burke. We don't want to create a panic. If only I'd known Phillip was ill last night, I would have done something for him."

"No, ma'am, Miz Rachel. If'n you been in here whilst the fever wuz on him, you'd be ailin' or be dead this mawnin' yerself. Twernt nuttin' you could do."

She knew Burke Wells was right, but it hurt nonetheless. When she had come to him early this morning, Phillip had appeared still drunk. The room had smelled horrible. She had opened the curtains, lifted a window for light and fresh air, then gone to check him. Phillip had rubbed an aching belly as he mumbled wild and crazy things in a desperate rush to warn her about some imminent peril. Then he had seemed to lapse into unconsciousness. She had felt his brow to

12

find him cold, not burning with the fever she'd expected, and his skin had looked withered in the faint dawn light. She had lit the lamp nearby to examine him closer. His drawn face had been a strange color and his pulse had been so weak she could barely find it. Before Rachel could summon Lula Mae to fetch a doctor, Phillip had roused for a short time, mumbled more dire warnings, then died while she stood there helpless and in shock.

Rachel eyed the bedside table where several whiskey bottles lay on their sides. "From the number of bottles he emptied, he was terribly thirsty," she remarked. "Even drunk and ashamed, he should have called to me. He wanted to be left alone, so I obeyed. I shouldn't have, because it was so unlike him to have behaved that way. I don't know why he did this to himself. We have to burn these garments and gloves and scrub our bodies. We can't risk spreading this disease or catching it."

"Yessum, Miz Rachel, Ah un'erstan," Burke agreed.

"I'll starts water boiling and warsh them dishes. You wants me to throw out the food left over? It might be gone to the bad."

"I don't think tainted food was Phillip's problem, Lula Mae, as you and I haven't become ill after eating the same things, but, yes, do it just to be safe."

"When me 'n' Mr. Phillip went fishin' day afore yesterday, I seed him drinkin' dirty water from dat river 'hind us. I tol' him black water wuz bad."

Rachel knew cholera was said to come from eating contaminated food or from drinking contaminated water, but she didn't think the contents of the Ogeechee River, which ran along the western boundary of the property, was the cause of Phillip's death. "Many people drink and fish from the river, Burke. If there was a problem with its water, we would have heard

13

about it. But it wouldn't hurt to mention that to the law."

"It's gonna be most awful when they comes."

"I know, but I'll have to report it soon. Phillip's gone, so it won't matter if I wait a while before putting myself through another investigation. He insisted the business is urgent, so I'll take care of that first. It's certain the law won't allow me to leave afterward."

"Dat law shouldn't be so bad to you, Miz Rachel."

"We know I didn't do anything wrong, Burke, but they won't see it that way. You can bet your life they'll give me trouble."

"You have witnesses dis time, Miz Rachel. Dey cain't hurt you."

"They'll only think you two are lying to protect me."

Burke Wells looked offended that anyone would dare question his word and honor. His dark eyes sparkled with anger and his fingers stroked his black mustache. "Deys bedder not go amessin' with me 'n' mah friends."

"Thank you, Burke, but I don't want you or Lula Mae getting into any trouble because of me. Just tell the truth, then it's up to them to believe us or not." She smiled as the strapping man mumbled under his breath about setting the law straight if they fooled with him and his loved ones.

Rachel and Burke stripped the linens from the bed, removed the feather mattress and pillows, and carried them outside to a clearing. They hauled several wash tubs there, then filled them from the well near the house so they would be prepared to battle any blaze that might sneak its way from the safe area. The black man tossed lantern oil on the pile and lit it. The empty whiskey bottles were broken and tossed into the roaring flames; later they would be buried after the fire killed any disease on them.

While the linens and bedding were being consumed

14

and dark smoke rose skyward, Rachel asked, "Burke, did Phillip give you anything to hide for him in the last month or so?"

"No, ma'am, Miz Rachel, why'd you akst me dat?"

She trusted and liked the manager and housekeeper, but she didn't want to draw either of them into this mystery. She offered a logical explanation, "Sometimes Phillip didn't want to worry me about business problems, but if there are any and he's hidden papers about them, I need to know, and now!"

"No, ma'am, Mr. Phillip didn't gimme nuttin' to hide for him."

Rachel sighed in disappointment, which Burke mistook as exhaustion.

"Why don' you git in the house and res', Miz Rachel? Ah kin tend dis fire. Ah'll holler if'n Ah needs help. You looks pow'ful tired."

The blaze was under control, so the new widow thanked him and went to the house.

Lula Mae had opened all windows in the guest room and kept the door closed to prevent the stench from wafting through the rest of the two-story house. When Rachel joined her upstairs to help with the repulsive but necessary task, Lula Mae had finished her kitchen chores and had begun to mop up splatters. Any area Phillip might have touched where a smidgen of the dreaded disease might have been left behind had to be cleansed.

Rachel looked at the woman who was working so hard. "I'm sorry you have to help with this mess," she said. "I can do it, if you mind."

"I reckon I cleaned up worse messes in my life. When Mr. William or his son was sick, they ruint many a cover and floor. When I'm done, I'll toss these rags on the burnin' heap and bury this bad water. Won't be no sickness left in this house when I'm finished. The air's better a'ready."

As Rachel went to work with hot soapy water on

the bed's woodwork, she murmured, "Why did this have to happen to me, Lula Mae? I'm not a bad person."

"A body hasta takes what the Lord keeps on his or her head. Don't let on it don't hurt bad. A good cry never did a body no harm."

Rachel halted to look at the woman whose stern-looking features made many think she was mean and cold. Today, concern and affection for Rachel seemed to soften them. Rachel knew Lula Mae to be one of the kindest people alive. The woman's words and her own thoughts stirred up memories.

As Rachel scoured the bedside table for smeared fingerprints and drops of whiskey that had escaped the fallen bottles, she murmured, "I wish I could keep his death a secret forever and not go through all that again, but I can't sell any of Phillip's holdings without exposing his death. How can I just walk away and leave everything that is rightfully mine? How can I start over somewhere else without funds?" And if she tried to flee, what all would happen to her if those faceless and nameless "enemies" tracked her down?

"I hate to see more trouble coming up the road," the woman said, "but do what needs doing. I'll stand by you."

She smiled. "You always have, Lula Mae, and I'm grateful."

Rachel slipped into deep thought as they continued their work. For some inexplicable reason, her kind and gentle husband had gotten heavily inebriated following a visit from Harrison Clements, his business partner in Athens. She didn't know what had transpired between the two men, but it had sent Phillip McCandless over the edge of a dark precipice. She wondered what Phillip's strange mumblings meant. In slurred speech, he had talked about her life and all she owned being in danger, about enemies who could get to her anywhere and any time and who would stop at nothing to get what they wanted, and about her selling everything to repay a debt she didn't know existed as it was the only way for her to stay alive and safe. What was the mysterious deal that she must honor, and where was the money she must return to its owner? And why was it hidden? She knew it had to do with guns and ammunition, with strange phrases like "you can't go to the law," and "you'll be blamed."

She didn't want to be blamed for whatever was involved. She remembered the terrible incidents—"all those warnings came"—over the last weeks to which he must have been referring. She had assumed they were unrelated crimes: the ship that was burned and sank, the warehouse that was vandalized, the two seamen who were beaten, and the dockworker who was slain. "Don't double cross Harry and . . . ." Scary words from him.

What if Harry did something wicked to Phillip last night? Rachel wondered in fear. *If it shows, I'll be blamed, not him. The law would never believe me over him.*

Whatever was going on, it was real and dangerous, as one worker was already dead. She couldn't go to the authorities with a wild mystery and become entangled in it. If she didn't solve it herself, she could be in even worse trouble than from a third investigation of husband killing and "Black Widow" gossip.

"That's all, Miss Rachel," Lula Mae announced. "I'll takes these rags and burn 'em. You git washed up and rest a spell. Supper'll be ready on time."

Rachel started to ask Lula Mae if the clues meant anything to her, but changed her mind. Some things were too personal or dangerous to confide in friends or employees.

Rachel didn't know any other woman who had lost three husbands, not even as a result of the war with the North. Yes, she reasoned, cholera did run its lethal course in a matter of hours to a few days, and death resulted from massive and swift loss of body fluids. But arsenic had the same effect as the symptoms Phillip had displayed. She knew about diseases and poisons, because she had lived on a plantation nearly all of her life where accidents and illness were commonplace and where items with deadly ingredients were used—both facts the law and townfolk knew, and had tried to use against her when William died.

Rachel glanced around the spotless room. Phillip was gone, forever. She couldn't believe it, even though she had helped wrap his body in clean sheets and hauled it to the site where Burke had dug a secret grave. She felt guilty over not washing and dressing him for a proper interment, but none of them had wanted to touch anything that might be infected by the cholera. Phillip didn't even lie in a coffin; his grave wasn't marked and he hadn't been given a service. None of that could be helped, she told herself, then closed the door to keep from looking into the room again.

Rachel's mind was in turmoil as she bathed and dressed. She had not wept over her husband's death because she was so angry with him. She was afraid of what loomed before her because of both his loss and the mystery he had mentioned for the first time on his deathbed. Phillip had been the one man she felt she could trust, the man who had taken away her wariness of all men; now, her faith in him was shaken. He had deceived her, endangered her, and deserted her. Yes, she fretted, she had a right to be angry and bitter.

As Rachel brushed her dark-brown hair, her thoughts returned to the path that had brought her to this point in her life. She had not had good luck with men. From the day the lecherous Earl Starger had entered her life, most had proven themselves untrustworthy and selfish.

Rachel dismissed Earl from mind. Maybe, she

speculated, the war had brought forth the animal instinct in men: survival at any cost and take anything you desire to prove you're the strongest. She wasn't certain what had happened to men, but she knew her father and brothers and male friends had not been this way years ago. Some day in the far future when all of this was years behind her, hopefully she would find—

Rachel's thoughts were interrupted by a knock at her door. She opened it. Lula Mae stood there, looking hesitant. "Is something wrong?" Rachel asked.

"You have cumpny. It's a man, a stranger, who wants to see Mr. Phillip. You wants me to send him away?"

Rachel released an annoyed sigh. She didn't want to be disturbed tonight, or have to begin her false tale on this horrible day before her mind cleared. "A stranger?" She repeated Lula Mae's words.

"Yes. He says he has important business with Mr. Phillip."

"Business?" She came to alert and her heart drummed in trepidation.

"Yes, Miss Rachel. What must I do?"

She witnessed the housekeeper's worried look. "Tell him I'll be down shortly. We don't want anyone getting suspicious. I'll speak with him."

"Should I serve coffee or spirits?"

Southern hospitality was expected, so she said, "Coffee will be fine."

The older woman nodded and left.

Rachel checked her appearance in the mirror. She summoned her wits and courage, then went to face her first challenge since Phillip's death. As she walked along the lengthy hallway toward the stranger, she saw that Lula Mae had left him standing in the entry hall, no doubt with hopes of her mistress sending him on his way fast. Rachel noticed how his size and presence seemed to fill the doorway and how they pulled one's full attention to him.

She halted her approach with a few steps left between them to prevent having to strain her neck to look into his face. Her gaze met his as she said, "I'm Rachel McCandless, Phillip's wife. How may I help you, sir?"

Dan had met beautiful women before, but this one possessed even more allure than he had noticed from a distance this morning. He wondered why she had chosen Phillip as her third victim. Surely there were plenty of men in town with more wealth. To begin his own ruse, he extended his hand and said, "My name is Captain Daniel Slade, Mrs. McCandless. I'm here to see Phillip. Will he be down shortly?"

Rachel accepted his strong hand and shook it, noticing how he stared at her. She forced a polite smile to her lips and replied in a serene tone, "I'm sorry, Captain Slade, but my husband is out of town. I don't expect his return for many weeks. May I be of service? I take care of business matters whenever he's away."

Dan feigned surprise and displeasure. "I don't understand. Phillip was expecting me. Is he in Athens or Augusta? May I join him there?"

Rachel tensed, but kept control of her expression and voice. "I'm afraid not. He's in Baltimore to check on several new investments. I don't anticipate his return until the end of April or middle of May."

To dupe her, Dan gave a heavy sigh and frowned. "That's too long to wait. Where can I reach him? My business is pressing."

Her anxiety mounted in fear of this handsome stranger causing trouble for her before she could leave home. Yet she retained her poise, a skill she had learned over the years when people were cruel to her. "I'm afraid I can't help you there, either. Phillip said he'd be moving around and he'd contact me, but he hasn't done so yet. What is the problem? Perhaps I can handle it, or tell you who can help solve the matter."

Dan watched and listened for clues to her personality and character. She seemed at ease, as if she were telling the truth. Nothing in her mood, expression, speech, or manner exposed her as a new widow—his brother's widow and Phillip's murderess. He put aside his grief to carry out his task. "The business is between me and Phillip. He offered an old friend a good deal on an arms and ammunition contract. I wrote him of my acceptance and arrival date. I don't understand why he left, knowing of my imminent arrival. My ship docked tonight, and I came straight here with the money."

Rachel glanced at a large carpetbag on the floor. "Money? For a weapons and ammunition deal?" Suspicion filled her.

Dan perceived a curious reaction to his false claim, but it seemed a logical fabrication. He thought fear and panic had registered in those odd-colored eyes before she hurriedly composed herself. Her response was strange and unexpected. He nodded as his reply.

"Why don't we sit while we talk?" she invited, motioning toward the formal parlor. She needed time to think and to recover her wits. As they entered the spacious room, she indicated for him to be seated on a floral sofa and she took the matching chair across from it. The positions allowed her to study him while conversing. "Special orders usually go through Harry in Athens, not through Phillip here. What was it for, a custom-made weapon and special-size ammunition?" she questioned, even though she had caught that the mentioned items were plural.

To make the alleged deal sound important, Dan corrected, "No, for three thousand rifles and enough ammunition for each one to last for months of fighting. There's a conflict raging in the Mediterranean area, and I agreed to buy and deliver needed arms."

21

Rachel decided she must lead him on to learn all she could about him and his curious business. "Isn't such a deal illegal?" she asked.

Dan looked surprised, then grinned. "Stars, no. The Americans are assisting the battle against Turkey, though not publicly, of course. Guns and ammunition are needed badly there. I'm a private shipper who will deliver them for a tidy profit. Phillip said he could arrange the order for me. Why would you think your husband would become involved in something illegal?"

Rachel eyed him intently as Phillip's warnings about "war, freedom, and need guns badly" echoed through her mind. But there were contradictions: the money "must return" and "hidden" did not match with the captain bringing along his payment, and "Cuba" was a long way from Turkey. Contradictions, yes, if Daniel Slade was telling the truth. "I didn't say I thought Phillip would do anything illegal," she said, "But it isn't past evil and greedy men to lie and cheat or kill to get what they want. Are you sure the shipment will go into the hands of the right side?"

Dan was cognizant of her quick intelligence. "Since I'll be delivering them into American hands, I presume so, unless our country is wrong to interfere. I don't get involved in politics, local or foreign. But I do try to sail on the right side of the law." He grinned again. "Of course, some things are never what they appear. I'll head to Augusta and Athens. Maybe his partners know about our arrangement and have my order ready for transportation to Savannah. Harrison Clements in Athens, isn't it?"

Rachel smiled and thanked Lula Mae as the housekeeper served the coffee. Both added sugar to their cups, but neither took milk. She waited until Lula Mae returned to the kitchen before continuing the conversation.

The use of Harry's name instead of George's or

22

that of both men seized her interest. A daring plan came to mind. "Yes, it is. If you can wait until Monday morning, Captain Slade, I'll be leaving by train for both companies. Phillip asked me to take care of business there during his absence. Please feel free to come along with me. I want to learn if Harry knows about this curious deal of yours that Phillip didn't mention to me, and I also want to make certain it isn't detrimental to our firm. I wouldn't want Phillip misused by an 'old and trusted friend.' "

"Don't worry, Mrs. McCandless; I would never do anything to harm Phillip or his businesses. And I wouldn't do anything, even for a lot of money, to get myself thrown into a boiling sea of trouble. I'd be delighted to ride along with you. I appreciate the assistance, and the lovely company. Phillip is a lucky man to have a wife with such beauty, charm, and wits."

"Did you know my husband well?" she asked, unaware she used the past tense, as Captain Daniel Slade was distracting and disarming. She sipped the sweetened black coffee as she observed her guest.

Dan caught Rachel's slip, but didn't point it out. As he summoned the best response, he sipped his coffee to conceal the slowness of an answer. Her appeal was potentially dangerous. Her unblemished skin was an olive gold, her features small and perfect. She looked delicate and angelic, though he knew she wasn't. Her brows and lashes were the deepest shade of brown before it became black, as were the silky cascading waves of her hair that flowed over her shoulders. Her eyes were a fusion of pale yellowy brown with just a hint of grayish green, encased by a dark-brown band. She was clad in a simple day dress in a hue of grayish green that almost enticed her hypnotic eyes to reflect the color of it, but fell short of victory. Her gaze possessed strange power and magic. He was astounded and vexed she could sit there so serene and poised after what she had done today. She seemed the perfect reflection of a genteel lady! He placed an empty cup on the table and replied, "A long time ago, Phillip and I knew each other well and were very close. I'm looking forward to seeing him again. We'll have plenty to talk about."

"You were close friends?" she probed after witnessing a curious look of affection and fond remembrance in his seawater-blue gaze.

Dan assumed she would be less doubtful of him if she believed they were close friends, not just business acquaintances. "Yes, years ago in Charleston. That's where we're both from. You knew that, didn't you?" he inquired to test her knowledge of Phillip's past.

"I knew Phillip was from Charleston, but he didn't talk much about his life there. With his family dead, it seemed to pain him too much to speak of the past. But I'm surprised he never mentioned such a close friend."

Dan again caught her use of the past tense. "I left Charleston in '71," he said truthfully, "and haven't seen him since. He contacted me through the mail. He seemed eager to make our deal. It must have been something urgent and unexpected to call him away like this."

Both were silent as Rachel rose to refill Dan's cup. She added two spoons of sugar as she'd seen him do earlier, then she replaced the silver pot on the matching tray, took her seat, and straightened her skirt. She retrieved her cup and sipped her coffee, as if waiting for him to go on.

As she served him, Dan concluded she didn't know anything about him, which was logical since Phillip had been told he was long dead. Fortunately, she couldn't cull anything from their appearances, as Phillip had favored their father and he favored their mother. His parents . . . But that was his tormented past. Right now, he had to deal with a painful present.

24

He had to use every skill he possessed to weave a web of his own around this lethal beauty. She would never get away with murdering his brother.

Rachel observed Dan as he drank his coffee and seemed to slip into the past. She noted the conflicting array of emotions that flickered in his stormy blue eyes. She perceived an aura of mystery, a hint of tragedy, and troubling secrets in his personal life. It was easy to recognize those feelings which matched hers. She was baffled by how such a strong male could feel, and suffer, so deeply. It drew her to him, despite her previous warning to stay wary of this potent stranger, this possible enemy. Perhaps she was too tired and distressed to think clearly.

She reflected on Phillip's dying words: "He'll come soon and help me." Dan could be an old and trusted friend. If not, he might offer clues to the perilous mystery. In hopes of making light of the strained moment and contradictory emotions tugging at her, Rachel remarked in a skeptical tone, "I don't recall any correspondence to or from you, Captain Slade. If you and Phillip were so close and he was looking forward to your visit and to renewing your old friendship, why didn't he mention you to me?"

"Call me Dan, please. We'll be traveling together soon, and I hope we will also become good friends. As for Phillip's . . . secrecy, if that's what it was, I can't explain it. Knowing him, he probably wanted us to meet before he related past tales of our. . . . " He paused intentionally, chuckled, then finished, "Our devilish misadventures. We grew up together, so we have a long and colorful past."

Rachel wished she could relax her stiff guard and strained nerves. Her emotions advised her not to suspect this charming man of evil and treachery. Since Phillip *was* in the arms business, it was natural to have more than one deal in the works. Daniel Slade's arrival and contract must be coincidental. Yet her survival instincts warned her to stay alert and wary in case she was misjudging him and being duped. It wouldn't be the first time a man had fooled her.

"Something I said annoy you, Mrs. McCandless?" he asked when she frowned, then looked angry.

Rachel calmed herself again and smiled. "No, my mind just drifted for a moment. To an unpleasant topic, I fear. Pardon my lapse in manners. It's been a diffi—" She halted and flushed. *Don't relax, Rachel.* "It's always strange if Phillip's away and business problems arise. I'm nervous about making a wrong and costly mistake."

Dan saw how her eyes and smile could cause a man to forget all else if he weren't careful. But there was an aura of wariness around her that kept him on guard. "I can't imagine a smart woman like you ever making a mistake. If you weren't married to an old and dear friend, I'd be tempted to . . ." He let his words trail off suggestively, then put on an expression of near embarrassment. "I'm sorry, Rachel, . . ." He switched to use of her first name in a husky tone meant to ensnare her interest. Women had told him he was handsome and charming. He had never used his appeal as weapons before today, but he must do and use any ploy necessary to entrap his brother's killer. Rachel Fleming had an abundance of similar traits and she had used them in sinister ways. "Pardon my lapse in manners, too. It's not that I've been at sea too long or don't have self-control where friends' possessions are concerned, but you're the most beautiful woman I've met and I . . . behaved badly for a moment. It won't happen again, so please don't be nervous around me."

As he smiled, Rachel saw bright white teeth amid a darkly tanned face with handsome features. His wide smile seemed to make his face glow and his dark-blue eyes sparkle with boyish mischief. There was a power, a magic, an energy that permeated the air around

26

him. His movements were fluid and effortless. He had manners, excellent breeding, and education. He was masculine and self-assured, but not arrogant—not that she had detected so far, at least.

She had buried her third husband this morning, so how could a stranger have such a stirring effect on her this soon? Because Phillip's death seemed unreal, her mind answered, and because this sea captain stole nearly all her sense of reality. *Be wary of him, Rachel.* "You're forgiven, Captain Slade, and thank you for the compliment. I can tell you're a southern gentleman, so I'm not worried about spending time with you." After he encouraged her to call him Dan again, she asked, "When did you arrive? And where are you staying?"

It took Dan a few moments to respond, as he was lost in the swirling depths of her eyes. They seemed to possess the power to penetrate his very flesh. If only she were genuine . . . But she wasn't. It riled him to realize how looking into that exquisite face made him feel warm and tingly. If he didn't know better, he couldn't imagine this vital creature as a cold-blooded murderess.

Dan lazed against the back of the sofa and lied. "I just docked and came straight here." He motioned to the carpetbag. "I brought along my things because Phillip invited me to stay with him. Since he's gone, I'll return to my cabin on the ship and wait there until we leave."

Rachel needed privacy to search for clues and that hidden money. Since he had docked tonight and was a stranger, hopefully he wouldn't hear the malicious rumors this weekend and form a false opinion of her. "I'm sure Phillip would expect me to extend our hospitality to his old friend, but I don't think it's proper for you to stay here with him gone. Gossip can be a vicious and destructive thing. We can meet after breakfast on Monday at the Central depot on Broad

27

Street, about eight-thirty. Buy a ticket to Augusta. After we finish there, we can continue on to Athens."

"That's perfect. Thank you, Rachel, for your help. I'll leave my first mate in charge of my ship and crew. I'll see you at the train station. I don't think we should mention our trip together to anyone," Dan suggested as he stood to leave. "As you said, we don't want to inspire naughty gossip. Phillip would never forgive even a good friend for sullying his wife's name. We'll talk again on the train."

Rachel liked that precaution. She smiled. "Thank you, Dan. I appreciate your kindness and understanding. I'll see you to the door."

Dan lifted his bag and followed her. He felt her eyes on him as he mounted a rented horse and rode into the encompassing darkness. He turned to see her close the door, then he halted. *He* would never fall prey to her powerful charms, but it was easy to understand how she had woven her webs and lured her victims into them before they realized what was happening.

Don't worry, Phillip; she won't get away with killing you, Dan vowed silently. *Damn you, Black Fate, for not getting me here in time to save my brother's life! I needed to see you, big brother; it was too long. Now you and Father are both gone before the past could be settled. He died hating me and mistrusting me, but you, Phillip, desperately sent for me in your hour of need. I failed you again, and I'm sorry.*

He dismounted, deep in thought. *I never wanted to be involved with lies and tricks again; they're too damn expensive. But I'll carry off my ruse, even if I have to lure that little enchantress into marriage myself to expose her. No matter how long it takes, I'll complete this task before I return to the sea. I swear that on your grave, Phillip, and you know I always keep my word.*

Dan glanced toward the area of large live oaks where his brother lay without a coffin and denied a headstone and burial service. The patches of visible

28

soil were a dull grayish brown. Spanish moss hung from the massive trees and appeared a ghostly gray in the light of a full moon. Shadows danced on the ground as a breeze stirred the "old man's beards" and silent spring leaves. The croaking of frogs reminded him there was a river, the Ogeechee, not far away where murky water flowed between banks where tree roots were exposed and swampy vegetation and moss-laden cypress grew. He heard crickets singing and caught the lonely calls of an unknown bird in search of something in the night.

The heavy-hearted man looked toward the direction of the river, westward from the house. That was how he had sneaked up on the secret burial this morning. He had rented a horse from a town livery, ridden to his brother's property, then dismounted before reaching the house. He had secured the animal's reins to a bush, then walked near the river as he moved closer to the lovely setting. He had wanted to slip up to the house without notice, to surprise Phillip, to be able to see the first expression on his brother's face at close range. Instead, he had spotted a husky black man, a plain older white woman, and a breathtaking young creature hauling a sheet-wrapped body toward an area of dense trees, then lowering it into the earth beside a freshly dug mound of sandy dirt. He had frozen in midstep, concealed himself, and spied on them.

He hadn't noticed anyone but those three around, and his heart had begun to pound. He had slipped from large tree to large tree without being discovered. But he had heard them, heard enough to pain his heart and infuriate his mind and demand vengeance.

When he docked in Charleston a few days earlier, he learned his father was dead, and his brother had moved to Savannah and was in deep trouble. "I may be killed if I don't do what they want," he had written to Dan.

They? Why didn't you put more facts in your hazy letter, Phillip? If I don't keep your death a secret for now, I'll never learn the truth. I have to know why and how you died. Hear me, big brother, I'll do it or die trying.

A chill crept over Dan's flesh at that intimidating thought. He stared at the lovely house and shook his head. *No, my little beauty, you won't murder me, too. I'll be camped nearby and watching every move you make until we leave. Take one false step tonight or tomorrow, and I'll get you for sure.*

Chapter 2

"That's all for tonight, Lula Mae," Rachel said. "Thank you for everything you've done today. Get to bed and rest. I'm sure you're as exhausted as I am."

"I knows you be bad off, Miss Rachel, but you forget your troubles and sleeps tight now. I left you a biscuit with fried ham in the server. You didn't eat enough for a biddy. If you needs anything, you holler for me."

"I will, but don't worry about me. I'll be fine."

"What did that stranger wants with Mr. Phillip?"

Rachel refused to draw the loyal woman into her troubles. "Just business. I handled it and sent him away. It's all right."

The older woman looked as if she wanted to press for more information, but she merely bid her mistress good night and left the room.

Rachel followed her to the back door. She watched the housekeeper move across the raised walkway to another matching structure that held the kitchen in the front and Lula Mae's quarters to the rear. On either side was a set of steps. To the left, a cobblestone path headed to the privy; at one point, it took a turn to the smokehouse, and at another veered off around the smaller building to the back gate. To the right, another walkway led to the well beneath a conical roof and separated to continue to a garden gate in one direction and to the wash shed in the other. Beyond the wooden fence to the rear of the home were a carriage house, stable, and corral. All structures were painted in slate blue with rust-red trim to form a picturesque sight.

Rachel closed the door and leaned against it. The Georgian house was lovely and comfortable. The hall where she stood traveled the width of the house, but a striking archway separated the span into two entry areas. All the interior doors, windows, moldings, panels, and fireplaces were painted a slate blue. The plaster walls were tinted off-white, and the floors were shiny brown wood with small rugs in strategic spots. The entire decor of the house was meant to evoke feelings of happiness, security, and beauty. But Rachel felt none of those things tonight.

She doused the lamps, returned to the back entry, and climbed the steps. As she went down the hallway toward the front of the house, she didn't even glance at the other rooms before she entered the bedroom she had shared with Phillip. She shut the door, needing to seal herself in a private and protective setting. So far from town and on a large plantation, she had never worried about peeping eyes and unwelcome intrusions during the night, so she didn't draw the drapes. She removed her garments and slipped on a nightgown.

As she brushed her long tresses, she looked into the mirror above her dressing table. The gown had been a gift from Phillip on her twenty-first birthday last February. She had laughed and told him the bloodred provocatively cut garment in Chinese silk was shameful and risqué, but it was the most comfortable one she owned. It clung to her body as if made to her measurements, and the material felt sensuous—almost delightfully wicked—against her olive-toned flesh. Phillip had loved it, and had paid a hefty price to get it. Maybe that was why she wanted to wear it tonight, to make her think of happier times and tender moments. She didn't want to remember him in the same light in which she recalled Craig Newman, but his betrayal caused those feelings to assail her nonetheless. Phillip had made her feel loved, trusted, and safe; so why had he deceived her in the end?

The bedroom suddenly felt stuffy, almost suffocating; she needed fresh air. Rachel entered the hallway and walked onto the wide porch which ran the full length of the house and matched the one below it. She leaned against a sturdy corner post.

Rachel stared at the full moon and wished it were bright and warm sunlight shining on her chilled body. The evening was not cold, or even very cool, but strange goosebumps covered her bare arms and raced along her body. She had the eerie sensation of being watched, but sighted no one in the shadows beyond the fence-enclosed yard. She told herself she was being foolish, that it was the events of today that had her on edge. Still, unable to shake the uncomfortable feeling, she returned to her room.

Phillip's belongings were everywhere to remind her of his past existence. Soon she must pack up or give them away, perhaps to Burke Wells and the other two workers. They only had four employees, as they didn't farm the land themselves; they used the sharecropper system.

Rachel had loved this plantation and house, and it had been a good home for her and Philip. But it didn't feel the same after today; it was . . . distant and cold. She felt a stranger in her bedroom, an unwelcome guest. When matters were settled, she must sell Moss Haven and leave. She had no one in Savannah to entice her to remain, as Lula Mae could go with her. She could never return home to White Cloud—the Fleming cotton plantation between Savannah and Augusta. But, she worried, where could she move to and what would she do when this was over? She didn't have answers yet.

Get to bed, she instructed herself silently. *You have a lot to do before you leave town. And you aren't guilty, so don't be forced to live like you are.*

Dan stood in the shadows beyond the house, still staring at the upper porch. He couldn't believe what he had seen—the scantily attired creature in that fiery red, seductive nightgown. He knew he hadn't been seen, but the apprehensive woman had been nervous about something; perhaps she had sensed his powerful gaze as he gawked at her. Yes, *gawked,* he admitted with displeasure. Stars above, she was ravishing in that seductive outfit with near-black hair tumbling around her shoulders! The moonlight had played over her olive skin like a lover's caress. At around five four and probably one hundred ten pounds or so, she was quite slender, but possessed a shapely body that made a man's hands itch to stroke it. Her lips—the full lower one and the heart-shaped upper one—enticed a man to cover them with kisses, and her silky hair urged masculine fingers to bury themselves within its luster. He understood how the other three men had fallen victim to this enchantress.

He had lingered near the house to see if anyone came to call tonight. Did she have a partner in this foul deed as "they" in Phillip's letter had suggested? The only surprise he had received was sighting Rachel McCandless on that porch like a sultry goddess bathed in moonlight. He wiped perspiration from above his lip, smooth after a shave earlier. He licked his dry lips, then took several deep breaths to calm himself. His reaction to her was perilous; he could not for a single minute forget who and what she was! If so, he was as big a fool as her past victims. *Sorry, Phillip.*

* * *

An hour later, Rachel left the bed where she had tossed and turned. Her roaming mind would not let her sleep. If something vital was hidden in the house, she wanted to know *now*. She lit an oil lamp, as a candle would not provide enough light for her task. With Lula Mae sleeping in her quarters and the workers' houses at a far distance, she felt she wouldn't be discovered. She decided to start her exploration downstairs.

She took Phillip's keys from the dresser bowl where he kept them and left the room to enter the combination private sitting room and office to the right of the back hallway. She set down the lamp and unlocked her husband's desk. She searched each drawer and compartment, finding nothing out of the ordinary. After she relocked the desk, she focused on the cozy room, probing the short sofa and two chairs, but her fingers detecting nothing hidden inside them. She looked behind the pictures, but found no concealed holes.

Rachel crossed the hall to check the serving area, a small room adjoining the dining room where dishes, glasses, and utensils were washed and kept. To prevent a fire hazard, the kitchen was in a separate structure. She knew Phillip would not hide something valuable in Lula Mae's domain, so there was no need to check there. Cabinets were above and below the L-shaped counter and the square table in the middle of the floor with its two chairs. Rachel looked inside each one, but as expected, discovered no clues.

She entered the dining room. It was spacious and uncluttered, with a long table, eight chairs, a serving buffet that stood on one carved leg and was mounted to the wall, a linen chest for tablecloths and napkins, a hutch for china and silver, and a few decorative vases and pictures. She looked under and inside each piece and behind all the pictures and the mantel mirror. She examined the edge of the fireplace to conclude the bolection molding had not been tampered with. She examined the plaster walls, wood dado, and chair rail. As far as she could tell, no area looked disturbed since her and Phillip's arrival last August.

Rachel knew she must not skip anything and she entered the formal parlor, noting its beauty and charm as always, and searched the room. She paid close attention to the fireplace where a slate-blue mantel with carved sides and top encased the brickwork. The large painting over the mantel was heavy, but she worked until she could inspect behind it. She sighed in frustration: not one clue found!

Rachel returned to the combination office/sitting room to search the desk once more. Nothing! She closed and locked it, then slammed her palm against the wood, which repaid her blow of frustration with a stinging hand. She winced and rubbed it until the discomfort ceased.

"Where did you hide that money?" she questioned her dead husband in frustration. "You said if I didn't find it, I would be as dead as you are. If the money and that arms deal are so important and dangerous, why didn't you give me better clues to this damn mystery? Why didn't you confide in me about your trouble? Tomorrow I'll search everywhere else. If I don't find anything, I'll search your office Sunday while Milton is in church. If I don't find anything there, either, I hope to heaven I learn something from George or Harry about what's going on. Someone must hold the key to this mystery! Oh, Phillip, why did you leave me in such a terrible mess?"

Rachel took the lamp and went to her room upstairs. She doused the flame and climbed into bed. She was restless and tense, but soon, her exhausted body and troubled mind let her sleep.

Dan saw the light go out in her room. She had gone to bed, a second time. He knew for sure that there was more to this situation than what he'd witnessed. Now he understood her reaction to his mentions of money and an arms deal.

Unable to sleep himself, he had watched the house after Rachel had left the upstairs porch. She had not remained in bed more than an hour before starting a search of the downstairs. The house had several windows in each room to provide plenty of light and fresh air, so he had gone from one to another as he observed her curious behavior. At last, thanks to the two-inch opening of the bottom sash, her angered words had told him what she was searching for and why she was so upset.

Dan tried to reason out the clues to this painful riddle, but he didn't have enough of them to form a clear picture. He grasped why her trip out of town was so urgent. But why had Phillip warned her about danger before his death?

"Why don't you rests today whilst I gits the warshing done?"

"That sounds good to me, Lula Mae," Rachel replied, as it offered her the seclusion she needed to continue her search. She watched the housekeeper lift the clothes basket and go to the shed near the well. The arrangement was perfect for doing the laundry, even during the winter, because coastal Georgia had such short and mild ones. Although there was a water closet upstairs, bathing was also easier to do in the shed.

Rachel went upstairs. She looked through everything in the bedroom, including a thorough examination of the fireplace. She searched the guest room where Phillip had spent his last night alive. The water closet and sewing room were next, but still the truth eluded her grasp.

Rachel sat down in a rocker in the room where she and Lula Mae did their sewing. It was supposed to be a nursery, when and if that time had come, which it hadn't. She didn't know if she had failed to become pregnant with Phillip's child because they hadn't made love but a few times or if it was the result of her difficult pregnancy with Craig's child and the subsequent miscarriage. The doctor who attended her had said she might either have trouble getting pregnant or might never be able to again. Phillip had known that possibility; it had dismayed him, but he had accepted it. Rachel did not think she could ever accept never having a baby. One day she wanted to have safety, happiness, true love, a real marriage, and that would include children.

She decided to go to the attic, before Lula Mae finished outside, but that use of time and energy were as fruitless as the rest of her search.

Lula Mae came inside to tell her mistress she would be in the kitchen working, as she needed the wood stove to heat the irons. Two were needed, one would get hot while the other was cooling during use, and they were exchanged as necessary. Her first loads had dried quickly in the fresh air and sunshine, and she wanted to finish the laundry today.

"I'm going for a walk to clear my head and to loosen my body," Rachel said. "I'll return soon and help you put everything away." She left by the back door, went down the steps to the left, and followed the cobblestone walkway toward the carriage house.

At the back gate, she glanced toward the vegetable garden where Burke and his two helpers were working. They should be busy for hours, so she wouldn't be disturbed during her task.

Rachel entered the structure that was painted and trimmed to match the house. A comfortable carriage, built by a local craftsman in town, sat cleaned and polished and ready for use, as Burke always took pride in and care with his chores. She glanced at the harnesses on the wall pegs, an extra wheel leaning against one side, and the repair tools on a workbench under which a stool rested. She looked through the chest where blankets were kept to cover legs during chilly or cold weather. Nothing!

Rachel strolled to the barn. Earlier, Burke had turned the horses and milk cow into the pasture to graze, drink, and exercise. She checked the stable and hay loft. Another futile search. After careful study, she decided nothing could be concealed in the small privy or wash shed and smokehouse where she and Lula Mae visited frequently. That left nothing else to examine, except the shipping office in town tomorrow.

Rachel was a skilled horsewoman, so she didn't use the carriage or have Burke drive her into Savannah Sunday morning. Whatever happened to her, she didn't want Burke or Lula Mae involved, and she told the housekeeper and manager of the plantation she was going for a long ride for relaxation. Moss Haven was about fifteen miles southwest of town, but the route was an easy one to travel. For protection she carried a derringer in her drawstring purse. Being in the weapons business, Phillip had given it to her and taught her how to use it.

Savannah . . . Rachel entered the edge of town and thought how much she enjoyed the loveliness of this city. As she walked her mount up Broad Street toward the waterfront, she looked at her surroundings.

She smiled as she recalled how Savannah was often compared to an exquisite woman—one conceived, born, and reared in beauty and charm. Thanks to Sherman's kind heart, her face and body remained unscarred by the vicious war years ago, unlike many other Georgia towns that had not fared as well beneath his crushing boots.

Savannah was desired by South and North, and long ago by British and Colonists. She was graceful, elegant. Built upon a forty-foot bluff and surrounded by marshland, she was situated fifteen miles from the Atlantic Ocean. The waters at her feet carried her name and provided a natural harbor for ships. She was a prosperous and generous creature who shared herself with planters, merchants, factors, bankers, shippers, and numerous other businessmen. She provided them with such goods as tobacco, rice, cotton, lumber, and indigo. Her limbs were adorned with spacious and pretty squares. Around those grids marked out by Oglethorpe in 1733 were beautiful homes whose various architectures—Georgian, Colonial, Greek Revival, Gothic, Regency, Federal, and Italianate—nestled up to one another and were trimmed with lacy ironwork as if a blend of expensive cosmetics adorned her appearance. The sizes and styles of the homes displayed the varying tastes and wealth of their owners. Around them were walled gardens, massive live oaks with lacy drapes of moss, and abundant spring flowers in all colors. Rachel could hardly wait for gardenias, her favorites, to show their lovely white faces this summer.

She preferred the plainer route she was taking over a more picturesque one which would take her past the homes she had shared for such short times with William Barlow and Craig Newman on two of the twenty-four town squares. She passed Central Station where she would catch the train the next morning and guided her horse to Congress Street, past the eighty-foot water tower and the town market near Franklin Square to reach Ellis Square. She rode up Barnard to Bay Street and turned left. She heard the striking of her mount's hooves against the ballast stones used to pave most of Savannah's streets, stones that were brought over on ships to give them weight until they were dumped in port to take on cargo.

Rachel dismounted and secured her reins to a hitching post. She sighted very few people, and none she knew. She glanced down the two blocks separating McCandless & Baldwin Shipping Firm from the custom house that cleared their imports and exports. She looked across the wide street at Factor's Row. She had been there many times with her three husbands. On the river's level, numerous adjoining buildings rose above Yamacraw Bluff. They were connected to the higher ground by iron bridges from the upper floors and by cobbled alleys or circular stairsteps. A retainer wall to hold the sandy bluff intact was made of those same ballast stones, as were the stairways and winding alleys.

Factor's Row was the heart of the cotton industry in this area and to those nearby. The lowest floors of the buildings held cargo to be shipped elsewhere, mainly cotton and other valuable southern crops and items. The upper floors provided offices for cotton brokers and other businessmen. One of the tall buildings on the far end, between Drayton and Abercorn streets, belonged to her husband's company. Since her husband was dead, it was partly hers now. It was used as a warehouse to store incoming and outgoing cargoes on ships owned by McCandless & Baldwin and by other firms. The warehouse that had been vandalized was on this end of Factor's Row.

Rachel glanced down Bay Street. She noticed the telegraph poles and gas lamps that lined it. Many people who lived in town now had gas lamps in their homes. Huge live oaks with their ever-present moss

41

trim were abundant and she heard birds singing, as spring was in bloom and they loved this time of year. In three days, it would be April.

"Stop looking at the sights, Rachel, and get on with what you came to do," she said aloud, warning herself against further dillydallying.

Upon her return from her trip, she must go to see their lawyer, banker, and insurance broker to settle Phillip's will and holdings. But first she would have to visit the location down the street where Police Chief Robert Anderson worked . . .

Despite the warmth of the late March day, shivers raced over her body and chilled her heart. She wouldn't think about that problem now.

Rachel used Phillip's keys to unlock the office door. She was glad church was in progress and that most Savannahians attended, whether it did them any good or not. Rachel scolded herself for that wicked thought, as not everyone in town disliked and ostracized her. Yet the ones who didn't seem to feel that way did not give her support when trouble befell her. But everyone had their own little worlds to tend and protect, she supposed. They couldn't be expected to defend another's, a stranger's.

Rachel's gaze traveled the papers in Phillip's desk, the books atop it, and the letters in a drawer: all shipping business, nothing about an arms deal with either the Athens or Augusta companies. There was no mention of "Cuba," and she didn't know anyone there. She wondered why Phillip had mumbled, "Go see him. . . . He'll help. . . . He'll stop them. . . . Only hope. . . ." She pondered the "he" in bewilderment. She, too, was sorry Phillip "got you into this mess."

Nor did Rachel find any notations about Captain Daniel Slade, which concerned her. She checked Milton Baldwin's desk, but all his drawers were locked with his own keys. She rummaged through the small corner desk she had used, but it was empty, as her position had not been filled since she quit work to marry her boss.

Rachel still suspected that Phillip had created the position just for her and had paid her salary out of his own pocket. The work she did—running errands, filling out reports, doing correspondence neatly, keeping the office clean, making appointments when the owners were gone, and notifying captains of their schedules—Phillip and Milton could have handled themselves. In fact, Phillip had never liked to send her on errands, especially to the warehouses or to clients, where someone might be rude or pushy. He had always been protective, and perhaps a little possessive, of her.

Rachel pulled the combination to the safe from its hiding place and went to kneel before the four-foot-high black box. Her nervous fingers twirled the dial, going from one number and direction to the next. She opened the heavy door, relieved the combination had not been changed. She sat down on the floor and reached inside to grasp a stack of papers to examine them. Beneath them was a packet of money, bound with a red ribbon.

Rachel lifted it in quivering hands, stared at the bills, then counted them. Some people, she concluded in disappointment, might consider five thousand dollars a lot of money, but she knew this wasn't the large amount Phillip had mumbled about during his dazed state.

A knock at the door interrupted her thoughts and startled her. She barely suppressed a scream as her head jerked in that direction and she dropped everything. *Discovered! Exposed! More trouble and accusations!*

Her heart raced, her mouth went dry, and her breathing altered to fast and shallow gasps. Milton wouldn't knock at his own office door. It could be a dangerous enemy spying on her. What if Chief Ander-

·son or one of his many officers had seen her enter and concluded she was up to no good? What if the law insisted on speaking with Phillip about her curious behavior?

Rachel turned to the gaping box to hurriedly conceal her action and herself, but it was too late. She heard the door open and then after someone came inside the room, heard it shut. She knew she would be sighted immediately and froze in panic, knowing how this would appear to Milton Baldwin or the authorities. Even if it were an enemy or thief, her purse with the derringer was out of reach. She gave a heavy sigh, put aside the money and papers, and stood to defend herself, if she could.

Rachel's eyes widened, then closed a moment as she sighed again, this time with relief. "Captain Slade, what are you doing here? You startled me. How did you get inside? I thought I locked that door."

She had, but the handy Captain Daniel Slade McCandless alleged, "Obviously you didn't, and that was careless of you, Rachel. Being here alone could be dangerous, especially with the safe open and money inside." He nodded in the direction of it, as she had walked forward to meet him. No doubt she hoped he hadn't noticed that fact, as she looked as if she had been caught committing a crime and was relieved *he* had found her here instead of someone else. There was no denying she was afraid of something and someone. "If you're finished working, I'll escort you home. I brought a light meal we can share here or have a picnic along the way."

Rachel glanced at the basket he was holding before her wary gaze settled on his merry one. He looked as tempting as his unexpected offer, but she wanted to get out of there fast. She came up with what she considered a good excuse, "Neither would be wise, Captain Slade. We might be seen together and inspire wicked rumors. Besides, I have packing to do for my trip. I came to fetch some papers I'll need to carry out Phillip's business requests. I just finished and was about to tidy up and leave."

Dan sent her a broad smile and a coaxing expression. "A beautiful woman shouldn't be on the road alone, Rachel. We can meet outside town and I can escort you home."

"There's no need. I'll be fine. We don't have many criminals around Savannah, and I have a derringer in my purse for protection if I should run into one. But thank you for your concern and offer. I don't know how long my business will require, so I plan to pack for a few weeks away. If that's a problem for you, Dan, you can return any time you wish."

Dan shrugged his shoulders. "It's not a problem. I can't sail until my order is ready for shipment. One doesn't find many wives so involved in their husbands' businesses. Phillip must have great faith in your capabilities."

"Before we married, I worked here for Phillip," she reminded him, "so I am acquainted with all of his dealings and holdings. That's why I'm baffled by not knowing about your contract and friendship with him, and furthermore I found no mention of you or your order in his files."

Dan grinned and murmured, "So, that's how you two met. I'm surprised to hear about a genteel lady working; that's most uncommon."

Rachel couldn't tell him they had met through her second husband, as Phillip had been Craig's main shipper. Nor could she tell Dan that Phillip had befriended Craig, whom he didn't like or trust, just to be near her as often as possible. Yet, she used part of the truth, which he might already know, "I needed to support myself, and Phillip offered me a job here. I accepted immediately because many men are hard to work for."

"No doubt because of jealous wives and sweethearts."

"Perhaps a few, but that wasn't my meaning."

"What was?" he probed, looking quizzical.

"Candidly, many men take advantage of a woman alone."

"I'm sure that would be a problem for a beauty like you."

Rachel felt uncomfortable about the topic she shouldn't have broached. "Looks have little to do with some men's wicked behavior. Some think you owe them more than a well-done job to earn a decent salary."

"Sounds as if you've had a rough time with men."

She noticed that his playful smile had been replaced by a serious look. "Not with all of them, thank goodness. But often it's hard to tell the bad ones from the good ones until you get to know them."

Her response sounded to Dan as if she didn't bear hatred and mistrust for the entire male sex, as a killer of them surely must; but he assumed she was only bantering skillfully with him. "You don't have to tell me Phillip was different, one of the good ones. I know he would never misuse an innocent young woman. As to finding no mentions of me and my cargo here, that doesn't seem odd to me. This is a shipping firm, and I have no need of one. I have my own clipper, remember? I would imagine my order would be listed in the books of his other companies, as my business is with them." Dan quickly protected himself against what she would, or rather wouldn't, find in those books. "Unless this was a private deal between old friends. Maybe Phillip didn't record our contract; he was having the order sent to him to keep me from paying a higher profit mark-up if I went through his partners. It isn't uncommon for a friend to do another friend a big favor. Phillip was like that, a good man bone deep."

46

Rachel didn't refute the fact that even if it were legal, that would be cheating his partners out of their rightful share of profits. In light of her husband's mumblings, she didn't know anymore if her deceased mate would do something illegal or unscrupulous. "How did you meet Phillip?" she asked suddenly, wanting to test him to see if his story would be consistent.

Dan noticed her skeptical look. "Living in close proximity in Charleston and being almost the same age, we went to school together, shared mutual friends and interests, and we were both in the shipping business. Phillip and I were not alike, but we became good friends."

"That would make you around twenty-nine?"

"Twenty-eight this past January, ten months younger than Phillip if I recall correctly. He did have a birthday the first of this month?"

Rachel didn't want to remember the young age Phillip had died. She nodded. "Did he tell you in his letters that he had married last August?"

"Yes, he did, and he sounded very happy about it."

"So why did you seem surprised to meet me? You stared at me when I introduced myself as Mrs. McCandless."

Dan sent her a wry grin and drawled, "Guilty as charged, ma'am, but I have a good defense. Phillip wrote you were beautiful and charming and well bred, but I assumed he was biased in your favor. He wasn't, and it caught me by surprise. Frankly, I expected pretty, not ravishing."

She stepped away from this magnetic man before his force overpowered her. "Thank you. I'm pleased to hear my husband bragged about me to his friends. What else did he say about me?"

"Nothing, except that you were a very special lady, his joy and pride. I think he wanted me to meet you and form my own opinion."

"I hope it's a good one. You didn't say how you knew I was here in the office."

Dan was ready with an answer to that expected question. "I'm staying at the hotel across the side street. I thought a change of scenery and diet would be nice for a while. I was about to take a walk around town when I saw you enter. I gave you time to do whatever work you'd come to do, purchased this basket, then came to join you. It *is* mealtime, so I hoped you might be hungry. Are you sure you won't sneak off for a picnic along the road home? We can get better acquainted. Since Phillip isn't here to fill me in on the last four years, you can do it for him. I doubt I'll still be in port when he returns from his trip." He was certain she was attracted to him, a feeling that clearly made her nervous. Excellent, he praised himself. If he had to romance the truth out of her, so be it, but he didn't want to appear a wife-stealer or a man who viewed women lightly. No doubt she would simply think he was enamored of her.

Rachel didn't know how to take his behavior, as merely friendly or flirtatious? "We can do that on the train and during our journey. It's unwise to be seen dallying with such a . . . an attractive man during my husband's absence."

"Thank you for the compliment, and I understand." Dan cautioned himself not to press and panic the skittish creature. "See you tomorrow."

Rachel walked to the safe, replaced the items, then locked it. She straightened anything she had disturbed to conceal her visit. "You leave first, then I'll follow shortly."

"You forgot your papers," Dan reminded.

"I don't need them. I have the information inside my head. Until morning, Captain Slade. The train leaves at nine sharp. Don't be late."

Dan chuckled and gave a playful admonishment. *"Dan,* remember?"

"Good-bye, Dan."

"Good-bye, Rachel. Nine sharp," he repeated, then grinned.

Rachel watched the tall and handsome man depart with his basket swinging on a strong arm. He had to be at least six two, and was well built. He appeared all lean and hard muscle. He was certainly tempting, and no doubt many women had fallen prey to his charms. She couldn't and mustn't; she had to stay on guard to protect her mission and supposed marital status. She hung the drawstring purse on her wrist, took one last look around, then left. This time she made certain the office door was locked behind her. She mounted and walked her horse down Bay Street to Broad, then headed for home.

Rachel was only a few miles from where Moss Haven property began when a shot rang out and rent the silence of the lovely afternoon. A bullet whizzed past her, close enough to be heard and almost powerful enough to be felt. She urged her horse off the dirt road, dismounted with agility and speed, then jumped behind the protection of a large tree.

She leaned against it as she tried to slow her rapid heartbeat and clear her head. She jerked the fabric bag from her wrist, relieved she hadn't hung it over the pommel as she was inclined to do while riding. She yanked on the string to open it and fumbled inside for her derringer with trembling fingers. Clutching the little weapon in her grasp, she waited and listened for an enemy's approach. She knew the small gun had a short range, whereas the rifle in her foe's hand had a long one.

Rachel's breathing came in shallow, rapid gasps that dried her lips and mouth. Panic surged through her. She struggled to regain her wits, to be ready to defend her life. Someone had fired at her! Was this a scare tactic or a real threat that had missed her by inches?

Time passed without another shot. Her frightened horse had calmed down and was grazing contentedly nearby. Hugging the tree, she peeked around it with caution. Her gaze searched the other side of the road and tried to pierce the concealing woods beyond it. She strained her ears to detect any footsteps. Nothing.

She wondered if it was only a stray shot from a careless hunter, but doubted it was an accident. She wondered if it could have been a warning by whomever was responsible for the destructive episodes Phillip had mentioned on his deathbed, done by someone who didn't know he wouldn't be affected by another threat. But if that was true, how would she know?

Rachel wondered if Daniel Slade was who and what he claimed and if he had had enough time to get a horse, trail her, and . . . But why would he want to terrorize her or harm her? He had seemed so nice and polite, and so sincere. Maybe she was wrong about him. She recalled the eerie sensation of being watched last night after Dan's visit, and had dismissed her feeling as raw nerves and fatigue. But . . .

Earlier, Dan had suggested escorting her home *safely*. If that had been a hint to her needing his protection, she had missed it. During their journey together, she needed to study him carefully. She could not afford to misjudge him or to relax to the point of exposing herself.

Maybe she had misunderstood one of Phillip's ramblings. When he had said, "Killing me," perhaps he hadn't been referring to his illness.

Tomorrow she would be on greater alert when she met Dan!

Chapter 3

"You been gone a long time, Miss Rachel. I had a good notion to send Burke looking for you. I thawt something bad had happened to you."

Rachel had taken time to recover her poise before reaching home. She had decided not to reveal the alarming incident to keep from worrying her servants. "I'm fine, Lula Mae; you worry about me too much. I've been riding and thinking. I have a lot on my mind."

"You bound to, Miss Rachel, but you'll be safe again soon."

"Right now I have to pack for my trip tomorrow. When Burke comes by, tell him I'll need him and the carriage at seven-thirty in the morning."

"Why cain't you jest sell everything and leaves, like he was still alive?"

"His partners wouldn't buy me out without contacting Phillip. I can't lose everything that rightfully belongs to me. Phillip doesn't have any other family, so I'm his only heir. Besides, if I tried to move away and sacrificed all his holdings, his partners would get suspicious of not hearing from him or seeing him and they'd begin an investigation. If the authorities had to hunt me down, which they would if I left mysteriously, I'd appear even more suspicious to them."

"I don't like you being hurt like this, Miss Rachel. It ain't fair."

"I know, Lula Mae, but I'll have to reveal the truth soon. If the authorities don't believe me, they can dig up his grave and examine his body."

The woman was horrified. "They won't dares to touch cholera dead."

"I hope not; I don't want his resting place disturbed. Once the news is out, I'll get a headstone to mark it. Now I'd better get packed. I don't have to leave any orders; you and Burke know what needs to be done while I'm gone. If anyone comes to visit, tell them Phillip and I are away on a trip. That should stall matters until I get back."

Rachel went upstairs and Lula Mae entered her bedroom to assist her mistress with folding and packing garments for her trip, even though the young woman had told her it was unnecessary. "I hate to see you leaves. Be careful out there alone. I worries about you when I ain't around to takes care of you."

The new widow looked at Lula Mae, smiled, and said, "Ever since I married William and moved into his house, you've looked after me. I couldn't have gotten through his loss and everything that happened to me afterward if you hadn't helped me, my dear and loyal friend."

"I shoulda been there when Mr. William died: I didn't knowed when I visited him that day, it was his last one; he seemed fit as a spring chicken."

"The doctor said it could have been his heart, but the law still isn't convinced. My opinion is that he never recovered from the loss of his son."

"That was a mitey strange fall that boy took when he broke his neck."

Rachel halted her packing. "That's why the law questioned me about it again after William died only two months later, leaving me as his heir. Most people still think I had something to do with both deaths."

Lula Mae patted her cheek. "I know you didn't, you sweet angel."

"I wasn't sure you'd believe me, either, Lula Mae," Rachel said. "You didn't like me when I married William. I was afraid you'd had your eye on him and felt I'd taken him away from you."

The thirty-eight-year-old spinster stopped working to laugh in amusement. "I was only worried 'cause you was so young. Mr. William and his son was like my brother and nephew. I 'bout raised that boy after his ma died when he was ten and I was hired to takes care of him and the house. But I saw how fonds you was of Mr. William, and I saw how he treated you like a daughter."

Rachel grasped her meaning, and stopped herself from blushing with embarrassment.

"Mr. William took good care of you, like I does. If I hadna been gone for three months at my sister's, you wouldna married that Craig Newman."

"It wasn't your fault, Lula Mae. I was young and scared. The law was harassing me, and people were saying such awful things about me. You know why I married William and why I left home." Rachel's gloom deepened. "So much happened after Sherman blazed across Georgia. If those carpetbaggers and Yankees hadn't put such high taxes and harsh rules on us, we could have saved the plantation. It wasn't fair or right, Lula Mae."

"Don't you be worrying over things that cain't be changed," the housekeeper soothed.

"That sounds easy, but it isn't. I tried to change things plenty of times, but nothing worked right for me. Craig appeared to be the only one who believed in me and tried to defend me. But I was certainly fooled by him."

"I'm sorry I wasn't there to help you, Miss Rachel."

"I was hurt when I thought you were ignoring my

messages. I was alone and scared. When you finally returned to work for me I was so happy."

"Me, too. Mr. Newman was bad. He didn't want me working for you."

"I'm sorry Craig fired you, Lula Mae, but I couldn't stop him. He was so angry after Governor Smith canceled those state bonds and he lost so much of my inheritance from William. He did it to punish me."

"We was both hopping mad when he gots rid of me," Lula Mae said with bitterness. "He had no call to do that; I done a good job in his house. He didn't even hires nobody to take my place. It wasn't right or proper for a lady to do her own cleaning, cooking, and warshing. Mercy be on my head, but I was glad when you was free of him. Bad men don't deserve to live and hurt people."

"Craig was a bad man, Lula Mae, but I didn't wish death on him," Rachel refuted. "You know how he was when he got angry or upset. You visited me the day he died and you saw what a terrible mood he was in."

"His brother weren't no better. Taking all your money and leaving you pore. The law shoulda been chasing them 'stead of you!" The overwrought woman slammed down the items in her hands so hard that she toppled a stack of neatly folded clothes on the bed. She scowled and went to work straightening up the mess she'd made. "Sorry, Miss Rachel, but it gits me worked up. You knows I was working for them Terrells. Mercy, they was hard folk to please! That was the worst year of my life. I couldn't work for you, 'cause you was near penniless, pore thing. I needed food and a bed."

"But you gave me a little money—as much as you could spare," Rachel pointed out. "And you came by to tend me every time you could when I was recovering from my miscarriage. I don't know what would

54

have happened to me if it hadn't been for your kindness and loyalty."

"It weren't right for peoples to be mean to you when you never done nothing wrong. They forget their Christian duties not to judge or be cruel to others. It was most awful how wicked men tried to bed you on the sly and how women wouldn't have nothing to do with you and talked about you something fierce, right to your face! Just mean and jealous witches."

"I wanted to stand on my own two feet," Rachel admitted, "and I could have if people had allowed me to do so. But what can one expect from people who welcomed that destructive Sherman into their homes and handed him their beloved city on a silver tray? Perhaps it was done, as they claimed, only to spare Savannah from the same fate as Atlanta and the other towns that evil Yankee razed, looted, and burned."

"Things seemed good for us after you married Mr. Phillip," Lula Mae reminisced, "but here comes that bad trouble again. It seems you cain't get away from it, Miss Rachel. It follows you around likes a black shadder on a sunny day."

"I know, Lula Mae, and I can't seem to shake it. Phillip seemed like good luck for a change. I hoped my past would be forgotten or ignored in time, when everyone saw how happy we were and how safe he was. Now he's dead after getting drunk like Craig did that last day. It's a scary pattern that frightens me so."

Lula Mae halted her chore and looked at the young woman. "You and Mr. Phillip acted more like good friends than husband and wife. Were you truly happy and in loves down in your deepest of hearts, Miss Rachel?"

Rachel wondered if the housekeeper knew her so well or was merely unusually perceptive. "Happy? To be honest, Lula Mae, I'm not sure I even know what real happiness is. Not since my family and home were

55

taken from me because of the war. We didn't believe in or practice slavery, yet, my father and brother are dead because of it, and my family and home were lost." That reality had ruined her life. "I don't hate all Yankees," Rachel murmured. "Many came south to be genuine reformers; but some won't allow us to forget our old way of life or grant us time to accept the new one." But today Rachel didn't want to think about the South's lingering dilemma. She had worries closer to home and heart to resolve.

"What am I going to do if the law comes and arrests me?" she plaintively asked Lula Mae.

"I won't let them or anyone harms one hair on your pretty head."

"Thank you, Lula Mae," she said, but knew there was nothing the kind woman could do to save her from whatever her fate would be.

Both worked in silence as the packing neared its end.

Rachel noticed that the bitterness she had seen in the housekeeper's expression and heard in her voice had vanished. She prayed hers would drain away, too, as she needed all of her energy to work on her problems. Somebody had shot at her today, but she would be out of that culprit's reach tomorrow. All she could do was wait to see if a message came to tell her who and what was behind this afternoon's threat. If it came to Phillip, she would be the one to receive and read it. If Phillip had been murdered and her life was in danger, she would take no risks that would allow an enemy to succeed again. She couldn't report the shooting to the police; that might entice them out to Moss Haven to ask questions. She would advise Lula Mae and Burke to be alert and careful during her absence, but not expose why. And soon, she would have the opportunity to study Daniel Slade closer.

* * *

56

As Burke and Rachel rode away in the carriage the next morning, Lula Mae observed their departure. She shook her head and frowned. "You be up to something, Miss Rachel, and you shoulda tolds me what it is," she muttered to herself. "I know you better than you know yourself. You always pluck the wrong man to marry. You're truly like me and don't need no man messing up your life and doings. Most men ain't worth nothing nohow. Most jest uses us and throws us away when they don't wants us no more. You should never let no man hurts you like that Newman beast did; I seed your bruises and such. No man deserved dying more than him!"

In town, Captain Daniel Slade McCandless was having his last talk for a while with Luke Conner. "Learn all you can," he said to his first mate, "but don't draw attention to yourself or to me. I don't know how long I'll be gone. Stay at the hotel; I'll send telegrams there to keep you informed." Dan thought Luke almost always looked as if he were about to grin over a joke; he had a playful air, a boyishly roguish charm, and a pleasant manner that Dan thoroughly enjoyed. They made perfect companions and had been best friends for four years.

"You be careful, Dan," Luke cautioned. "If all we've heard about your sister-in-law is true, she's a dangerous woman."

Dan saw how concerned his friend was. "I know; her own words at Phillip's grave incriminated her. That story I told her made her plenty nervous, Luke, and I can tell she doesn't trust Phillip's partners. And from what I sense, she doesn't know whether or not to believe me."

"What if she knows who you are?" the brown-haired man ventured. "You did give her part of your real name. What if she recognized it?"

"She didn't react as if she'd heard it before."

"If she's a good actress, she wouldn't; and no woman would be a better one than a successful murderess."

Dan reflected on that. "I don't think Phillip ever spoke about me or even knew I stopped using my last name after I left home. She said Phillip told her his family was dead and that he didn't want to talk about them."

"Then, why did she invite you, a stranger, to travel with her?"

"Obviously to study me to see if I'm embroiled in her mystery. Somehow Phillip was forced into a trap. I told you what his letter said about needing help fast and about not telling Rachel anything or he would be in more trouble and danger than he already was. That makes me even more suspicious of her. Maybe she got him into a raw deal and something happened to the money. She was searching hard for it yesterday, so I know she doesn't have it, and that scares her. Phillip must have hidden it as insurance, but died without revealing its location. Then he must have warned her she would be responsible for returning it. I wonder why he would do that, Luke."

"If Phillip didn't tell her about the deal and money until he was dying," Luke speculated, "it could be his revenge against her for killing him—put her into an enemy's peril. She has to find it and return it or her own scheme could be exposed. If she does know or suspect who you are, my friend, maybe she thinks you know where the money is hidden, so she's turning her charms on you to extract that information. Why else would a one-day widow who loved her husband be sailing toward you so fast?"

"I don't think that's her motive for inviting me along. Phillip had to love and trust her to marry her, especially with her bad reputation, but I doubt she loved my brother or any of her husbands. Besides,

Rachel hasn't listed that far in my direction, Luke, though I admit I have caught her eye."

"Not yet and not here. She has to protect herself against more gossip and suspicions. Wait until she gets you away and see how she behaves then."

Dan didn't want to think about that possibility. "This would never have happened if she'd known Phillip had a brother who would come after her. It's because of that damned ship we were supposed to sail on in '71! If we hadn't changed to another clipper at the last minute because of the problems aboard, we'd be at the bottom of the sea with those unlucky sailors. We were in too much of a rush to have our names removed from the seaman's role in port. I didn't even remember that mistake until I was given Phillip's letter last week. I never knew they thought I was dead. Phillip was desperate, so he prayed it wasn't true. He wanted me to get him out of trouble again. It all comes back to the arms deal and missing money. Rachel's true motive is in that mystery; she's not just after an inheritance."

"She probably wants the hefty profit from it, but you'll foil her," Luke said with confidence in his friend. "If anybody can romance the truth from her lips, it's Captain Slade. You've never let a pretty face and shapely body sway your judgment before."

"Not even when I bedded the woman my father loved and wanted to marry?" Dan scoffed. "Damn that scheming bitch!"

"That was different, Dan, a mistake, and we both know it."

Agonizing memories flooded Dan's head. "I let that flaming-haired vixen get her claws into me. My father never forgave me, Luke, and I don't blame him. From the time I was born, he had a grudge against me. I couldn't help looking like my mother, and it wasn't my fault Mother died giving birth to me. If anyone's to blame, it was he. He shouldn't have got-

59

ten her pregnant again a month after Phillip was born. That was too soon and she was too weak. I told him so one day when we quarreled; I think he hated me even more because I forced him to face the ugly truth; it was cruel of me."

"That's over, Dan, and you can't change the past. I thought you'd resolved all that bitterness and anguish, but Phillip's loss has apparently brought it back to the surface. Don't let it eat away at you, Dan. Bury it now."

"That's easier said than done, Luke. If only I could have seen Father and Phillip one last time to make peace with both of them, it would be over, one way or another. At least my conscience would be cleared by my overtures. Now, it's still hanging over my head like a sharp cutlass."

Luke clasped Dan's shoulder with a firm pressure and sent him an expression that revealed his love and support.

Dan nodded in gratitude. He dropped the matter and returned to their original conversation. "Rachel wouldn't be concealing my brother's death if she's after his money. His partners would never let her drain the companies of enough money to make murder worthwhile anyhow. If Phillip died of natural causes, that would be simple to prove."

"Maybe it isn't," Luke speculated, "or doesn't look that way to her. If she's innocent this time, she could be afraid she'll be arrested and convicted unjustly. That would be ironic."

"If my ravishing sister-in-law isn't guilty, my friend, the law wouldn't be so interested in her. They don't believe her, and neither do I."

"If she *is* scared and was looking for escape money, why didn't she take that packet you saw in the safe? As you said, she was searching for something particular, something important."

Dan picked up his bag to leave. "But if not that money, what could it be?"

"Damaging evidence that needs destroying? Or clues to this deal?" Luke surmised.

"Could be either one, Luke. I aim to find out everything soon."

"If she sets her eye on you, Dan, protect yourself. I'll see what I can learn about her family and servants. And about that Earl Starger she mentioned."

"I have a few tricks of my own to use on our pretty prey . . ."

Rachel purchased a ticket at Central Station while Burke placed her luggage on the loading platform for a porter to put it aboard the train.

"Don't you worry none while you're gone. Me 'n Lula Mae'll takes care of ever'thin'. You can depen' on us."

"I know, Burke, and thank you."

"Mr. Phillip'd be proud of you, Miz Rachel. You be handlin' dis real good. And don't you be scared. Ole Burke won' let no harm come to you."

Rachel smiled and embraced him. She didn't care what anyone in the South said about a white woman showing affection for a black friend.

"Bye, Miz Rachel," he said. "You takes care now."

"You, too," she said.

She hadn't seen Dan outside, and she didn't see him inside the car she was assigned to use. She sat down and waited.

"Good-morning, Mrs. McCandless," the familiar voice said over her shoulder. "May I join you since we're the only people occupying this car?"

The wary widow smiled as she put her ruse in motion by teasing the grinning man. "Since our mischief can't be observed, please join me."

Rachel moved her skirt out of Dan's leg room. She

61

was wearing a simple outfit—a promenade polonaise and a demitrained skirt that lightly swept the floor in the rear. The material was a brownish green that enhanced the color of her eyes, a dye Phillip had mixed just for her.

"You look lovely this morning," he remarked as he settled himself in the aisle seat next to her, getting his own deceit underway.

"You look nice yourself, Cap— Dan."

"That's mighty kind of you, Rachel," he drawled.

Yes, she had noticed his appearance. He was clad in an obviously expensive suit that was tailor-made for his manly physique—a deep-blue waistcoat with striped trousers in blue and brown and a neat cravat with a tiepin at his throat. Beneath was a brown vest over a tan shirt. He looked comfortable in his dress garments. He cut a dashing figure this morning, and seemed in high spirits, yet she wished he would stop smiling at her as he did and wished the sparkle would leave those seawater eyes. This man was too irresistible for his own good, for *her* own good. It was hard to concentrate on deluding him when he stole her wits and breath with ease and swiftness.

A whistle blew—loud beneath the covered platform—to indicate their impending departure. They heard hissing steam and felt the tug against the tracks as the train began to move. It did not increase its speed until they cleared the town, then headed northwest at a steady, rocking pace with its wheels sending forth clickity-clack repetitions as they struck the iron rails.

As she gazed out the window, Rachel opened a safe conversation. "I hear they're having a terrible railroad strike up North," she said. "The papers say working conditions are so awful and dangerous that men have walked off their jobs and refuse to return until changes are made. They've reported all sorts of crimes they say are the work of a group called Molly

Maguires. I hope it doesn't spread to here. Most of the interior crops and goods are sent by rail to Savannah for shipment to other ports, and things they need are sent inland by rail. Of course, if goods can reach Augusta by wagon, they can be sent downriver by steam or keel boat."

"You seem to pay close attention to anything that might affect your affairs. That's smart, Rachel."

"Phillip taught me well. The '73 Panic and Depression warned people to watch for danger signs and to ward off trouble before it struck. My father was smart like Phillip, too."

"Does that mean he's dead? Of course he is, or you wouldn't have been working to support yourself. I'm sorry, Rachel."

"He and my older brother were killed in the war. We owned a beautiful plantation between here and Augusta: White Cloud where we raised cotton. That's how it got its name. When the fields were ready and you gazed out over them, it looked like a giant snowy cloud covering the earth."

This was what he needed, more information about her. "Did your family lose it during the war? Was it burned and looted?"

"No, we were lucky there," she revealed in a bitter tone. "But postwar taxes and expenses were destructive."

"What happened to your home? Where is the rest of your family?"

"Another brother drowned shortly after the war. The others . . . If you don't mind, I don't want to talk about this anymore. We won't be passing near the plantation; it's farther east than our route."

Dan realized these were all clues to her dark past, ones he needed to probe later if Luke didn't have the answers when he returned. He saw how the conversation had dulled her eyes with remembrances of bad times. Her voice and expression exposed the strain she was experiencing, which told Dan she wasn't totally unfeeling. Despite his suspicions and caution, her soulful mood tugged at his heart. While he regained his control, he pretended to gaze out the window beyond her, when actually he watched the baffling array of conflicting emotions that flickered on her face and in her golden-brown eyes.

For a time they both looked out the window at the stretch of pines and cedars with intermingled hardwoods that seemed to go on forever. At some points, they passed plantations and farms and saw workers in the fields. One pasture was dotted with cattle and a few horses. They came to an area where several boys and girls were waving and yelling at people on the train. He observed how she smiled dreamily as she watched them.

The bartender had told him she had been married three times but had no children, just large inheritances from each. Dan tried to imagine his brother and this beauty as a wedded couple, but he couldn't. "You and Phillip don't have a child; that's a shame. Your expression says you're fond of them."

"We've only been married eight months, remember?"

"Then you two want children someday?"

"Yes, if it's possible. Some couples . . . Look, isn't that lovely?" she asked, changing the subject. "Everything is so green and alive. I love this time of year. I suppose you miss many seasons while at sea."

Relax her, old boy. Let her think she's learning all about you. "A world of blue can be peaceful and enjoyable, Rachel. I love the sea. I was born to be a sailor. The *Merry Wind* is my home and family. She's never failed me. She's sleek, fast, and beautiful. A clipper with three masts, miles of rigging, and sails enough to fill a big house. She's the most beautiful sailing vessel ever made—long and lean with sharp bows and raked masts. You've never seen a more

64

thrilling sight than a clipper knifing through a wind-swept sea with a white curl at her bow as she tosses aside an occasional spray. She doesn't have that bone-jarring lift and plunge into the water like other ships. She just skims across the surface like a strong hand over a calm pond. Her flapping sails are like musical heartbeats to me. Yep, she's my home, family, and love."

"I take it you're not married?"

"Only to the sea. She makes a challenging, unpre-dictable, and bewitching wife. She'll steal your very heart and soul if you let her. But she'll take your life if you don't master her."

Rachel didn't mean to relax in his company for a single moment, but she couldn't help herself. "I've never been on a clipper before, only a large steamship once. You make it sound so exciting."

His gaze met hers. "It is. It makes the blood sing through your veins. Maybe I can take you on a voy-age one day."

"That would be won—" Rachel halted and com-posed herself, dashing aside the contagious emotions he had evoked within her. "I'm sure Phillip and I would enjoy a trip on your . . . lovely wife." She laughed.

The train made a few stops at small towns with tiny depots. The whistle would blow on approach and departure. Steam would hiss like an angry snake and send clouds of misty white breath billowing away from its sides. It would move onward with its steady sounds and lulling motion.

Despite the numerous stops, no other passenger entered the car they were sharing. They remained se-cluded in the quiet and intimate setting, sitting side by side with shoulders touching and occasionally one's knees rubbing the other's as the engine took them around bends.

"Somehow I can't picture Phillip McCandless as a plantation master," Dan commented.

Let him think he's getting to know you, Rachel. "He isn't. We use the sharecropper system at Moss Haven. Our plantation is divided into large parcels where other families live and work. They pay us by giving us half of their crops, mostly cotton and indigo. We own the land, houses, work animals, and tools. We supply the seeds and other necessities. Phillip sells the crops to brokers in town, and the profits are split down the middle. We only have four people who work for us: Lula Mae, our housekeeper, Burke Wells, our manager, and two helpers. Burke takes care of our private property and sees to the needs of the sharecroppers. We only keep a few stock and raise a family garden. This method saves us a lot of time, work, and aggravation. If their crops fail one year, we have other holdings to see us through. So far, that hasn't happened."

"Your staff is mighty loyal. That housekeeper looked annoyed with me for bothering you the other day. She's mighty protective, isn't she." He chuckled.

"She's always been that way. She calls me *Miss* Rachel and has trouble forgetting I'm a grown woman. But I don't mind. She's been good to me."

The train halted for a time at Tennille. The passengers were allowed to get off to stretch their legs and to buy a snack if they wished. Dan went to purchase them something to eat. He returned with a napkin of cold fried chicken, still-warm biscuits, hunks of cheese, and an open bottle of wine.

He spread another napkin across her lap, then one across his thighs. He held up the food for her to make her choices. Rachel took some of each and thanked him. Dan pulled two glasses from his pockets and poured wine into one. He passed it to her, then filled his own.

"I'm sure you paid a pretty sum for this lovely feast."

"We're worth being pampered today, aren't we?" he jested.

"Yes, and it's fun." How curious that he should make her feel so relaxed and happy while simultaneously making her tense and worried.

"Do you like Savannah, Rachel? Are you and Phillip planning on living there permanently?" He listened as he ate a chicken thigh.

"It's a beautiful town. Phillip never mentioned moving again. He seemed happy with his change from Charleston. Why do you ask?"

"I just never thought about him moving away. He loved it there. But Savannah does put him closer to his other businesses. Why did he merge the McCandless shipping firm with Milton Baldwin's?"

She chewed, swallowed, then answered, "Savannah already had several shipping firms, and both of theirs were smaller. To be competition for trade, they needed to be large and powerful. I also think Phillip wanted someone helping to run the firm when he was in Athens or Augusta."

"How did he get into those businesses? They're both odd choices for a gentle man like Phillip who was never a hunter or a fighter."

"I don't know. I assumed he always owned partnerships in them. He didn't inherit them from his family when they died?" she asked Dan. *Listen close, Rachel.*

"No, the McCandlesses were never involved with arms and ammunition."

"I can't answer. I never thought to ask him that question."

"Did he spend much time with them?"

"A few days every five to six weeks. He seemed content to let George Leathers and Harrison Clements run those two companies. That's why I found

67

it strange that he worked out a personal deal with you."

"Probably because we're old friends." Dan was confused. Since Rachel was a clever actress and cunning murderess, she shouldn't make the mistake of using the past tense so often when she talked about Phillip. Why did she?

They finished their meal as the conductor yelled, "Awl-la-board!"

Dan put away the leftovers and napkins, but refilled their glasses with pale-red wine. "To an interesting and successful journey together," he toasted, then tapped his glass against hers.

"I hope it will be," she concurred, and smiled at him. She relaxed in the comfortable seat, sipped the wine, and viewed the landscape.

The Coastal Plain of the lower part of Georgia was flat in most areas. As they journeyed toward Augusta, the terrain began to alter. Hills with gentle rolls and fertile valleys appeared and increased in frequency. The soils changed colors where the hard brown or red clays of the northern section met with the sandy yellow and gray ones of the southern section. They crossed tree- and vine-shrouded streams and rushing rivers that wound through the land like wriggling snakes. Wildflowers and bushes bloomed and displayed new cloaks of verdant leaves. Forests of pine—some tall and slender, others short and thick, both laden with brown cones—and hardwoods of oak, maple, poplar, hickory, and scattered dogwood ran for miles along the tracks and for miles backward from the front rows. Recently planted fields of cotton, tobacco, corn, and vegetables showed green sprouts in their fertile brown beds. The train moved past houses, farms, barns, pastures, stock, workers, and dirt roads. Soon they would arrive at their first destination.

Augusta . . . Where Savannah was comparable to a

genteel lady, Augusta was like a child—busy, impatient, eager, growing constantly, ever-altering, but always retaining some of its original appearance and traits.

Phillip had told her it was the primary manufacturing city in Georgia, was the first inland trade center, and one of the state's largest cities. Named for Princess Augusta, mother of King George III, it was nestled against the Savannah River. Because the winters there were short and mild, it was a resort for northerners and rich inland planters. Augusta was a rail center, large cotton market, and a textile giant with her numerous mills, factories, and foundries.

As the train slowed at the edge of town, they went over rolling hills and through verdant flatlands. They moved past open spaces of rusty-red dirt and areas crowded with pines. They saw mills on both sides— some as high as five stories, their chimneys making them appear even higher. Twice the tracks crossed the city canal system that furnished the companies with power.

They reached Union Station on schedule, a huge complex of buildings that covered many blocks. The train halted inside a large depot with wooden platforms and wide windows.

Rachel wondered if Dan noticed her trembling, both from his touch as he helped her descend the train and from the task that loomed before her.

"I'll get a porter to bring our luggage out front. Wait for me there."

"I'll hail a carriage and be ready to leave when you join me."

Rachel walked outside and glanced around. Plenty of public carriages were nearby, as well as private ones and wagons waiting for freight. She caught one driver's eye and motioned him to her. He reined his team and jumped down beside her. "My companion is claiming our luggage," she informed him. "We're staying at the Planter's Hotel on Broad."

Dan and the porter joined them and the men loaded the baggage. Dan tipped the man, thanked him, then assisted Rachel into the carriage and climbed in behind her. When they were settled, the driver clicked his tongue and flicked the reins to urge the horses into motion.

The carriage headed up Campbell Street. When they reached Greene, Rachel pointed to a structure in the middle of the intersection of the next block. "Look at that, Dan." The driver halted a minute for them to get a good view.

"George lives nearby. He said it's called Big Steve. They ring it for fires and other emergencies. The tower is five stories high and the bell in the cupola weighs six thousand pounds. I wonder what it would feel like to climb all those winding steps and look out over the city."

"About as scary for you as it would be exciting," he responded. Dan had scaled riggings much higher than the bell tower, a few times even while swaying in bad weather. It always gave him a surge of power and burst of heady stimulation to see his sleek ship and the rolling sea far below him.

"While we're here, we must see the sights."

"That sounds nice," he agreed, but was miffed by her cheery mood when she was a recent widow.

The carriage moved on toward the hotel. The streets were wide; some were paved with cobblestone and Belgian blocks. In the middle of many of them were lovely parks or landscaped areas. Azaleas and other flowers were in full bloom. Trees—redbuds, pines, magnolias, dogwoods, and assorted hard-woods—also lined the sidewalks. They saw lovely homes in Victorian, Classic Revival, Greek, and Georgian architecture. Occasionally upper porches were shaded and decorated by entwining wisteria.

The carriage reached Broad and the driver halted until he could cross the street which was congested with wagons, carriages, riders, and walkers. It was aptly named, as twenty wagons could sit side by side in its great width. Brick-and-wood buildings two and three stories high stood shoulder to shoulder in both directions; some displayed balconies where owners lived above their businesses. Telegraph poles stretched out along one side on Broad, and lampposts lined both sides. Two blocks down and six blocks up in the middle of the street were two city markets, one with a large cupola that held a giant clock that revealed the time as ten minutes past five.

When it was clear, the driver urged his team across the tracks of the horse-drawn city trolley and turned left. They rode half a block to the corner of Macarton Street where the Planter's Hotel was located.

Dan's alert senses detected the nearness of the Savannah River, two blocks away.

"I hope this hotel will suit you, Dan."

"It looks impressive," he said, noticing that it filled the width of the block.

Rachel looked at the large structure. A street-level veranda stretched across the front and down one side. Above it, a porch offered guests a tranquil area for relaxing, with one side covered to provide shade in hot weather or cover during a shower. "We should take third-floor rooms if possible. That way, our rest won't be disturbed by talkative late strollers."

Dan paid the driver after he returned from carrying their baggage inside. The man flashed him a toothy grin for the large tip and left.

"You mustn't keep paying for everything, Dan. I have my own money."

"It wasn't much; it won't ruin me," he jested, then grasped her elbow and guided her to the registration desk. "Two of your best rooms, preferably on the top floor and side by side, please."

71

While the clerk studied his book, Rachel glanced around. The lobby was all done in polished oak with matching pillars for ceiling support; clustered around them were sitting areas for socializing with friends, with business associates, or with strangers who needed to be welcomed in the proper southern style.

"Three-eleven and three-twelve are available, sir. Ten dollars a day, including breakfast. We have the finest dining room in town with reasonable prices and delicious meals. How long will you be staying with us?"

Dan looked at Rachel for the answer.

"One week, please. We'll leave on Monday, the fifth of April." She watched the clerk record the dates, but didn't look at her companion.

Dan was surprised by her response, as it was a long stay just to carry out simple business. He'd know her motive soon, because he didn't plan to let her out of his sight except to sleep and dress, or not at all if she decided he would make an excellent victim number four. Under the grim circumstances, that wouldn't be a betrayal of his brother. Yet he assumed she would not pursue him or another man until she found a safe way to expose her husband's death—unless, of course, she was so confident and bold that she would do as she pleased. She seemed taken with him, but that could be another pretense.

"The bellman will see you to your rooms and deliver your baggage. I hope you have a pleasant stay with us. If you need anything, let me know."

In her most polite tone, she said, "Thank you, sir, I'm sure we'll have a lovely time in your city. Come along, Cousin Dan, let's get settled in and have dinner. I'm ravenous."

As she joined the bellman nearby, Dan followed behind her swishing skirt and swaying hips. He noticed how dark her hair looked against the ripe-olive-colored garment. This woman utterly amazed and perturbed him. She behaved as if she truly were on a holiday, as if she didn't have a care in the world!

They reached their rooms and waited for the bellman to separate their baggage. When that task was done, Rachel and Dan tipped the sunny-haired young man, who nodded his gratitude and left.

Standing in their doors, Rachel smiled and said, "I'll be ready in one hour, Captain Slade, as soon as I unpack and freshen up."

"I'll knock on your door at six-thirty sharp." Dan noted that her cheeks were lightly flushed and wondered if sharing that bottle of wine on the train was the reason for their rosiness and her merry mood.

Rachel locked her door and walked to the bed, beside which her trunks had been placed. She unfastened the buckles and unpacked them.

As she looked into the oval mirror, Rachel observed how pink her cheeks were. As far as Daniel Slade was aware, she was a happy woman, wed to one of his oldest and best friends. She had to be very careful how she behaved around him or he could become suspicious of her morals.

Dear Phillip . . . She spoke silently to her dead husband. *I tried to love you as a wife and to desire you as a man, but I couldn't. I believed you understood and accepted that reality. Perhaps you didn't and you're punishing me with this dangerous mystery. Somehow I must find the key to unlock this prison you've placed me in. If you truly loved me, guide me to the clues I need for release and freedom.*

Rachel donned a simple but lovely cornflower-blue dress that was trimmed in ivory lace and small ribbons. She pinned up her long dark hair in a stylish manner, then secured a matching blue silk flower just above her ear. As she finished putting on her hose and slippers there was a knock at her door. She glanced at the clock on the dressing table and smiled.

73

"I see you're punctual, Cousin Dan," she greeted the captain at the door. "I'm ready."

"Why *Cousin* Dan?" he asked.

"That's how I'll introduce you along our journey so no one will think anything wicked of our traveling together."

As they strolled down the lengthy hallway toward the stairs, Dan asked, "How many times have you been to Augusta with Phillip?"

"Only once. We came around the Christmas holidays. We spent two days with George's family, and another two with Harry's in Athens. Phillip considered his business partners the closest people to his family. As you know, his real family are all deceased. The men spent time with business and socializing with their friends. I was left in their homes with their wives. I didn't get to see much of either town, so I'm looking forward to this holiday. I'd also like to get to know his partners better. With Phillip not around I can do that better."

"You sound as if you don't trust them," Dan hinted as they descended the steps.

"Why would you think that? I hardly know them."

Dan couldn't say that when she was relaxed her eyes looked like a pale yellowy brown of melting honey and when she was tense or guileful, they looked more greenish brown, the hue they were now. She also seemed to hold them open wider when she was nervous. So he merely commented: "The way your voice sounded, and the fact that you're staying around more than a day or two."

"Will that interfere with your schedule?"

"No. In fact, I can use a holiday myself. I've been at sea a long time and I'll be heading there again soon. I can use a little fun. Right now, a delicious meal will be perfect." He gestured down the hall. "There's the way to the dining room."

They were met at the door and seated at a table

near a window. The eating area was busy tonight. After their orders were given to the waiter, they looked at each other across a white-linen-covered table with glowing candles and fragrant flowers in a shallow cut-glass bowl. Soft music from a violin filled their ears helping to calm their tensions.

Rachel realized this evening was not going to be easy while staring into that handsome face with its enticing blue eyes and smile as bright as a thousand candles. She had to lighten the heavy romantic aura and distract them both. "Tell me about your travels around the world. I imagine you've been to many exciting places and had countless adventures. Entertain me with colorful tales."

Dan recognized her ruse and concurred it was a good and needed one. She was far too ravishing and enchanting tonight to be ignored. As their turtle soup came he began to relate tales of some of his voyages. He was well into his third story when their dinner arrived: baked ham, stewed tomatoes, green beans, and biscuits with honey. The meal was served with coffee and a heady red wine. Between bites, Dan continued his stories, and she listened or asked questions or made comments.

The candles between them were burning low when the waiter set down their dessert plates, which were heaped with fruit dumplings covered with a hard butter sauce.

Rachel glanced at the enticing sweet and laughed. "I'm stuffed. I don't think I can hold another spoonful."

Dan swallowed his second bite, licked his lips, and tempted, "It's worth the pain, Rachel; it's a wonderful dish—sweet and spicy at the same time, so very crispy, and with a sauce that slides down your throat with ease. Surely you can't deny yourself such a treat just to prevent a little discomfort later. Some things are worth doing, then paying the price for later."

For a moment, Rachel had the wicked thought that he wasn't talking about the dessert. His blue eyes seemed to leap with flames that could consume her. She had the thought of leaning over and licking the sweet sauce off his full lips. Or slipping into his arms and covering his mouth with hers, right here in front of everyone. Rachel used her lagging strength to free her gaze from his. She took a bite of the dessert, then said, "Very good."

The waiter asked if they'd like more coffee. Dan looked at Rachel, who shook her head and said she was too full to finish the tempting dessert and was ready to leave. Dan instructed the man to add the meal to his hotel bill.

"If I can't tempt you with finishing your treat, let's leave. Would you care for a stroll down the street? It's well lighted and looks safe."

"No, thank you, Dan, not tonight. I'm tired from a long and busy day. I'll meet you in the lobby at eight for breakfast. Afterward, we'll go visit George Leathers. Perhaps he knows about your contract."

"Ah, yes, business first and play later. Wise choice, Mrs. McCandless. Shall we go?" When Rachel put down her napkin, Dan assisted her with her chair, then put his hand at the back of her waist and guided her toward the lobby stairs.

At her door, Dan smiled and bid her good night.

"Good night, Dan. I'll see you in the morning."

Dan watched the door close and heard it lock, just as he heard it squeak when it was clear she remained there leaning against it. He wondered what she was thinking and feeling, and plotting. Whatever her plan, it would get under sail tomorrow. He went to his adjoining room.

Rachel heard his departure and wondered why he had lingered. Who and what was Captain Daniel Slade? What role did he have in her destiny? Whatever it was, it had begun the moment he arrived at Moss Haven last Friday. Was Dan a villain or a hero? she wondered. *Worry about this tomorrow—whatever it brings,* she instructed herself.

Chapter 4

Breakfast passed in light conversation between Rachel and Dan. Their waiter returned, cleared away their dishes, and refilled their coffee cups.

When the tables nearby were empty of hotel guests and they had privacy, Rachel moved their talk to a serious vein. "When we visit George this morning, don't forget you'll be introduced as my cousin from Charleston. I plan to tour the company and pretend we're on a holiday. If George offers to entertain us, I'll accept. As far as he's concerned, we're here on vacation. After I soften him up in a few days, I'll ask to see the company books. Hopefully by then he won't object."

"I'm confused, Rachel. If you're here on business, why not say so?"

"Because my task is a secret for now."

"You don't trust me? How can I help out if I'm in the dark about what you're trying to accomplish?"

Rachel pretended to ponder his words. Phillip hadn't mentioned Daniel Slade to her, but neither had Phillip told her much about his past, so maybe that wasn't too strange. She had come up with a plan that would seem to include him, yet not enlighten him to her motive. "All right, Dan, I'm going to trust you because you're Phillip's good friend. He's thinking of selling his shares of the companies, but he doesn't want his partners to get worried about him pulling out or checking up on them. I did his books at the shipping firm, so I understand records. He wants my opinion about their values by studying the assets and liabilities."

"Doesn't he get business reports from his partners?"

"Yes, but he wants to make certain they're accurate."

"I see, you hope to catch them off guard to get an honest figure."

"Neither man should suspect me or what I'm doing. The two companies are separate, but they do joint deals. I want to see if either or both partners act suspicious or nervous as if they have something to hide."

Dan noticed that her eyes had that greenish cast again and were held wider than normal; it told him she was lying through those beautiful white teeth and soft lips as easily as she was breathing through them. "Do you know enough about guns and ammunition to be a fair judge?"

"Yes. I've read all of their reports, and Phillip's taught me all he knows about them. For comparison, we've gotten prices, models, sizes, and lists of materials from other companies. I've studied the diagrams of weapons and types of cartridges. I know enough to spot when something's wrong. I know how gunpowder and shells are made. I know how different guns work, and who owns their patents. Phillip wanted to make certain that if anything happened to him, I could take his place if I wanted to. Besides, I find it all fascinating." She had refreshed herself with those manuals and papers Sunday night to make sure she had the facts clear in her head.

"Guns and bullets are fascinating?" he teased the woman whose eyes were now that amber shade that might indicate honesty. But for all he knew, it could be only an effect of lighting.

"Yes, how they're made and how they work. Isn't it the same with your ship? You want to know how every inch of her works."

Dan smiled. "That's right, Rachel, and I do."

"I'm certain that's so. You seem like a man who needs to know everything that's going on around him, especially if it involves you."

"Do you and Phillip think he's being cheated? Is that why he wanted to handle my contract himself?" He complimented himself for being astute and alert enough to throw in his last question to supplement his cover.

Rachel hoped her ruse with Dan would make her questions and curiosity about George and Harry sound logical. "Perhaps. Both businesses were earning nice profits until mid-'73, at which time Phillip was told things had slacked off. They said orders were lower, and material prices and salaries for skilled workers were higher. After the war ended and things settled down, surplus arms and ammunition were sold off. With the fighting over, not as many weapons were needed. Big companies like Remington and Winchester gobbled up the foreign markets. But Phillip figured that most southerners would replace weapons confiscated from them after the war—for protection and hunting." She sipped at her coffee before continuing. "I'll be able to tell if more supplies are being purchased than make the amounts of the sales listed that he's paid for. I plan to check items ordered against items made against items sent out or in inventory against recorded sales and profits. Any discrepancy should stand out. For example, if large amounts of supplies are ordered to make cartridges, but only a few sales are recorded and the inventory is low, that would point out an inconsistency—that unrecorded goods were going out. Phillip doesn't believe that sales have dropped off or as much as they're telling him. He thinks secret deals are being made. That would be easy for his partners to accomplish since he isn't around much to see what's going on."

If he didn't know better, her fabrication would sound convincing. "Phillip certainly did himself a good turn when he captured you. I see why he didn't hesitate to leave you in charge or to send you here on this clever mission. Do his partners know how enlightened you are?"

"No, not yet." She liked the way Dan seemed impressed by her wits and skills. True, she did know all those things, and would continue to pretend that was her task. "And I won't behave as if I am. I want them relaxed enough to make slips. One last caution, Dan. If your deal with Phillip isn't recorded in those books, don't mention to either George or Harry that it was a previous arrangement. Perhaps his secrecy is a kind of test. We'll tell them we came to place your order, then see if they already know about it. If they don't, since you need your arms in a hurry and Phillip isn't here to tell us how to handle it, we'll put it through the books. Is that all right?"

"I'll go along with you. Problems with either or both companies could affect my order. I came a long way to carry out my business, so I don't want it to be a waste of time and energy or a loss of a nice profit."

"Profit is what concerns Phillip, too. If the companies aren't making hefty ones, he wants to rid himself of those drains on his finances. He's checking out replacement investments now, so he's serious about this."

Dan set down his cup and asked, "What kind of investments?"

"I don't know. He said it will be a surprise." She didn't care for the foul taste of this deception, but it couldn't be helped. She liked Dan and wished she could solicit his assistance, but she couldn't risk trusting him.

Dan didn't point out the hole in her fake tale, but she must have caught that oversight, because she came up with a valid explanation.

"Phillip didn't want to arrive and demand to study the books himself because he was afraid, if things were accurate, that it would create ill will. That would tell his partners he had suspicions of them. It probably wasn't wise, but he's always accepted their word and reports without question or intrusion. Since they're out of town and he lets them run the firms, he stayed out of the accounting end. Phillip was actually a silent partner or more like a shareholder. I've been trying to get him more involved; that's why he wants me to get the facts for him. If I'm smart and lucky, I'll find a clue in the records to help him make his decisions."

Dan thought he should reason with her. "If they're taking orders on the sly or not recording the full profits, that wouldn't show in the books, would it?" he asked. "Surely they would conceal such devious actions. Why would they act nervous or suspicious if they know nothing can be found or traced?"

"Isn't it human nature for a man who has something to hide to worry he's made an error someplace that someone might catch?" she asked. "Something overlooked, like a freight wagon rented when no order is listed to be hauled to the wharf or depot that day? No matter how clever a criminal is, doesn't he usually make at least one tiny slip that eventually gets him exposed and caught?" She observed him closely.

"In most cases that's true." Dan decided not to press her further and make her skittish. He worried about how easily and thoroughly she lied and how fast she caught and covered her mistakes—except for that recurring use of referring to Phillip in the past tense. He needed for her to make slips, big ones! Dan

82

cautioned himself to keep a keen eye and clear head. *Move slow and careful, but let her think you're bewitched by her. Maybe she'll try to use you to save her, then you can snare her.*

"Are you ready?" Rachel asked when his cup was empty.

"Let's go entrap our first villain."

Rachel witnessed his roguish grin and the devilish glint in his dark blue eyes. "You like confronting challenges and dangers, don't you?"

His smile broadened and made deep creases near his mouth and eyes. "Yep, I do. They keep one alive and alert. Entertained, too."

She observed his expression and listened carefully to his tone. "You're not like Phillip in that area. He likes things calm and safe and simple, as I do. He doesn't want his life to be complicated or to change drastically. Nor do I."

"He's still reserved and mellow? Still prefers smooth sailing? I thought moving, new ventures, and marriage would have changed him."

For a while, Rachel needed to have pleasant thoughts about the man who had rescued her from a terrible situation and who had shared eight peaceful and safe months with her. "He hasn't changed since I've known him. He's sensitive, caring, and even-tempered. He enjoys life and having a good time, but he's soft-spoken and quiet. He's a kind and special man."

Dan watched her gaze into empty space as if calling Phillip's image to mind and remembering the good times with him. He was unprepared for her remarks. If one didn't know about her, one would think that was real affection and respect in her now limpid gaze and softened voice. She was clearly so talented in deceit that he couldn't detect bitterness, resentment, or hatred for his brother in spite of what she had done and why she was here. He was angry, but made certain his feelings were cloaked. "Phillip was always that way. Fair and honest, but restrained. He never liked trouble or problems, and he was almost generous to a fault. Growing up, he was shy, a mite withdrawn and self-protective. But I rid him of some of that and got him into a few mischievous deeds."

In view of her perilous dilemma and how little she knew about Phillip's life before she entered it, she realized how secretive he had been. He had never discussed his past, claiming he liked to live in the present. She thought she had known him and his work; it was obvious now she hadn't. There was another side, another personality, to him that he had guarded and hidden. She had witnessed only the good and tender side of her husband, but there was also a dark and unknown one that had made an illegal deal with dangerous men. "I wonder why Phillip was like that," she murmured, partly for her own curiosity and partly to coax needed revelations about him.

Dan figured that if he kept talking about Phillip, she would, too; and he'd learn more about his brother since their separation. Dan wanted to discover how and why Phillip had changed over the years, as his brother would never have done what Rachel hinted at that night when she searched their home. Yet Phillip must have gotten himself into a bad situation: his letter, her remarks, and this trip were leading to a perilous road Dan knew he must travel if he wanted truth and justice. No doubt she was testing him to see if he knew enough about Phillip to be who he claimed.

"His father. Stephen McCandless," Dan replied, "was a tough man in business and at home. You could say I was a mite reckless and spirited when I was growing up, so McCandless thought I was a bad influence on his son. He raked me over several times for taking Phillip off the straight and narrow, but I didn't want Phillip to be like his old man. I'll admit I went too far sometimes to give him spunk, but it was because I loved him. At times he was too gentle and tender-hearted for his own good. Phillip toughened up some after he went to work for his father and started dealing with other men. Gave him mettle and a new perspective." Dan saw how attentive and interested she was. "I don't mean to imply he was a weakling; he just didn't care for ill feelings and disruptions or embarrassments. He wanted everyone to get along and be happy. He would have made a good diplomat; he preferred peace and love. He never liked to see anyone or anything harmed. He took up for me plenty of times when I was mischievous or stubborn."

"He's still tender-hearted and protective," Rachel remarked. "His gentleness and understanding were two of the things that drew me to him. He would go to almost any length to keep from hurting someone he loves."

"That's Phillip McCandless all right."

"Was his father cold and mean?"

Dan quelled the bitter memories that question evoked. "Not to Phillip or to his wife. Phillip was born with the old man's image, was his pride and joy. Fortunately, he didn't inherit his father's worst traits."

"You obviously didn't like Mr. McCandless."

Dan was ready to get off this painful subject. "I never got to know him that well. We didn't get along or see eye to eye. He was afraid I'd corrupt or mislead his . . . son, maybe pull him off to sea with me." Dan caught himself before using the accurate word *favorite* son. *Watch it, old boy.*

That last comment astonished Rachel. "Was Phillip ever tempted to become a sailor or ship captain?"

"No. He didn't like water or ships. He got seasick." Dan didn't tell her his brother had been scared of the deep ocean and of drowning ever since a near-fatal mishap when they were young boys.

"Maybe he was afraid of them," Rachel surmised. "There was a storm when we took our short trip to

New Orleans, and he almost panicked. He checked the weather several times before our return home and was nervous during the entire trip. But he didn't like to expose his fears to anyone. If he was afraid of anyone or anything, he always tried to conceal it. I suppose he thought it would make him appear weak to admit them."

After that childhood mishap and Dan's alleged loss at sea, he could understand Phillip's fears and hatred of the ocean. "No man wants to expose his flaws to others, Rachel. We all have some, but we like to hide them, keep them under control, not allow them to rule our lives."

Both wondered why Phillip had changed and how he had gotten into his dangerous predicament, but neither could broach that subject.

The dining room had quieted down with the departure of most customers. Their waiter arrived and asked if they wanted more coffee. Rachel and Dan told him they were finished and leaving, but both hated to end the informative conversation.

They hired one of the drivers of the three phaetons that were lined up outside the Planter's Hotel to take Augusta visitors to their destinations. Dan assisted her into the carriage and sat beside her. Rachel gave the driver the address, then settled herself into the comfortable seat.

"Did I tell you how lovely and refreshing you look this morning?" Dan asked. "If not, it was an oversight."

Rachel smiled and thanked him. The dark-haired beauty opened her parasol and held it over her head to protect her eyes from the sun's glare. She was attired in a ladylike ivy promenade outfit that nonetheless flattered her figure. Her hat of tightly woven straw with its sprigs of flowers and an ivy ribbon band had a curved brim that Phillip had said called attention to her face. A fabric drawstring purse rested in her lap. Her husband had helped her select this outfit down to the last detail, and she loved it.

The phaeton headed up Broad with the click-click of hooves striking the pavement and with a dipping bounce as the wheels made contact where the stones were put together. The street was busy with freight wagons, carriages, mounted riders, and a horse-drawn trolley that was making its way along the tracks on the other side of the street. They passed various businesses, a few warehouses that ran the depth of the block, and the west-end town market. Behind it was Citizen's Fire Company # 8, with men working on equipment in preparation for an emergency. To assist the firemen, there were water pumps and fireplugs at intervals in the long street.

At McKinne, they turned left. Houses mingled with businesses. Dogs chased each other and barked. Birds sang in trees that were in or near blooming: dainty dogwoods dressed in ivory gowns, radiant peaches adorned in pink, majestic magnolias eager to open their large shell-shaped flowers, and lovely redbuds with tiny clusters of crimson petals. Some yards were aglow with color: sunny daffodils, flaming red, pale-pink, and snowy-white azaleas, rose-hued quince blossoms, and sprawling yellowbell bushes. Grass was as green and supple as spring leaves; so were countless wild onions and pesky weeds. It was a glorious day and tranquil setting.

Rachel studied Dan while he looked the other way. His dark-gray jacket hugged his broad shoulders and a single button fastening at the tapered waist exposed his narrow torso. His striped trousers did not fail to hint at the long and lean legs beneath them. He didn't look discomforted at all by the standing collar of his shirt or the cravat tied neatly at his neck. He was a man who took pride in his appearance.

To her relief, he had seemed to accept her devious explanation this morning. Unless she was wrong, he had looked and sounded as if he had known Phillip too well and had too deep an affection for him to have been lying about their mutual past. Surely Dan would despise and mistrust her when he learned she had beguiled him. But it couldn't be helped, she excused herself. Too much was at stake—her life and freedom. She tried to calm her apprehensions, but it was hard with her next challenge looming ahead.

Dan sensed her attention to him. Phillip's widow had looked at the sights, smiled, and chatted as if relaxed; but she wasn't, and he knew why.

They halted at the corner of Mill and Ellis streets. The Augusta Canal was in sight, as were tall buildings with towering chimneys atop them.

"Is this it?" the driver asked when neither person moved nor spoke.

Rachel glanced at the structure with a large sign reading AUGUSTA AMMUNITION COMPANY and said, "Yes, thank you."

Dan got out and extended his hand to Rachel, who lowered her parasol and grasped it. He felt her tremors as she exited the carriage, and he was glad she was nervous, as it made her vulnerable to his plans.

After the phaeton left, Rachel's gaze met his with anticipation.

Dan looked over the building with a two-story center section, a small one-story connection on the left, and a large wing to the right. Constructed of wood painted gray with blue trim, it had many tall windows and one chimney. On the two front doors were signs with red lettering that read: ABSOLUTELY NO SMOKING INSIDE. "Let's begin our work," he suggested.

Rachel knocked on the office door. No one responded. She tried the door; it was unlocked. "Let's go inside," she said.

George's office was neat and clean and uncluttered. In the front right corner stood a tall rack with a hat and double-breasted jacket. In the left corner was a easel holding a board with a display of the company's cartridges.

Rachel walked to George's large oak desk. On its surface were yesterday's newspaper, a lamp, a box of cigars and a clipper, an inkwell with pen on a carved base—a gift from Phillip last Christmas—and two letters. Rachel lifted the mail and read the names, but did not recognize them. The trash can beside it was empty. No company books or papers were in sight for her to sneak a peek. It was a good thing, as the part-owner opened a side door to the adjoining building and entered his office.

George Leathers' eyes widened in surprise. "Rachel McCandless, how nice to see you." He came forward, held out his hand, and smiled.

Rachel accepted the polite and friendly gesture and replied, "Nice to see you again, George. This is my cousin and dear friend, Captain Daniel Slade from Charleston." As she introduced Dan, she noticed no unusual reaction in Phillip's partner, who was clad in a brown vest and pants and a white shirt with sleeves rolled up a few turns.

George Leathers stepped closer to his second guest, extended his hand, smiled again, and said, "Pleasure to meet you, Captain Slade."

"Dan, please, and it's good to meet you, sir. Cousin Rachel has spoken highly of you."

As they talked, Rachel observed the older man. His hair was almost all gray and the matching mustache almost concealed a thin upper lip from view, but it was neat and made George look distinguished. He had heavy brows over long and narrow brown eyes, but not the kind that gave one a feeling of deceit. His nose was large, but suited the squarish face whose angles were broken only by drooping pockets of age-weakened flesh on either side of his chin, as George was of medium height and weight, though not stocky.

George glanced around and inquired, "Where is that partner of mine? Did I miss seeing him? I was in the laboratory on the other side."

"No, Phillip isn't with us," Rachel told the fifty-two year old man with a pleasant expression and genial manner. "He's in Baltimore for several weeks on business." She didn't detect any suspicious reaction to that news. "Dan came to visit me and has business here and in Athens, so we're making a holiday of it while Phillip's away. Dan's been at sea on a long voyage, so he needs time off to enjoy himself. He's never been to either town and I didn't see much when I was here last time, so we're staying until Monday morning."

"That's nice, Rachel. I'll be delighted to show you two around while you're here. I can use a little relaxation and entertainment myself."

Rachel put on her prettiest smile. "That's wonderful, George, and very kind of you, if it doesn't interfere with work."

"Have a seat while we chat." George took his chair and motioned to two others for his visitors. "Unless you have plans, I can fill your schedule except for Friday. I have appointments that day, but in the evening there is a big party at a friend's home. I'm sure he won't mind if I bring you two along. It will give you a chance to meet some important and nice people."

"Sounds marvelous, too tempting to resist. Don't you agree, Dan?"

"Sounds like what we both need, Cousin Rachel. Thank you, sir."

"We accept your hospitality and kindness, George."

He leaned back in his chair and smiled. "Excellent. Of course you'll join me and Molly Sue for supper at our home tonight, won't you?"

"We'd be delighted to come. I look forward to

90

seeing Mrs. Leathers again. The last visit, she gave me some wonderful recipes. Naturally our housekeeper, Lula Mae, doesn't cook them as good as your wife, but we have enjoyed them nonetheless. Perhaps she'll share more special ones with me."

Pride and love glowed in George's brown eyes. "I'm sure she will. Molly Sue is the best cook I've ever known. It's too bad Phillip couldn't come with you. He's working too hard. He looked tired the last time I saw him. I hope he gets a little rest while he's away. How long will he be up North?"

Rachel feigned a look of dismay. "Six to seven weeks, he said. I miss him already, and he's only been gone a few days. Thank goodness I have Dan to keep me company and this trip for diversion."

George's fingers toyed with the gold chain to his vest-pocket watch. He glanced at a calendar on one wall and looked concerned. "That's a long trip."

"Yes, I know. Is there any pressing business?"

George stroked his mustache. "Not before his return. I did want to chat with him about some changes I have in mind, but they can wait."

"I suppose you're busy working on that large and important order Phillip mentioned," Rachel remarked in a casual tone.

George curled his fingers around the arms of his chair. "Yes . . . Did Phillip send me any special instructions? Or send anything else?"

He had hesitated, as if unsure of what to say, or perhaps wondering what or how much she knew about it. She thought it wise to put the nervous man at ease. "No. Is there a problem? Did he forget something in his rush to leave? His urgent trip did come up unexpectedly."

"Not really, but he said he was sending word soon on a new project. I'm sure he'll handle it when he returns. Nothing to worry about."

"He didn't mention anything to me, but you men

91

never tell us wives very much about business. I hope it won't slow you down to entertain us."

"Certainly not. We have good men working for us. They don't require much supervision. You're a ship captain, Dan? Do you work for Phillip?"

Rachel and Dan both noticed how George changed the subject.

"I have my own clipper, work for myself, and live on my ship, the *Merry Wind*. I have friends and acquaintances who hire me to deliver cargoes for them around the world. When I'm not doing that, I usually pick up my next job and shipment wherever I'm docked. My base is Charleston; that's where I receive my mail and most job offers."

"It sounds as if you stay busy and on the move."

"Most of the time. I had to bring a load of iron-work to Savannah last week, so I took time off to visit with Cousin Rachel and her husband. It made better ballast than stones, and there was a good profit in that heavy load. If you ever have need of a private shipper, George, I'm for hire at reasonable prices."

"Sorry, Dan, but I either use the railroads or Phillip's firm. I always try to refer any business I can to him. He's been a good friend and partner for years. Since you're both from Charleston and in shipping, I suppose you knew Phillip before he moved to Georgia and married your cousin."

Dan wanted to ask how many years and how the two had met and gotten into this business together, but it was better for that to wait until later. Too many questions could make the man even more nervous than he was. "No, I'm from Alexandria, Virginia. I started using Charleston as my home port after Phillip left. Most of my regular customers shipped out of there, so it seemed a good idea to change locations. It didn't matter much to me, since I'm not around often. Before we leave town, I do have an order I'd like to place with you."

George assumed it was a small and personal one, so he didn't press it at that time. "That sounds good to me; I can use the business. We'll discuss it during the week and make out a contract. Have you ever been in an ammunition factory before?" After Dan shook his head in the negative, George asked if they would like a tour of the company.

"We'd enjoy that very much, if you aren't too busy," Rachel answered enthusiastically.

"Certainly not, Rachel. Besides, your visit is long overdue." He stood and said, "Follow me, but stay close and don't touch anything."

As they trailed behind George to the door to the adjoining structure, Rachel looked at Dan and smiled. She was delighted by how he had handled himself and by how quickly he came up with appropriate answers.

Dan grinned and winked at her, also pleased with his performance.

Rachel enjoyed Daniel Slade's company and attention. She hoped he was trustworthy. She had never met anyone like this fascinating man who exuded virility and confidence. She was certain there would never be a dull moment with him.

Sometimes it was awful to be a woman whose life was controlled by men and their whims. Perhaps Lula Mae was lucky in not needing a man to protect and support her, but most women did and wanted it that way. It was the natural way of life for a father to have that role while a girl was growing up, then for a husband to take over when she was older. Women were born to be obedient daughters and helpful sisters, then dutiful wives and good mothers. But where did the single woman fit in the scheme of life? If she were moral and genteel, only with a man, in wedlock. If she lost one mate, she was expected to find another. That was what southern society taught and demanded of her. But what happened if cruel fate kept defeating her life's purpose? Rachel knew that answer too well. A southern woman could not afford a stain upon her honor. If she earned one, it was as damaging as a witch's mark burned into her forehead for the whole world to see as a warning to avoid her. Somehow, some way, she had to destroy the unjust brand on her, the brand of Black Widow that alleged her to be a destructive predator of men.

They had climbed the stairs to the top floor of the middle structure. She pushed aside her crazy thoughts and listened to George Leathers.

"This is where it begins," he said with pride, waving one hand over the large area. He picked up blocks with indentations of different sizes and explained bullets molds and ball-making. He motioned to a hot cupola in use and informed them that they melt the lead there, "one of the few locations we allow a fire, but away from anything explosive."

He guided them to another area of the floor. "These men are making shell casings. The rims are marked to indicate rim or center fire," he said, then related the differences and how each worked. George looked at his guests to make certain he was talking in terms they understood before he urged them onward to the front of the second floor.

Far from the fire in the vertical furnace and separated by a thick wall was the shell-loading area. "Powder is measured or weighed, poured into a shell, and the ball seated atop with the right amount of pressure."

"Fascinating," Rachel murmured. "So many steps to make one."

"That isn't all," George said, but didn't know she knew that.

They went down the steps to the first floor. "This is where boxes are made and labeled with sizes. Over there is where the finished cartridges are stored until they're packed." George continued strolling as he talked and pointed to different tasks in progress. "In here, we store our chemicals and materials." He moved to the next room. "Boxes and cases are shelved and orders are filled from here. We box by fifty cartridges with twenty boxes per case to make one thousand cartridges, unless it's a special order for less. Supplies come by river or rail, and are sent out the same ways."

"There's so much to this business. How do you keep it all straight?"

He beamed with pride. "Been in it a long time, Rachel, so it's second nature to me. One last stop, the most dangerous and delicate one. Make sure you don't touch anything in here or lean against any counter."

They entered a large and well-ventilated laboratory. It was cluttered with work and storage stations, laboratory equipment and instruments, chemicals, and packing containers. Three men were busy, but only one halted his task a moment to glance at the guests with his boss.

Rachel and Dan both noticed that nowhere along their tour had George interrupted his workers to introduce either the men or them.

"This is the dangerous and delicate area of powder-making. We treat cotton or wood pulp with nitric and sulfuric acids to make nitrocellulose. Nitrocel is unstable and volatile. It decomposes rapidly to explode. The power of the explosion relies on how much it's nitrated and the sizes and shapes of the granules. You don't want any flames or accidental impacts in here. We have mild winters, so little heat is needed to keep these workers warm. If the weather gets too cold, we close down this area." George was serious as he said, "I don't like to take any risk, no matter how small, of blowing up this place. We get our power from the canal system that runs through this part of town. The white chemical is potassium nitrate. That yellow crys-

95

tal-like is sulfur. The dark one is charcoal. They're mixed in a seventy-five to ten-to-fifteen ratio, then all you need is nitrocel and it's finished. Any spark or impact will ignite that blend, and it has to be keep dry until it's weighed or measured and put inside shell casings."

Rachel looked at the large stores of chemicals and final mixtures. "Doesn't this create a terrible danger of accidental explosions? This is a wooden structure; a fire would burn it to the ground in no time. I hope you and Phillip have plenty of insurance and a safety plan to evacuate men."

George and the nearby worker, the one who had glanced at them earlier, looked as if her question was strange. "Insurance is expensive, which is understandable for this business, but we're well covered and have safety drills often. My employees are skilled and experienced, and we don't allow smoking near the building. We sit alone on this site, so there's no threat from other burning structures reaching us."

"That's a relief, but it still seems so dangerous. Wouldn't a brick building be better? Have you and Phillip thought about that change?"

"Wood burns faster and easier, but brick would explode, too. We've never had an accident, and I don't expect any in the future."

"I hope not," Rachel murmured, and wondered why the man with the wire-rimmed glasses kept sneaking peeks at her over them.

George removed his watch from his vest pocket and looked at the time. "Oh, my, it's almost one o'clock. I wish I could spend more time with you this afternoon, but I have errands to run. I'll tell Molly Sue to expect you for supper at six. You remember where the house is located?"

"Yes, I think so."

"Are you staying at the Planter's Hotel again?" George asked Rachel.

"Yes, it's so lovely."

George gave them directions to his home and suggested they use the trolley. "That should be fun for you, and the weather's nice. I have my carriage outside. I can take you back to the hotel."

"That's kind of you, George. We'll have time to rest and freshen up before we come to your home. And we thoroughly enjoyed the tour."

"Yes, sir, we did," Dan concurred.

At the hotel, Dan and Rachel enjoyed a light snack in a cozy corner, as it was too long to wait between breakfast and the evening meal.

"George sounded as if he was expecting an important message or delivery from Phillip," Dan remarked, "then passed over it lightly when you questioned him about it. Wonder what that was about?"

"I don't know. Phillip didn't mention anything pressing before he . . . left home. George certainly has a lot of men employed and they seemed very busy for a company whose business has slacked off. He didn't even seem that enthusiastic about your order, as if he has more trade than he needs."

"He probably thought it was small and personal, and I didn't want to distract him with its size. Maybe they're working on that big special order."

Rachel's thoughts had drifted when Dan made his remark and caught her off guard. "What big and special order?" She tensed, fearing he had made a slip that proved he was involved after all.

"The one you mentioned to George earlier."

"I guess my mind is elsewhere, such as on dinner tonight at his home. I hope we can learn more than we did this morning, which wasn't anything other than George acting a little tense and that man staring at me."

A waiter came and offered more coffee. Dan let him

fill his cup, but Rachel said she was finished. The man took away their dishes and left.

"I noticed that, too," Dan commented. "The one in the laboratory. Maybe he was just taken with your beauty and charm, Mrs. McCandless."

"Thanks, but he gave me an eerie feeling." Rising, she said, "I'm going to my room to rest before I freshen up for tonight's adventure. I'll meet you at my door at five-fifteen. Does a trolley ride sound fun to you?"

"It surely does. I'll finish my coffee and see you later. Rest well."

Rachel was glad one of the water closets on this floor was only a short distance from her room. She had washed off in a basin last night and this morning, so she wanted a long and soothing bath before tonight's adventure.

When she finished and returned to her room, she began to gather what she needed to dress for the upcoming episode. Within moments, she halted and frowned, then checked the room with thoroughness. Alarm consumed her. As she had certain ways of folding and placing items, it was obvious someone had searched through her things but tried not to make it evident. Yet nothing was missing! A thief would have stolen her jewels, so she ruled out that possibility. Surely, she surmised, a maid wouldn't risk being caught or reported for nosy mischief that could get her fired.

A daring sneak had explored her room. George or Harry or the unknown client? Maybe the culprit was seeking that missing money or written clues to her involvement. Someone, she reasoned in dismay, was trailing her and had known she was absent. It could be the same villain who had spied on her at home and shot at her!

What about Daniel Slade? Rachel didn't want to think of him, but she had no choice, as she must consider any potential foe. In each instance, he had the opportunity to be responsible. If Dan was guilty, his only motive could be some entanglement in the mysterious deal. At times she believed and trusted him; at others, she didn't. Mostly he appeared open and honest, saying and doing the right things for an old friend. Yet sometimes she sensed he was holding something back. Maybe that was normal behavior for a man who was trying to resist a friend's wife, or maybe it was something else . . .

Rachel cautioned herself to be more leery of him and everyone. She didn't like being watched and intimidated, especially when she didn't know why and by whom. She wondered if she should mention to Dan that she had noticed the search, but she decided it was best to keep the matter a secret for now. She prayed it wasn't him behind the evil deed.

The trolley stopped to pick up passengers. Dan assisted Rachel and another lady aboard. Everyone took their seats and the driver urged the horses onward past the railroad tracks on Washington Street.

It halted near a fountain for several people who lived nearby to get off and for one to get on. While they waited, Rachel and Dan glanced down tree-lined Monument Street to their right to see the fifty-foot signer's obelisk in the center of Greene Street, standing tall and proud of its meaning before City Hall with its cupola of the temple of justice.

"Phillip told me the last time we visited that it's made of granite blocks from Stone Mountain," Rachel said. "He said two of the three Georgia signers of the Declaration of Independence are buried beneath the obelisk. Isn't that fascinating? Important men resting there forever."

"It certainly makes an unusual headstone. When I die, I want a small and simple one above me, just large enough to let people know someone is buried there so they won't trample my grave in ignorance," he remarked as if teasing, but it was actually to prick her about the lack of a marker on his brother's grave.

"That isn't funny, Dan," she scolded.

Dan witnessed anguish in her multicolored eyes, an unexpected emotion that caused them to shine with moisture. He wondered why she employed this ruse. "I'm sorry, Rachel," he said. "Death never is a laughing matter."

The trolley was moving along the city tracks again. They passed the east-end town market with Fire Engine Company #4 behind it. They went right onto Lincoln, down three blocks in silence, and halted at Telfair.

Rachel got off while Dan was paying the driver. When he joined her, she began walking toward Elbert Street where George lived in the corner house.

Dan captured her arm to halt her movement. Something was amiss, and he couldn't allow his clever groundwork to be destroyed. "Wait a minute, woman. All of a sudden you're giving me an icy shoulder. Did I hurt your feelings back there? If so, I said I was sorry."

His expression and tone seemed so genuine that for a moment she forgot her doubts of him. "I'm the one who's sorry, Dan, for being so rude. It wasn't intentional. You see, my father lies buried somewhere in an unmarked grave. With so much fighting going on, all the soldiers could do was dig a hole, drop a body in, then cover it and leave a man resting where he'd fallen. His entire unit was slain before any of them could report where the ones to die first were buried. Sometimes there are good reasons why a man doesn't have a headstone on his grave. It's sad, and shouldn't be that way. When you made your joke, I thought of

100

people walking and laughing and children playing on the earth covering my father without even knowing he was there."

Dan gazed into her misty eyes of dark honey and reluctantly concluded she was telling the truth. "I understand, Rachel. That must have been hard to accept."

"I don't think I ever will. That war should never have happened."

"I agree. Things should have been settled other ways. I was fourteen when it started and eighteen when it ended. I didn't do much fighting, but I sneaked through enemy lines many times carrying messages."

She gaped at him. "You were a Confederate spy at that age? How could your parents allow you to do something so dangerous?"

For a brief time, Dan lost his wits as their gazes fused. "My mother had died and my father couldn't have stopped me, even if he had wanted to or tried. I like to think of it as being a blockade runner on land. I witnessed some pretty awful things, enough to keep me away from fighting as much as possible. I guess I'm as peace-loving as Phillip."

Rachel caught how quickly Dan rushed past his first sentence, as if he regretted making that painful confession. This man had suffered during his lifetime, as she had. That similarity and their intimately secret work together on this trip drew her closer to him, even though she failed to grasp that steady weakening. An exchange of smiles caused her to unwillingly lower her guard. "I'm sure Phillip's father was glad you didn't take his son along during those adventures. We'd better move on; it's almost six. This is one adventure and challenge we'll share, Captain Slade."

"The first of many, I hope. Let's make sure to stay on extra alert tonight."

Chapter 5

Dinner was delicious, and passed in polite conversation between the four people. George told them about Augusta, which Rachel and Dan found interesting.

While Molly Sue was clearing away the cups after the final coffee service, Rachel asked, "How did Phillip get into the ammunition business with you? With him in Charleston and you here, how did you two meet? I've never thought to ask him before, but realized this afternoon I didn't know."

"Harrison Clements introduced us in January of '73," the mild-mannered man replied. "Harry and I both needed an investor to add capital to our businesses. Phillip wanted to get into other interests, so he joined both our companies. He was a good choice, particularly since he was moving to Savannah the next month and could handle our shipping needs. That saves me and Harry money because Phillip gives us a low rate."

"How did Phillip meet Harry?" Rachel inquired in a casual tone.

"I don't know. I've known Harry since the war ended, but we aren't close. We've done joint contracts many times over the years. Phillip joined my company and Harry's in February of '73, and it's been good for all of us."

Rachel watched George as she said, "I'll have to

ask Harry when we reach Athens next week. Dan wants to place an order with him, too."

"It's good to keep the earnings in family businesses," George replied.

Rachel concluded the man didn't appear tense or suspicious about her visit to Harry. She was glad, because she liked George and Molly Sue. Perhaps, she reasoned, George was only supplying ammunition without knowledge of it being illegal. She hoped so. "It's late, so we should be going," she said. "It was a marvelous dinner and evening."

"Yes, it was," Dan concurred. In fact, he had enjoyed himself too much! This skilled woman had a hazardous way, regardless of how hard he fought it, of making him relax and respond to her. This weakness was a threat to what he must do. He couldn't allow himself to forget who and what she was for a single moment. He didn't comprehend why it was so difficult to remember that at all times. Perhaps because this creature seemed to have an awesome power to beguile him. He must toughen his resolve and chill his heart to ensure she became his victim, not he, hers.

"I'll bring the carriage around front and take you to the hotel. The trolley has stopped running, and it's too late to catch a phaeton or walk back in the dark. This area is safe, but no need to take chances."

While he was fetching the carriage, Molly Sue said, "George has wonderful plans for you this week," and related them. "I hope it's all right with you that he's filled up your time here. He so enjoys doing things like this."

"It sounds wonderful. You will join us as much as possible, I hope?"

"Of course. It's like a holiday without leaving town. I'm so glad you came to visit, Rachel, and brought this nice cousin of yours."

"You and George are most kind and hospitable. Thank you."

"I've never had a better meal, Mrs. Leathers," Dan complimented. "I hope that when I find a wife, she can cook only half as well as you."

Molly Sue blushed with pride. "A real southern gentleman. We don't see enough of them anymore. Stay this way, Captain Slade. Some lucky woman will thank heaven for a good man like you."

"You're most kind and generous," Dan replied with a broad smile.

Everyone said good night, then Rachel and Dan departed.

"It was fun, wasn't it?" Rachel said at her door.

He lazed against the frame and murmured, "Yes, it was. I could get used to living on land if it were like this all the time."

"Divorce your wife and leave the sea?" she jested.

"That would depend on my finding a better one to replace her."

Rachel studied Dan. "You haven't searched very hard. I'm sure plenty of women would leap at the chance to become Mrs. Daniel Slade. I'll bet you have females in every port around the world pining over you."

Dan kept his gaze on hers. "Pining over me isn't the problem. I have to find one I pine over."

"That does make all the difference, doesn't it?"

"Absolutely. Trouble is, every time I see one that might suit me, she's taken. I don't think it would be wise or safe to snatch another man's love. It's a shame you aren't available, Rachel. You and I seem much alike and we get along well. That's rare for a man and woman."

Rachel felt a warm flush cover her body and rose her cheeks. "Thank you for the compliment, Dan, but you don't know me that well yet. I could be a terrible person masquerading as a proper lady."

Dan sent forth a chuckle, but was intrigued by her reaction. "I've met plenty of women around the world, Rachel, and I know a real lady when I see one. You're just too modest and nice to agree with me."

She looked at the muscular man leaning against the doorway with his arms crossed over a broad chest. He was so alluring and special, if he was genuine. "I do try to be a lady, Dan," she joked, "but it's hard sometimes."

Dan laughed and straightened himself. Stars above, she was tempting and dangerous! *Cool your loins and clear your head, old boy. She's only your target, not an ordinary woman to dally with or pursue.* "Probably as hard as it is to be a gentleman at all times."

Beneath his smoldering blue gaze, Rachel became apprehensive. His husky voice was trailing over her flesh like a gentle caress. His masculine smell was attacking her senses. His nearness was tantalizingly perilous. "It's late," she said in a strained tone. "We'd better say good night. I'll meet you for breakfast at eight before our first tour."

"Good night, Rachel. Thanks for including this lonesome old seadog in your lively existence for a while."

She was confused and touched by his last remark. "You don't seem to be a man who would ever have reason to be lonesome."

"That's because I'm masquerading as a carefree bachelor."

"One day that will change. Don't rush into any relationship until you're certain it's the right one for you though," she advised in a serious tone.

"How does one know when and if it's the right one, Rachel?"

She lowered her gaze, lost her smile, and replied, "I don't know the answer to that, Dan. I just know that misjudgments can be painful and costly. When you choose, make certain you aren't wrong."

"That sounds like the voice of experience talking. Why?"

Rachel forced a smile to her lips, met his probing gaze, and said, "I was referring to my mother. She made a terrible choice for a second husband. After Papa died and things were so bad, she was frightened and alone, so she rushed into marriage with an awful man. It was wrong for her and her family. It's caused us a lot of anguish, and we're all paying for it."

Dan perceived that she was being only half honest, that part of her words included her own experiences. But which ones?

She berated herself for that disclosure. "That's enough reminiscing tonight. It solves nothing and keeps pain from healing. I'll see—"

Dan caught her cold hands in his warm ones. He realized with annoyance that his heart was racing and that he didn't want to leave her. "I understand. I had a hard time growing up myself. We can't change the past, but we have to find a way to keep it from hurting us the rest of our lives."

She made the mistake of gazing into his blue eyes and was engulfed by their flames. "What way did you find, Dan?"

"I haven't yet, but I'm still looking and trying," he admitted.

"Maybe we'll both succeed this year."

"I hope so, Rachel, for both our sakes. It's never too late to try."

Is it too late for me this time to keep from being destroyed unjustly? Rachel wondered. *Too late to find a man like this who would—* "Good night, Dan. Thank you."

Dan released her hands and moved a few steps away. "Sleep well, Rachel McCandless. I'll be waiting for you in the morning."

Rachel entered her room. She walked to her bed and sat on its edge. *If only you would truly be waiting*

106

for me in the morning, she thought, then let her tears flow. She wept for the loved ones she had lost, for the unhappy changes in her life, for what might have been, for Phillip, and for what she knew could never be with Daniel Slade—the first man to reach her "deepest heart," in Lula Mae's words, and the first to enflame her passions. She knew she couldn't pursue him. Even if he were for real, he was married to his ship and the sea. Even if he were attracted to her, she couldn't win him, not with her black past and with the lies she'd told him. Except for the loyal Lula Mae, she was alone again, with more malicious gossip and another vile investigation looming before her. She yearned for her lost parents and siblings. She craved peace of mind, safety, and happiness. She hoped she had not misjudged Phillip, as she had Craig. She hungered soul deep for Captain Daniel Slade.

Dan stood at the secret entrance to her room and listened. The desk clerk had told him about the hidden doorway between the two rooms, concealed by the movable chests. He had unlatched his and pushed it aside to see if she said anything enlightening, as she had that night in her home, but so far she hadn't. He was relieved the freshly oiled hinges didn't squeak. He was baffled by her loss of restraint. An evil and dangerous woman should be colder and have more self-control. . . .

Dan heard the bed squeak as she stood to undress. With caution, he pushed the chest in place and relatched the hinges. The truth eluded him, taunted him, and tormented him.

Rachel was satisfied with what she saw in the mirror. She felt better after purging her pent-up emotions last night and was relieved her eyes were not red and puffy from it, thanks to a restful sleep. She had slipped a note under Dan's door, changing their breakfast from eight to nine to give them less time together before their appointment with George at ten-thirty. Until her troubles were solved, she had decided to keep their relationship in check, limit it to friendship and proper behavior. All she should concentrate on was carrying out her reason for this trip. She must not flirt with Dan again, or allow him to flirt with her, as they had done last night at her doorway. It was too dangerous, too soon . . .

Rachel joined him in the lobby. Dan rose from the chair where he was sitting with a newspaper in one hand and a cup of coffee in the other. She smiled and said, "I hope you aren't starving. I needed more time this morning to make myself presentable after our late night."

"You always look more than presentable, Rachel. Are you ready to eat?"

"Ravenous," she said, then gave a merry laugh.

Dan offered his arm and guided her toward the dining room. The yellow dress flattered her olive skin and dark-brown hair. She seemed calm and cheerful, which surprised him after what he'd heard last night. She was so unpredictable and as enigmatic as the mystery that brought them here. "We've a busy day ahead, so it's good you got plenty of rest."

"I feel much better this glorious morning. No more depressing talk like we had last night. We're supposed to be having fun while we work."

"Reprimand noted, Mrs. McCandless, and I fully agree. Being drawn into the dark past is no fun at all. We'll make sure it doesn't happen again."

"Good," she remarked as they were seated at a window table. She glanced outside. "Isn't it a lovely day? Not a cloud in the sky."

Dan's eyes scanned the horizon. "Looks like smooth sailing to me."

* * *

"There's our guide approaching in his carriage," Rachel said.

They joined George and rode west on Broad Street with Rachel in the front seat, a yellow parasol held over her head, and Dan in the back one. Their host pointed out sites and talked about them as they journeyed toward their first destination miles away.

George halted the carriage. "There's a major part of our heritage—the old Confederate powderworks," he related. "During the war, it was the largest gunpowder factory of the South, actually one of the largest in the world." As he told them about it and pointed out various structures, Rachel and Dan gazed at the enormous span of buildings whose architecture reminded both of a Norman fortress.

"Since Sherman didn't raze Augusta and we had the canal and plenty of mills, we were able to recover quickly from the war. I suppose he didn't think he needed to destroy us after he sliced the Confederacy in half and cut us off from our supply center. Most of our employees worked here during the war. That's why they are so skilled and experienced."

"That's good news," Rachel said. "After you told me how explosive and sensitive gunpowder is, you know, I was concerned about fires and safety."

"No need to be worried. Augusta has fifteen fire stations, underground water pipes, and pumps around town. Let's head on; there's a lot to see."

Rachel saw Dan out of the corner of her eye when she faced George to talk. She quelled the desire to turn and look at him. It was good they were not sitting together, so she could *almost* keep her mind off him, off the question of whether or not he was a physical, as well as emotional, threat to her.

At the toll house for the planked Summerville Road, George halted and paid the charge. They went right and rode into a verdant hill section which slowed the team and carriage. "Many of these houses were built in the late 1700's and early 1800's by rich folks as retreats from the summer heat, floods, and insects downtown," George informed them. "Some of them belong to inland planters or rich northerners who spend their winters here. If you look behind us, you can see a grand view of our beloved city."

Rachel and Dan simultaneously twisted in their seats. Although three miles away, Augusta was in full and splendid view on the flatland. As Dan turned frontward before Rachel did, their gazes met, locked for a moment, then were broken as she, too hurriedly, he noticed, faced forward once more.

George halted the carriage at a long road to their left and said, "This is the Augusta arsenal. Most of it was shut down after the war. You could say it ended for us on May third of '65 when the arsenal surrendered." He reveled in telling them all the details.

George guided his team up that roadway toward the structure with architecture similar to that of the Confederate powderworks. The parade ground still showed traces of past use. Trees were planted along both sides and every so often there were pyramids of old cannon balls.

"There were four major arsenals in the South, and three of them were in Georgia. We had the supplies, power, rails, river, and ocean to make our state crucial to the Confederacy. Even when the Yankees blockaded our coastline, our ships still got in and out of Savannah. That's why it was so important to Sherman. After he destroyed our rail center in Atlanta and took control of Savannah, the back of our nation was broken. I don't know why he left those vital cities intact: Augusta with her powderworks and arsenal, and Athens with her manufacturing of arms, but I'm sure glad of it."

"Didn't Harry say that private arms were made here at one time?" Rachel asked.

"Yes, by Leech & Rigdon, then Rigdon–Ansley.

Ah, there it is, your surprise for today," George announced with a cheerful grin.

Rachel glanced down the drive, lined with mounted cannons and stacks of their black balls, to a large and lovely cottage. She didn't have time to question her host further about how Harry got into the arms business or if he was a native Athenian or if he was involved in the war's arms manufacturing.

"Bellevue Cottage, home of Octavia Walton Levert. Her grandfather was one of the signers of the Declaration of Independence; he and Lyman Hall are buried beneath the signer's obelisk downtown. She lives here with her aunt, Mrs. Anna Robinson. We're to have lunch with these fine ladies. You'll enjoy them immensely. It's one o'clock, so we're right on time." He tucked away his pocket watch, then told them about Octavia.

Rachel's nerves became as tight as a French corset two sizes too small. Whatever, she fretted, would she talk about with such an intelligent, widely traveled, educated, and polished woman? A woman so well known around the world would surely find her dull and simple. If she had known about this important lunch, she would have dressed differently, better. She trembled as the carriage stopped before the residence.

Dan noticed her apprehension. He smiled and whispered, "Don't worry; they'll adore you, as everyone does. Just be yourself, Rachel."

That's easy for you to say, she scoffed silently, *you handsome and charming rake! They'll love you at first sight, like all women must do.*

Hours later, Dan assisted a smiling Rachel back into the carriage. A few pleasantries followed, then the visitors rode away with the two ladies waving and Rachel and Dan responding in like manner.

"That was wonderful, George. I don't know when

I've had a better time. They were wonderful, special ladies. Thank you for bringing us to meet them. Octavia is lovely, so well bred and well mannered."

"They keep our Old South ways alive and fresh, don't they?"

"Yes, George, they certainly do," Dan agreed.

"You had a good time chatting about foreign places and people with her, didn't you?" Rachel asked, her body half turned in the seat as she spoke to Dan.

He rested his arms along the back seat and carriage side. His blue eyes trailed over her serene face as he answered. "It was quite enlivening and refreshing. I also enjoyed reading that poem to her from Edgar Allen Poe. It was much lighter than his usual style."

"You like to read?" Rachel queried.

"Sea captains have plenty of time for books during voyages. Jules Verne, Mark Twain, and Thomas Hardy are three of my favorite authors."

"Ah, the adventurous tales for a man with a wild heart and restless spirit," she jested, and watched him grin in amusement.

"You'd be surprised how much their works teach you about people."

"I've read many things by all of them. I love to read, too. Perhaps I should become an author and write down my adventures for sale." Rachel wanted to bite off her loosened tongue after it made that foolish mistake.

When she appeared dismayed over her slip, Dan subtly rescued her. "I'm certain you would earn a fortune on them. Wait until we complete our trip and you'll have many more, like today's, to add to them."

"I saw the photograph of Dr. Levert on the piano. He was a fine-looking gentleman. I'm sure she must miss him something terrible."

Dan grinned at how the cunning creature changed the subject from her past. "We should locate a photographer's studio and have a picture taken of us on our holiday as a souvenir remembrance."

"I know a good one downtown," George interspersed.

Dan leapt on that assistance from the man who didn't guess they weren't related. "Give me his name and we'll see him Friday afternoon. We can do our sitting dressed in party clothes to look our best for posterity."

Rachel laughed. "You're such a joker, Cousin Dan."

"I'm serious. It would be fun, and will give us a nice keepsake."

"He's right, Rachel. You should capture pleasant times in pictures."

"If you two insist, it's fine with me."

"I insist," Dan murmured.

"Friday it is," she responded, then faced forward because his sensual grin was weakening her resolve not to be more heavily attracted to him.

The entertaining tour continued as they made their way back to the hotel where they parted company for the day.

"Either George is a nice and sincere man," Rachel speculated at dinner, "or he's cleverer than I can ascertain and he's keeping us occupied and away from the company. What's your opinion of him?"

"If he's a dishonest and treacherous man, it certainly doesn't show in his personality and behavior. I like George; he impresses me as kind and generous. I think the reason he acted strange at the company when you spoke with him is because he didn't want to discuss business with his partner's wife or with a woman. Other than changing the subject to distract you from an uncomfortable topic, he seemed open and trustworthy."

"That's good, because it matches my opinion of him and his conduct. I would hate to think of George being guilty of my suspicions."

Dan knew which suspicions she really had in mind. "We are having a wonderful time, and you're getting good information for Phillip."

"Yes, I am. I'm enjoying your company and assistance. Thank you for coming along and for being such a gentleman."

Dan grasped her implications and sly warnings. "Me, too, Rachel, and you're welcome. Have you contacted Phillip yet?"

Rachel lowered her fork from her lips. "What?" she asked.

"Have you sent Phillip a telegram to let him know how things are going?" he explained to see how she would react.

"No. I told you at home, I don't know how to reach him. He knows where I am and what I'm doing. If he wants news, he'll contact me. I'm sure he realizes it's too soon for me to have any facts for him."

Dan swallowed his piece of ham. "You're right. Maybe he'll cable you in Athens. Then we can let him know I've arrived and that I'm with you. That should keep him from worrying about you being alone on this journey."

Rachel calmed herself. "I'm sure he'll be delighted to learn his best friend is protecting me for him. If a telegram is delivered to my room along the way, I'll tell you immediately, so you can respond with me."

When a bellman came to their table and told Dan he had a message at the front desk, he said, "I'll check on it while we're waiting for dessert."

Rachel observed his retreat with intrigue, as it was odd for their dinner to be interrupted unless it was an emergency.

When Dan returned after ten minutes, he seemed

winded to her, as if he'd rushed to do something. "A problem?" she asked.

"No, but I'll tell you about it later," he hinted with a sly grin.

They finished eating and walked to her door. Rachel unlocked it and turned to say good night, to find him grinning. "What is so amusing, Dan?"

"Your surprise," he murmured in a husky voice and pointed inside to a vase of flowers. "You said this was your favorite season, so I thought a little bit of spring would brighten your room and give you pleasure."

She looked concerned as she asked, "How did you get them in here?"

"They arrived while we were dining. The bellman came up with me to unlock the door so we could put them in place. You don't mind, do you?"

"Of course not. It was kind and gracious. Thank you. Good night."

"Good night, Rachel. See you in the morning." He assumed she made her hasty escape because she was worried he had seen her perfidious mischief on the bed.

Rachel walked to the table and roved her gaze over the lovely and colorful arrangement. She couldn't decide if his gesture was friendly or romantic. The card with them did not help answer her query: "Rachel, they can't compare with your beauty, but I hope you enjoy them. Dan."

She withdrew a daffodil and smelled it, smiling with delight at the heady fragrance. She went to the bed to place it on her pillow to give pleasure during the night, as she often did with gardenias during their season.

Something was lying there—a folded note and a small vial of white powder. She tensed as she put aside the daffodil to grasp the two items. A sick feeling caused her heart to drum. She read the note on hotel stationery. Dread and panic made her heart race faster and her hands shake.

She read it again: "I want you and I'll get you, whatever it takes, in life or in death. Leave your husband or you'll soon be a widow once more. Divorce him or desert him or use this on him; I don't care, but get free and be mine this time or else you'll be sorry. I need you and must have you."

Rachel gaped at the vial of poison in her trembling hand. She had to get rid of it fast before it was found in her possession! Whoever had written the note didn't know Phillip was dead, but was following her and scaring her. Anyone who saw it would think she had penned it, as the script matched hers! She didn't know if the contents were the insidious truth or a cruel joke. Who, she fretted, had done this horrible deed, and how?

Dan didn't have an alibi this time, either, but he couldn't forge her handwriting without a long sample and lengthy practice. The brief message she had slipped beneath his door this morning was not sufficient. She had no tangible reason at all to distrust or suspect him.

As quietly as possible, she left her room and went downstairs. She located the bellman who had summoned and accompanied Dan earlier. She questioned him about anyone else being let into her room for any reason during her stay. He told her no one could enter a guest's room without permission from the desk clerk. Rachel checked with the other man, to learn that only one person had done so—Daniel Slade, and tonight.

"Did you notice anything lying on my bed?" she asked the bellman.

"A note and a small bottle of medicine. I put them on your pillow. I didn't read it or bother anything, ma'am. Ask Captain Slade; he saw me."

"Did he read the note and see the . . . medicine?"

116

"He saw them when I moved them, but he didn't touch either one. Is something wrong, Mrs. McCandless?" the desk clerk inquired.

She smiled and lied. "No. It's only that the note was very private; so, when I found it moved, I wanted to make sure no one had read it."

"I swear we didn't, ma'am. Delivering the flowers only took a minute."

"Thank you, and don't worry about it again." The bellman left and she said to the clerk in a pleasant tone, "I have important personal papers in my room, sir, so please don't let anyone inside for any reason. Have future messages and gifts left with you, then contact me to come for them."

"Yes, ma'am; your request will be obeyed," he replied politely.

"Thank you, and good night." As she returned to her room, she prayed Dan had mistaken the vial for medicine, too. She hoped he wouldn't remember her having it when he heard the horrible rumors about her soon. If he did, she knew what he would think!

Rachel took her same precaution of a breakfast that allowed only enough time to eat. Last night it had been difficult to share a leisurely dinner in the cozy dining room. She didn't want every meal to be a chore where she had to stay on strenuous alert against reaching out to Dan or risk making slips when she became too disarmed.

She pushed aside her fears and worries over the recent threats. She needed a clear head to concentrate on George and Dan. She reminded herself that the original incidents in Savannah had begun before Daniel Slade's arrival, so it was doubtful he was behind them; that made her think he couldn't be blamed for the ones dogging her on the road. Still, she would

117

keep an alert eye on the enticing sea captain and on her surroundings.

George picked them up at nine-thirty and gave them a detailed tour of the inner city. When they reached the waterfront, he halted the carriage and they got out near the city wharves. Steamboats and keelboats plied their trades at the location, which was loud and busy with workers. Homes, businesses, and enormous warehouses were lined shoulder to shoulder along Bay Street. Two covered railroad bridges crossed the river less than a block apart. Nearby was another bridge for use by the general public.

Rachel saw the sparkle that entered Captain Daniel Slade's dark-blue eyes as he gazed at the wide and swift Savannah River and the boats. He appeared filled with energy and excitement to be near water again. When George asked Dan a question, she listened closely to his response.

"Ever been tempted to give up the sea, Dan?"

The captain didn't take his softened gaze from the rapid currents. "Not yet, George. Haven't found anything worth replacing it and my ship."

"I understand that feeling. This river is a powerful and unpredictable one. She serves us well until heavy rains cause her to flood into the city."

"Flood the city?"

"That's right, Rachel. She usually overflows a little once or twice a year, but Augusta has suffered four terrible floods. What we need is a levy to control her overabundance. We sit close to her banks and we're low. When she's too high and dumps water into the canal at a heavy rate, it spills over into the town and residential areas. Where Molly Sue and I live, it's been pretty safe over the years from much damage."

"What about at the company?" Rachel questioned. "Since it's beside the canal, is there much danger of things getting ruined when it floods? You said the powder and chemicals had to be kept dry. A flood there could create a terrible financial loss for you and Phillip."

"No problem so far. Let's continue on," George suggested.

At their next stop, without leaving the carriage, George said, "This is Cotton Row, one of our most important locations, our life-blood. We still do well with tobacco, but that white stuff is the ruler. King Cotton—what a history and tragedy that's been for the South," he murmured before going on. "We're second only to Memphis in the cotton trade, and second only to Savannah in shipments of it to northern and foreign markets. Our buying and selling spans the world. You've never witnessed such a commotion and such excitement as the height of the season in September."

George stared off into space with a dreamy gaze. In a few minutes he shook his graying head, and said, "If you two are hungry by now, I know a special little cafe not far from here. Wonderful food and clean as my home."

"That sounds good to me, George. After we finish, I'd like to go to your office to get my business with you settled, so I can forget about it."

"Suits me," George agreed with a genial smile.

At the Augusta Ammunition Company, Rachel and Dan were in for several surprises and new clues to her mystery.

"How do you keep track of different orders, George? Can you show me the books so I can see and understand how it's done? I'd like to learn more about Phillip's business so I can talk with him intelligently about it. I'm sure he would be surprised and pleased by my interest and knowledge."

George looked anxious about her unexpected request. "I wish I could help you, Rachel, but it's impossible on this trip. The books aren't here; they're with our accountant, and he's out of town this week. He's working on financial reports for us, hopefully to show us where we can cut costs to save money. They'll be finished by the time Phillip returns. I'm sure he'd be delighted to teach you all you want to know."

Rachel sensed that George was deceiving her, but not because of the mystery engulfing her, but rather because he didn't want to show the reports to her without her husband's approval or to expose his private earnings. "That's fine, George," she said to relax the nervous man.

Dan spoke quickly to lessen the tension and to distract George from Rachel's intimidating request. "I did my figuring, and I'll need eighteen hundred cases. I'll pay cash in advance before I leave town so I won't have to worry about hiring someone to deliver the payment to you later." Dan knew he would have no problem selling that size order somewhere during his future travels, so he wasn't risking the investment in his cover story.

George's brown gaze widened in astonishment as he scribbled notes. "That's 1,800,000 cartridges! It's . . . $30,006! I didn't realize you meant an order this big. I would have discussed it and taken it sooner. I can use the cash. Do you mind if I ask why you need so many cartridges?"

"Certainly not. We have a small force in the Mediterrean area, and they're expecting trouble by the end of summer with Turkey and her surroundings. I was in port when they mentioned sending an order for arms and ammunition. I requested the assignment and received it. When Rachel planned this holiday, I decided to mix business with pleasure. I want Phillip's two companies to fill my orders. I'll try to stay in port until it's ready. When can you have the cases in Savannah ready to be shipped out?"

Rachel leapt at the chance to gain information.

120

"Will that be a problem or take long, George? I know you're already working on that other big contract Phillip mentioned before he left home."

"I had it started before Phillip canceled it, but Harry stopped by last Friday and told me Phillip had changed his mind again and to get back on it fast. I have my men working as quickly as possible to make our deadline. It'll be in Savannah by May fourteenth as promised."

His words reminded her of Phillip's frantic mumblings. May fourteenth was six weeks away. "I forgot who Phillip said it was for."

"I don't know, just Phillip's name is on the contract. He's handling the order, delivering it, and collecting the payment."

"Harry didn't mention the customer's name, either?"

"No, Phillip's handling the arms deal the same way."

Rachel did not point out how preposterous that sounded. "It's big and important. How many cases are involved?"

"Thirty thousand."

Rachel's eyes widened this time. "That's . . ."

"Thirty million cartridges." George supplied the amount for her. "We're charging $16.67 per case, so the contract is for five hundred thousand dollars. We give a discount on large orders like that; normally we charge eighteen dollars a case. I'll give you the same lower rate, Dan, because your order is large."

Dan didn't get to thank him, because Rachel murmured, "Five hundred thousand dollars for your end of the deal? With Harry's share added to it, that's a huge amount of money. How are the companies supposed to be paid? When? If anything happened to stop the order after it's made, we'd have a terrible loss."

The gray-haired man nodded agreement. "The balance is to be paid on delivery by Phillip's ship, to Phillip himself. He assures us nothing can go wrong. I hope he's right. I'm working on borrowed money to fill this size order. You're right, we could be ruined if the deal fell through. Who else would take such a load off our hands?"

"You said *balance,* George. What does that mean?"

"Phillip already has an advance of half the money owed to both companies. He's to collect the other half on delivery."

Rachel speculated that with Phillip dead, George and Harry stood to earn a great deal of money. They could pretend the deal didn't exist or fell through, then keep and divide the large payment. But if George was telling the truth about not knowing who the buyer was, how could she discover his identity? Unless Harry lied about knowing. What if Harry had received the advance already, perhaps when he visited Phillip last week, but her delirious husband didn't recall that fact? Worse, what if something had happened to it while in Phillip's keeping? Whoever it belonged to would demand it or the merchandise. Unless George and Harry were paid, it was doubtful they would honor "Phillip's" deal. That would leave her responsible for what had to be a . . . million-dollar-at-least trap! "You say it's to be delivered to Phillip in Savannah on May fourteenth?"

"That's right; then he's supposed to come straight here to settle the account. He did promise to send half of the money for working capital by now; that's what I was concerned about the other day. With him gone until the deadline, I'll have to borrow more money to work with until his return."

"What about my payment and order, George? Won't that help out?"

"It will help some, Dan, but supplies and salaries are expensive. What caliber do you want?"

Dan gave the size for the rifles he planned to order in Athens.

"Rim or center fire? We can make them either way."

"Centerfire gives less trouble on the battlefield."

"I have some in storage that size. I can have the others ready and send them on the same day I rail down Phillip's contract. Is that all right?"

"That's perfect timing, George," Dan said. "Thanks."

Before they retired to their rooms to dress for the theater and dinner with George and Molly Sue Leathers, Dan remarked to Rachel, "That's a big contract Phillip worked out with somebody. Seems he's bringing more orders and profits into the companies than his partners are. He'd probably earn more if he was in business by himself."

Rachel recalled her fabricated tale to Dan and felt she must defend it to prevent suspicions at this vital point. She could only come up with one idea, a rather strong one. "This doesn't make sense, Dan. If the companies are on the verge of such large profits that Phillip knows about and can't be cheated out of, why would he be thinking of selling them? Why would he be concerned about secret deals by his partners when he's made two himself? I'm utterly baffled."

Dan perceived her ruse. "You'll have to let him explain when he either contacts you or you both return home. That deal is large enough to supply an army somewhere. If a soldier fired fifty bullets a day every day, it would keep ten thousand men in shells for months of fighting. He surely became lucky; it's even better than my deal. That's a big shipment of questionable cargo to clear customs. I wonder how he plans to get it past them. I have a letter of clearance for my arms," he alleged, knowing he could get one

123

from a friend before he left Savannah. "It seems strange he would take off like this when both his partners are waiting for partial payments from him and he was expecting my arrival and business. That doesn't sound like the Phillip McCandless I know; he's always dependable. It will be interesting to see what Harry has to say about all of this when we reach Athens."

Rachel hadn't thought about clearing the shipment through customs, but Dan's mention aided her ruse. "Yes, it certainly will. Perhaps that's where Phillip's really gone, to work out a problem with customs—and he didn't want to worry his partners. He might have sent me here just to distract them during his absence. I'm afraid I'm confused and annoyed, so I'll excuse myself before I say something I shouldn't. I'll be ready to answer your summons at my door at six-thirty."

As she turned to enter her room, she halted and faced him again. "Dan, if you have so much money with you, please be careful. Don't let anyone overhear you talk about it; that could provoke a robbery."

Dan had mentioned the money with hopes this rumored seductress would think him rich and would come closer to him as choice for her next victim. Yet she appeared genuinely worried about his safety. That was odd . . . "Don't fret, Rachel. I've taken care of myself since I was a boy."

"I've taken care of myself since I was a girl, but sometimes things come up one can't control or handle alone. Just be careful, will you?"

"I promise, and I'll take care of you, too. Get dressed, so we can have a great time and forget our troubles," he urged, his hands nudging into her room before he rashly yanked her into his arms and kissed her.

"I'll be prompt and shipshape on time, Captain sir." She gave him a mock salute and closed her door.

124

She had obtained a few clues, and they frightened her. With Phillip's protection gone and perils confronting her from two directions, the temptation to entice Daniel Slade became overwhelming. She asked herself if she should resist it or surrender to it. Perhaps tonight would provide an answer . . . First, she had to bathe and dress.

Dan surmised Rachel hadn't shown him the clever note she had written to herself because she realized he would recognize her handwriting. Too, the reckless contents would reveal her Black Widow past, which she surely hoped was unknown to him.

She almost always caught her slips before they could damage her! Perhaps she had wanted to use it to make him jealous, to entice him to pursue her faster. Perhaps she had hoped to use it later as an alleged threat against Phillip to make her appear innocent of his murder.

Dan wondered how she would react when she received a real note in a few minutes. He had taken the precaution of having Luke Conner pen it for him before leaving Savannah. He had sent a message with the flowers so she could compare his script to that of his deceitful note; the difference should dupe her into not suspecting him. He wanted to make her nervous and afraid so she would make mistakes or would turn to him for protector and confidant. He slid the note under the water-closet door while she was bathing and left in a hurry before he was sighted by anyone.

Rachel heard a noise and glanced in that direction. Her eyes widened as a paper was shoved under the door. She froze for a moment, then leapt from the tub. She wrapped a bath sheet around her, crept to the door, then unlocked and opened it. She peeked into the hall, but it was empty, so she rebolted the door. The wary woman lifted and unfolded this second note. It was not on hotel stationery and was not a forgery of her script.

"Weave me an enchanted web, my beautiful love. Capture me with your magical strands. I will gladly risk my life to spend only one blissful night in your silken arms. I must have you or perish. I will give you any amount of money and all the jewels you desire to become my mistress or my wife. I am a rich and handsome man, and a skilled lover who will pleasure you as you have never known before. I will never harm you and I will never allow others to hurt you. I will take you anywhere you wish to go, far away from your past troubles and sufferings. I will make you happy. If your answer is yes, wear silk flowers in your hair tomorrow as a sign. If it is no, I will keep craving you from afar until you change your mind and need me."

Rachel trembled. The words were meant to sound romantic, but they were intimidating. Was it from the same person? If so, what did the sneaky man really want from her? She dreaded to imagine. She had torn up the first note, then discarded it and the poison in the chamber pot. This one she would keep, to see if she could discover whose handwriting it was. It did not look familiar. And its tone was not menacing like the first note . . .

Rachel finished her bath and returned to her room. She compared the script to Dan's card. As hoped, they had bold differences. Yet she couldn't show it to him and reveal her predicament; it would expose her past at a delicate time. At least this proved that the threats weren't coming from Daniel Slade. Didn't it?

She couldn't contemplate the matter further, as she had to hurry to prepare for dinner and the theater with the Leathers and Dan. But the next day she would do her best to unmask her wicked spy.

Chapter 6

Rachel had told Dan she would skip breakfast this morning, sleep late to rest up for the night's activities, and meet him for lunch and a long stroll.

The meeting in George's office yesterday kept racing through her mind and troubling it deeper. When Phillip had mumbled about money, never had she imagined it was at least a million dollars! That was more than enough to provoke an evil man to recover it at any cost or to seek lethal revenge. When Phillip didn't deliver the shipment on schedule, the client would be forced to come and check on it. She dreaded to imagine what would happen in six weeks when he arrived and challenged her.

Rachel thought she must contact Milton when she returned home to see if Phillip reserved a ship. To solve this mystery before the deadline, she needed a destination and client's name. If the deal was legal, maybe something could be worked out to everyone's satisfaction. But then she realized she was fooling herself; no one—especially that client—was going to believe she didn't have the money or know what was going on. If only she could ask Dan to help her solve this mystery, but she couldn't because he might learn the truth about her. He'd never understand or accept what she'd done, not after she reported Phillip's death. *But at least after that's handled, you can . . .* she thought.

Rachel frowned, and spoke aloud to the empty room. "You can what, you stupid fool? Let him deceive you like Craig and Phillip did? You can't trust him. Phillip rants all those crazy things on his deathbed, then his supposedly old friend shows up the same day. You sense you're being spied on, then someone shoots at you. Your room is searched, then you receive two intimidating notes. No doubt someone thought you'd be fool enough to keep that vial of poison and get caught with it when you returned home. That would certainly get you blamed for Phillip's death, just like all the others. He's so clever and evil that he forged your handwriting so you couldn't show his first note to anybody. Every time, Daniel Slade had the opportunity to be behind those sinister deeds. I'll wear the flowers in my hair today and see who responds to that message. If only you are who and what you claim, Daniel Slade . . ."

As Dan sat on the floor and listened through the secret entryway between the two rooms, these were not the words he had expected to overhear. He asked himself if he could be wrong about Rachel, if she could be innocent of all four deaths. He wondered if cruel fate could be to blame or if a jealous rival could be framing her. If she was innocent, he couldn't harm his brother's widow, his sister-in-law. Maybe his curious doubts were nothing more than the results of having not seen Phillip in so long, or seen him dead, or known her in the past. What he had been confronted with was a beautiful woman who was charming, tantalizing, and genteel appearing.

He had observed Rachel's proper, but cheerful and relaxed, behavior during the last few days at Octavia Levert's home and at the theater last night. With her cloudy past, and this hazardous mystery hanging over her, how she could be so poised and so lighthearted?

Once in a while, he glimpsed moments of panic, sadness, and confusion in her face. If only he knew the real Rachel, knew the whole truth. But he didn't. How would he feel and behave if she weren't guilty of those crimes? Being attracted to him didn't make her a bad person. Nor did marriage to Phillip mean she had loved his brother. For certain, there was more to the puzzling situation than Rachel McCandless being a Black Widow. There were the curious arms deal, an enormous amount of missing money, and Phillip's involvement with them. If only she weren't so skilled with her pretenses!

He was responsible for the spying, room search, and the second note, but not the other incidents. But if Rachel wasn't, then who was? Dan recalled that he hadn't seen the first note and vial when he examined her room on Tuesday, a search she hadn't mentioned to him. Either someone had put the items there during dinner or she had them with her in the water closet.

Don't be tricked, old boy, Dan warned himself. *She's putting on a superb performance for you in there. She knows about the secret passageway and she hopes you're listening so she can be certain you're duped and duped good. I doubt she knows you're Phillip's brother, but thinks you're an enemy. You'll just have to convince her you aren't. Get your sly romance sailing faster, old boy.*

"I set up an appointment for us with the photographer George suggested," Dan told her as they ate lunch. "We're to be in his studio at six, dressed in our finest. He says we'll be finished in thirty to forty-five minutes, and can make our seven o'clock party on time. He isn't far away."

"You've been out this morning?" she inquired. *Doing what else?*

Miffed I didn't overhear your little ruse? he mentally

129

scoffed, but smiled and jested, "Of course, sleepy-head. I'm unaccustomed to lying abed late. I walked down to the riverfront and enjoyed the fresh air and exercise. I ate breakfast, too, but I was ready to eat again."

"I shouldn't have skipped it; I'm starved. This is delicious," she remarked of the chicken and dumplings.

"For certain Buelly isn't this talented. Do you cook, Rachel?"

"I can, but don't do much of it; Lula Mae gets her feathers ruffled if I try. You don't know Lula Mae Morris. The kitchen and housework are her domains, her prides and joys. She doesn't believe in a lady, the mistress of the house, doing menial chores. She doesn't accept the death of the Old South. I'm supposed to be a pampered and spoiled southern belle who doesn't lift a finger."

"I can tell by the laughter in your eyes that you're teasing me."

Rachel grinned and nodded. "You're learning me too well, Dan."

"I hope so; I'm trying," he admitted. "You're a fascinating woman."

"The truth is, I help her with some of the chores, but cooking and ironing are two things she prefers to do alone. I plan the menus, set the table, and help with the dishes. She likes for me to spend my time reading, sewing, and taking care of my appearance. It makes her happy to wait on me, so I try to let her do so as long as possible. But when I get bored or annoyed, I put my foot down and dig into work. When I'm in that kind of mood, she ignores me and lets me have my way."

Dan reflected on the heavyset nanny and house-keeper who had raised him and Phillip. Maw-maw had been a kind, intelligent, and gentle black woman. She had been like a protective aunt—no, a mother—

to him, one of the few people who could and would stand up to Stephen McCandless about his ill treatment of his youngest son. She had come with his mother from their cotton plantation when she married Stephen McCandless, a woman freed as soon as she was purchased, a woman who had loved them and been loved and deeply respected by them. Her death couldn't have hurt him more than if she *had* been his mother. She had died shortly before his last quarrel with his father. That loss had pained him deeply. Perhaps suffering from it was why he had bedded Helen and—

Rachel witnessed the unknown memories that evoked a pleasant, then tormented, look on Dan's face. She wondered what he was thinking about. "Tell me more about you and Phillip in Charleston," she encouraged, then realized she had broken into his thoughts when his eyes rushed to her as if he'd been caught doing something he shouldn't have.

Dan could not tell her about Maw-maw in case Phillip had mentioned the woman who had raised him. "Curious about those devilish things we did?" he teased as he obtained control of himself.

"Yes. I haven't learned much about Phillip's past, so it's about time I do, don't you think?" What she wanted to learn more about was Dan.

"We men are protective and defensive about our mischievous years and deeds, but I'll tell you, if you promise not to tell Phillip I exposed us." He waited for her to nod. "We got into the regular boyish pranks and troubles. You had brothers, so you know how they are, always into something they shouldn't be." When he saw the reaction his last statement inspired, he hurried on to get her mind off her own tormented past. "One of our favorite pastimes was playing hide-and-seek in the McCandless warehouse near the wharf. We especially liked the fall when it was filled to capacity with cotton bales. We'd jump from one to another all around the building until we were covered in dust and had white fuzz in our hair and stuck to our clothes. It'd take an hour to get cleaned up to go home so the evidence wouldn't expose us. We weren't allowed to play games like that because they were dangerous; a fall that far could break a neck or limb."

Reared on a plantation, Rachel had similar memories of picking and playing in cotton—but piles of unginned, unbaled, and dusty clouds of white. She didn't want to distract Dan by mentioning that fact. "You love dangers and challenges, don't you?"

"Guilty as charged, Mrs. McCandless," he confessed with a broad grin. "I remember one time when we sneaked aboard this ship and vowed we were going to stow away to conquer the world together. We even had food and water with us. But Phillip turned coward at the last minute and sneaked off the vessel. I wound up in Alexandria, and in big trouble. Was my father angry with me! But Phillip came to my rescue; he took the blame, said we were only playing hide-and-seek and the ship took sail."

"Did you still get punished?"

"In a way," he answered, but didn't explain.

"What happened to your family and shipping business?"

"My family all died, and I lost control of the firm. After I left Charleston in '71, I worked as a sailor for three years until I earned enough money to buy my own clipper to work for myself. Fortunately I've been very successful and prosperous."

The waiter arrived to refill their coffee cups, clear away the dishes, and serve their dessert. As the man did so, they remained quiet.

Dan recalled the day he left home after the fight with his father over his mistake with his father's intended. He loved his brother, but there were times when he had resented Phillip for being his father's favorite—no, *only*—son. Growing up with Stephen

132

McCandless had created hard times during childhood and teenage years. Poor Phillip had been caught in the middle—wanting to please their father and wanting to be friends with his brother. Sometimes Phillip had enjoyed and taken advantage of being the favorite, but that was normal for a young boy. Other times Phillip had hated being trapped between their father and his younger brother. When he started sailing on McCandless ships, it had kept him away from home much of the time, which suited him and his father. During those years, he only saw Phillip when he was in port for short periods. After he had left home and stayed gone so long and became successful, he had mellowed and matured. He had wanted to return home to set things right with both Stephen and Phillip. Now . . .

After the waiter left, Dan discarded his past and continued the conversation. "I've been on my own for years and have managed fine. What about you, Rachel? How did you reach this point in your life?"

Rachel decided to tell Dan a few things about her, as he could discover them if he checked on her. If he had done so already, it would make her seem honest and open. If he hadn't, it might evoke empathy and understanding when she needed them later. Besides, Phillip's wife and best friend would share this type of get-acquainted conversation.

Rachel selected her words with care and spoke them slowly. "I was born and reared on the plantation. Mama married Papa when she was sixteen. Within nine years they had five children: three boys and two girls. They were so in love, and we were all close and happy. Then the war came. My father and Robert were killed in battles. Things got bad at home. Mama did her best to shoulder the responsibilities, but she was scared and lonely and didn't know how to run a big plantation. When taxes and expenses worsened, we almost lost everything, and that terrified her.

I was twelve when she panicked and married a Yankee carpetbagger who promised to take care of her. Earl was four years younger than Mama, but she was so beautiful that it didn't make any difference. Our friends and neighbors were angry with her for surrendering to the enemy while wounds from the war were still too fresh. He pretended he was rich and in love, but all he wanted was to get his hands on White Cloud. It would have been better to lose it than to let that snake take control."

"What about the rest of your family?" Dan coaxed.

"Randall drowned the next year while he was fishing with Earl. He was a good swimmer, but his shirt got caught on an underwater limb and Earl said he couldn't rescue him before it was too late. The twins, Richard and Rosemary, ran away from home in '69 and '70 and no one knows where they are, not even if they're alive. Lordy, how I miss them! None of us got along with that Yankee. I think he was mean and hard on us on purpose to drive us away from home. He didn't want a houseful of children who weren't his. He succeeded, but Mama refused to believe it was her husband driving away her children. She still thinks we all betrayed and deserted her. I left home in '72 when I was eighteen because I couldn't get along with him, either. I wish Earl Starger had never entered our lives. I hate him for what he did to us."

Dan remembered her cold words about Starger over Phillip's grave. "What happened after you left home?"

"I moved to Savannah. I met Lula Mae when I arrived and we became friends. She's been a big help to me over the years. I went to work for Phillip in January of '74, and I married him in early August of last year."

Dan noticed the gap of time in her story, but she *had* spoken the truth without revealing too much. That surprised him. "George said Phillip moved to

Savannah in February of '73. Did you meet soon after his arrival?"

"We met in April of that year through a mutual friend who's dead now." They had met through Craig Newman, but she dared not mention her second husband. "Speaking of George and Phillip, did Phillip mention this big contract to you in his letters?"

Dan knew she changed the subject to get attention off herself. "No, but he had no reason to. If he'd been home when I arrived, I'm sure he would have boasted about it. *I* would have. It should make a nice profit for all three partners. At least one third of the contract has to be profit, and divided three ways would make a hundred thousand dollars each. That's an excellent return on an investment. If he's thinking of selling two of his partnerships, what about the third one—the shipping firm?"

For a while she didn't know what to say. "I don't think so," she finally managed.

"Maybe he's planning to sell all three and become a full-time planter."

"He hasn't mentioned anything like that to me. Would he do that?"

"It wouldn't surprise me, Rachel. He never liked ships or water. He would make the perfect country gentleman. I'd bet he loves plantation life. It could be why he bought Moss Haven and not a house in the city."

Phillip had told her that he bought the plantation with winning her in mind, to get her out of Savannah, but to still be near it for business. "Dan, may I ask you a personal and serious question?" she asked suddenly.

He put down his fork and leaned forward. "Of course."

Rachel decided how to phrase her queries to simultaneously cover her ruse but also to obtain information. "You said this mysterious order is large enough

135

to supply a big army. What if it isn't legal? What if Phillip can't get it cleared through customs? If it falls through, the Augusta and Athens companies could be ruined. Would Phillip do something like that to destroy his partners? To punish them for cheating him? Even if the two companies were no longer profitable, he would lose his original investments in them, whatever those amounts were. But if he's being cheated and deceived, he might not care about that money. Does that make sense?"

"Phillip never courted problems, but he was always honest and kind-hearted. Your reasoning makes sense for some men, but it doesn't sound like the Phillip I knew."

She was happy with his answer. "Who could make such a large and expensive order?" she asked.

Dan played along with her probe. "Don't worry, Rachel. It isn't for another rise of the South; the contract isn't that large. And Phillip would never supply arms to men trying to overthrow a government somewhere, and it's too big for an outlaw gang. Maybe it's a secret military contract; there are plenty of problem areas around the world, some even in our own West with Indians. Phillip has a good head for business, and he never liked trouble. The contract must be legal or he wouldn't go along with it."

Cuba, her mind hinted, but she didn't have time to speculate on that possible clue from Phillip's dying words. "Didn't you hear George? He said Phillip canceled it last month, then he and Harry talked last week and reinstated it. That means Phillip had doubts about it. Maybe he feared he was being duped. I don't like this secrecy. Something is terribly wrong."

Dan agreed. "Has Phillip kept important secrets from you before?"

"I don't know," she admitted. "I didn't think he kept anything from me until this came up. Then there's you . . ."

"What about me?"

"Why did Phillip keep you, his past, and your deal secret?"

"Am I the reason you're doubting him, because you didn't know about me? If so, Rachel, that's not valid; men often don't mention such things."

"Not even to their wives?"

"I can't answer that one; I've never had a wife."

"If you love someone and marry them, it seems to me you tell them everything. There isn't anything about me from the time I was born until last Friday that Phillip didn't know."

"Everything, Rachel?"

"Yes, Dan, *everything*. That's how it should be. If a marriage is good and going to last, it must be based on love and trust, on sharing and caring, the good and the bad."

"You're a wise woman, Rachel McCandless."

"I learn from observation and experience. I've witnessed good and bad marriages and I know what makes the difference." How she wished she had learned that truth long ago, but she knew it now. She wouldn't make another mistake with another man and another marriage, even if she had to remain unmarried the rest of her life, even if she lost her inheritance from Phillip and was dirt-groveling poor, and even if she were defenseless and terrified.

Dan forced himself not to ask about her marriage to Phillip or about her first two marriages. Her gaze was a mixture of emotions. She seemed upset, uncertain, and vulnerable—yet resolved and strong. "We could speculate on this for weeks, Rachel. Let's keep searching for clues together. If we don't get answers from Harry in Athens, we'll have to wait until we see Phillip and he explains. Don't let this mystery ruin our holiday; worrying over it won't help. Let's go for our stroll, relax, and enjoy ourselves. Let's forget about work this afternoon."

"You're right, Captain Slade. Why don't you take command and steer us to a happy port?"

"That's the most tempting offer I've ever had. Let's ship out, mate. I'm going to help you forget all your troubles today."

"I'll hold you to that promise, sir. I'm ready."

They left the hotel and headed eastward. When they came to the town fountain in the center of the street, they walked over to it and sat down on the wide ledge around the rectangular pool. The day was sunny and clear, a beautiful early April afternoon.

Rachel trailed her fingers through the water and listened as it trickled over the compote-shaped levels of various sizes. "Do you miss the sea, Dan? Does all water remind you of it, like the river did the other day?"

"You're very perceptive, Rachel. I suppose it's true, because it's the only thing I've known and had for years. It's a vital part of me."

She watched him gaze in the direction of the Savannah River only two blocks away as if the currents in it had a powerful pull on him. The city wharves were straight beyond their location, and they could hear the sounds of steamboats and workers. She wished she could have that same potent effect on this unique man. How wonderful it would be to have his eyes sparkle or glaze over dreamily because of her as they did over ships and water, to be the only important thing in his life. She wondered if Dan would believe the terrible gossip about her, and if he would be interested in her once he learned she was not married. It was foolish to be thinking such reckless things until she was certain he wasn't involved in her perils. "Do you ever think of leaving the sea and giving up your ship and voyages?" she asked.

"If a good enough reason came along, I suppose I would."

"What kind of good enough reason would it have to be?"

"Something that fills my life, heart, and soul more than they do."

"That's the perfect, best, and only answer."

"That's the only reason anyone ever does anything, isn't it, Rachel?"

"People search for better choices, but they don't always make them. Or they don't turn out to be the best after one's made them."

"Mistakes give us experience, knowledge, and growth. Mine have accomplished all those things. Have yours, Rachel?"

"Some have and some haven't. It all depends on whether the action affects only me or includes others. If something involves other people, you're not always in control." Rachel stood. "You aren't keeping your promise, Captain," she teased. "You're letting your first mate get gloomy on you."

Dan grasped her hand and tugged on it. "Come along, woman. I'll keep trying until I succeed."

They reached the busy east-end market with its tall pillars and high tower displaying a cupola and large clock. They turned right onto Centre Street, strolled to Greene, and turned right again. They slowed to look at the Confederate cenotaph, obelisk, city hall, and "Big Steve" bell tower. They didn't break their meditative silence or stop holding hands. They absorbed the lovely sites, balmy weather, and each other's company. They took another right onto Campbell.

At Broad, Rachel glanced at the market clock and said, "It's four, Captain; better steer us into port for repairs for tonight's activities."

"At your command, Mrs. McCandless. Come with me, please."

Both noticed that no one followed or approached them during their stroll. Dan had seen her play with the silk flowers in her hair, but he made sure he did not mention them. Rachel wished her signal had worked, but presumed Dan's presence had foiled a meeting. If anyone was trailing and spying, she couldn't see or sense it.

Dan gaped at Rachel when she opened her door after he knocked.

"Is something wrong? Isn't this appropriate?" she questioned, looking down at her dress.

"You're absolutely ravishing. Stars above, woman, are you trying to enchant every man who'll be present tonight?"

"You are far too kind and generous. Come inside while I finish pinning the flowers in my hair. It will only take a moment."

Dan didn't tell her it was improper to enter the room where she dressed and slept. He came inside and closed her door, but stayed near it, almost afraid to get any closer to the alluring beauty.

Rachel was dressed in a satin gown of dark rose with rich pink trim. The square neckline was edged with pink ruffles and lace and creamy pearls. The puffy short sleeves ended with ribbon bands and ruffles. The bodice drifted down into a fitted waistline where a wide silk ribbon banded it, then was bowed in the back. Its tails were joined by two others to make staggered drops of three different lengths near each hipbone. The front of her skirt was in three layers, the first ending at her knees, the last at the floor, and the third between those two. Each layer was bordered in delicate embroidery of pink flowers with pearl centers. The longest was cut apart in the back, pulled up and over to each side, secured near the bow, and allowed to settle into soft folds as the decorated hem drifted lazily to the floor. The exposed section from waist to floor was frilled in many vibrant pink lacy tiers that flowed into a sweeping train.

He had seen her slippers and stockings when she lifted her hem to walk to the dressing mirror. Both were dark rose to match her gown, as was the fashion. Her silk slippers revealed the same pattern of embroidery as on her evening dress. Her only jewelry were pearls on her ears and a gold wedding band on her finger, but she needed nothing more to enhance her breathtaking image. He watched her finish securing several sprigs of silk flowers in her hair, which was pulled away from her face, pinned in the back near her crown, and cascaded into curls and ringlets to the top of her neckline. She lifted an ivory silk shawl with a swingy fringe border, tossed it over one arm, and collected her satin bag.

"You look splendid, Captain Slade," she said, approaching him. "Evening clothes suit you. Turn around and let me admire you for a moment."

Dan did as he was asked. She liked the low-cut waistcoat with its wide lapels, narrow velvet collar, velvet cuffs, and lengthy tails. The straight-cut trousers and vest matched its dark-blue color. The vest was tailored low, and the jacket was to be worn unbuttoned, so his fancy white shirt with a pleated frill completed his perfect look.

"With you on my arm, I'll be the envy of every woman present. Shall we go and capture our moment of perfection forever?" she teased.

"The sooner, the better," he murmured.

In the photographer's studio down the street, the man had them posed for their first picture. Rachel sat on a velvet stool while Dan stood slightly behind and to her right. The man positioned them, moved back a few steps, and checked them from head to foot.

"Perfect, ye look elegant an' bonny," the photographer said in his Scottish brogue. "Dinna move a muscle." He walked behind his camera on a tripod, checked the shot through the lens, looked back at them, and said, "Smile as tha happy couple ye are." As they obeyed his instruction, he took the first picture. "I'll be wan'nin' two ta be sure ta get a guid one. Stay still."

Dan didn't move as Rachel's heady perfume teased his senses. Her curls grazed the skin on her back, near where his fingers made contact with that enticing bare flesh. His genial expression did not change as worries stormed his mind. If Phillip had had the cash, it was more than enough for someone to kill him for. If she was determined to keep it, all she had to do was claim she didn't have it or know about it, and no one could do anything to prove otherwise. After inheriting Phillip's estate, she wouldn't have to touch it for years and risk exposing her deceit and theft. Maybe that was what she had in mind with this trip, to initiate her defense. Maybe he was along to aid it, to be used as a witness, to be set up as her next protector and victim. If only she didn't look so . . .

The photographer told them to switch their positions. Rachel's hand rested atop Dan's broad shoulders, an action which aroused both.

As they awaited the shots for the second sitting, Rachel inhaled Dan's manly aroma that blended with his Bay Rum cologne. Her body was touching his, but she yearned to be even closer. She wanted to run her trembling fingers through his head of glossy, midnight hair. She longed to snuggle into his strong arms, to seal her mouth to his. He was appealing and magnetic, powerfully and dangerously so. He was a man she could respond to with passion, a man who could steal her heart. But he could break it just as easily if she weren't careful.

The photographer changed their positions a last time, placing them side by side on a longer velvet seat.

142

As they moved, they exchanged quick smiles. Their bodies touched and warmed, their scents mingled and enticed, their spirits tempted and taunted and tormented.

When the session was over, Dan paid the photographer and ordered the best copy of each pose for both of them.

"I'll hae them at yer hotel by Sunday. Check with tha desk clerk. If there be a problem, dinna hesitate ta contact me."

"I'm certain they'll be perfect," Dan assured him.

"Thank you," Rachel added before they departed.

As Dan paid the carriage driver, Rachel stared at the enormous Palladian Georgian home, awed by its size and beauty.

A servant answered Dan's knock at the door. The immaculately clad man with excellent manners bowed, welcomed them, and ushered them inside a lengthy hallway. He took Rachel's shawl, then escorted them to go, into an oversize drawing room.

Dan and Rachel paused beneath an archway sided by fluted pilasters. As with the outside, rococo detailing was used inside on the woodwork. The drawing room extended the length of the house, but was skillfully separated into three areas by a series of columns to match those at the entrance and archways. There was no mistaking the craftsmanship and designs of Chippendale furnishings, again in the rococo style. The decor was obviously done by someone with superb taste and plenty of money.

"It's breathtaking," Rachel murmured to her companion, who agreed emphatically.

The sitting areas were filled with guests. George had told them there would be forty tonight. A talented female played a piano in the center section, sending forth soft music into the well-lighted setting.

George and Molly Sue Leathers came forward with the Powers to greet them. "May I introduce your host and hostess, James and Jane Powers? This is Rachel McCandless, Mrs. Phillip McCandless, wife of my business partner. This fine gentleman is her cousin, Captain Daniel Slade from Charleston, who owns his own ship and business."

Pleasantries were exchanged, then Rachel complimented, "Your home is the loveliest I have ever seen. Thank you for having us here tonight. It was most kind of you to accept George's request to include us."

"Please make yourselves comfortable. Ask for whatever you desire. Meet everyone and enjoy yourselves. Dinner will be served at eight."

"There are plenty of people for you to meet," George said. "Come, and let me introduce you to some of them before dinner is announced."

Rachel took her place and looked around the table to see who was sitting with her and Dan—all twelve appeared important and wealthy people, all were nice and charming. She was relieved.

A bevy of servers and butlers bustled around three tables. Red and white wines, coffee, tea, and water were poured into an assortment of crystal glasses at each plate. The menu was thorough and delicious. To avoid having to pass along and possibly spill something, the servants brought around each choice for the guests' selection. Tiny silver bells sat before each plate to ring for another helping or assistance.

Dan observed Rachel's conduct and found her charming, well bred, and an excellent conversationalist: a southern belle to the finest degree of training. She knew how to behave in this opulent setting, and looked the perfect image of a lady.

Dan continued to watch her from the corner of his eye as she dined and chatted with those nearby. She seemed to be having a marvelous time. Her olive complexion had a glow of health, merriment, and self-confidence. He wished she didn't look so ravishing and radiant, as it made her too distracting and appealing. The more he was around her and the more he learned about her, the more he was confused. He had met devious, scheming, and heartless types before. How could Rachel conceal those traits so expertly and without dropping clues to expose her true nature? As she had said earlier, no matter how clever an evil person was, one couldn't hide a true self from everyone and all the time . . . It was frustrating to entice her physically closer while trying to stay distanced emotionally. He couldn't allow himself to forget his behavior was only an entrapping fantasy. He just wished his chore weren't becoming so difficult.

While after-dinner liqueurs were being served in the drawing room, the men enjoyed their pipes and cigars, and people gathered in groups to converse, Rachel excused herself to visit the powder room.

Before she could rejoin Dan near the piano, she was halted by Jane Powers and a stranger near the archway.

"This gentleman wants to meet you, Rachel. His name is Harold Seymour; he's here with his aunt. He's taken with your beauty and charm, my dear, but I've warned this smitten bachelor that you're married."

"You do me an injustice, Jane," the neatly dressed man drawled in a thick Southern accent. "I told you, this lady looks familiar to me, and I haven't had the opportunity to make her acquaintance yet."

Jane laughed and sent him an incredulous look. "Harold, this is Rachel McCandless, *Mrs.* Phillip McCandless, from Savannah. Her husband is the partner of George Leathers."

"Ah, yes, the lovely Mrs. McCandless from Savannah. Now I know why your face is familiar. You've had quite an interesting life, Rachel. As a newspaper reporter, I've read many articles about you and your adventures. Would you do me the honor of granting me an interview?"

Rachel was caught off guard. How dare he mention something so private and embarrassing—and revealing—in such a luxurious, social setting! How dare he use her first name in that intimate and suggestive tone!

"Rachel is famous?" Jane Powers inquired, showing great interest.

Rachel sent her a fake smile and said, "I'm afraid not, Jane. My husband is the important one in our family. I was simply mentioned in stories about him." Before she could try to extricate herself further from the alarming situation, one of the guests summoned Jane to answer a question.

Rachel focused on the newspaper man to bring his damaging idea to an instant stop. "An interview with me, Mr. Seymour, would be dull and useless to you. Besides," she continued sternly when he tried to interrupt and persist, "I do not grant them to anyone. I'm afraid I haven't met many reporters who write the truth as the person involved relates it. Most have been rude, aggressive, and insensitive. I try to stay clear of such men, as my life is private, not a tasty treat for public consumption."

Harold had his eyes glued to hers. "Ah, yes, protection of privacy would be important to a beautiful and famous lady like yourself, but—"

"It is, Mr. Seymour, and thank you for the compliment. If you'll excuse me, I must be leaving. It's late, and I have an early train to catch in the morning. I must thank my host and hostess and bid them farewell."

"Are you sure you can't spend a few moments with me tonight or in the morning before you depart?" he wheedled. "I won't be rude or callous. I find your story utterly fascinating and the gossip surrounding

146

you misinformed. Isn't it past time you tell your side and call a halt to nasty rumors?"

Rachel did not smile as she responded, "No, Mr. Seymour. I neither have the time nor the inclination to do so. Good night and good-bye."

Rachel walked to Jane and James Powers. She waited until they finished their talk, then said, "It's time for me to leave. The evening was delightful. Thank you for including me and my cousin. If you visit Savannah, please allow me to repay your hospitality and kindness."

They chatted for a moment, then parted. Rachel's eager gaze located Dan. He appeared to be enjoying himself and having no problem in this formal setting. She presumed he had come from a wealthy and refined family and had training and plenty of practice in the social graces. She went to Dan and told him she was ready to leave.

Dan knew she was upset and in a hurry to escape from what had appeared to be an unpleasant and apprehensive chat with a man across the room. He had asked the gentleman with him for the intruder's identity. The moment he learned it was a newspaper reporter, Dan assumed the man had recognized the "Beautiful Black Widow" from Savannah and was harassing her. It was obvious she had handled the man with expertise, but he didn't want to give Seymour another chance to expose her. "I'm ready. I need fresh air, exercise, and sleep," he said.

Dan paced his room as he made plans. He had to put his romantic ploy in motion tomorrow, convince her he was falling in love with her.

Chapter 7

As Rachel dressed for her breakfast with Dan, she prayed she wouldn't run into Harold Seymour. She hoped he wouldn't check with the hotel clerk to make certain she'd told the truth about leaving. Being caught in a lie would make the aggressive reporter more curious and bold, as he already aroused her suspicions. He could have seen her arrive, recognized her, and, hungry for a juicy story, searched her room and left those two notes to make her susceptible to his interview request. If he didn't pester her again, she would ascribe last night's meeting to coincidence, which would mean she hadn't unmasked her tormentor.

For a while she had suspected her stepfather of spying on her and perpetrating all the insidious deeds. White Cloud wasn't too far from Savannah and Augusta for him to make quick trips to harass her as always. She had discarded that angle, though, as Earl Starger had been very direct with his wicked desires in the past. So, she mused, who did that leave?

The more she was with Daniel Slade, the more she was tempted and persuaded to trust him. She told herself she mustn't confuse his emotional threat with a physical one. Perhaps she would learn enough about him if she become more—but carefully—responsive to him.

If that inquisitive reporter came around and asked revealing questions, how would she explain her dark past and lies to Dan? Yet it would be too suspicious to everyone, including Dan, if she made a sudden change in departure plans.

She met Dan in the lobby. "Did you rise early again this morning?" she asked.

"Always, Rachel; it's in my blood. Did you sleep well?"

"Yes I did, and I needed it. Wasn't the dinner party marvelous?"

"I had a splendid time. But I always have a good time with you. I'm going to miss you, Rachel, when I ship out again. I'm afraid I'll be hard pressed to find such perfect company and good friendship elsewhere."

"Hard-to-please man, are you?" she teased, warmed by his words.

"One of those flaws you haven't noticed yet."

"Being discriminating isn't a flaw, Dan. What's more precious than one's time, pleasures, and friendships?"

"You're right, woman. It's a strength, not a weakness."

"I wouldn't imagine you have many, if any, weaknesses."

"You'd be surprised to learn I probably have plenty of them."

Rachel laughed. "That's a sneaky way of not admitting to having any."

"I should have left out *probably,* because I do have some."

"Such as?" she probed, unwisely sealing her gaze to his.

Dan imprisoned it. "No way will I expose them to you, woman."

"Why not? How else can I get to know you better?"

"With you as such a good influence, maybe they'll

vanish, so there's no need to tell you about them to hold against me later."

"I would never hold anything against you, Dan. People change over time, and hopefully for the better."

"You don't, Rachel."

She was confused. "What do you mean?"

"How could perfection be improved?"

"Perfection? Me? Surely you jest. Or you don't know me well."

"I hope to by the time we return to Savannah. If not, it won't be my fault or from a lack of trying."

"I wonder if you like me as much if you really knew me?"

"What a crazy question," he said.

"I'm on my best behavior, of course. When I'm not . . ." She grinned and left her brazen implication dangling in midair.

"So that's it, you're a skilled actress who's pretending to like me."

"Certainly not. Of course I like you, Daniel Slade. Who wouldn't?"

"Because I'm Phillip's friend and you're a well-bred young lady?"

"Certainly not. I like you because you're nice and fun to be with, because you're a real gentleman and I can trust you."

"I'm a gentleman only because it's necessary with a friend's wife. If you weren't married to Phillip McCandless . . ." He left his suggestion hanging.

"You wouldn't be a gentleman around me?" she quipped.

"That isn't exactly what I meant," he replied, looking embarrassed.

"If I weren't married, Daniel Slade, I wouldn't be a lady around you."

The waiter intruded at that moment and silenced their provocative words.

* * *

George and Molly Sue came to fetch them and they traveled for a few miles on the road toward Washington, Georgia, chatting about the party and the guests. When they arrived at their destination, George drove slowly so the couple could get a good view of the impressive driveway that was lined with majestic magnolias, some in bloom with their eight-inch shell-shaped flowers. At the far end of the drive stood a square, two-story house with white pillars around all sides, a gallery that encircled the second floor, and a cupola atop the roof.

When the carriage halted, the Berckmans came to greet them. They were shown into the house with its thick cement walls that held in winter heat and kept out summer blazes. They chatted for a while with the Belgian family, then left with Prosper on a tour of world-famous Fruitland Nurseries.

They enjoyed walking among the flowering trees and colorful bushes. Bees darted here and there, collecting nectar. Graceful butterflies fluttered around the countless blossoms and cheerful strollers. Birds sang and flitted about. Brown thrashers searched among dead leaves for bugs and worms, rapidly tossing debris in all directions during their task. The day was clear and sunny, and Rachel and Dan were at ease for a while.

They returned to the house to share tea and small cakes with the family. When it was time to leave for their next activity, she and Dan thanked their host and departed with the Leathers.

A mile down the road, George asked Rachel if she wanted to stop to purchase honey from a beekeeper, some of the best in the state.

"That's sounds wonderful, George," she said. "Thank you."

George halted the carriage on the edge of the dirt

road. Rachel and Dan walked to the wooden stand to make their purchases from an elderly gentleman. Rachel bought a case of six jars, while Dan bought two cases to take to his ship. He paid for all three.

"You must like honey," she commented.

"I love it. When you're happy and relaxed, it's the same color as your eyes," he remarked as he accepted his change and waited for their order to be placed in crates. "I've never seen that shade before, sort of a pale golden brown with a very dark ring encasing them."

"I get this color from my father's side of the family, the Flemings. I take after them. I don't favor Mama or her side. She has blond hair and green eyes. Even at forty-five she's beautiful and slender and looks my age."

The packaging was finished. Dan lifted the small crates with ease.

"Yours are the color of the deepest sea," she said.

"Do honey and water mix?" he asked with a roguish grin.

She couldn't answer, because they reached the carriage and because she couldn't think of a clever response to the romantic query. He noticed so much about everything, including her. That both pleased and panicked Rachel.

Dan placed the cases on the floor between them and the carriage left.

"You two get along well," George remarked. "It's nice to see families and kin who are so close."

Rachel and Dan exchanged guilty looks, then conspiratorial smiles.

"Yes, sir," Dan murmured. "We do get along better than most people. Cousin Rachel and I are best friends. We have a long history together."

"I hope you get back this way again soon, Dan. We've enjoyed your company," Molly Sue told him.

* * *

They headed to the city parade grounds, which were composed of ten acres with a group of trees near the center. Wagons and carriages were parked along the four streets and people milled around, chatting and laughing.

"Winter is our season to play baseball, because harvest is over and it's still mild here. The team gathers one Saturday a month to practice during the spring and summer. Men and older boys from town make up the opposing team. It's fun and relaxing to come over and watch. We usually have a picnic afterward. It draws the community closer together."

Molly Sue handed the two men quilts for them to sit on to observe the practice and to join the merriment. As they strolled across the grassy lot toward the gathering of people and players, George made a shocking but unintentional revelation to Rachel and Dan.

"Phillip loves baseball and horse racing season. We have our races in the winter, too, at the Lafayette Course south of town. Gamblers of all ages and sexes visit during that time. I'm not a gambling man, but Phillip surely loves to place bets. He even likes to wager on the cockfights and billiard tables. We have a few gambling establishments, but I don't frequent them. I've always let Phillip go alone or with others. Hard-earned money is too valuable to toss away on games and horses. I've seen Phillip almost lose his shirt some days," he chuckled.

"I didn't realize Phillip liked to gamble," Rachel murmured.

"Oh, my, have I talked out of the wrong side of my mouth?"

"Don't worry, George, I won't tell him you mentioned it. There are certain pleasures we women shouldn't interfere with, right, Molly Sue?"

"You're a smart woman, Rachel," she complimented, then frowned at her husband in a way that told him to keep silent on the matter.

Gambling? A regular bet maker? Phillip McCandless? Enough to be an expensive and hazardous weakness? Enough to lose . . . Rachel didn't want to ponder those possibilities any further at the moment.

"Here we are. Just spread your quilt, have a seat, and enjoy yourself," George said.

Rachel glanced around the crowd and searched for Harold Seymour. She didn't see him and sighed in relief, though he could still come later, she knew.

Dan witnessed her tension and noticed her scan the crowd. He knew why. As he pretended to watch the teams practice, he drifted into deep thought. His brother had never been a gambler, but it sounded as if Phillip had gained a love of that expensive and risky sport. Dan prayed it hadn't become a weakness, a dangerous threat. If a man owed someone a lot of money, he would be tempted to do anything to settle that debt. Or if a man gambled with someone else's money and lost all or part of it . . . Dan didn't want to think his brother could be so foolish. If—

"Did you see that, Dan? It's going for a mile before it lands!"

"He's a hard and straight hitter, George."

"Some of these boys amaze me. We have a good team this year."

The practice continued for another hour before the picnic began. Molly Sue and George fetched the food basket from the wagon and spread out a feast on a tablecloth on the grass. They chatted as they feasted on cold fried chicken, pickles, biscuits, and strawberries.

Dan watched Rachel lick her greasy fingers and use her tongue to collect the crisp pieces of chicken that clung to her lips. "Don't let anything get the best of you, Cousin Rachel," he jested.

She leaned forward and pushed a ripe strawberry into his mouth. "Aren't they the finest you've eaten?" she asked, then licked her fingers.

"Sinfully so. I should also buy two cases of them for my ship."

"They would be ruined by the time you set sail."

He stopped nibbling on the chicken to reply, "I keep forgetting my holiday is so lengthy; I'm unaccustomed to being in port so long."

"Do your men stay aboard the ship when it's docked?"

"Some do at all times. They rotate taking shore leave. It isn't wise to leave a ship unguarded in port even if your cargo's been unloaded."

"I know what you mean. One of Phillip's ships was robbed, burned, and sunk last month. It was loaded to sail, but fortunately no crew was aboard to be attacked. Phillip's firm had to cover the client's loss, and it was a very big one."

Dan scowled at that news. "Did they catch the culprits?"

"No. We also had a warehouse vandalized last month, then a dockworker was murdered. It seems trouble comes in bunches. The police are too busy chasing people for minor offenses to spend the time needed to catch real criminals."

"That happens everywhere, and it's a shame. I'm sure those incidents upset a peace-loving man like Phillip. If Phillip hasn't taken the precaution to hire men to guard his possessions, he should. Sounds to me as if that bunch is rotten and needs attention."

"That's a good idea; I'll tell him." Rachel concluded Dan hadn't known about those threatening episodes, and congratulated herself for her cleverness in mentioning them.

"If you two don't mind," George said, "Molly Sue and I are going over yonder to speak with some friends. We'll return shortly."

"So, you were the baby of your family," Dan remarked when he and Rachel were left alone. "What was it like to live at White Cloud? If you don't mind talking about it," he added.

"Until the war, wonderful. It was one of the most beautiful and prosperous plantations in Georgia; I suppose it still is; I don't know, because I haven't been there in years. Mama and Papa knew how to throw such grand parties and everybody loved them—my parents and the splendid events. People came from miles away to attend. Sometimes I would sneak out of bed, peek through the railing, and watch the dancing for hours. Until I was caught," she added with a laugh.

Her tone and expression became somber as she went on. "After my father died and Earl came, it was awful, like living in a prison. Nobody was happy anymore; nobody smiled and joked. The air in the house always seemed cold and hostile. We'd get up, eat, do chores, eat, study lessons, eat, and escape to our rooms until bedtime; then repeat that depressing schedule the next day, and the next, and the next. After the twins left, things didn't get any better. Earl kept me and Mama on the plantation like captives, as if he was ashamed of us. I was educated at home by private tutors and taught the social graces every southern girl should know. But Earl rarely gave me a chance to practice them on others, unless he gave a big party to show off to everyone. Then he'd flaunt us like expensive possessions. Some old friends and neighbors wouldn't attend White Cloud functions or even speak to us anymore. I can't blame them for viewing Mama as a traitor and weakling. She changed so after Papa died. By the time I was eighteen, I was suffocating; I couldn't wait to get away from there. I still don't understand why Mama can't see how terrible he is," Rachel murmured with sad eyes, then went silent as the Leathers returned to join them.

* * *

As they entered the hotel, Dan tried to imagine a proper young lady of eighteen being thrust into the world alone to support and defend herself. Did that harsh experience and her losses explain why her first choice was a man old enough to be her father? Yet he suspected there was more to her reason for leaving home than she had confessed. Why wouldn't a killer of men get rid of the one she despised and resented the most?

As they strolled through the lobby, a waiter approached them offering them two mint juleps, as the drink was a hotel treat on Saturday nights.

Dan looked at Rachel in askance, then grinned before she could reply and said, "Yes, that should relax us nicely for a good night's sleep."

The waiter lowered his tray and handed each a tall glass filled with ice, which was covered with a golden-brown blend of sugar, bourbon, and mint leaves. It was a potent mixture, a symbol of Southern tradition and hospitality.

Rachel and Dan took their drinks and strolled onto the second-floor veranda to sip the juleps and chat before parting for the night. Others were there for the same purpose, so the couple sought a quiet and private area. They sat in comfortable rocking chairs with a small table between them. For a while, they only enjoyed the pleasant evening and heady refreshment. Their moods mellowed, their spirits soared, and their bodies warmed with the intoxicating drink and the close proximity of the other.

"Tell me about Turkey and why arms are needed there," Rachel coaxed, needing a distraction from Dan's overwhelming pull.

Dan lowered his glass from his lips, licked them, and replied, "If you're not familiar with that area, you'll need some background on it first."

"I'm not, so a history lesson is required."

"At one time, Turkey pretty much ruled that part of the world under the Ottoman Empire. Years ago, people of certain areas started demanding better treatment and independence. The Tanzimat Reforms were issued to appease them." Dan related the problems for and between the Christians and Muslims of the region, then halted to sip his drink to wet his throat. To keep from staring at her, he rested his head against the chair back and gazed toward the building across the street.

It was night, but the waning moon and gas lamps cast soft glows on the cozy setting and highlighted their features. Most of the other people had left the porch for late dinners, strolls, visits, or to retire to their rooms. It was becoming more intimate and romantic in the shadows.

Rachel was partially turned in her rocker to watch Dan as he spoke. He had the most compelling smile and arresting blue eyes she had ever seen. His complexion was darkly tanned from hours on his ship's deck beneath the sun. His features were bold and rugged. His hair was as dark and shiny as a crow's wing in the moonlight. He caused her heart to flutter and her slumbering desires to awaken.

Dan lowered his glass. "Some reforms worked, despite opposition. But the sultan was left with too much power and control. The rebelling peasants asked for help from other European and American powers. The sultan has run up a big foreign debt, and one he is unable to repay since the '73 worldwide financial crisis and Depression."

Rachel remembered that panic, an event that had helped push her into Craig Newman's arms and life, into his wicked power.

"No nation will loan him more money, so he isn't about to give up any of his profitable possessions. When war breaks out, other nations will get involved, mainly Russia; the United States can't allow her to steal control of such a large and important region." Dan hoped his truthful explanation would satisfy her curiosity.

"It sounds awful, but crucial. Everyone wants freedom," Rachel said and thanked Dan for the interesting information. "It's late now and we have church early in the morning. If you've finished your drink, we'd better go to our rooms and retire. My glass is empty, and I feel it working on me from head to toe." She laughed and rubbed her tingly nose. She hadn't intended to consume the whole drink, but had, she was so distracted by him.

Dan held her elbow as they walked up the steps to the third floor. In her weakened condition, it was the perfect moment for his next move, as he could always blame his own light head for his loss of self-control.

The hallway was empty and quiet. Dim lights cast seductive glows and shadows. He guided Rachel to her door. Dan asked for her key to unlock it. After doing so, he led her inside. "I'd better help you, woman," he said as excuse, chuckling all the while. "You don't seem too steady afoot right now."

Rachel gave a soft laugh. "I'm not," she responded. "I shouldn't have drunk all of that mint julep. I'm not used to strong spirits. My head feels like a bird in dizzy flight."

"I know what you mean; I'm not a drinker, either, and that mixture was potent. You need any help with unreachable buttons?" he offered.

"I don't think so, but thank you." She looked up into his eyes, and their gazes locked. "You're the kindest man I've ever known."

"And you're the most bewitching woman I've ever known. It takes a strong will not to caress this satiny skin, this silky hair, and these soft lips." As he mentioned those forbidden areas, his defiant fingers trailed over each one with sensuous caresses. His

159

thumb rubbed over her parted lips as he fused his eyes with hers. He felt her tremors of arousal, and he witnessed kindled desire in her gaze. He noticed how her breathing became fast and shallow and how her cheeks flushed even brighter.

Dan's eyes never left hers as he slowly lowered his head and sealed their lips, bringing fiery flesh into contact. His arms circled her back and drew her against him. He closed his eyes as his lips feasted on hers. His deft tongue explored her mouth and danced wildly with hers as they savored the taste of each other and the lingering one of the drinks. Dan groaned in need, tightened his embrace, and deepened his kiss. She was responding to him. Was it her unleashed passions or the debilitating bourbon controlling this blissful but wanton behavior?

Rachel allowed the rapturous feelings to continue for a while. Flames of desire leapt throughout her body. Her heart raced and she felt weak and shaky. She had never experienced anything like this with any man. She yearned to give free rein to the emotions, to let them sweep her away. She couldn't, though, not yet, not until the mystery of Phillip was clarified between them. She didn't want to give Dan the worst—a wicked—impression of her. She decided the best path of escape was to go limp in his embrace as if she'd passed out.

Dan caught her sinking body and carried her to the bed. He sensed it was a defensive ploy, but he had learned what he needed to know. Tonight wasn't the time to further explore her weakness for him. They still had work to do before their return to Savannah, work that could be halted by a guilty conscience or fear of a repetition of their behavior. He removed her shoes, covered her, and gazed down at her. Assuming she was awake, he murmured, "Stars above, Rachel McCandless, you're too much of a temptation to resist. I wish you weren't married, at least not to a good

160

friend of mine. I can't steal Phillip's wife or compromise her. You're much too special for that. It's best to ignore this accident; it wouldn't have happened if we hadn't taken those drinks. If you recall this weakness tomorrow, I hope you forgive it and don't mention it. For us to discuss it would expose things better left hidden. Sleep well, my fetching siren." He kissed her forehead and left the room. He locked the door and shoved the key under it into her room.

Rachel rose quietly, removed her clothes, and returned to bed without donning a nightgown. The cool sheets rubbed against her flaming flesh. She curled to her side and nestled her face against the pillow. She had made a thrilling discovery; Dan did want her, and, if not for his friendship with Phillip, he would pursue her. She had to trust Dan, and couldn't think of a tangible reason not to do so. For a while she would pretend their indiscretion hadn't happened. What she had to worry about was Dan's reaction to her deceptions. She must pray, and pray hard, it wouldn't destroy any chance she might have with him in the future, because she wanted him. Forever.

Fears attacked her. If no man who married her could survive long, could she endanger Dan's life? Wouldn't it be wiser and safer, she reasoned, to try to become his lover, not his wife? It couldn't injure her reputation, as that was already ruined. Besides, Dan loved the sea, his ship, and his adventurous existence. With her as his mistress and waiting in port for his visits, that arrangement should suit the carefree bachelor fine. Besides, there was a strong possibility she couldn't have children, and Dan would surely want them.

"Please don't hate me and spurn me when you learn the truth about me," she murmured to herself. "I swear, I'll promise you forever as your mistress."

Rachel heard a squeak, leaned up, and glanced toward the armoire. She listened, but heard nothing more. She surmised that Dan was putting away his clothes in the next room. She would enjoy doing all Dan's chores for him, but probably would never get the chance. Besides, it might only be a physical attraction to her he felt. He might never want to marry a three-time widow, one husband having been his old friend. Then again, she could be mistaken, and prayed she was. She cuddled into the soft mattress, closed her eyes, and went to sleep to dream of Captain Daniel Slade.

As the singing of hymns finished and the crowd took their seats in the large church, the pastor rose to stand behind his podium. He passed his gentle gaze over his flock, smiled, and opened his Bible.

He began with shocking words: "In Exodus twenty, verse thirteen, the Good Book says, 'Thou shalt not kill.' Most people believe that only means not to take another's life. I tell you, brethren and sisters, it means far more. There are many other ways to kill. You can murder someone's reputation with cruel lies or by spreading destructive gossip. You can murder someone's spirit by crushing it until it dies. You can murder someone's hopes and dreams by preventing them from coming true. You can murder someone's will by forcing him or her to be weak and useless so you can be stronger. I say to you, obey the Fifth Commandment in all ways."

Rachel hadn't attended church in a while, but had been reared to do so and taught to honor the Bible's words. She had tried to obey the Ten Commandments she had learned as a child. Even if she had surrendered to Dan, she wouldn't have committed adultery. "Until death do you part," the Book commanded, and it had, from all three husbands. Yet, she couldn't vow she hadn't broken the last one. She had coveted, hungered, and envied what others had: good names, friends, respect, honor, and happiness. Sometimes she was jealous of others for having what she wanted, and experienced bitterness and resentment for being denied. She wished every person who had been cruel to and judgmental of her could hear this message and obey it.

Dan observed Rachel from the corner of his eye as the minister talked, but didn't see a smidgen of guilt exposed on her face. They had eaten their early meal in a hurry, and neither had mentioned the heady incident last night. Both had put on cheerful moods and sunny smiles and chatted like good friends. He had seen Rachel relax the moment her gaze finished scanning the church and found no reporter. After the service, they were to have Sunday dinner with the Leathers, say their farewells, then return to the hotel to pack.

At the hotel, Dan collected the photographer's envelope from the desk clerk. He went to Rachel's room and knocked at her door.

She opened it and smiled, but looked tense. "Are you all finished this quickly?"

"I haven't even started yet. I went downstairs to get the pictures. They were just delivered as promised. They're excellent, beautiful. I'm well pleased." He withdrew and handed her three photographs. "Those are yours. These are mine," he said, shaking the envelope and grinning. "Real treasures."

Rachel looked at all three. She smiled and concurred, "Yes, they are wonderful. He did a splendid job. Thank you, Dan. I would invite you in to chat, but that wouldn't be proper."

He nodded agreement. "Besides, I have to pack, and you have to finish your chore. I'll meet you downstairs at seven for a light meal."

"I'll have something sent up, so I won't have to

stop work. This takes a long time. And after I finish, I need to rest. We have to rise, dress, and eat early to get checked out and to the station by eight-thirty. The train leaves at nine, and we first have to buy the tickets we ordered."

Dan reasoned her plans were meant to protect them from another untimely temptation. "That's fine with me. Tomorrow will be a long and busy day. I'll see you in the morning at seven. Good night, Rachel."

She almost sighed aloud in relief for his understanding. "Good night, Dan, and thank you again for these lovely pictures."

After she closed her door, Rachel recalled what George had said today about telling Phillip to send that advance to him as soon as possible.

Rachel knew George was worried, but she believed—hoped—he had told her everything he knew about the mysterious order. She still wanted a look at the company books, but that wasn't possible, not on this trip, at least.

They boarded the Georgia Railroad train at Union Station. Everything had gone as planned this morning. They settled back in their seats and waited for departure. It wasn't long in coming. The engineer gave several blasts of the whistle, then put the train into motion. At first it traveled slowly and carefully through the southwestern side of town, but when Augusta was left behind, it increased its speed. Soon the wheels were rolling with their clickity-clack sounds, steam was rolling over the top of the line of cars, and passengers relaxed to enjoy the day-long trip.

This time, their car was filled with people, and Rachel and Dan were sitting across from each other. The noise made conversation difficult, so they soon ceased trying to communicate with curious listeners nearby.

For a while, they gazed out the windows as they passed forests of pine and hardwoods. Grass was long and green in the fields, wildflowers were abundant and colorful, and stock grazed in contentment. Fields were plowed and planted with a variety of crops, many in cotton or wheat or oats, but sometimes in seemingly endless rows of tobacco and corn.

Both held books they had purchased to while away the hours, but mainly used them to keep from staring at each other. Their knees often touched as the train veered around a bend or they altered their positions, as the seats faced each other. They would glance up then, smile, gaze a moment, then focus their eyes on pages which hadn't turned in a long time.

The sea captain watched his bewildering sister-in-law from beneath lowered lashes. He wondered if Rachel could suffer from a strange mental derangement that compelled her to mate and kill. What if she couldn't help herself and didn't even remember doing those vile deeds once they were over? How could he find out for sure? Marry her and let her attempt to murder him seemed the only answer.

He speculated about a pattern to the mysterious deaths. Nothing about the three men or her mating schedule seemed to match. If the devastating war had done something to her mind, and her motive was determination never to be poor or vulnerable again, but she had the missing money hidden and would soon have Phillip's inheritance, she could spend a year in disarming mourning as she had before marrying Phillip. That lengthy timing would put a snag in his ruse to romance, wed, and then expose her.

It was easier to blame a madness that she wasn't even aware of for her insidious actions than to believe this woman could be capable of plotting and carrying out four cold-blooded murders. That would explain why she didn't act guilty and how she kept from dropping any incriminating clues.

If he doubted her guilt in the least, he couldn't do anything necessary to destroy her. But if she were only clever, dangerous, and daring, and if she had defeated the law many times and gone free, he had no choice but to use any ploy to entrap her. Soon he would know which course to sail with her.

There were routine stops in numerous towns along the route to let passengers on and off and to unload or load freight. They had their longest one at Union Point, where the tracks forked to head either right with a branch to Athens or left along the mainline to Atlanta. They ate lunch at a small cafe near the depot. Afterward, they took a muscle-loosening stroll. They didn't stray far from the small station as they walked along the tracks on a dirt road and looked at the landscape. Verdant leaves mingled with white or pink flowers on plum, peach, and pear trees. Sunny daffodils and purple rabbit's ears blossomed in a profusion of beauty nearby.

"I love spring," Rachel murmured as she watched bees and butterflies at work amidst the blooms. She saw birds searching for worms, bugs, and insects. She noticed tall green pines reaching for a sky that was cloudless and a rich blue. A mild breeze stirred the flora and leaves. "Everything is so alive and vivid, as if all things are filled with magical energy and eagerness. Everything's reborn, given a new chance to be better than before. It's inspirational, isn't it?"

"I've never thought of it that way, but it's true. You're a very sensitive woman, Rachel McCandless. You constantly amaze me and—"

The whistle blew its warning to reboard, to which the conductor added his shout. "We'd better get back to the train. We don't want to get stranded here until the next one comes along tomorrow."

* * *

The engine and line of cars halted on Carr's Hill, across from the one-hundred-fifty-foot-wide Oconee River and east of Athens. No trestle had been constructed for it to continue on into town, and wouldn't be until 1881. Warehouses, a depot, and several freight, stage, and carriage companies were located at the terminus of the Georgia Railroad and lined both sides of the tracks with structures of various sizes. Hack drivers, drayers, and freight haulers met the train to compete for business. After the baggage was unloaded, separated, and claimed by passengers, returning residents and visitors were taken across the bridge and into town.

Rachel and Dan's carriage climbed a steep slope which was lined with homes, a canebrake, woods, and cornfields. Their driver, a student at the local college, filled their heads with facts. Athens, located below the stirrings of the Blue Ridge Mountains, was nestled among the rolling hills of North Georgia, which were covered with pines, hardwoods, and red clay. Named after Athens, Greece—another city of beauty, prosperity, and culture situated atop scenic hills—it was a town of wealth and refinement, of education and industry, of enormous homes, and a mixture of both hurried and relaxed lifestyles. If they wished to tour the city later, he asked that they please hire him as their guide, as he needed the money for tuition. Rachel told him of course they would if their schedules matched.

The driver halted at their hotel. Across the street was the University of Georgia campus, established ninety years ago. Dan paid the student, who eagerly rushed away for another pickup.

The Newton House Hotel was a three-story, redbrick structure with white decorative work over its numerous windows. On the second floor, a free-hanging covered porch ran half the length of the Broad Street side and half the width of the College Avenue side. Double doors with glass sidelights and oblong fanlights led into a well-furnished lobby. Two polite bellmen lifted their baggage from the stone sidewalk and carried it into the hotel. It was lovely, the couple remarked, as grand as the Planter's Hotel in Augusta.

They registered and were shown to their rooms, which were across the hall from each other. It was six o'clock and they were hungry, so they decided to eat before unpacking and resting. They locked their doors and went to locate the dining room, to find it another cozy setting.

"Tomorrow morning we'll visit Harrison Clements and see what he has to tell us. I wonder what it will be . . ." she murmured.

Chapter 8

On Tuesday, the sixth of April, Rachel and Dan hired a carriage that took them down Broad Street to the Oconee River to the Athens Arms Company owned by Harrison Clements and Phillip McCandless.

Before they knocked on the office door, Rachel reminded Dan: "Don't forget what I told you at breakfast; Harry is smart and tough, so we have to move slower and easier with him than we did with George."

Dan eyed her. "You don't like him very much, do you?"

"I don't know him well, but he hasn't made a good impression on me. He seems smart in business, but there's something about him that makes me wary. I'm sure you'll see what I mean. It's his eyes. He has a disconcerting and sneaky way of squinting them or lifting one brow. I never feel comfortable around him. See if he strikes you the same way. Phillip claims I'm being foolish."

Dan shook his head. "I've never seen you be foolish, Rachel. I'll watch him closely. I'm sure you're right. Something has to be lurking below his surface or you wouldn't have doubts about him."

"Thanks for your confidence in me. Let's go face the lion in his den," she jested with a smile.

Dan heard men talking, so he didn't knock. He

simply opened the door to catch the part-owner off guard. He pushed the door aside and stepped back to allow Rachel to enter first.

The man who had been sitting lazed back in a chair, his legs propped on his desk, got to his feet with speed and agility. The two men with him merely turned in their seats to see what had caused their friend's curious reaction.

"Rachel McCandless! What are you doing here?" Harrison Clements asked, sounding as if she were an annoying intrusion.

"Harry, how nice to see you again," Rachel murmured in a sweet and soft southern drawl. She smiled as she slowly walked toward his desk. "I do hope I'm not interrupting anything, gentlemen."

"Not really," the man with thick and wiry flaxen hair replied. His light-blue eyes narrowed, then one brow lifted quizzically. "What are you doing here?" he repeated as he came around the desk to meet her.

Phillip's warning, "Don't double cross Harry and the . . ." raced through her mind. She cautioned herself to be careful around Harry, who possibly was her enemy. With feigned vivacity, she related the same false tale she had told George about Phillip's sudden business trip up North and her holiday with her "cousin," whom she introduced. If Harry recognized Dan's name, it didn't show, and Rachel was relieved. "I thought a visit with you and a company tour would be nice today if it's no bother. If you're busy . . . ."

"Let me finish with these gentlemen, and I'll be with you two."

Rachel watched Harry guide the two men to the door, step outside to speak a few words in a lowered tone, then return to her. While he was doing so, she studied the man's boxy face, chiseled features, and deep-clefted chin. He looked as if he spent a great deal of time outdoors, as his skin was dark and his hair appeared sun-streaked. Harry held himself stiffly, as if he were annoyed and on alert; and she was certain it was her unexpected arrival that caused his reaction. She noticed there had been no introductions of her and Dan, which seemed rude.

Harry joined the couple inside his office, next to the arms company along the Oconee River. His ice-blue gaze roamed her face as he asked, "Now, what's this about Phillip taking off to places unknown?"

Putting on an innocent expression, she shrugged. "He left on business right after your visit," she said casually. "He said he'd be gone for six to seven weeks. Baltimore was his first stop, but he could be anywhere by now. That naughty husband of mine hasn't even contacted me yet."

Harry glued his eyes to Rachel's face. "Why did he go? What kind of business?" he asked in an almost demanding tone.

Rachel grasped the man's surprise and suspicion. "I haven't the faintest idea, Harry. Phillip said it was urgent and unexpected. He said he had to handle it promptly and it would require that long."

"That should put him back home the first or second week of May."

After he frowned and narrowed his gaze once more, Rachel asked, "Is there a problem? Phillip didn't mention one before he left home suddenly."

"No, I just wanted to see him before the fourteenth of next month."

Harry sat down, but didn't ask Rachel or Dan to take seats. He looked worried, and she surmised that it was because he would be out of a big profit if Phillip spoiled their secret deal. He probably wished he himself had handled the negotiations and collected the advance. He had to be angry with Phillip for concealing the money and perhaps refusing to pass it along to the company, or to him. "May we sit?" she asked.

"Of course. I'm sorry, but I have things on my mind today."

He didn't appear sincere, but Rachel pretended not to notice. "We just left Augusta and a wonderful visit with George and Molly Sue. They showed us around town and kept us busy for six days. They're so nice and hospitable, but of course you know that about them. George mentioned a large arms and ammunition deal the two companies are doing together. Is that what you're concerned about, Harry? I know Phillip's a partner and he's away now, but he doesn't normally handle much of the two companies' affairs. He leaves most of that to you and George."

Harrison Clements stared at her a moment, his probing gaze digging into hers to uncover clues. "We don't have any problems with any of our contracts, Rachel," he answered, "I only wanted to discuss an expansion during the early summer with him. I was just wondering why Phillip didn't mention this trip to me when we talked on the twenty-fifth."

He's probably asking himself if I know anything, Rachel mused. *Did Phillip send me here on a fact-gathering mission? What did Phillip's secret trip mean?* Rachel pushed aside such speculation. "I don't know. Unless," she created with a bright smile, "it was because he didn't know about it when you were there. A telegram arrived early Friday morning and he left soon after your departure by train. A little sooner, and you two might have run into each other in town."

Harry leaned forward. "A telegram? From whom? From where?"

Rachel felt a surge of power and excitement at tricking this unlikable man. "He didn't say. He only said he had to sail to Baltimore for six to seven weeks about a new investment, something urgent and sudden. You sure there isn't a problem? You seem disturbed by this news."

Harry straightened. "No problems, Rachel. I just need an agreement about the expansion before May fourteenth so I can sign the contract and hire a builder. This time of year, they get busy and filled up fast. When you hear from Phillip, tell him to contact me immediately. Maybe that urgent business was why he was in such a bad mood during my last visit."

Rachel noticed he didn't say to ask him, but demanded to tell him. She also caught the sarcasm in his voice during his last statement. As sweetly as she could manage, she replied, "I didn't notice a foul mood before or after your visit with us. He did seem preoccupied, but not upset. You know Phillip; he always keeps his worries to himself. He was excited over a new prospect when he left; he said he would surprise me with good news when he returns. I can hardly wait to see what he's getting involved with this time. He needs so many different interests to keep him interested."

"Just tell him to cable me as soon as possible."

"I will." She changed the subject. "May we tour the company? Dan and I would love to see how guns are made."

Harry glanced at the stranger with her. "It has to be quick and quiet; the men are busy and I don't like to distract them. Errors in products cost money, and even lives sometimes. Follow me," he instructed.

As they did, Dan winked at her and nodded his approval of her conduct.

Rachel sent him a warm smile of gratitude. He had kept silent but watchful during her talk with Harry and she appreciated his assistance.

Harry showed them into the factory where many men were laboring to make parts or to assemble them. They stopped only a few minutes at each work station, and no introductions were made. Harry pointed out the construction methods and gave them the names of parts. He showed them how breech action worked on a rolling block rifle and moved on to where a lever-action rifle was being put together and explained its functions.

As if she was ignorant of gun-making, Rachel observed and merely asked a simple occasional question. Yet she paid close attention to the diagrams the men used, and made an astonishing discovery. She stared at the weapon design, an old Henry model that had been improved later by Winchester. When Harry exhibited the next model, she recognized it as a Spencer, a lever-action repeater with a spring mechanism that held the cartridges in the butt . . . She knew those facts from the manuals Phillip had given her to study.

"We also make and sell slings, swivels, and sights. We have a testing range outside town; I do most of that job. Laying a rifle gives me a thrill. Pardon me, Rachel, that means to adjust the sight to compensate for any left, right, or downward drift of a cartridge after it's fired."

Expert with a rifle, like the villain who shot at me? "How fascinating. You must be an excellent shot."

"I am," he admitted without modesty.

Rachel wondered how Harry and Phillip had gotten their hands on registered designs. Had they purchased the rights to use them, or had they stolen them and used them illegally? She thought it best not to ask any questions in that area, since they would reveal her knowledge on the subject. If stolen, exposure could ruin the company and could lose her the truth. She could not understand why Phillip, if he had known, could be involved in criminal activities. Had she misjudged him, as she had Craig? Whatever the truth, she must wait until later to deal with it.

On the way out of the factory, Harry remarked, "We used to make arms for Winchester and Remington when they were too busy to fill all their orders. After the weapons were constructed, we'd ship them to their companies to have their trademarks placed on our superb workmanship. When they expanded, they didn't need our help anymore. I hated to lose those valuable contracts, but that's how things go in business."

Rachel remembered being told how surplus arms had gone on sale after the war. It would have been simple for a skilled gunmaker to get his hands on certain models, take them apart, study their workings, then draw his own patterns. No matter that it was stealing the inventors' ideas, works protected by law. Phillip had never mentioned buying licenses to use those patents; since he had taught her so much, he wouldn't have overlooked that important fact. Yet, how could Harry do that foul deed without Phillip's knowledge and consent?

"You two will have dinner with me Friday night," Harry said. "I'll send word where to meet me. You are staying at the Newton House again?"

Rachel faked a smile. "Yes, we are, and thank you for the invitation."

"Well, now if you don't mind, I do have work to do this afternoon."

Not so polite a dismissal, she mentally scoffed. "Thank you for taking the time to show us around. We'll see you Friday night."

"You said you're planning on sightseeing?" Harry hinted.

"Yes, we're going to do just that," Dan said.

"Nice to meet you, Harry, and thanks for the tour," Dan said. "I've never been inside a gun company before. Quite interesting."

"I'm certain you'll have a good time with your cousin this week. If you need anything, send word to me."

"You're most kind and thoughtful, Harry."

Rachel and Dan halted at the top of the hill to catch their breath at the five-points section, three blocks from the hotel.

"He didn't even offer to act as our guide or even to entertain us at night after he finishes work. He probably wants to avoid me as much as possible. I'm sure you noticed how fast and reluctantly given our tour of the factory was. At least George offered us one and did it with leisure. I thought it rude neither man introduced even me to the workers; I *am* a partner's wife. And that stupid excuse about expansion! He was lying, covering himself for needing to get in touch with Phillip soon. He's probably worried about Phillip checking on him and his deals through me."

"Why didn't you tell me Phillip had just sailed when I arrived?"

Rachel was stunned by his query. She expected comments on her observation of Harry. "You didn't ask when he departed. Does that matter?"

"No, I was just wondering if there was a reason."

"Phillip left home the morning you arrived in town. You just missed seeing him." She got off that unsettling subject fast. "Harry rushed us through the tour so swiftly, I didn't have time to learn or see much. They're certainly busy for a company making so little profit."

"It's probably work for that big contract all of you mentioned."

"That's what I assumed, too. I'm glad you decided to wait a few days to place your order. It will give us the opportunity for another visit, as I'm sure Harry won't extend another invitation. That man can be so rude."

"I noticed," he concurred. "Your opinion of him seems accurate to me. I can understand Phillip liking and working with George Leathers, but Harrison Clements isn't his kind. That friendship baffles me."

As they walked to the hotel, Dan said, "You go inside and rest until supper. I'm going over to the telegraph office to send word to Luke Conner, my first mate. I want to let him know we've reached Athens in case he needs me for anything. I'll also locate that young student about acting as our tour guide for the next few days."

Rachel looked puzzled and Dan gave her his explanation.

"Because Harrison Clements struck me as a careful man. It wouldn't surprise me if he has us watched and followed. If we don't play the holiday game, he'll get suspicious of us. We'll give him a few days to be duped and disarmed, then work on him again Friday night. That suit you?"

She was pleased and impressed. "You're clever, Daniel Slade, very clever. I'm glad you're here to prevent me from making mistakes. You and Phillip are so different for best friends."

"We didn't used to be. I guess we've both changed a great deal."

"I suppose so."

Rachel and Dan enjoyed a late breakfast as they waited for their guide to finish early morning classes and fetch them. When Ted Jacobs arrived a little after eleven, he was bubbling with energy and excitement. The fair-skinned, auburn-haired youth was slim with hazel eyes. He announced they would begin their tour across the street at the University of Georgia campus, as he was between classes and had two free hours. The couple followed the jaunty youth across the dirt street to the sidewalk.

"This cast-iron arch is patterned after the Georgia state seal," he explained. "Only seniors and graduates can walk through it. Other students and visitors have to use these stone stiles. Follow me, please."

Rachel and Dan obediently used the stepway over a cast-iron picket fence. They began at the library and Ivy Building, where Ted related their histories and functions. They continued on to Demosthenian Hall, behind which stood Moore College for the agricultural and mechanical arts—two skills of importance to this agricultural and industrial location.

Ted halted them to say that the Demosthenian Society was established in 1803. "It's a debating society," he explained, "to improve the mind and to give practice with speaking. I'm a member. With a little more practice, maybe I can become a famous politician. Our biggest rivals and competitors are the Phi Kappas. That's their hall across the way." He pointed across the quadrangle to the left side of the campus. "Phi Kappa was created to give Demoses something to think about and practice on. They have secret signs and meetings; their favorite prank is to steal our notes before a big debate."

The college chapel was next, a Greek Revival structure with six tall columns and windows that almost stretched from roof to floor. They came to New College as the chapel bell signaled the changing of class. Students—male and female—hurried to and fro: some silent and thoughtful; others laughing and chatting. They waited there until the activity ceased and all was quiet again.

Ted guided them past Old College, the campus's oldest building. "Students used to meet under trees for classes," he said. "Some families, especially wealthy planters and businessmen, moved to Athens for their sons to attend this college. Most liked the town and stayed. My father owns a large cotton farm near Danielsville, too far to travel every day, so I room and board here. We had a fire in our barn last year that destroyed nearly all of our cotton before we could haul it to market. I take jobs like this to see me through until this year's picking and selling. You were kind to hire me."

Rachel perceived that the young man was a little embarrassed about his confession and predicament. She smiled and said, "Everybody has hard spells, Ted, and needs help. We were lucky you needed this job or we might have stumbled around on our own and missed your informative lessons. This is more enlightening and enjoyable."

"She's right, Ted." Dan concurred. "Besides, you'll appreciate your education more by helping to pay for it, and you'll probably study and learn more this way. If you're interested in politics, it's good to meet a lot of different people."

Ted beamed with delight. "That's very true, sir, ma'am."

After Philosophical Hall, they strolled toward the campus entrance. Ted told them about two colorful town characters: Joe Keno and Deputy Marshal William Shirley. "You'll see both plenty of times during your visit."

At the arch, they halted to chat a while longer, then the bell in the chapel rang loudly to signal the changing of periods again.

"I have to go to class now, but I have all day tomorrow free," Ted said, "Would you like to continue our tours around town?"

"That will be nice, Ted. What time shall we look for you?"

"Let's start at nine; that will give us plenty of time to see many things. Bring a picnic with you for noontime. We'll take all day, if that suits you."

"It sounds perfect. We'll see you at nine in the hotel lobby. Hurry to class before you're late," Rachel coaxed with a smile as she noticed students rushing from building to building with books burdening their arms.

"You want to take in those sights he mentioned during our stroll?" Dan ventured after Ted left them. "He told us all about them. And," he added with a grin on his face, "we need to stay busy having fun, because, as I suspected, we're being watched and followed. Don't look around," Dan cautioned as she started to do so. "I have my eye on him, so don't worry. We'll play the holiday guests as alleged. Come along, partner."

The couple crossed the street and strolled up College Avenue. There was a gentle rise to the terrain that did not urge them to strain as they walked along the tree-shaded street. At the intersection of College and Market, they looked at the confederate monument in the center of it. The Athens Baptist Church, with its tall white belfry atop, was on one corner.

Businesses and homes intermingled and complemented each other with their lovely architectures and neat facades. They turned down Market Street and walked toward Town Hall in the center of the street one and a half blocks away. Rows of china trees grew to its rear. Ted had told them the first floor was used as the city market and jail; the second, for town meetings, entertainment, school events, community suppers, trials of men incarcerated downstairs, and debates for local and state politicians. Until the new courthouse was completed, it served in that capacity, too, as the county seat had been moved to Athens from Watkinsville three years ago.

"Do we still have our shadow?" Rachel inquired, acting casually.

"Yep, about a block behind, but keeping step. Make sure you pretend not to notice him. He doesn't come close enough to make a threat. If he does, let me handle him. I'm in a protective mood today."

"Aren't you always?" she teased, sending him a radiant smile.

They stopped at a cafe for lunch. That day's specialty, which both ordered, was fried ham, red-eye gravy, biscuits, and buttered grits—a true southern meal that could be eaten and savored at any time of day or year. The busy cafe was popular with the local citizens and the tables were close, so Rachel and Dan only talked about the sights.

180

When they finished, they strolled to the Stevens Estate at the corner of Hancock. They stopped to admire the enormous Greek Revival mansion with its two formal boxwood gardens, numerous outbuildings, several wells, a fruit orchard, and vegetable garden.

"Ted didn't exaggerate; it's wonderful," Rachel murmured.

"That it is, and a large place to keep up," Dan remarked.

"Do you ever miss having a home?" she inquired.

"I do have one—my ship," he corrected with a lopsided grin.

"I meant one on land."

"Not since I left my family home in Charleston. I suppose I'll want one some day when I get too old and feeble to sail the world."

"You're teasing me, Daniel Slade."

"I know, but your question isn't one I can think about at this time."

Rachel thought it wise not to probe him on the matter.

The couple strolled toward the hotel and passed it. The block beyond contained Long Drug Store, owned by Dr. Crawford Long, a noted surgeon who discovered ether anesthesia. Standing outside the store was a wooden statue of a man grinding medicine in a large metal vase with a wood stick shaped like a baseball bat. According to Ted, the town citizens affectionately had named the statue "Tom Long." Rachel and Dan didn't halt until they returned to Jackson Street and entered a gallery of art. With leisure and enjoyment, they examined the paintings on display and for sale.

Dan paused before one of a three-masted ship, its hull tossing whitecapped waves beneath a stormy sky, her sails billowing in an invisible wind. "That's a beautiful clipper. Reminds me of the *Merry Wind*."

Rachel eyed his wistful expression and the powerful painting, and decided she must have it. It didn't seem to surprise Dan when she purchased it, and she wondered if he thought she had done so to remind her of him after they parted.

Dan carried the wrapped painting to the hotel. Rachel halted abruptly as they entered the room, then he heard her gasp. His astonished gaze took in the same sight over her shoulder.

"Look at this mess!" She scanned the ransacked room, then began to check her belongings. "Nothing's missing," she finally said, "so it wasn't a common thief. It's probably Harry's doing! He must not have believed that tale we told him." She noticed something white at the edge of the rumpled bed and she retrieved it. "What's this?" she murmured, examining the clean handkerchief to find the initials D. S. on them.

Dan watched her make that stunning discovery. "It's one of mine, Rachel, but I didn't drop it here. How could it fall out of my pocket? Besides, I still have mine," he said, drawing a matching one from his back pocket.

"You don't have to worry about convincing me of your innocence. You've been with me every minute since I left my room. I was wondering who and why someone would try to frame *you* for this."

"I don't know, but I certainly don't like it. It seems inconceivable that Harry would go to such trouble to leave this here when he thinks we're cousins." Dan peered out the window. "Rest before dinner," he suggested. "I'll meet you downstairs at seven. If I hurry, maybe I can trail our shadow to his boss. That could give us answers about who's doing all this to you."

Dan left in such a rush that Rachel didn't have time to ask questions or to give cautions. She went to her window and looked down on the street. Her gaze located the man who had followed and watched them all day, who had lingered a while to make sure they didn't leave again. He headed down Broad toward the river in the direction of Athens Arms Company. She watched Dan sneak along behind him at a safe distance. She prayed the captain wouldn't be seen and caught and that he wouldn't attempt to get too close to eavesdrop on the imminent meeting of spy and boss. Clues were one thing, but his safety came first.

Don't you dare get hurt or killed helping me, Daniel Slade, Rachel silently instructed. *Harry Clements is dangerous; I should have told you that. You don't know what you're getting yourself into with me. I would die if anything terrible happened to you. Please don't take any risks, and hurry back.*

Worried, Rachel stared out the window for a long time, until the sun set and dusk appeared. She saw the lamplighter going from lamppost to lamppost lighting them one at a time, a stick in one hand, a lantern in the other, and a three-legged dog tagging along behind him with a running-hopping motion.

At least she knew Daniel wasn't behind this new incident. Maybe he wasn't responsible for any of them. Until today, she hadn't seen or sensed anyone following her. For all she knew, Dan hadn't written that card which had come with the flowers, and the script on the second note could be his! But how could he have forged hers on the first one? It was a vicious cycle of guilty or innocent.

She glanced at a clock on the mantel. Seven-fifteen. She poured water from a floral ewer into a matching basin and refreshed her face and washed her hands. After brushing her long hair, she checked her garments. She hadn't straightened her plundered room and she was a little mussed, but there wasn't time to now.

Rachel glanced around the lobby, but Dan wasn't there. They had scheduled to meet at seven for dinner. *Where are you?* she fretted.

Chapter 9

Someone tapped her shoulder, and Rachel turned to respond. "Dan!" Forgetting all else, she hugged him in joy and relief. "Where have you been? I was worried sick over you."

Dan embraced her for a moment and found himself wishing he could hold her longer, but too many people were in the lobby to risk exposure of their kinship ruse. His hands grasped her upper arms gently and he leaned her away from his enflamed body. He chuckled to release his sudden tension. "Why? You're the one who's late," he jested.

"I watched you leave from my window and stayed there until dark. I didn't see you return. I've been so frightened," she admitted.

Dan knew she hadn't created the plundering incident, so she might have told the truth about the other ones he had overheard her mention in Augusta. If so, she had a persistent enemy and a reason to be afraid. Still, nothing had proved her innocent of Black Widow allegations. "I returned by the side entrance. I've been on the porch reading the newspaper. When I didn't find you here, I checked in the dining room, then went upstairs to see if you were delayed."

"We must have just missed each other. What happened?"

"About what?" He forgot his earlier task, as she

was so tempting and distracting, so touchingly moved by fear and concern for him.

"With our spy," she whispered, her gaze staying locked with his. He was safe. He was with her.

"Oh, the spy." He released his hold on her arms. "He went into Harrison Clement's office and stayed about ten minutes," Dan answered in a low tone. "I couldn't get close enough to overhear anything. I didn't want to chance being discovered."

"So Harry is having us watched and followed. I wonder why."

"Probably doesn't trust Phillip any more than Phillip trusts him, and he must not have believed our ruse about why we're here."

"Did I act suspicious when we saw him?" She fretted aloud.

"Not that I could tell; a skilled actress couldn't have done better." But, Dan recalled, she had noticed something during their tour, some clue she hadn't shared with him—not yet. It had to do with the weapons the men were constructing, and she had told him she knew all about arms-making. Her expression and reaction had given away that fact to him, but probably not to Harry who didn't know how smart and informed she was.

"I was about to send for the marshal to report you missing. If it hadn't been dark and I was familiar with this town, I would have come looking for you myself. Next time you check in with me when you return," she chided.

"Yes, ma'am," he said playfully as she dropped the touchy subject.

"It isn't funny, Dan. I was worried and scared."

"There wasn't any reason to be, Rachel; I'm always careful. I never challenge uneven odds."

"Such as the powerful ocean?" she quipped.

"Ah, but I'm acquainted with all her phases, so there are never any surprises."

"She's never beaten you, Dan, never defeated you?"

"Not yet, thank the lucky stars."

"But that luck might give out."

Dan grinned, as if failing to perceive her seriousness. "Rachel McCandless, are you asking me or warning me to give up the sea?"

"We've become good friends, Daniel Slade. I wouldn't want anything to happen to you. Every day at sea is challenging danger, isn't it?"

"Ocean violence is rare, Rachel. And there's no more peril than on dry land. Probably less."

"Are you sure?"

"As positive as I can be, Rachel, so stop worrying. Let's eat. I'm ravenous." He was confused by the curious change of topic.

As they dined, Rachel coaxed, "Tell me about this Luke Conner."

"Luke's thirty," Dan related, between bites and sips. "He has brown hair and lively blue eyes, the kind filled with boyish mischief. He looks as if he has a permanent grin on his face and in his eyes. He's so good-natured, it breaks free a lot."

Dan thought a minute about Luke. "He's cheerful, smart, dependable, and level-headed. The men trust and respect him; so do I. He stands by me in any situation, good and bad. He loves the sea and sailing. We're both adventurers at heart. Luke's easygoing, but he can be tough and strong when the situation demands." Dan sipped his tea, which was spiced with fresh mint. "We've been tight friends and constant companions for four years. Where one goes, the other goes. We met on the ship I took when I left Charleston in '71. We forged a tight bond during that voyage, and we've been together ever since. After I purchased my ship, I signed Luke on as first mate, and I've never been sorry for a moment. The *Merry Wind* has been my home for years, and he's been my family. Luke's like a brother to me, and he feels the same way about me."

Rachel was warmed by those revealing words and the strong feelings behind them, was even a little envious of that relationship. Hearing about the kind of special relationship that she had been denied through no fault of her own made her a little melancholy and bitter. "That's wonderful. I haven't had a best friend since I was a child. I played with the plantation workers' children until Mama married Earl. He said it wasn't proper and stopped it. Earl didn't like for visitors to come around much, so I didn't meet many girls my age who were acceptable to him.

"Of course," she conceded, "we didn't have many close neighbors with daughters my age because the plantations were so large and far apart. After I moved to Savannah, I wasn't given the opportunities and time to make friends with other young women. Oh, I had acquaintances, just not close and best friends like you described. I've missed that." She sighed heavily, then forced a smile. "Lula Mae is my friend, and so is Burke, the manager. But they're older, and I'm their mistress. Sometimes I think Lula Mae still views me as a child. She tries to protect me and teach me and discipline me as if I were her daughter. I suppose that's why I don't get any closer to her; it could cause a problem if I had to overrule a decision of hers or reprimand her. I owe her a great deal, so I let her get away with things I might correct others for doing or saying. If it doesn't seem that important, I allow it to pass unchallenged."

"Everybody needs a good friend, someone to confide in, someone who stands by you no matter what comes along, somebody you trust and respect."

"But how do you find such a person, Dan? How

can you be sure they'll stand by you in dark times or not betray you?"

Dan sensed she was serious, perhaps even testing his feelings, his reaction to even bigger revelations. "You found *me*, Rachel. I promise you can speak freely to me. I would never betray you, to anybody. I could make a good best friend even if I'm not a female."

We'll soon see if you mean what you say . . . "This topic is gloomy. However did we sink into it? Order me a tempting dessert and put me in better spirits." She laughed softly with her voice and expression, but not with her gaze.

Dan noticed, and it curiously pained his heart. He believed those admissions were true, tormenting, and difficult. The fact she could reveal such private and poignant feelings told him how close she was getting to him and how much she trusted him in certain areas. If only he could trust and believe her, and didn't have to betray her.

On Thursday morning, they met with Ted Jacobs in the lobby. The hotel cook had prepared a sumptuous picnic basket, even loaned them glasses to go with the wine, along with a tablecloth and utensils. They got into a rented carriage and headed off to tour Athens.

Rachel and Dan were both amused by the redhead's enthusiasm, but they suppressed their laughter at the way he often leapt from topic to topic like a jumping frog. It was only when he turned his back to drive, that they exchanged grins and soft laughter. They realized how much fun they had together. They were relaxed and content, even though their shadow was tailing them again.

As they turned onto Milledge Avenue, Ted pointed out how much larger the lots were in an area which had many trees and meadows and a few branches.

The streets and roads were dirt, but the hard-packed Georgia clay gave up little dust at their slow pace and that of the carriages they encountered. He pointed out many homes of famous residents along the picturesque route—mostly in Federal, Greek Revival, and Victorian styles.

Their next stop—a long one—was at a female institute. Ted reveled in telling about it being "one of the highest honors to be known as and be called a 'Lucy Cobb Girl.' Now, families from the North send their daughters South to get refinement and culture and social graces. That's ironic."

The sun was high, so Rachel held her parasol over her head and leaned closer to Dan to shade his eyes, too. Their shoulders and legs touched. The heady contact affected both of them, and they had a difficult time paying attention to their guide's words and the sights.

They reached Lumpkin Street and turned left, back toward town. Ted soon pulled to the side of the street. "Let's stop here for our picnic."

The serene, woodsy, flower-filled meadow bordered the estate of an ex-governor and the college campus. It was a perfect selection. Tall oaks and thick magnolias presented a lovely setting and welcome shade. They spread out the tablecloth and sat down on the grass around it. As they feasted on the delicious fare and sipped tepid wine, they chatted about what they had seen and would see.

When Ted asked questions about them, they related the same tale they had told Harry and George. It was doubtful, but George could have warned Harry of their impending visit and Harry could have hired this innocent-faced boy to meet them and to stay with them during their visit. The couple had discussed that possibility, then dismissed it because of their shadow. Still, it paid to be careful and alert. Dan and Rachel watched everything they said and did in his presence, which took extra effort, but it didn't prevent a good time.

Their tour continued along Lumpkin past the university to the cotton-factoring location. There, the student, a fountain of information and overflowing with energy, said, "Athens is one of the largest cotton markets in the South and probably in the world. Outside of town in every direction are farms and plantations of immense sizes. After cotton is picked, hauled in, ginned, and baled, you see stacks of them everywhere, I mean *everywhere* along the streets nearby. It's a big and profitable business."

They traveled up Thomas Street toward the area called Lickskillet, the original location of the rich gentry, which now belonged to Prince and Milledge avenues. Ted pointed to a large Victorian home on the corner and said, "I suppose you know that's where Harrison Clements lives."

"Yes, I was there for a short visit before last Christmas," Rachel revealed. She waited to see if Ted would make further comments, but he didn't. Neither did she.

At the hotel entrance, Ted informed them that he had tests the next day and was visiting his family Saturday. "But I can show you around Sunday afternoon," he said. "You must see the old botanical gardens before they go to ruin."

Rachel smiled genially at the slim youth. "That sounds like a delightful way to spend Sunday afternoon, doesn't it, Dan?"

"It certainly does. We'll be waiting for you after church." Dan paid the agreed hourly fee and added some more money to it.

The youth beamed as he saw the large tip. "You're most kind, sir."

"You are most informative and interesting, Ted," Rachel said. "You've shown us a wonderful time. Thank you. Until Sunday afternoon."

As they watched the student head down the street to return the rented carriage, Rachel asked, "Is he still there?"

"Yep, our spy has stuck to us all day. I bet he's starving if he didn't bring along a picnic, too. Just for meanness, we should stroll until dark and exhaust him, but we won't. Let's just get washed up and have dinner."

Friday they walked up and down and in and out of blocks of town. They halted here and there to shop, having fun together and relishing the merry chase they were leading their shadow on. She purchased several sweets, including fresh baked cookies and candy called "bucket mix" from a confectionary store. She waited outside the hotel while Dan carried those items to his room, and she pretended not to see the spy who had to guess they were leaving again soon or she would have gone inside.

Dan returned and their adventure continued. They stopped to have lunch at a restaurant, but hurried to prevent their spy from having time to eat or risk losing sight of them. It was amusing to punish and outwit the hired man, who couldn't even stop for a drink to wet his dry throat or to be excused. Afterward, Rachel bought gifts for Lula Mae, Burke, his wife, and the other two workers at the plantation.

As they strolled along, Dan carried her packages, but didn't make any purchases himself. He had a pleasant time just being with and watching Rachel play the perfect holiday traveler.

The more they were together, the closer they became and the higher their desires increased. They cared about what happened to each other; as they worked in intimate secrecy as a team and they shared—without knowing it—common goals, dreams, hopes, and interests.

191

When Rachel and Dan were too weary to continue with their mischievous ruse, they returned to the hotel to relax before bathing and dressing for dinner with Harrison Clements. His message, more like a summons, had awaited them at the front desk telling them where to meet him.

At eight o'clock, the couple entered Fabeer's, a restaurant known for fine and leisurely dining. They were shown to Harry's table, to find him alone and sipping Irish whiskey without water or ice or a mixer. As they were being seated, Rachel asked where his wife was tonight.

"She's visiting kinfolks out of town. I must have forgotten to tell you. It will just be the three of us for dinner. I hope you don't mind."

Rachel didn't believe him. She guessed that his wife was at home or he had sent her away. No doubt it was to provide an excuse not to socialize with her and Dan and to prevent the woman from making a slip. "That's a shame, Harry; I was looking forward to seeing her during my visit. Please tell her I inquired about her and shall see her during my next one."

"When will that be?" Harry asked, then sipped his drink.

"I have no idea. I suppose whenever Phillip asks me to come along with him, perhaps during the summer or fall."

The waiter arrived and asked if the couple wanted a drink before ordering dinner. Rachel and Dan didn't glance at each other as they shook their heads, but Harry insisted. "Bring them champagne—your finest, William. This is a celebration. We're here to enjoy ourselves."

Later, as they dined, Harry questioned, "Are you and Phillip doing all right? Are your problems over in Savannah?"

Rachel grasped his meaning and panicked. "Everything is fine, but thank you for your concern." She quickly changed the subject. "When we were visiting with George, he mentioned something I'd never thought about: How did you and Phillip meet, and how did he become your partner?" *Focus the attention on him, Rachel, and off you.*

Harry couldn't hide his surprise at her unexpected queries. "Phillip's never told you?" he asked, stalling.

Rachel laughed and replied, "If he had, I wouldn't be asking you. George said you introduced him to Phillip and helped them become partners. Suddenly I realized I didn't know how you two had met or how my husband had gotten into the arms business, or even when he had done so. Surely there's no reason why I can't be enlightened, is there?"

"Why would there be?" he asked as his answer. "Phillip and I met when I was visiting Charleston in late '72. A mutual friend introduced us, and we liked each other from the start. During a conversation one day, we both discovered we wanted business partners and came to an agreement he would join my firm. After his father and brother died, Phillip wanted to leave Charleston and start fresh in another place. He wanted to get away from all those bad memories and gossip. I suggested Savannah as his new port and introduced him to Milton Baldwin. Milton's shipped for me for years, and he needed a partner just as George and I did. Arms and ammunition go together, and it made a nice circle to have Phillip involved in all three companies. The idea appealed to Phillip, so he joined all of us in early '73. So far everything's worked out well for everybody involved."

Two things stuck in her mind: Philip's brother and Harry's prior relationship with Phillip's shipping partner. Harrison Clements was like a ringleader who had created that little "circle" he used. Once more she realized how little she had known about the man she had married and buried. She echoed, "Brother? I didn't know Phillip had one."

It was Dan's turn to panic. He hadn't thought about either partner knowing about him or knowing people in Charleston. Since Phillip's wife hadn't known about his existence and alleged demise at sea, he had assumed his brother hadn't told anyone about them. Of course this cunning man could have investigated Phillip's history before or after taking him on as his partner. If Harry knew the whole story, he himself was in deep trouble! He waited and listened to see if he would be exposed to her. Since Harry didn't know Phillip was dead, wouldn't he think such revelations might create problems between him and his partner? He recalled that Harry had visited his brother the night before Phillip died and that Harry had a strong reason to be angry with Phillip.

"I can understand why Phillip wouldn't mention his lost brother," Harry said. "It's still much too painful for him, even after all these years."

"But Phillip told you about him," she said in an accusatory tone.

Harry shrugged broad shoulders and responded, "Only once and just a few words, because he knew I knew about him. He was drowned at sea in '72 when his ship went down in a violent gale. Another vessel witnessed the sinking, but couldn't help. The captain and crew didn't get the sails down in time; the waves flipped her on her side, and the weight of the sails and masts dragged her under too fast for rescues. The entire crew was lost."

"They were certain his brother was aboard?"

"No doubt about it at all. The crew registers in port with the ship's company before sailing. His name was on the role and he's never returned."

Rachel observed a look of unconcern and a lack of sympathy about the matter. "How awful for Phillip and his father," she murmured.

Without sensitivity or caution, Harry related, "The worst part was the nasty scandal his brother left behind before he sailed to his doom."

Why, she wondered, was Harry telling her such private and painful things? Was he angry with Phillip and trying to punish him by causing trouble between husband and wife? "What scandal, Harry?" she asked.

The man did not hestitate to answer, "I don't know the details, but it was a nasty triangle between Phillip's father, brother, and a woman they both wanted. The McCandlesses tried to keep it quiet and concealed."

"But Phillip told you about it?" she probed in visible intrigue.

"No, James Drake, that mutual friend who introduced us, told me. You're from Charleston, Dan. Did you ever meet James, Phillip, or Mac?"

"Mac?" she echoed.

"Phillip's brother—Mac," Harry clarified. "That's all the name I know."

Dan did not expose his relief. "No, the McCandlesses were gone when I moved there from Alexandria, and I haven't made Drake's acquaintance yet. I'm not in port very much or for very long periods."

"Is that how you met Phillip, when he married your cousin in Savannah?"

Dan put a genial smile on his face as he used his ruse. "That's right, but I've only seen him a few times, and not in a very long while. I docked the afternoon of the day he sailed in the morning. Rachel and I decided that while we were catching up on family and old times, we'd take this trip and have fun. A few more days of relaxation and entertainment, and I'll have my land legs back." Dan was aware that Harry had not asked them if they were having a good time in town or what they had been doing for the last few days. He knew why, because Harry was having them followed. Yet, as clever as Harry seemed, in Dan's eyes that was a reckless oversight. Perhaps the man's second one, since he had searched her room too casually and made no attempt to have it appear a robbery.

Everyone ate in silence for a few minutes as they studied each other.

Rachel worried that if Dan had grown up with Phillip and they had been best friends as he told her, he should have known about this brother and the scandal. Doubts about him returned. He could be one of her enemies after all, and Captain Daniel Slade might not be his real name. Maybe he had come along to investigate the mysterious arms deal for himself or his partners. She would question him later about these inconsistencies. If she didn't ask natural questions, he would be suspicious. No doubt Dan would come up with a cunning way to explain his deceits and she would be compelled to let him do so and pretend to believe him. Again . . .

"So," Harry spoke first, "you two are enjoying yourselves here. That's good. Athens is a nice town and has plenty to offer visitors."

"Yes, it does." Rachel concurred with an amiable smile. "We hired that university student I mentioned to you. He's made a splendid guide. He knows so much about Athens, so our visit has been fascinating."

"I know something you'll enjoy even more than sightseeing; I'm attending a party tomorrow night at the Fabeer's, the people who own this restaurant. I mentioned you were in town, so you two have been invited. It's at eight o'clock; no dinner, but plenty of treats and drinks, and there'll be dancing. Would you like to attend?"

"That sounds marvelous, Harry. Thank you," Rachel accepted for both her and Dan.

"I'll give you the address before we part tonight and see you there. Make certain you save several

196

dances for me, Rachel. With your husband absent, a beautiful woman like you will be popular with the men."

"You're too kind, Harry. Thank you for the compliment."

"I speak the truth," he said, then, changing the subject, added, "The evening will be formal. Did you come prepared for special events?"

"Dan and I are prepared for anything," she said with a false smile.

"Excellent. More champagne?"

Rachel sent forth faked merry laughter. "I fear I've had too much already. If I don't stop now, I'll become all giggly and sleepy."

"What about you, Dan? It's a superb bottle."

"As with Cousin Rachel, I've had my limit, but thank you."

The meal and polite talk went on for a while, then they all departed.

Dan asked, at Rachel's door, "What did Harry mean when he asked if you and Phillip were all right and if your problems were over?"

Rachel tensed. "It's a personal matter, if you don't mind."

"Of course. Sorry I intruded. You looked upset, so I was concerned."

"Only because of the curious way Harry mentioned it. He isn't involved in that matter, so he should keep his nose out of it."

"I hope it isn't trouble with Phillip in your marriage."

"Certainly not. We're . . . fine in that area."

"Then I won't mention it again."

"Speaking of not mentioning things, why didn't you tell me about Phillip's brother and that scandal Harry revealed tonight?"

Dan was ready with the response to sate her normal curiosity and to quell her new doubts with part of the truth. "Phillip didn't like to talk or even think about them. When I realized you didn't know either story, I decided it wasn't my place or right to expose them and create problems between you two. Harry shouldn't have betrayed Phillip's confidence. If he was a close and true friend, he wouldn't have."

"Did you know Mac, too?" She witnessed a look of anguish and sadness on his handsome face that appeared sincere and honest.

In a strained voice, he admitted, "Yes, and we were very close. I didn't learn about that ship sinking until after Phillip left Charleston."

"But you said you left in '71 and haven't seen him since then," she pointed out. "So how do you know how he felt about those two matters?"

His gaze fused with hers. "From his letters, Rachel. James Drake was not a friend of ours and he's not a nice fellow. I don't know how or why Phillip got involved with that despicable character after I left town. James and Harry shouldn't gossip about Phillip behind his back, especially to you."

So Phillip had been tormented by wicked gossip, just as she was. That could have been the reason why he was drawn to her and wanted to protect her—kindred spirits of a sort. "I've been wondering why he did."

"It sounded spiteful to me. I think there's a problem between them."

Rachel thought that perhaps the deaths of his father and brother had changed Phillip from the man her companion had known, *if* he had changed. She still couldn't trust him and decided to do some more probing. "Was Phillip ever secretive with you and his other friends? As he was about this new deal, according to his partners?"

"Not exactly. Why?"

198

"This long trip he's on and this secrecy about his past," she partially invented. "It wasn't like him not to confide in me. He has a surprise in store, but it has me worried. Harry, too, from his behavior and expressions." *Something strange is going on, and it makes me nervous.* "Phillip should have told me everything before he . . . left home."

"I'm sure he'll explain all matters when he returns, so don't fret."

"And if he doesn't?"

"Then it's nothing to worry about, Rachel. Phillip never did anything illegal when I knew him and hasn't mentioned anything like that in his letters to me. He was always too afraid of getting caught and being humiliated to be careless or to break the law."

Phillip a coward? "Explain," she coaxed without a hint of a smile.

"Just teasing. Relax, woman. Everything will be fine soon."

"I hope so. One last question, what was the scandal about?"

Dan exhaled loudly. He frowned. "I don't know if I should—"

"Yes, you're the perfect one to tell me the truth," she interrupted, "and it's past time I knew what made Phillip like he . . . is. His brother drowning at sea explains why Phillip is so terrified of ships and the water. It explains why he suddenly moved to Savannah. We've learned how, why, and when he got into the arms and ammunition businesses. If you tell me about the scandal in his family, it might clarify other things about Phillip. Please, I need to know. Phillip won't object; I won't tell him."

Dan tried to stall, as he didn't want to delve into Mac's—his—past tonight, particularly that agonizing mistake with his father. He hadn't thought of or been called that nickname in years. He was positive Harry didn't know Captain Daniel Slade was Mac McCandless and he hoped the offensive man didn't do any checking on him anytime soon. "This isn't the place to keep discussing private matters, not in the hall where we can be overheard. I'll relate the story tomorrow as we stroll."

"No, tonight. Come into my room to talk. It shouldn't take long."

"What if somebody sees this improper behavior?" he reasoned.

"We're cousins, family, kin, remember? We'll behave; I swear it."

The chilliness in her gaze and tone warned Dan that her doubts had returned, her confidence and trust in him were shaken, and she was afraid of him. Yet her need to know the truth outweighed the fear of being alone with a possible threat. Her courage impressed him, and matters needed repairing fast. "All right, Rachel. On your terms," he added.

Chapter 10

They sat down in two chairs placed before a window and with a round table between them to form a small sitting area.

Dan tried to relax, but couldn't. His heart raced in dread. He prayed Rachel wouldn't realize he was talking about himself, as he had no choice except to reveal the cruel situation to win back her trust. "This is difficult, Rachel; I was very close to Mac."

Rachel sensed deep anguish that couldn't be an act, and tried to help him begin. "Who was he like, you or Phillip?"

"Me," he murmured, gazing off into space across the room.

"So you two were closer than you and Phillip?" she prompted.

"Much closer."

"What happened?" she coaxed. "Harry hinted at a romantic triangle."

Dan leaned forward, rested his forearms across his thighs, and interlocked his fingers. "Not exactly. In fact, not at all, but that's how it seemed to McCandless. It was a tragic misunderstanding, and it tore that family apart. Stephen—Mr. McCandless—and Mac died before they made peace. It started years ago with a greedy and treacherous woman Mac saw on occasion. Nothing serious, mostly social and physical—if you know what I mean—but she wanted to capture Mac as her husband."

"I understand your meaning. He saw her to satsify himself physically, but she wanted to snare him as her husband."

"That's the truth, Rachel. All three were wrong, if you ask me."

"Everybody makes mistakes when they're young, Dan. Men do those kinds of things without stopping to think of the consequences. Often a woman agrees to a liaison because she loves a man and thinks he loves her and will eventually marry her when he doesn't have the same feelings or intentions. Sometimes the woman is trying to entrap the man; and sometimes he's only using her and misleading her to get what he wants. Those are cruel and reckless tricks with high prices. So, how did it involve the father and create a scandal? How did it all affect Phillip?"

"I suppose it actually began long before that. You see, Mac and his father never got along; there was always trouble and bad blood between them. Sometimes Phillip was caught in the middle of their disputes. Mac never could please old man McCandless, so he eventually stopped trying. Mac was a sailor for his father's firm, while Phillip did the office work. During one long voyage, that sorry vixen decided that if she couldn't win young McCandless, she would ensnare his father, getting her into their wealthy and well respected family one way or another. While Mac was gone, she became involved with Stephen. But Stephen fell in love with her, wanted to marry her, and didn't know about her relationship with his son. When Mac returned, she gave it one last chance to see if she could win him. Mac wasn't interested, but he'd had a terrible quarrel with his father, so he used her to help him settle down. As you said, that can lead to costly mistakes. Stephen found them in bed together and believed his son was being vindictive by stealing his intended. With their troubled history I can understand how Stephen would feel betrayed, embittered, and spiteful. They had a vicious fight that almost came to blows. Mac returned to sea, but not on one of his father's ships. He signed on with the one that sank, leaving no survivors. Stephen and Phillip got word about the tragedy. I was gone, so I didn't hear the news for a long time. I still can't believe what happened."

"Somehow people found out and gossiped about them?"

"Probably overheard their last quarrel. Stephen broke his betrothal to that selfish witch. I heard she left town and disappeared. I can assure you, Rachel, she was a heartless and conniving female who would do anything to get what she wanted. In Mac's defense, I have to say she had him fooled, too. He honestly believed she wanted the same things from their relationship that he did: a fine time in bed, nothing serious or permanment. And I promise you that isn't a biased opinion."

"So the father and son never made up before they died."

"No, but I'm certain Mac would have settled the matter in time."

"You liked him and trusted him, didn't you?"

"Nobody has ever been closer to me."

"I'm sorry, Dan, but that explains a few things to me."

"About what?" he asked, meeting her comforting gaze.

"About you and Phillip. I can understand why neither of you would want to discuss that painful affair. A lot of people were hurt, and it's terrible that so many have died without making peace. Did it cause trouble between Phillip and his brother when their father made those mistaken accusations against Mac?"

"Yes. At first Phillip was angry and hurt; he didn't know which one to believe. He loved and needed both of them. I tried to tell him Mac's side, but he wouldn't listen; the matter was too fresh. You see, if he sided with Mac, he would lose his father and his inheritance. If he sided with Stephen, he would lose his brother. Phillip never got a chance to make that choice, since Mac got on that ill-fated ship. I don't know what Phillip would have done if Mac had returned from that voyage. I like to think he would have believed Mac and helped him convince Stephen of the truth. Perhaps Phillip feels guilty over both their losses. It's too late for him to ever settle the matter now."

Naturally Rachel thought Dan meant because Stephen and Mac were dead. The unknown truth was that a father and two sons were dead with a bitter tragedy buried with them.

"This news made you mistrust me, didn't it?"

"Yes," she admitted. "What if Harry checks on you and learns we lied to him? That can cause more problems."

"That's the risk I'm willing to take to learn the truth. Even if he discovers I was close to Phillip for years and we aren't cousins, it won't matter soon. Your problem with him won't take much longer to solve." Dan moved before her on his knees. He captured her hands. "I'm your friend, Rachel; you can trust me. Haven't you realized that by now?"

She looked at the ceiling to avoid locking gazes with him, as that always disarmed her. "I want to trust you, Dan."

He wiggled her hands to force her gaze to meet his. "Then why can't you?" he asked. "What have I said or done to make you doubt me? I only kept a secret I didn't think I should reveal, and you suggested the deceits in my cover story. I merely embellished it to prevent doubts in Harry. If I had exposed the truth of us growing up together, Harry would have gotten nervous about our closeness and suspected Phillip sent his old and trusted friend here to investigate him." *And surely would have checked me out!*

"You're right, Dan, but trust is hard for me sometimes. Phillip was the one person I felt I could trust completely, but now I find he deceived me several times."

"Keeping a painful episode in his life from you isn't exactly deceit. I'm sure you'll be told the truth one day."

She freed her hands, and the captain stood. "But there's more, Dan. This trip, this secret deal . . ." She stood, but looked at the floor.

"I'm sure Phillip has good explanations for them," he said, but knew what her real meanings were. Dan grasped her chin, lifted her head, and locked their gazes once more. "Being ignorant of something important has a tendency to make one nervous, even afraid. But I'm here with you."

Rachel needed and wanted him so much, she was tempted to throw herself into his arms, confess all, and surrender to him. "I suppose I'm just tired and being foolish."

"Then get into bed and get some sleep. We'll talk again tomorrow." He bent forward and placed a light kiss upon her lips. "I won't let anything unjust happen to you, Rachel McCandless."

Would you feel that way if you knew the truth? she wanted to shout. Instead, she said, "Thank you, Dan. I don't know what I would do without your help. I'll see you in the morning."

He kissed her again on the forehead as a father would a weary child about to retire. "If you need anything, Rachel, I'm across the hall."

She needed him to hold her, to kiss her, to take her away from this perilous nightmare. The black truth would kill that golden dream. She walked him to the

205

door. Before he opened it, she said his name and he turned. She placed her hands on either side of his bronzed face, pulled his head downward, and gave him a quick and light kiss on the mouth. She gazed into his eyes a moment. "Thank you, Dan. Good night."

"Good night, Rachel." He left, and heard the door lock. He knew he had repaired some of his broken rigging, but not all of it. She was weakening toward him and he could have pressed his advantage with her, but something deep within him hadn't permitted it. It would be wrong and cruel to seduce her tonight. Years ago, he had taken Helen whenever he needed his lust satisfied, but it was different with Rachel. Helen had been eager, willing, persistent, and experienced. With Rachel, there were strong feelings involved, contradictory feelings he didn't quite understand, powerful feelings he couldn't deny or ignore. Despite his fierce battle, she had gotten to him. She had woven her magical spell around him. She had spun her silky strands over his heart and body. She seemed willing to give him a night in her arms, perhaps a few months in her golden web. But could she promise him, or any man, forever? That was a tormenting mystery he had to solve soon, as he couldn't allow his traitorous heart and loins to cloud and overrule his head.

During the next morning and afternoon, Rachel washed her hair and stayed in her room while it dried. She rested and tried to read, and constantly thought about Daniel Slade, her stormy past, her shadowy present, and her cloudy future.

At seven forty-five, Dan knocked on her door to escort her to the Fabeers' party. Rachel put on a sunny smile and cheerful disposition and answered it.

"You look exquisite, Mrs. McCandless," he murmured.

Dan was wearing the same suit he had worn in Augusta, as it was the only formal outfit he had brought on the trip. Rachel was clad in an off-the-shoulder gown in sapphire satin that was edged with black lace and blue silk flowers, as were the short puffy sleeves. A row of black ruched trim journeyed from the neckline, over each breast, and down to the bottom of the first of three layers of her skirt. Her fabric bag matched the gown, as did her silk slippers. Around her neck and on her ears were black pearls, gifts from Phillip. Her dark hair was secured into leafy curls, and received no accessory tonight. A black lace shawl was over one arm.

"Ready on time, Captain Slade."

"How do you do it, woman?"

"Do what?"

"Get more beautiful every day."

Rachel smiled and quipped, "The same way you get more handsome every day, kind sir. Shall we go? We don't want to be late."

They reached the Fabeer home, a majestic and enormous Greek Revival mansion with ten Doric columns and a long wing attached on each side near the rear. Fancy gas lamps provided light for guests.

A well-dressed butler escorted them inside the foyer, led them down a hall, and halted them at a columned archway. "Madame, sir, this area is for quiet conversing," he instructed. "Through the arch there is the ballroom for dancing. A small sitting parlor is near the front door. Refreshments are provided in all rooms. The privies are located to the right of the drawing room. If you do not find what you require, tell one of the servants. Your hosts are in the ballroom if you care to greet them first. I will see to your wrap, madame. Have a pleasant evening." He took her shawl, bowed, and left them standing in a large and formal drawing room decorated in the French style.

Women were begowned and bejeweled in their finest, and men were attired formally for the elegant event. "My goodness. This is—"

"Intimidating and impressive," Dan filled in for her with a grin.

She laughed and agreed. "Quite accurate."

Harry came forward. "The first dance is mine, Rachel," he said. "I'm sure your cousin can find a partner. The rooms are filled with ladies eager to be noticed and whirled around the ballroom floor."

Rachel didn't have time to accept or refuse as the man seized her hand and pulled her into the brightly lit room where musicians were playing in one corner. She went into Harrison Clements' coaxing arms and away they danced, her fabric bag swinging from a ribbon tie around one wrist.

Harry looked her over from head to waist. "You look ravishing tonight, Rachel. No woman should be as tempting as you."

She smelled the alcohol on his breath, but knew he was not drunk. "Such flattery from a man can swell a woman's head, Harry. You must be careful with your extravagant compliments, kind sir."

Harry removed some of the distance between them. "It's the truth, my lovely vixen. It seems our mates had a simultaneous need of privacy and diversion. We shall have to keep each other company tonight. Will it be a burden to such a coveted prize as you'll be this evening?"

Rachel played the coquettish southern belle to the height as she laughed once more and murmured, "How could it be?"

"Splendid. I wonder if Phillip McCandless knows how lucky he is."

"I beg your pardon?" she hinted as if confused by his meaning.

"To have such a treasure for a wife," he clarified with a sly grin.

She sent him another false smile, then lowered her voice to a silky whisper as she replied, "I hope he does; but I'm lucky, too, to have him. Phillip is a wonderful and special man, the perfect husband."

"Ah, too bad," he said, then chuckled as if teasing.

Rachel did not appreciate the way Harry was behaving tonight. She did not like Harrison Clements at all. She didn't trust him, and she didn't enjoy the amorous game he was playing. If he was testing a lack of morals, her fidelity to Phillip, the rumors about her, or a possible attraction to him, he would be disappointed in all areas. No matter how much she wanted clues from him, she would never behave the wanton to obtain them. As they danced in silence for a time, she wished she were in Dan's arms. She saw him dancing with a lovely young lady attired in a gown with a soft bustle. The two were laughing and chatting and seemed to be enjoying each other's company. A surge of jealousy and envy shot through her.

"Is there a problem, Rachel?" Harry inquired. "You've tensed."

She met his ice-blue gaze, smiled, and apologized with cleverness and skill, "I'm sorry, Harry. I was thinking about Phillip. Your words reminded me of him, up North and alone, while I'm having such fun."

"Don't worry about Phillip; he always takes care of himself."

"Whatever do you mean?" she asked, feigning an innocent look.

"If there are gambling parlors around, he's being entertained."

There it was again, she fumed, a mention of a weakness for gambling. She laughed merrily. "Phillip McCandless a serious gambler? You jest."

Harry was vexed as he scoffed, "No, I don't. You mean you haven't witnessed how much he loves and how often he engages in that costly sport? But, of course," he added with that sly grin and narrowed gaze, "he wouldn't tell his beloved wife about such a weakness, now would he?"

"Are you serious, Harry? Phillip has a weakness for such things?"

"To the point I worry about it, Rachel."

"Oh, my, I didn't know. That's dreadful, Harry. I must speak to him about it when he returns. It could get out of control if he isn't careful."

"I just hope it hasn't done so already," he murmured as the music halted. "I shall fetch a drink to quench my thirst. I'll see you again soon."

Rachel moved to the side of the dance floor and watched Harry's departure. He held himself rigid, as if angry. It was true she didn't know Phillip loved to gamble, not until George mentioned it earlier. And she fretted over why the important money was missing. Surely Phillip wouldn't . . .

Dan came to join her. "What did he have to say tonight?"

Rachel did not hesitate to expose Harry's curious and bold conduct.

"He's up to no good, Rachel. Be wary of him," Dan warned.

"I know, but why, and why tonight? He's never done this before."

It didn't escape Dan that Harry's wife was called away suddenly and that Harry was making an amorous move toward Rachel. He recalled his wild speculations about a jealous lover or envious male who desired Rachel enough to kill to win her. "When did you meet Harry?" he inquired.

"After Phillip and I were married. Why?"

"I just wonder if he tried to romance you while

Phillip was doing the same. That might be what he's up to, trying to romance clues out of you."

"Well, he's wasting his time and energy. It won't work."

"Or maybe he's trying to provoke you into making slips."

"That won't work, either. I don't like that man."

"It doesn't show when you're with him; that takes skill and practice, woman. Why don't we dance before others claim us?"

"I think we should find our host and hostess, meet them, and thank them for our invitation," she suggested.

The Fabeers were nice but showy people, they both decided after the brief encounter, and they were glad when the two were summoned away by friends.

As they danced, Dan said, "He's watching every move you make."

"Who?" she asked, too distracted by being in Dan's arms, one hand on his powerful shoulder and the other clasped within his.

"Harry. He hasn't taken his eyes off of you. I can't blame him. You are the most exquisite creature here."

"Phillip never used such affectionate terms. On whom have you used them, Captain Slade?"

He chuckled. "I haven't used them, but I've heard plenty."

"I see," she murmured with a skeptical tone.

"You don't believe me. You think me a cunning seducer of women?"

"Are you?"

Before he could answer, Harry intruded for another dance, which passed too slowly for Rachel's liking. Afterward, several men requested the "honor" of dancing with her. Five dances went by before Rachel could rest and return to Dan's side. A pretty girl of about eighteen was flirting openly with the dashing sea captain.

"Cousin Dan, I'm exhausted. I have great need of refreshment. Would you two care to join me while I fetch something to quench my thirst?"

Dan introduced the two women, who smiled and spoke politely to each other. "May I bring you something, or would you prefer to come along and select it?"

The girl looked miffed by Rachel's interruption. "Later perhaps."

As they entered the adjoining room where beverages were being served, Rachel whispered, "She didn't like me."

"Who?"

"Your little conquest. She was about to pounce upon you, Dan."

"I would much prefer for . . . What would you like to drink, ma'am?"

"Champagne. Let's have another toast. The other one is old."

Dan ordered two glasses of pale gold liquid. "It's your turn."

"Mmm, let's see . . . How about, to best friends forever?"

"Perfect, if you mean it."

"I do."

He tapped his glass against hers, and they both took sips from their own. "You're having fun tonight?"

"Yes, except the times I have to put up with Harry."

"Speaking of the demon, here he comes again to steal you from me." "I shall save you," he whispered, taking her glass and quickly setting it down to whirl her away before Harry reached them. "See, I told you I would protect you from all evil."

The remainder of the evening passed in delightful moments with Dan, pleasant ones with other notable guests, and distasteful ones with Harry.

At eleven, Dan whispered, "Our hosts are at the door. Why don't we say our thanks and farewells, then sneak out while Harry is fetching another drink? Our carriage is waiting outside."

"That's a grand idea. Lead on, sir. I'm in your care."

They followed his suggestions and returned to the hotel. At Rachel's door, they said good night until morning.

The champagne had made Rachel thirsty, but her ewer was empty. She took it to the water closet down the hall to refill it, leaving her door unlocked a short time. When she reentered the room she headed for the other side where the table was located. She had taken only a few steps when a hand clamped over her mouth. Startled, she dropped the pitcher; it shattered and splashed its contents onto her dress.

A chilling voice whispered in her ear, "Do not scream or fight, *Señora* McCandless or this knife will slide into your heart."

Rachel felt the blade tip pressed against her back. She froze in panic.

"This is only a warning for your husband. Tell him not to double cross me or his beautiful wife is dead. He has taken my money, so he must honor our deal. Do you *understand?* Nod your head."

Rachel obeyed, trembling, as her alarm mounted.

"I am going to blindfold you so as you cannot see me when I release you and leave. If you do, *señora,* you must die. *Comprende?*"

Rachel nodded again. She held silent and still as he tied the dark band across her eyes. She was shoved to the floor and ordered not to move for five minutes. She heard the door open and started to yank off the cloth.

"No, no, *señora,* not yet," the icy voice scolded.

Time passed and she detected no noise or presence, but she was afraid to disobey her tormentor in case he was still lurking nearby.

"Rachel, why is your door—" Dan didn't get out *ajar* before he saw the astonishing sight. He rushed to where she lay on the floor, face down, with broken glass and water around her. He helped the shaking woman to a sitting position as he asked her what happened.

He removed her blindfold as she related the terrifying episode. Her frightened gaze locked with his concerned one. "What is this all about, Dan?"

"I don't know, Rachel, but it won't happen again. From now on I'll come inside and search your room every time we return to the hotel. When you're alone, keep that extra bolt pushed into place . . . Are you hurt?"

She looked at her hands and arms. "I don't think so. He must have been hiding beside that chest," she surmised as she motioned to the tall piece of furniture near the door. "When he put that knife to my back, I didn't know what he was going to do as a warning to Phillip."

"Let me see if you're cut back there." As she leaned over, his keen gaze found a prick in the satin between her shoulder blades, but no injury. "Sit in the chair while I pick up this glass."

Rachel watched him gather the broken pieces of the ewer. The rug was soaked, but she would ignore that tonight. It was time to enlighten Dan to a few things, as the incidents were becoming perilous and frequent. "This isn't the first warning I've been given."

He glanced at her. "You're referring to your room being ransacked?"

"No, but that was one of them. That Sunday after I left Milton's office when you visited for the picnic, somebody shot at me on my way home. He followed me to Augusta and my room was searched there, too.

214

His first one wasn't messy like the second one, so he must have been in a rush."

Dan placed the collected shards in the basin until morning. "Why didn't you tell me about these threats?"

Rachel intentionally didn't respond. "He, or somebody else, sent me two notes while we were in Augusta. I don't know if they're connected to this trouble, because they were . . . romantic."

"Romantic? What do you mean?"

Leaving out all hints to her past and reference to the vial of poison, Rachel told him what the messages had said. "I took them as jokes or flirtations."

"Why didn't you give the flower signal to draw out the culprit?"

"I did, but no one responded."

"That was risky to attempt alone. You should have included me."

"I realize that now. I won't take any more chances of getting hurt. I don't think the two matters are related. I believe the two notes were mischievous pranks of somebody in Augusta; I haven't received any here. The other incidents, however, are clearly results of Phillip's mysterious deal. I think it's illegal and that he's gotten involved with unsavory characters."

"You're probably right. The best thing we can do is keep probing Harry for clues, then discuss it with Phillip when we all get home. It sounds to me as if he should return the advance and cancel this contract. No amount of profit is worth these risks. But don't worry, I won't let any harm come to you. I'll deliver you safely back into Phillip's arms."

Rachel shuddered at that horrible thought.

Dan grasped her reaction, but said in a gentle tone, "You're still shaken. Why don't I leave so you can retire? Lock the door after me."

As he headed for it, she halted him. "Dan?"

He halted and faced her. "Yes?"

"How did you find me tonight?"

"I went for a walk and saw your door cracked when I returned." He had done so to release his tension and frustrations, to keep his pleading loins and treacherous heart from ignoring the cautions inside his head.

"Thank you for checking on me and for cleaning up the glass."

He thought of something he had overlooked in his concern. "Did you notice any clues to your attacker's identity? Voice, size, accent, or such?"

"He was about your height and spoke in a whisper, with a Spanish accent, I think; and he used a few Spanish words. We haven't seen or met anyone he reminds me of; if we do, I'll tell you. Thanks again, and good night."

"Good night, Rachel. If you need me for anything . . ."

She smiled. "I know, you're nearby."

They attended Sunday services at Athens Baptist Church. After dining at the hotel, Ted Jacobs arrived for their next tour. It was a pleasant day under a clear, sunny sky for their downhill walk on West Broad to Finley Street. Rachel held a parasol and Dan's hand to steady her balance on the steep decline. They soon learned that Ted had not exaggerated. The botanical gardens were still lovely, despite years of little care. The landscaping was magnificent. One of the willows was grown from a cutting from Napoleon's tomb. Other trees, shrubs, plants, and flowers—thousands of varieties and species—had come from all over the world. There was a serene lake and countless walking trails, and all were laid out with skill and beauty. As they strolled through still passable and pretty sections, Ted talked about past and present Athens.

As the vivacious student got a little beyond them on

one path, Dan whispered, "Our shadow didn't follow us here. I haven't caught a glimpse of him since the entrance. He's probably hiding there because he knows we'll return by the same route." That was why he hadn't released Rachel's hand and denied himself that pleasure. She must be enjoying their contact, too, because she made no attempt to break his grasp. She appeared to have settled down from her scary experience last night, one that still had him worried and angered.

Ted chatted about his home, the techniques of growing cotton, past days of Old South glory, and the war. He brought Rachel to full alert when he said, "The Yankees confiscated all arms and ammunition; people couldn't even hunt game for food. That's why Mr. Clements's and your husband's firm grew so prosperous and important: folks had to replace their weapons to hunt and for protection against foraging Yanks."

"In peacetime people don't require many arms or much ammunition. That's wonderful for the South, but less profitable for our company," Rachel commented.

"It's still busy, Mrs. McCandless. I tried to get a job there after classes hauling arms to the train depot, but Mr. Clements already has wagons and drivers he uses. When I pick up passengers, I see their wagons moving all the time to their warehouse at the terminus. They must rail out regularly, because that warehouse can't hold that many long crates."

"I'll put in a good recommendation for you with him, if you'd like," Rachel offered, and Ted thanked her enthusiastically.

Before they reached the last bend in the path and would come into view of their spy, Dan released his hold on her hand. Rachel knew why. They returned to the hotel and after Dan paid and tipped the student and said they'd let him know if he was needed again, bid farewell to Ted.

Rachel and Dan freshened up before eating downstairs, then retired to their rooms, after watching their shadow go off duty for tonight.

The next day they had lunch at a cafe, then stopped at the Clements & McCandless Gun Company on Lumpkin Street. They entered the store, which was partly Rachel's now, and were greeted by a friendly clerk.

"What may I show you nice folks today?"

"I'm Rachel McCandless, Phillip's wife, and this is my cousin, Captain Daniel Slade. We are in town on holiday and thought we'd look around in here to see what our store carries."

"Help yourselves, folks. If you need anything, call me for service."

"Thank you, sir," she said to the man who suddenly looked nervous.

As Rachel checked over the weapons, ammunition, and items offered for sale, Dan observed the clerk as he went into a stockroom and spoke with a young boy who left in a hurry by the back door. He joined Rachel and told her the man was no doubt warning Harry about their presence.

In less than twenty minutes, Harry arrived at the store. He looked surprised to see them. "Rachel, Dan, how nice to see you today. I missed your farewells at the dance the other night."

Rachel put on her most ladylike expression. "When we were ready to leave, we didn't see you anywhere to say good night and to thank you for obtaining us that invitation. The evening was splendid."

"What plans do you have for today?"

"Not much. We've stayed so busy that we're taking it easy today. We were strolling and noticed the store

218

so we came in to buy gifts for friends. My manager will love one of those carved and engraved knives. You carry more varied items than I realized. As you know, I didn't see the store when we visited before Christmas. I'm very impressed and pleased."

"Select what you want, then have it placed on Phillip's account."

"How delightful, purchases without payments," she jested.

"I was going to contact you two earlier about joining me for the opera tonight. I've been so busy that I allowed too much time to slip by. I hope it isn't too late. Do you have other plans for this evening?"

"Only for dinner at the hotel. We'd love to join you at the opera. Is that all right, Dan?" she asked her companion.

"Sounds entertaining to me, Cousin Rachel."

"Excellent. I'll pick you up in my carriage at seven-fifteen. The performance begins at eight. That should allow plenty of traveling and seating time. See you later." He spoke to the clerk, then left.

Rachel made several purchases to cover her tale to Harry. Dan did the same with one of the superb knives for Luke Conner.

During the evening at the Duepree Opera House very little conversing could take place while listening to one traveling Italian group. That relieved Rachel and Dan, who put on faces of enjoyment.

As Harry dropped them off at the hotel, Dan said, "I want to place an arms order with Phillip's company before I leave. What time is convenient for me to speak with you tomorrow and to sign a contract?"

"One o'clock?"

"Fine, see you then." After Harry rode off, Dan pointed out that Harry didn't seem surprised about his news or ask any questions about the number of rifles he intended to purchase. "That's strange," he observed. "I wonder if George sent word to him about my intention or if he pressed George for information about us."

"How else could he have known you'd do business with him after our arrival? That disappoints me. I was hoping and believing George could be trusted. Ted, too. I pray I'm right about those two."

"I think it's best if we don't trust anybody completely, Rachel. We know it was curious that the clerk summoned Harry as there shouldn't be anything odd about Phillip's wife visiting his store. We must stay alert. We only have a few more days here."

Rachel and Dan sat down before Harry's desk, and the part owner of the company relaxed in his chair. She listened and observed as the men talked.

Dan explained his cover story about the imminent conflict in and around Turkey and why he was purchasing the arms. He related his order for ammunition from George Leathers in Augusta, with a delivery date to Savannah of May fourteenth. "How close to buying three thousand weapons can I come with a hundred thousand dollars? I have the full payment with me, so you'll get the money in advance. How soon can they be ready?" Dan told Harry he wanted the lever-action repeater with the tube loader through the butt, and gave the cartridge size of a center-fire shell he had ordered.

Harry was surprised and pleased. "That's a big purchase, Dan. I received a telegram from George on Saturday about your order from him and impending one from me, but he didn't reveal it was this large. Since you hadn't mentioned it to me yet, I thought you'd changed your mind about using us. Can you get it cleared through customs in Savannah?"

"I already have a letter of permission," Dan lied,

"so no problem there. I also want gunsights and slings on them."

As Harry did figuring on paper at his desk, Rachel concluded George had not alerted Harry of their arrival, so Harry's astonishment had been real. Perhaps after spending time on Tuesday and Friday with her and Dan, Harry had telegraphed George for information about their Augusta visit. George must not have told Harry anything intimidating, considering his amorous behavior Saturday night. As they had played their holiday ruse well, Harry should be fooled about her motives for coming to see him.

Harry looked at Dan. "I can let you have 2,860 rifles with attachments for that amount. They can be in Savannah by May twenty-fourth. How does that suit you and your schedule?"

"Perfect. I was impressed by that rifle you showed us the other day. I'm certain the soldiers will be more than satisfied with that model. I'll keep one for myself and give a few to my men."

"It's a good choice, Dan, and a dependable weapon."

"Won't that interfere with our deadline for that big order Phillip obtained?" Rachel inquired. "How can you make that many in such a short time?"

"Ten thousand rifles doesn't take forever to construct, Rachel. I already have the dynamite ordered. It should arrive soon. The entire order will reach the port there on time as promised, as will Dan's."

Rachel struggled to hide her astonishment at those revelations. "Dynamite? From you? Why not through George?"

"We hope George doesn't find out about that part of our joint deal," Harry continued. "Phillip wanted me to order it elsewhere, because it was cheaper than their Augusta company could make, and our Athens company profit will be higher. Of course, everything depends on Phillip getting the money to me soon, at least the advance for half of it. A five-hundred-thousand-dollar order that goes wrong could ruin us. That's a lot of weapons to lie around long."

"Five hundred thousand dollars? That certainly is a large deal, especially when added to the matching one with George. My goodness, a million-dollar purchase!"

Harry's frosty blue gaze narrowed. "Phillip didn't tell you? I assumed you knew after what you said earlier." He frowned when she shook her head. "He didn't give you the details, but I guess it doesn't matter if I do. We're getting three hundred thousand for arms and two hundred thousand for dynamite, gunsights, and slings. By the time Phillip collects his share of our profits here and his share from George's order, he'll make a tidy earning on one deal. Before long, you'll have a lot of money to spend. I'm delighted he obtained that contract, but I can't do much more about it until I get the advance. Partner or not, I can't take risks like that. He should have let you and Dan bring the money to me, or brought it himself before he left town for so long. It puts me and our company in a financial bind. I don't like doing business this way, but Phillip assured me nothing can go wrong at this point."

"Why didn't you collect the money when you visited him?"

"He had a silly excuse about wanting to deliver the advances to me and George on that following Monday," Harry scoffed. "I hope nothing's happened and that isn't where he's really gone, to repair the damage. I must say, George is worried, too. We both have our necks out on this deal."

"Because Phillip backed out of it once before, you're afraid he'll do so again?" she ventured.

"Yes, and that was foolish. You can't sign a contract, take five-hundred-thousand dollars in advance, then cancel the deal. That's bad business. When he balked in late February, I was worried. But after a serious talk with him during my visit he told me and George to get on with the orders."

Rachel realized the two partners had restarted the orders the day Phillip had died and that both could be ruined if that deal didn't take place, a deal her husband had wanted terminated.

"I can't deliver arms and George can't deliver ammunition on May fourteenth if we don't get the advance first. The client could take possession, then not pay the balance. I don't even want to think about that."

Rachel tried to appear calm. "I'm sure that won't happen, Harry; Phillip wouldn't allow it to fail. Who is this rich and important client?"

"I don't know, and that worries me. Phillip said it was confidential and that he would assume full responsibility for all facets of the deal. He took the order, he's to deliver it on one of his ships, and he's collecting the money. Are you sure you don't know where I can reach him?"

Rachel didn't believe Harry was that uninformed about business so vital. "I'm sorry, Harry, but he's out of touch. I'm sure nothing will go wrong. If Phillip doesn't return by the fourteenth of next month, surely the client will come to the house to check on his late order. If that happens, I'll contact you and we'll handle the final details. We certainly don't want to jeopardize a deal of this size, or risk damaging the companies. If Phillip doesn't return on schedule, I'll help out any way I can."

"Why wouldn't he return on time?" Harry asked.

Rachel shrugged her shoulders. "Storms at sea, sudden illness, or a problem on the ship could slow him," she speculated. "I doubt any of that will happen, but I'll keep alert for a problem and for our client's arrival."

"That still doesn't account for the unpaid advances, Rachel—a half a million dollars," Harry retorted. "As soon as Phillip contacts you, ask him where it is, then hire a guard to deliver it to me and George."

"Perhaps Milton can give us the client's name and location. Since Phillip is using one of their ships, it's probably recorded in their books."

"It isn't, because I've already telegraphed Milton for assistance and he says he doesn't know anything about it. I don't like the way matters are going and I don't like being kept in the dark. Phillip shouldn't have left at this time or withheld those advances. I hope nothing's happened to them, because I don't know how he could repay that much out of his pocket. We'd appreciate any help you can give us, Rachel, to carry out this deal. You can begin by locating that money and getting it to us fast. If we fail, everybody is out of a big profit and we can all lose our shares of the companies."

Rachel knew those warnings were true; and it sounded as if Harry was directing them straight at her, not as messages to relay to Phillip. She'd examined the Savannah firm's books to find no shipping schedule for the order or for that date, as Milton had claimed. She possessed no client's name, no destination, and no advance, yet, a million dollar order and the companies' survivals were at stake, and maybe hers, too . . .

"Do you mind if I see the company books while I'm here?" she asked. "I can give Phillip a report about how much that advance is needed."

"He's already received a financial report, Rachel, so he knows the condition of the company. Besides, I couldn't allow anyone to study them without a letter of approval from Phillip, not even his wife."

She faked a smile. "I understand. It is not a problem. I would like to see the warehouse at the depot; it's the only part of the company I haven't visited."

Harry shook his head of flaxen hair. "That would be a waste of time, Rachel. It's just a big, empty, and dusty storage building."

"You're right; I wouldn't want to get filthy seeing nothing. We'll be returning home early Thursday morning, so I doubt we'll see you again during this visit. I want to thank you for those lovely evenings."

"You're welcome. Just tell Phillip I need word from him immediately."

"I will, Harry, but don't worry; I'm sure this delay isn't serious."

"It had better not be," Harry said with barely suppressed anger.

"So, what do you think, Rachel?" Dan asked.

"I don't know, Dan. That mysterious deal has everyone crazy."

"Phillip will settle them down after he returns."

"Harry and George are right to worry; I'm worried, too. Something about this deal, the money, and Phillip's sudden . . . departure is strange."

Dan pretended not to notice her near slip. "You aren't suggesting Phillip stole the advance and ran off with it?"

"Of course not. He would never leave me behind."

To get closer to her, Dan sounded skeptical as he remarked, "I hope not, Rachel, because as Phillip's wife and heir, you'd have plenty of enemies after you for their payments or goods. You don't suppose Phillip's been paid the entire million dollars, do you?"

She hoped and prayed not. "I honestly don't know, Dan. The more I hear and see, the more I'm baffled."

"Stars above, Rachel, there's no telling what they would do for that amount if someone took it from them. Money can make murderers of some men. Don't forget, you've already been threatened several times."

"If Phillip didn't return, do you think I'd be in greater peril?"

If she were terrified, she might turn more to him, so he said, "Damn right I do. It's a good thing I'll be around to protect you until this mystery is solved. I have to stay in Savannah until after the twenty-fourth when my guns arrive. By then we'll know if there's trouble in the wind for you. I won't sail until I know for certain you're safe."

"Thank you, Dan. You're the best friend I have." She hesitated, then entreated, "May I ask you one other thing?" He nodded. "Was Phillip a big gambler like George and Harry implied? Do you think he could bet with another man's money? Gamble enough to possibly lose that advance?"

Dan gave serious consideration to her question. "Not the Phillip I knew. But we've been separated for years, Rachel, so I can't answer for certain. You've never picked up any clues about him having such a weakness?"

"No, never." She closed her eyes and murmured, "I pray it isn't true."

Dan sent up that same prayer, but he replied with half-truths and clever guile. "Maybe there's a good explanation for Phillip's actions. Maybe he hasn't given them the advances because he doesn't trust them fully. Maybe his trip is his way of avoiding them so he can hold on to the money until the last minute. If they drew him into their companies in '73 with lies about their conditions, then claimed slacked-off trade to cover those deceptions, Phillip may just want to handle this deal himself, protect and take his profit, then sell out like he told you."

"Do you think, when Phillip backed out in February, it angered Harry or George—or both—or the client so much that one or all of them were behind the incidents I mentioned to you, sort of as warnings to get it started again?" When he looked confused, she clarified. "You remember, the ship that was destroyed, the warehouse that was vandalized, the two seamen who were beaten, and the dockworker who was killed?" He nodded again, and she continued. "The shipping firm had to compensate those clients and families, so it cost Phillip and Milton a lot of money, and Milton wasn't happy about it. You don't suppose Phillip felt responsible or felt his client was guilty so he used the advance to cover those payments, do you?"

Dan was impressed by her intelligence and her reasoning powers. "I don't know what to think at this point, Rachel. Let's wait until we return home and ask Phillip for answers before we jump into the wrong ocean looking for them ourselves." Dan stretched and yawned. "It's late and we're tired, so I'll see you in the morning. Get some rest and sleep."

Dan needed to check out a suspicion fast. The more he learned, the more confused he became. He was having strong feelings that this mysterious deal could have something to do with his brother's death and that Rachel McCandless might be innocent.

By the next evening, their last one in Athens, Rachel and Dan hadn't seen much of each other. He had gone to the telegraph office across the street to send cables to Burke and to Luke telling of their arrival schedule for pickups at the railroad station in Savannah on Friday.

Rachel had a lot of packing to do and stayed in her room most of the afternoon, sorting and folding items. At seven, after a light meal taken in the room, someone knocked on her door. Rachel hoped it wasn't Harry and was tempted not to respond. Besides, she couldn't see him or anyone, as she was wearing only her red silk nightgown. "Who is it?"

227

"It's Dan, Rachel; I need to speak privately with you. Now."

She hesitated as she looked down at her scanty attire. It was reckless, but she called back, "Just a moment, Dan; I'm not dressed." She pulled a concealing housecoat over the gown, secured the belt snugly, and answered the door. To keep out of sight of a guest who might be passing by, she stood behind the door as she allowed him to enter. She closed and bolted the lock. "What is it? A problem?"

Dan stared at her with mouth agape and blue eyes wide. He had seen edges of red silk near her ankles and knew what she was wearing beneath that shorter robe, and remembered all too well how it looked on her.

Rachel flushed and murmured, "I told you I wasn't dressed properly, but your voice sounded as if it was important?"

"I sneaked to the depot warehouse last night. That storage building was filled with crates, oblong, rifle-size. Harry lied to us."

"Why did you take such a risk? Harry is dangerous."

"Because I knew that if he had lied, he would rush to move them in case you sneaked a peek inside as we were leaving in the morning. I went back just now, and he does have men moving them to another building. If something deceitful isn't going on, he wouldn't take that action."

"What shall we do about it?"

Dan used the best words he could think of to give her an opportunity to confess everything to him. "Nothing this trip. We'll report it to Phillip when he returns. Let him investigate and discover what's going on. Don't get more involved, Rachel; you've had tastes of how dangerous this matter is. Phillip shouldn't have sent you here to nose around, and I think that was a devious story he told you. I think he

228

was hoping, with your wits, you'd stumble across something he wants to learn. Frankly, I'm disappointed and annoyed with him for placing you in peril."

"I'm sure it wasn't intentional, Dan. Surely Phillip wouldn't endanger me. I'll go home and try to solve the matter from there."

Rachel was convinced Dan wasn't a threat to her. He was too caring, helpful, and protective to be wicked. He had become a good and close friend. They worked well together. She was heading home to face her other problem, one that could destroy her budding relationship with Daniel Slade. She could lose him before she could win him.

Dan could not resist her allure. He pulled her into his arms and lowered his mouth to hers. She did not resist him, but responded with mutual desire and eagerness. His mouth feasted on hers, then left to trek over her face, to press his lips against each feature.

Fires leapt within Rachel's body, powerful and unfamiliar ones. Her heart raced. Her breathing changed to short and shallow gasps between heady kisses and a fierce hunger chewed at her core and urged her to feed it.

A matching hunger gnawed at him. Dan's body felt hot and shaky all over as it reacted to her intense response.

What will he think of me if I surrender to him while he believes Phillip is alive? Rachel suddenly wondered. *After he hears the awful rumors about me, will he think I yielded to ensnare him as my next "victim"?* She told herself she should wait until after he knew the truth. If he wasn't genuine and he spurned her, it would be better for her if she never learned what it was like to have him only to lose him. In a near breathless whisper as his teeth nibbled at one ear, she said, "We mustn't, Dan, not yet, not tonight."

He felt her stiffen and heard her words. He looked

229

into her flushed face and tormented eyes and he took a deep breath to steady himself. "I'm sorry, Rachel, but I just can't seem to resist you. I've never met a woman like you. Stars above, I wish you weren't taken!"

In a ragged voice, she confessed, "I've never met a man like you, Daniel Slade. I've never felt this way before, and it scares me."

"Not even with Phillip?"

She lowered her lashes as if ashamed to admit the truth. "No, and that troubles me. We must fight this attraction for each other, at least for the present."

"We've been trying hard to do that, Rachel, but it's there. We both felt this pull between us the first time we met and it gets stronger each day."

"I know, I shouldn't have brought you on this trip with me."

His hand lifted her chin to lock their revealing gazes. "That wouldn't have changed our feelings. You needed me here. You wanted me here."

"Yes, but it isn't right. Not now, not yet. Soon, when things are different, we can test these feelings and decide what to do about them."

"This might be the only time we have together, Rachel, but I would never force myself on you or beguile you into surrender."

She craved him so much that she panicked. "It's too late for us, Dan." He wouldn't believe her or trust her again after her impending exposures.

"It's too hard to resist you, woman, and impossible to reject you."

"Give us more time, until everything's settled after our return."

"What if it isn't settled like we want it to be? We have a serious decision to make. I want you, if only once before we're forced to part."

Her heart fluttered in suspense and she wondered, *What decision?*

"I know it's wrong and cruel to pursue another man's wife, especially when that man is so close to me. But our relationship is real and it's right. No two people are more suited to each other than we are. Phillip will have to understand and accept that reality, accept your loss. We didn't set out for this to happen, but it has. You feel the same way about me, don't you?"

To Rachel, it sounded as if he was referring to more than a casual relationship, to more than enjoying stolen moments for a short time. There was only one reason why Phillip would have to accept her loss, and that was so he could win her. With courage and boldness, she replied, "Yes, Dan, I need you. But I don't want to make a mistake and get hurt again. After everything is revealed, you might not want me anymore."

He did not probe her hint on purpose, not tonight. "I will never betray you or desert you, Rachel, no matter what. I'll accept as much or as little of you as I can have, for as long as I can. Is that being selfish?"

Lost in the swirling depths of his ocean-blue gaze, she murmured, "No, Dan, it isn't; and I feel the same way."

As Dan's mouth covered Rachel's, each knew it was too late to prevent what must and would happen between them tonight.

Chapter 11

Dan doused all lamps except one, which he lowered to a soft glow. He flung aside the covers of the bed, removed his boots, then his shirt. He looked at Rachel, who hadn't moved or spoken during his actions. He studied the luminous eyes demurely glued to his bare chest. She appeared unsure of herself, as if she weren't familiar with an intimate situation. She had been married three times, so she couldn't be a nervous virgin. She looked so delicate, so graceful, so enchanting. He was mesmerized by her potent allure.

He admitted that Rachel McCandless had stolen his mind, his heart. She moved him in strange and powerful ways. He neither totally distrusted or believed her. He knew he should resist her, but wanted to surrender to her. He yearned to comfort and protect her, but feared he must punish her. He longed for her to be innocent, but wasn't convinced she was. The contradiction of emotions and thoughts was eating at him. He felt in control of his ruse, but out of control of himself. If circumstances were different, he would be wooing her. He had never met a woman who intrigued and bewitched him like she did.

Rachel watched Dan's movements with panic. Love and desire—what did she really know about such emotions? No man had ever made her feel warm and tingly and helpless inside. She had never lost herself in the smoldering depths of any manly eyes or experienced the overwhelming urge to boldly fondle a virile chest or to surrender wantonly to any man. Surely love and passion were unique and all-consuming, and she did love and desire Daniel Slade beyond reason or will to resist.

Dan wondered how she had the power to make him ignore all else except his yearning for her. "Come to me, love," he murmured. He did not have to ask twice or rush to her side to guilefully seduce her.

Rachel obeyed his husky enticement. He gently grasped her chin and pulled it toward his to seal their lips in a heady kiss. He was too near and too compelling to refuse. There could be so little time left to explore their feelings and to strengthen their bond. Her heart rebelled against the possible loss of him. His embrace was strong and comforting. His mouth left hers to nuzzle his chin against her hair. His lips claimed hers with hunger and possessiveness; they burned those sweet and forbidden messages across her unsteady senses and hazy brain.

A dizzying sense of power and unruly desire coursed through Dan's body and mind. His passions soared at her touch. She was warm, willing, and bewitching. Her allure was too powerful to resist. His mouth sought hers in an exploratory kiss. He was trapped in a world of fiery need and didn't want to seek freedom, not now, not ever.

Yet Dan perceived a tension and uncertainty in her. He leaned back and gazed into her beckoning eyes of melting honey. He observed the ever-changing emotions which flickered in them. A tug of tenderness suffused his taut body. He saw that she was afraid and doubtful.

Rachel's gaze traveled each line of Dan's handsome face. He was the most striking man she had ever seen. She had never imagined any male could be so devastatingly magnificent, so overpoweringly attractive.

His kisses were so insistent, so demanding, so persuasive, so wit-stealing. It alarmed her to be like soft clay in his hands, ready and willing to be molded into any shape he wanted.

Dan pushed a lock of darkest brown from her face. His eyes roamed the olive surface of satiny smoothness. He worried when she lowered her head and gaze. Something told him she was a rare gem ready to be cut into a valuable and precious stone by the right craftsman. He savored the heady task before him. "Don't be afraid of me, Rachel, I would never hurt you. Look at me, love."

All of Rachel but her eyes responded to his tender and coaxing voice. She fretted that she wouldn't know how to respond correctly, how to pleasure him, how not to disappoint him. What if the act wasn't like the blissful preludes? What if she froze up as with Phillip? What if it hurt or became rough as with Craig?

When she married Craig Newman, she hadn't even considered the conjugal bed. Lordy, how naive and innocent she had been! He had taken her without gentleness or romantic inducements. When he discovered she was a virgin, he had joked about William Barlow denying himself of her treats. After that horrible first night, he had taken her only three more times during their four months of wedlock. Each had been swift and rough, as if he was trying to hurt her.

With Phillip, it had been different. He had shown her sex didn't have to hurt or humiliate, and had been furious with Craig for ravishing her so uncaringly. Even so, she hadn't been able to relax and enjoy the act as Phillip urged her. Because he knew she didn't care for the physical intimacy, he had initiated it only a few times during their eight months of marriage, while hoping it would change one day.

Now she was facing a new challenge. The difference this time was that she wanted this man. She met his gaze.

Dan read her anxiety, and dreaded a last-minute withdrawal. "Relax, love," he coaxed, "This isn't an unpleasant chore to be done quickly and gotten over with. Yield completely to the waves of ecstasy," he entreated hoarsely. He knew he must use all his talents to rekindle the heated response she had felt earlier. His head lowered once more and his tongue deftly plundered her mouth. His masterful lips seemed to brand her mouth, cheeks, and throat—every inch of her face and neck. All restraint left her as he guided her toward total submission. Flames of passion leapt and burned rampantly within her. She wanted and needed this to happen, and tonight.

Dan trailed his tongue over her parted lips, nibbled at them with his teeth, then tasted the sweetness of her mouth again. His hands untied the sash at her waist. He eased the robe from her shoulders and let it fall to the floor. His lips trekked over the flesh he had bared. His fingers quivered as they moved under the straps of her red gown and slipped it off her shoulders. The material flowed down her shapely body to expose skin that was even silkier than the garment. With leisure and delight, his hands caressed and fondled and stroked the areas he had exposed to them. He set out to tantalize, stimulate, and pleasure her.

His mellow tone whispered soft and stirring words into her ears. She trembled within his grasp. His embrace was blissful, and his romantic onslaught was captivating. A curious mingling of lanquor and tension surged through her. Her mind was rapturously dazed by a fierce longing for him and she never wanted those breathtaking sensations to halt.

Dan lifted her naked body and placed her on the bed. Quickly he discarded the remainder of his garments, as he didn't want any of those flames he had lit and fanned to go out or burn low. He joined her and pulled her into his arms. His mouth covered hers.

Rachel cast her inhibitions and doubts aside. She

stroked the virile body touching hers. Its strength and beauty titillated her senses. His hands, calloused from hard and steady labor, did not hurt her. They were strong and skilled hands, gentle ones. From his sable hair to his firm middle to his warm feet, Daniel Slade was appealing. His actions were slow and deliberate, as if he were memorizing every inch of her body and attempting to enflame every part of it. Never had her breasts been sensitive to a man's touch, pleading to be caressed and kissed. Her body and mind throbbed with need.

Dan groaned as his own desires burned wildly with the urge to consume her. She was like a drug, powerful and addictive.

As Dan's head drifted down her throat and his lips worked at her breasts, Rachel watched him in the glow of the lamplight. Her tension was heavily laced with anticipation, but she wasn't sure of what. She was eager to explore the mysteries of love and sensuality with him. Her hands played in his midnight hair and stroked his bronzed body. She enjoyed the way his muscles moved beneath her fingers. When Dan's face returned to hers, she murmured, "I don't know what to do, so you'll have to tell me or show me."

That confession—honest from her golden brown gaze—surprised and confused him. "Are you sure you want to do this, love?"

Her voice was constricted by desire as she replied, "Yes."

His fingers caressed her flushed cheek. "All you have to do tonight is relax and enjoy yourself," he told her. "Do whatever seems natural or pleasing. There's plenty of time to teach you anything you don't know."

Without shame or reservation, Rachel beseeched, "Teach me all, Dan, tonight; I want to experience every sensation and emotion with you."

That plea captivated and thrilled him. Confident in

his prowess, he vowed, "You will, Rachel, tonight and forever. There's no need to rush. We belong together." Dan was perceptive to her desires and insecurities. As his mouth roved hers, his fingers drifted into her dark hair and played in its silky fullness.

Their tongues touched, teased, and savored. Their hands caressed, stimulated, and enticed. Their bodies demanded closer and more intimate contact. Tonight, there was no turning back. They would delve into the magic that enchanted and united them. They would be anchored together in heart and flesh.

Rachel was nervous about her lack of skill, but Dan was being patient and gentle and stirring. His broad shoulders were followed by a flat waist and narrow hips that extended into long and supple legs to form a splendid physique and she responded to and devoured every kiss and caress, every unspoken promise of what was yet to come. Her hands roamed his neck and shoulders. Her fingers played in the black curls on his muscled chest, then traveled his hard back of rippling hills and satiny planes. The bud of her womanhood came alive and tingled with previously unknown pleasure as he stroked it. Her pulse raced and her breathing labored. Every spot he touched was responsive. She knew why she had never felt this way before. Love made the difference; she loved and desired Captain Daniel Slade!

Dan had difficulty breathing, thinking, and mastering his cravings. He felt as heavy as a rock, but as light as a feather. The range of emotions he experienced astonished him. When his lips and hands aroused her to writhing and coaxings, he parted her thighs and entered her as he murmured, "Ride with me, my love. Capture me and hold me tightly. Be mine, now and forever." As she did as he entreated, her exotic scent called out to him even more than that of seaspray. She intoxicated him more than strong whiskey could, a thousand barrels of it.

Rachel tensed, inhaled, and panicked for a moment when his manhood slipped within her, but she instinctively arched to meet him. As he entered and withdrew many times, she was astounded by how wonderful it felt. The hair on his chest stimulated the peaks on her breasts. His mouth held hers captive. A curious tension built within her, slowly at first, then rapidly. She clung to him and responded in the ways he whispered into her ear. She was being fed a delicious meal yet her hunger increased and her tension mounted, and she didn't know why.

Dan moved with caution and gentleness, but he didn't know how much longer he could keep control. He had delivered women into the throes of passion before, but none had ever responded this way or ever affected him like this. His rhythmic strokes were sending her along an upward spiral, but he was climbing just as fast as she was. He took her with an intensity and hunger that were new and stirring, with tantalizing leisure that erupted into a turbulent fervor. He scaled heights he had never reached before. He couldn't understand why she knew so little about the act of love, yet he sensed that was true. She caught his pattern and tried to match it, but it was an instinctive reaction.

Rachel was swept away in a flood of ecstasy. She inhaled sharply several times and stiffened and clung to him. She moaned as her first climax seized her and carried her away. "O-o-o-oh, my, what's . . . ha-penning? O-o-o-oh . . . O-o-o-oh . . . Oh, Dan . . . This is wonderful. I never . . . knew—" Her breath caught in her throat as the powerful sensations assailed her body and stole it.

Control deserted Dan as she moaned, writhed, and clung to him; and the truth of the thrilling matter reached his mind. Wave after wave crashed over his fiery body. He allowed the raging storm to carry him away with her. As overwhelming spasms conquered the woman beneath him, his molten juices mingled with hers. His release spilled forth joyously. He plundered her mouth and womanhood until every ounce of need was sated. The release was powerful and stunning; he trembled from the force of it. Unknown satisfaction and unfamiliar contentment engulfed him.

A golden aftermath seemed to glow in the room and within them. She lay in his arms, as breathless and tranquil as he.

As Dan trailed kisses and strokes over her flushed face and body, Rachel was calmed by the tenderness and gentleness of them. Surely he wanted her as much as she did him. Surely everything would be all right when he discovered the truth. Surely nothing this powerful and special could be destroyed. "I've never felt anything like that before."

"I know, love, and I'm glad you found it first with me."

"Is that how it's always supposed to be?"

"Yes, but it only happens between certain people."

"People who . . . desire each other as much as we do?"

"Yes, Rachel." He sensed a vulnerability in her. He cuddled her. Maybe he had found the missing piece to the puzzle of Rachel McCandless: no man had ever captured her heart or won her surrender. She had not given herself to any of the three men she had wed, and buried. That meant she must feel differently about him. If that was so, she surely wouldn't try to murder him after he tricked her into marriage. If he had won her heart and changed her, though, he might never learn the truth. . . . If she did suffer from a form of mental disease and she couldn't help herself. . . .

"I never expected anyone like you to come into my life, Captain Daniel Slade. I hope you don't sail out of it for a very long time."

He knew why she was worried and afraid, and he

was, too. He didn't know if his reply was the truth. "I won't, Rachel," he said. "I swear."

She closed her eyes and prayed it was true. Monday would tell her if it was or wasn't. Even if it was, it might not make a difference when . . .

Rachel and Dan left Athens on the Georgia Railroad train. They did not peek into the company warehouse so the man watching them would have good news to report to Harrison Clements. They surmised the crates would be replaced as soon as they departed.

They sat side by side, but played their kinship roles with perfection to fool a possible spy Harry had put on the train. It was wonderful being together, even if they couldn't touch and had to battle with their eyes to keep their gazes off each other. After the passionate and blissful night they had shared, each felt more confident about the other's feelings. Each knew what was facing them soon, but they ignored that problem for now.

The train halted at Union Point for a lengthy stop, and they had lunch there again and another peaceful stroll. It continued on to Augusta, following those same numerous stops in small towns and at water tanks.

They dined and spent the night at the Planter's Hotel, but did so in separate rooms in case anyone was spying on them and because people there knew them as cousins. If Harry and George were in cahoots, George could be having them watched at this point. Or one of the travelers who had gotten off the train and registered here could be Harry's hireling. It was best not to let either partner discover how close they were, not yet.

Dan had wanted to request the same rooms they had occupied before, but he couldn't without revealing knowledge of the secret passage between them. It wouldn't be wise to spark doubts in her, not when their relationship was so new and fragile. He, like Rachel, had to be content to gaze at the three photographs taken during their visit here and yearn for their second union.

After an early and quick breakfast, they went to the station and this time boarded the Central Georgia Railroad. During the last leg of their adventurous trek, they whispered and made plans.

"If Phillip has returned home, send me a message," the cunning Dan advised. "I'll come out to speak with him about our business. I won't cause you any problem if you decide you want to stay with him instead of me."

Rachel's heart pounded in dread before he could finish. When he did, she was relieved and ecstatic, which showed in her honey-colored eyes.

He said what he knew she needed to hear, "If you choose him out of some sense of loyalty and conscience, I'd be tempted to battle for you, but that would be destructive to all of us. Please, Rachel, don't take him over me for those reasons. I'll make you happy, and you'll never be sorry."

Her reply was curious. "I can't see you this weekend, Dan, even if Phillip isn't home. We must be careful until our problem is resolved. I have to come into town Monday morning to handle pressing business, so I'll meet with you afterward. Then we'll have our serious talk, I promise. After you hear what I have to say, you can tell me if it changes your feelings."

Dan comprehended what she had to do—see the authorities about his brother's death and secret burial, then confess everything to him. After she did those two things, he would know at last what to do about her. If she deceived him again or failed to make a full confession, he would know he couldn't trust her and he must proceed with his original plan of expos-

241

ing and punishing her. "I'll check on my ship and crew while I'm waiting to see you. You're mine now, Rachel McCandless. Don't forget that for a minute."

"I hope so, Dan. I can hardly wait until we're alone again Monday. It seems like the end of time, but it's only a couple of days. No matter what happens after our return, I do want you, I swear it."

They reached Central Station in Savannah at four o'clock. Burke Wells and Lula Mae Morris were waiting in a carriage for Rachel, and Luke Conner was standing on the boarding platform waiting for Dan. "We'll get off separately and not speak here," Dan instructed. "We don't want your servants or any observers to know we've been traveling together. Until Monday, my love."

"Until Monday, Dan." She gazed at him as if dreading to part, as if she feared it would be their last time together.

Dan understood and sent her a smile of encouragement and support. "Don't worry, Rachel, everything will be all right. We'll be together soon."

"I hope so, Daniel Slade," she whispered, then left her seat and the train to join Lula Mae and Burke. As she did so, she glanced at Luke Conner, Dan's first mate and close friend. They exchanged smiles, and she wondered how much he knew about her, about them. *What if he's heard the false gossip about me and he tells Dan?* she fretted. Yet she detected no repulsion or anger in his sparkly blue gaze. *Please, God,* she prayed, *don't let them hear the ugly rumors until I can explain them to Dan.*

Rachel smiled at the black manager as he met her. "I'm afraid I have more baggage than I left with, Burke, but some are gifts for all of you. The porter will help you with my trunks and packages."

"You be too kind, Miz Rachel. I'll fetch 'em fur you."

242

The housekeeper smiled and greeted her warmly, but didn't ask questions.

At home, Lula Mae said, "We been missing you more 'an a starving man misses a good meal. You rest them weary bones a spell. I'm fixin' your most favorite supper. And thank you for my presents. You've always been a kind girl with sweet thinking and a good heart. How dids the trip pass?"

"Phillip's partners were nice to me, but neither will be pleased by the telegrams I send them Monday after I visit Chief Anderson. I didn't tell them Phillip was dead; I just weaseled information out of them."

"They bounds to be hopping mad when they hears Mr. Phillip be gone to heaven. They'll be all over you like insects in August to buys out them cumpnies. Men don't wants no woman partner. You oughta sells them fast. After you tawks to the law Monday, it's bound to be bad off for a spell."

"I know, Lula Mae, and I dread it but I can't wait any longer. I can't do anything with the three companies until I report Phillip's death."

"When it's done and over with, why don't you go visit your ma for a spell and git away from this sad house and mean town? Folks gonna be at your neck again, trying to strangle the life from you."

"No, I can't. Earl's there. I never want to see him again."

Lula Mae came to Rachel and placed a hand on her shoulder. "When times are most awful, a girl needs her ma. This trouble's been eating at you since you left home. Makes peace with her, Miss Rachel."

"I told you why I can't go home, Lula Mae. He's terrible and wicked."

"Why don't you write your ma and aks when he's gonna be gone away on business?" the housekeeper suggested.

"Earl might find out I'm there and return before I leave. I hate him."

"I'll goes with you and protect you. I won't let him or no man hurt you again. I know you don't like him, but you need your ma and I'm a betting she needs you. It jest ain't right to be living like this."

"You're right, Lula Mae, but that isn't my fault. Mama chose him, and that choice drove her children away. She's the one who has to make peace with us. She won't do that if it means losing that vile husband of hers."

"I'm real sorry about this, Miss Rachel. It's a good thing you got me to tend you, since your ma won't."

As Rachel snuggled into her bed, a mixture of joy and sorrow and fear plagued her. She wondered if it were plausible to be cursed to walk the earth alone, to be fatal to any man who wed her, to be doomed to bear no children. Dare she test that incredible theory by risking Dan's life? What if she was allowed to love and be loved, but not to have any man as a mate? Maybe she was jinxed through no fault her own. Who could answer such frightening questions with knowledge and not think her mad? A man of God, a physician of the mind, or a scientist? She certainly couldn't visit a fortune teller, as she'd been taught they were the servants of the devil.

If there was no such thing as a curse, what or who had killed her mates? Surely, as the law and public kept telling her, and she had even suspected, it was unnatural to lose three husbands in less than three years.

How she loved Dan, and wanted him, but she feared he was out of reach. Merely thinking of him warmed her heart and stirred her body. She recalled what he had said in Athens and on the train, but would an evil curse spoil the first happiness and real love she'd known since before the war devastated her life?

At the hotel, Dan was talking with his best friend and first mate. He related what he had learned and done during his near three-week absence. He hadn't risked sending his news to Luke Conner by telegram, so the developments astonished the brown-haired man.

"If you have serious doubts about your sister-in-law's guilt, you must have good reasons. You've become a good judge of character and situations, my friend. I know you to be a fair and just man, so you won't harm her if she's innocent."

Dan scowled. "That's the hard part, Luke, determining if she is or isn't guilty. I don't like being duped, and she's done that to me plenty of times; but I can understand her motives. I want the truth, no matter what it is. I don't know what to think or believe anymore."

"Maybe that's because you've gotten too close to her to see clearly."

Dan frowned again as he admitted, "You could be right, but it seemed the only way to get information out of her. If Rachel has a partner, I haven't found any clues to him; nor have you, obviously. When Phillip said 'they' in his letter, I assumed it meant Rachel had selected victim number four and they had killed him."

"You don't believe that now?"

"Not from what I've seen and heard."

"You mean because she's listed so far in your direction?"

"Yes and no. Just because she's attracted to me doesn't prove she killed Phillip or she doesn't have another lover somewhere. I keep telling myself it's possible she hasn't acted guilty because she hasn't committed any crimes. Some of her conduct could

245

have to do with concealing resentment toward Phillip for getting her embroiled in danger. I've tried not to let gossip, those past investigations, her inappropriately gay conduct, and Phillip's last words mislead me. If she didn't love my brother, and with her struggle for survival weighing her down, she could be hiding her true feelings. Stars above, I did as good of an acting job as she did! I finally won her trust and affection. With the right motivation, anybody could dupe another person. I have to admit, under the circumstances, she had no choice but to delude me."

Luke was concerned for his captain. "Even if those deaths are only strange quirks of nature, she seems to be a hazard to the survival of the next man she chooses."

"Or she's being framed," Dan said. "If the deaths weren't her fault, somebody close to her might be behind them. They could be the work of a female rival, someone who hates her and wants to destroy her. Or a rejected lover who keeps making her available so she can pick him the next time she's free."

"That isn't impossible, Dan," Luke concurred, "nor any wilder than your sister-in-law being a Black Widow."

Dan jumped up to pace off his rising tension. "I know; that's why I'm so baffled and frustrated. What if it is insanity, Luke?"

"I don't know about such things, my friend; that calls for an expert. But I did learn her opinion of Earl Starger doesn't match anyone else's. From what I've been told, he's well liked, well respected, and good-natured. He's never been in trouble and doesn't seem to have an enemy in the world. He's smart, hardworking, and devoted to his wife. Nobody even hinted at trouble between Rachel and her stepfather. From all appearances, he's done his best to help her after every problem. If he's mean and cruel, only she knows those traits."

"That doesn't prove Starger doesn't have them," Dan reasoned in her defense. "There has to be a reason why she hates him so much."

"Maybe she resents him for taking her father's place. Yankees did kill her father and brother. And you told me another brother was with Earl when he drowned. She could hold him responsible for all three losses . . . I used a pretense when I visited White Cloud. It's a beautiful and prosperous plantation, now, but from what I discovered, Earl brought it back from the brink of ruin. Rachel's mother is quite beautiful herself, and appeared happy. She was ill and on medication, so I only spoke with her a few minutes."

"What day did you visit there?"

"On the first. Why?"

"Was her stepfather at home?"

"Not in the house, but out in the fields. Why?"

"The night before was when note number one appeared in her room."

"I was camped nearby. I didn't see or hear him return during the night. That would have made a long ride home, but it's possible. Didn't you say the note was in her handwriting?"

"Yes, but Starger would have samples of it, living in the same home. And a rich man could find someone to make accurate forgeries. What else did you learn?" Dan asked, almost sounding desperate for another suspect.

"I couldn't find a single hint about a spurned suitor. The only female rival I could find is a woman named Camellia Jones. She had her hook out to catch both Newman and Phillip, but was defeated by Rachel. She's from a wealthy and prestigious family, a bit spoiled and hot-tempered, but no scandals. If she's a vengeful murderess, it didn't appear that way. I think you stand a better chance of romancing information out of her than I would."

"I'll work on that angle later. What about her servants?"

"The housekeeper's been with her for years, loves her and defends her. She was working for Barlow when Rachel married him. Nobody seems to know much about her. Wells was on the place when Phillip bought it and I didn't hear anything bad about him. I didn't get to search her home; somebody was always around when I checked, so it seemed too risky."

"Anything else?"

"Very few people I approached were reluctant to discuss their local legend. Those who refused didn't defend her or have good things to say about her. I noticed that most people relied on gossip for their knowledge; few actually knew Rachel herself. I found one big inconsistency: Craig Newman. Remember how the bartender and others said all her husbands were rich and she was the only heir?"

"Yes. What about it?"

"That isn't the case for husband number two. Craig had a brother named Paul . . ."

Luke went on to expose several shocking revelations and when he finished, Dan realized this pit got deeper and darker every day. Could Rachel McCandless ever climb out?

Saturday morning was a cloudy and gloomy day that promised rain by nightfall. At nine, Lula Mae rushed to Rachel's room and told her she had company, that same stranger who had "bothered" her before she left home.

Rachel glanced out the window and saw Dan in the front yard. Her eyes widened and she was confused about his reason for coming today. "It's all right, Lula Mae; I'll go outside and speak with him."

"I don't trust that man, Miss Rachel. Something about him . . ."

248

"Don't worry. Just go about your chores."

Rachel joined Dan in the yard, and they walked a short distance from the house for privacy, as Lula Mae was standing in the doorway and eyeing them. "What are you doing here, Dan? I thought we agreed—"

"I'm sorry, Rachel," he interrupted her chiding, "but I had to see you. I went to Phillip's office so I know he hasn't returned. Baldwin is miffed, but he accepted that message you left him about Phillip's trip."

"What's so urgent that it couldn't wait until Monday? If anyone sees you here this weekend, it could mean trouble for me, for us."

"You worried me, woman, with the way you talked yesterday. You implied that what you have to tell me Monday will change my feelings about you. It also sounded as if you doubted my pledge to you. The more I thought about what you said and the way you looked, the more concerned I got. What's troubling you, love, besides telling Phillip about us?"

Rachel took a deep breath, held it a moment, then exhaled. "I guess it doesn't matter whether I tell you today or Monday, or if you hear it before the authorities. It's something terrible, Dan, a secret. I was going to confess it to you after I saw Chief Anderson. Phillip died the morning you arrived in Savannah. I couldn't tell you that day because there were serious things I had to investigate first, in Augusta and Athens. Please, let me explain everything before you get angry and lose all trust in me. I—"

"Miz Rachel, the law's acomin' up the road!" Burke suddenly appeared to give the warning.

Rachel went pale and trembled. "They must know. Why else would they be coming now? This is going to complicate things. I buried him in secret, without reporting his death to anyone. With my past—"

"Stay calm, Rachel. It might be nothing," Dan

advised, pleased she was about to reveal everything to him, but dreading what that might be.

"You don't understand," she fretted aloud in panic. "They'll try to hang me this time. I'm innocent of everything, I swear it."

"This time?" Dan echoed, as if ignorant of her dilemma.

"I can't explain now," she hurriedly said. "They're here. I'm sorry, Dan. What I'll say is the truth; I hope and pray you'll believe me, because *they* won't. I'll explain everything in detail later, everything, I swear."

Two men with badges on their jackets dismounted, secured their reins to the picket fence, and looked at the couple approaching them.

"Mrs. McCandless," one said, "we're here to ask a few questions for Chief Anderson. And who might you be?" he asked the handsome stranger.

"Captain Daniel Slade of the *Merry Wind*. I'm an old and close friend of Phillip's. I came to do business with him."

"That's difficult, isn't it, Captain, since Mr. McCandless is dead? Tell me, ma'am, why didn't you report your third husband's . . . death?"

Rachel didn't like the way this interrogation was beginning. She knew Dan was observing and listening as intently as the lawmen. She was relieved she had begun her revelation to him to prevent him from being totally shocked by the news. At the word *third,* he had glanced at her. There was nothing she could do except stand there helpless and hurting while he learned about her past in this vile manner. "I was coming into town Monday morning to see the authorities."

"Isn't that a long time to wait, ma'am? He died three weeks ago. Why bury him in secret and wait so long to report it? What happened out here on March twenty-sixth?"

Rachel realized he had some of the facts, and they looked bad. She hated for Dan to discover the truth about her like this, and wished belatedly she had told him everything sooner. "I didn't know there was a time limit involved, sir. I had pressing business to tend for Phillip in Augusta and Athens at his two companies there. Before he passed away, he asked me to handle it immediately. I didn't think it made any difference if I took care of it first. Does it?"

The man looked her up and down with a surly expression. "It seems mighty strange that business is more important than obeying the laws."

"It isn't, sir, but circumstances couldn't be changed. There are some serious problems with our two out-of-town companies. I promised Phillip I would go check on them. I assumed an investigation would ensue and cost me valuable time, so I made my trip first. As you can see, I'm here now. Have I broken a law by delaying my report?"

He didn't answer, but asked instead, "Why did you bury him in secret, ma'am? No doctor was called that I can locate, so he must not have taken ill. A quick death happened with Mr. Barlow, too, didn't it? Was it from another . . . accident, as with Mr. Newman or Mr. Barlow's son?"

Rachel didn't like the sarcastic and suggestive way he spoke. She worried over what Dan must be thinking, but she warned herself to try to remain in control and to stay polite; but that was near impossible with the hateful man. "He died from cholera, sir. He took ill late Thursday night and was dead by early the following morning. My people and I buried him and burned everything he'd touched. I didn't want to create a panic in town. You know how people are terrified of that contagious disease. I didn't run away, sir; I returned from my trip and I was coming to see you on Monday."

"How do we know that's the truth?"

Rachel wanted to shout, Because I said it was!

Dan answered for her. "It *is* the truth, sir. I was here when Phillip died. It was from cholera, as Mrs. McCandless said."

"How do you know it was cholera?" the offensive man asked Rachel, after eyeing Dan from head to foot as he'd done with her.

She tried to maintain her poise as she related the symptoms.

"Don't you think it's mighty strange you've lost a third husband in such a short time?" the lawman asked. "Less than three years, isn't it?"

There, she fumed, Dan had heard the worst about her. "Yes, sir, but none of them from crimes I've committed."

"Why would you use that word, ma'am?"

The man looked as if he had cleverly pounced on a slip she'd made. Outrage and torment flooded her. She narrowed her gaze and said, "Because after every one of them died—of natural causes or true accidents—you lawmen have come and interrogated me for hours and harassed me for weeks, made not-so-subtle accusations, and behaved as if I did away with them. We all know the rumors and gossip, sir." Vexed and angered, she challenged, "If you doubt me, come along and I'll show you where Phillip's buried. You can dig up his body and have a doctor examine it—as many doctors as you please. Just glove your hands and burn anything that touches it, because you can catch or spread that awful disease if you don't take those precautions." The two men looked as reluctant as she'd imagined they'd be about examining an infectious and decomposing body. The longer that threat worked, the better it would be for her, as the more his body would . . . "I have nothing to fear, because I'm not to blame, this time or the other two times."

"Three times," the daring man corrected. "You

certainly have bad luck with husbands and marriages."

Rachel no longer tried to conceal her anger. "What are you implying, sir?" she demanded, gluing her fiery gaze to his cold one.

"Just what I said, ma'am. As for you, Captain, tell me more about why you're here and why you didn't convince Mrs. McCandless to report this matter."

Dan was furious about Rachel's treatment, guilty or not. He disliked these two despicable men. He grasped why she had dreaded and postponed this exposure. "Phillip and I are old friends. We grew up together in Charleston. We have a pending business deal. I docked Thursday night the twenty-fifth and came here early Friday morning. It was when I asked to see him, Mrs. McCandless went and found him ill. Phillip passed away too quickly to fetch a doctor."

"But you said he took ill late Thursday night, ma'am."

Rachel knew she had to explain with an honesty that she hoped would be apparent to even these disbelieving men. "I didn't know he was sick that night. Phillip did some heavy drinking after a talk with his Athens business partner about those serious problems I mentioned earlier. He had started vomiting and was feeling embarrassed, so he slept in the guest room. I found him very sick the next morning and realized it wasn't from drinking, as I'd thought the night before. It was too late to save him or to send for help." Rachel was baffled and intrigued by Dan's prior words, his bold lies, but she didn't have time to think about them. No matter what he had alleged, she stuck with the truth to avoid entrapment.

"Slept in another room, you say?"

Rachel glued her gaze to his to make him uneasy. "Yes, sir. Wouldn't you spare your wife of such foolishness? I regret I didn't learn he was so ill before it was too late to help him, but I can't be blamed for an innocent and natural mistake. There were several empty whiskey bottles on the bedside table to lead me to that erroneous conclusion."

Lula Mae told the investigators in a sharp tone, "It happened jest like she said. I he'ped clean up that awful mess. It was cholera."

Burke related his story about the fishing trip and Phillip drinking from the river. "Miz Rachel said it wasn't the wahter. Ah he'ped bury him an' burn stuff. Ah's seed dis afore. Miz Rachel didn't do nuthin' wrong."

In a blatant attempt to frighten the two employees, the investigator said, "You two will sign sworn statements it was cholera? You know you can go to prison for lying, for helping to conceal a crime if one was committed?"

Burke and Lula Mae looked offended and angered.

"Don' be threatenin' us. We done tol' the truth. Ah'll put mah hand on the Good Book an' swear it," the black man warned with boldness.

"I will, too," Lula Mae added, "You ain't gots no right to say such things to us or to Miss Rachel. A gooder body never lived and suffered such troubles."

"You have Mrs. McCandless's word and that of three witnesses, sir," Dan asserted, "so I don't see a reason to doubt what happened here weeks ago, yet, you seem to be implying you do. I'm confused about the way you're asking your questions and treating a fine lady. You appear to be interrogating her as if she were a dangerous criminal."

The chief's investigator scowled at the sea captain. "You'll sign a sworn statement, too, Captain Slade, before you leave?"

Dan sent him a scowl in return as he replied, "Of course."

"When will that be, Captain?"

"I can follow you to town this morning or come by any time you say."

"I meant, when are you sailing?"

Dan grasped the insinuation. "Not until May twenty-fourth."

"Why is that?" the man was forced to ask.

"My business. I have orders in with Phillip's partners that will be delivered here on May fourteenth and then the twenty-fourth. That's what I came for and what I'm waiting for, if you care to check, sir."

"How long have you known Mrs. McCandless?"

"I met her after I docked last month. Phillip wrote me he was married, but this was our first visit."

"Do you mind if we examine the house and grounds, ma'am?"

Rachel knew what they hoped to find—evidence against her, so she could be charged, arrested, and convicted of murder this time. She was positive they would look for poison in any form or container, but she knew none was present. Still, she asked their reason in an almost surly tone.

"To make our investigation thorough," was the answer. "I know you weren't expecting us today, but I'm sure your home is presentable."

"Go right ahead, sir. Lula Mae, show the *gentlemen* around the house. Burke, when they're finished inside, let them see any place on the grounds they desire. We have nothing to hide from such *upstanding* lawmen. Answer any questions they have. I'll wait here for you, if you don't need me along. You didn't say, sir, how you knew Phillip was dead and buried?"

"We received a message at the office. We don't know who sent it."

"Do you always act on anonymous notes?" Rachel asked in a cold tone. "Or did you make an exception this time because I was involved?"

The man scowled once more, then followed Lula Mae into the house.

Rachel and Dan watched the lawmen enter her home to search it. She thanked Burke, and the manager, who was still fuming, returned to his chores until he was summoned to guide them over the grounds.

"They're looking for evidence I killed Phillip, but they won't find any, because I didn't. They won't give up on this matter easily. They'll try their best to prove I murdered him."

"Try to relax, Rachel, until they're gone. One of the men is peeking out the window now, watching us. Let them leave before we talk."

Rachel sat in a swing, swaying back and forth as her mind filled with tormenting doubts. She couldn't understand why Dan had corroborated her shocking story when he couldn't know whether or not it was true. And how had the law discovered this deed? The only person who could have known and summoned them had to be responsible for Phillip's death . . .

Dan perceived what Rachel must be thinking and feeling. Even if she were guilty of his brother's murder, he had to keep her out of prison to get at the truth. He had to wait until that mystery was solved. He had assumed her servants would not expose his lies, either out of loyalty and love or out of complicity with the alleged crime. But some deep instinct told him she wasn't guilty. Or was that only his desire and love influencing him?

When the two lawmen returned later, one said, "We have no evidence to arrest you on, ma'am, but this investigation isn't over. This case will stay open until we're convinced your third husband died of natural causes. Chief Anderson might want a doctor to check the body, so don't go moving or hiding it. I'm sure we'll be seeing you again real soon. You do understand that some poisonings look like cholera, so we have to be certain."

That was too much to take without lashing out. "How dare you! Charge me and arrest me, or get off my land with your vile thoughts and wicked minds. I'm not a Black Widow, and there's no way you can prove I am. Unless you have undeniable evidence, don't you speak to me like that again. If you do, I'll be the one pressing charges against you."

"Don't go getting upset, ma'am. You can't fault us with only doing our duty. You have to admit these deaths are strange."

"Why shouldn't I get upset and angry? You've put me through this three times. I'm tired of the innuendoes and implications and hateful gossip. I am innocent of any wrongdoing."

"If that's true, ma'am, you have nothing to worry over."

"If that's true," she mocked scornfully. "How foolish and cruel you are. I suffer three tragic losses, and you want to imprison me for crimes!"

"You must admit, ma'am, four deaths in a short span are suspicious."

"Uncommon perhaps," Rachel corrected, "but not suspicious, not when there isn't any proof I did something wicked."

"I beg to disagree, ma'am, but four strange deaths have to create suspicions, especially when you inherited so much money afterward."

"I didn't inherit anything from Craig Newman," she argued, "His brother even took all I inherited from Mr. Barlow, and the law did nothing to stop him. That was an injustice, and I was left in near poverty."

"Until you married Mr. McCandless. He was rich. Now's he's dead."

She didn't let the other matter drop. "What motive did I have for killing Craig? I was left with nothing. I didn't marry Phillip for a year. I worked and supported myself, which I'm sure you know."

"You didn't know he excluded you from his will, isn't that right?"

"That's correct. What wife would assume such a wicked thing? Everyone in town knows what a mean

257

and spiteful and adulterous man Craig was. But I didn't kill him because he was evil. I didn't kill him, period."

"With Mr. McCandless dead, you're a rich woman again. Correct?"

"No. I told you earlier; two of his companies are in financial trouble."

"But you still have the shipping firm and this plantation."

She ignored the comment. "Phillip was a good and kind man. I loved him," she said, but didn't add, as a brother. "If it were any woman besides me involved, would you feel the same?"

"I would certainly hope so, ma'am."

"I doubt you would," she scoffed. "If that's all . . . ?" she hinted.

"For today, ma'am. Good-bye. I'll be speaking with you again later, Captain Slade. You staying here?"

"No, I'm at the hotel on east Bay Street. Room eleven."

"You want to ride back to town with us?"

"No, I haven't finished my business discussion with Mrs. McCandless."

After the men rode off, Dan murmured, "It won't look good if they learn we took that trip together and told everyone we were cousins. They're going to wonder why you didn't tell George and Harry their partner is dead. What's really going on, Rachel? Why did you dupe me, too?"

She glared at him. "I want to ask that same question, Dan. What happens when they learn you lied about when you arrived and about being here when Phillip died? That could get us both into trouble."

"I didn't lie to them about my arrival time, Rachel. I knew your staff loved you and were loyal, so I assumed they wouldn't expose me for trying to help you. I didn't tell you I'd docked earlier because I didn't want to make you uneasy wondering if I'd heard the terrible gossip about you."

"You knew about me when you visited?"

Dan nodded.

Her gaze narrowed in mistrust and anger. "You lied so you can extract your own vengeance? Is that why you seduced me? You hoped to prove to Phillip I was an adulteress as well as a murderess to save him from my evil clutches?"

Dan seized her arms and shook her. "It wasn't like that, Rachel. It *isn't* like that. I didn't know Phillip was dead, and I didn't believe the gossip. With Phillip gone, I didn't want you to feel uncomfortable around me. I know the rumors can't be true, because Phillip wouldn't have fallen in love with you and married you. He was a good judge of character. I've gotten to know you and have come to those same conclusions. Damnit, woman, I love you and believe you! Why did you tell me so many lies?"

"You . . . love me?" Distraught and frightened and hoping to be persuaded his words were true, she asked, "Why should I believe you?"

"Because it's the truth, and deep inside, you know it is."

Still, she had to challenge, "You're only saying that to beguile and disarm me. You're only trying to dupe me into making a confession of guilt, but I can't, because I'm not guilty of any crime."

Dan read her feelings and knew what she needed to hear. "How could you make love to me and doubt me this much?"

"In my experience, men are liars and users. Phillip was the only one I could trust, or I thought I could. But he lied to me, too, and I don't know why."

In a gentle tone, Dan asked, "How did he lie to you, Rachel?"

"Don't you know?" she accused in anguish. "Aren't you in on that mysterious deal? That's why you're really here! That's why you lied to them—to keep me out of prison to honor the deal or to return your money! I don't have it. I don't know where he hid it. Without the advance, George and Harry will never supply your arms and ammunition. Beat me or threaten me or kill me, but I don't have your money."

"I don't know what you're talking about, Rachel. The only deals I have with Phillip's companies are the ones you know about. This big and secret deal all of you are dancing around each other about isn't mine. That missing money isn't mine. If it were, I would tell you."

"I don't believe you. I can't," she said, hoping to be convinced.

"If it were my deal and lost money, wouldn't I be calling you the liar now?" he reasoned. "Wouldn't I be demanding you carry out Phillip's bargain or return my advance, or threatening you if you didn't? Think, love, and feel. We've become close. Don't you know you can trust me?"

Rachel met his tender gaze. "I want to trust you, Dan; I need to trust you. But it's hard and scary. My life and freedom are at stake. I've lost control of everything, and I don't know how to get it back."

"Let me help, love, please," he urged. "I can't do that in ignorance. What is the truth, Rachel? Don't I deserve to be told? You were starting to tell me when the authorities arrived. Finish it now. Even if I were your culprit, what difference would it make if you told me the truth?"

Rachel knew she had to take a chance he was being honest and sincere. Even if he weren't, it might save her life. "I pray to God I can trust you. If I'm wrong, I'm either in deep trouble or I'll clear myself with Phillip's enemies. It's a long and painful story, so be patient while I tell it. Let's sit over here," she suggested and guided him to a grassy spot beneath the shady live oaks dripping their moss.

Chapter 12

Rachel settled herself and began. "This is not a short and simple tale. It's going to be difficult for me, and it isn't going to be easy or pleasant for you to hear. I hope you'll be kind and understanding, even if you can't forgive me. When a person is backed into a corner, as I was, one is afraid and desperate and wary of others; it's only natural to be secretive and defensive when one's life and freedom are in peril. I know how terrible this is going to sound, but please listen patiently and try not to judge me harshly."

Dan nodded and waited to hear what she had to say.

"I need to start where it all began long ago when the horrors of war and losing Papa changed Mama. When things became so bad afterward, she seemed to panic. Maybe Papa was the one who gave her strength and courage, and she lost them after those tragedies. My mother was raised as a pampered and genteel southern belle with privileges and without worries. I'm sure it was hard for her to shoulder the responsibilities of a plantation and family. As things got worse, she couldn't face poverty and humiliation. She thought she needed a man to take care of her, southern women are reared that way. She was only thirty-seven and quite beautiful when that Yankee opportunist Earl Starger convinced her he had the money and power to protect her and her children. It didn't take long before all her children were gone. But she blamed us, accused us of hurting and betraying her after all the sacrifices she had made for us 'ungrateful' and 'selfish' children."

Dan grasped the bitterness within her, but kept silent.

"It wasn't like that, but Mama can't face the truth. I've only seen her once since I left home, and that was by accident. She acts as if she truly believes I've brought a terrible scandal on the family name. One day she'll be unable to ignore the truth, and I feel sorry for her when that happens. The reason I left home was because Earl was mean and evil; he wouldn't keep his pawing hands off me. If I were going to murder any man, it would be him!" She halted to calm her anger.

"The older I became and the more I blossomed into a woman, the worse it got with Earl. Oh, he tried to hide his groping behind games, teasings, and affection, but I wasn't fooled. When I was brave and angry enough to scold him, he played innocent and told me I was the one with a wicked mind. After one incident, he even warned me no Union judge or marshal would listen to the wild rantings of a vindictive southern belle against her devoted and respected Yankee step-father. He must have thought I was scared of him and that threat, because he became even bolder.

"William Barlow was a friend of the family and our cotton factor, too. He was a true southern gentleman, kind, and generous. When I was eighteen, he caught Earl trying to ravish me in one of the cotton storage sheds when he came to do business. William was furious; he already detested Earl Starger, so his hatred increased."

Rachel shuddered as she recalled that offensive day. "William had always been like an uncle to me and the others. When he witnessed Earl's lechery and my peril, he asked me to marry him to get me away from the dangerous situation. He didn't want me as his wife; he couldn't be a husband to any woman because of a physical problem. He said I could divorce him when I found someone I loved and wanted to marry. In November of '72, I became his wife, but it was really more like his daughter. Then, the next month, his only son had an accident. We lived in a large, three-story home in town. His bedroom was on the top floor with a balcony, and he fell from it. I heard a scream and found him. I summoned help, but it was too late; his neck was broken. The doctor said he was sick and possibly feverish and dizzy. He must have gone onto the balcony to cool off and fell over the railing."

"Was anyone else present in the house?" Dan had to ask.

"Not that I know of; William was at work and Lula Mae was shopping, so I was alone with him. When William died two months later, on my birthday, the authorities thought it was strange for a healthy and rich man to die suddenly after three months of marriage and leave his young wife wealthy. The doctor said it could have been a heart attack, but the law wasn't totally convinced. We didn't share a bedroom, so I didn't find him until the next morning after he'd died during the night." She related how Lula Mae was with her ailing sister from February to April, so she had been alone with her husband.

Rachel gazed into space as she envisioned that awful scene. "He had a look of terrible pain frozen on his face, but the doctor told the chief that he didn't detect any almond odor on William's mouth which would expose a poisoning. They were suspicious of me, but couldn't find any evidence to charge me with two murders. It didn't take long before those nasty rumors started about me being a Black Widow. Most people wouldn't have anything to do with me. I didn't know the cotton factoring business and I was tormented by vicious gossip. Lula Mae was still at her sister's taking care of the house and family until the woman got well. I hadn't seen her since she'd visited the day William died. That selfish woman was so determined to keep Lula Mae around as long as she needed her help that she destroyed all my letters to Lula Mae so she never realized my plight. Without my only friend for comfort and advice, I was completely alone. When the Panic and Depression of '73 struck, I was afraid I'd lose everything William had worked so hard to earn. Earl was hounding me to come home, but I knew couldn't ever return."

Rachel shifted her position. As she did so, she noticed Lula Mae observing them from a window. She knew the housekeeper was worried about her and was no doubt wondering what was taking place. She would explain to the woman later. "Craig Newman was a business acquaintance of William's. He was in textiles and milling. I'd met him plenty of times. He was twenty-four, polite, charming, and almost handsome. I was so vulnerable and frightened that I foolishly allowed Craig to convince me to marry him two months later. It didn't take long to realize he had married me for my money. Isn't that a twist, but who would believe it?"

Dan sealed his gaze to her eyes, and found them honey-colored. If he had gleaned that clue correctly, she was being honest so far.

"The trouble was, Governor Smith announced that many of the state bonds were fraudulent. He canceled almost eight million dollars in bad ones. People protested, but it didn't do any good. That's where William had many of his investments, so half of my inheritance from him was lost, and that made Craig mad. When he died from a fall down the stairs, his will left everything, including William's money, to his brother; and that was legal. We'd only been married four months, but I had discovered what a cunning and evil man he was; I had no respect or affection left for him at his death. Of course the law was delightfully intrigued and started another investigation of me. I was in the backyard working in the garden and came in to find him dead at the bottom of the steps, his neck broken, like William's son. They finally had to rule it an accident, because I had no motive and he was drunk. I didn't tell them I didn't know I had been excluded from the will."

"You were alone with him?" Dan had to ask again.

"For most of that time, yes. Lula Mae came back to work for me in May, but Craig fired her in July, out of meanness. I did all the chores at home. The law thought it was strange that no servants were employed and present, as if I'd planned his murder and didn't want any witnesses. They didn't seem to believe it was Craig's doing to be hateful. Lula Mae explained to the law that I was telling the truth, so they couldn't charge me."

Rachel didn't look at Dan as she disclosed, "Craig Newman was a bad man, but I didn't wish death on him. Lula Mae knew how he was when he got angry or upset. She visited me the day he died, and saw what a terrible mood he was in. He began drinking first thing that morning; that's why I was working in the garden, to stay out of his reach until he calmed down. When he was in one of those black fits, he became violent."

"I'm sure it didn't help matters you hated him by then," Dan probed.

"No, it didn't, and it was hard to conceal those feelings. I dared not tell the police how cruel he was and give them reason to doubt me." Rachel felt she should reveal an important fact. "I only slept with Craig a few times as his wife; he had a mistress, and everyone knew about it except me. I never made love to him, Dan. I didn't even like the act because it was so painful and violent those few times. I realized later that he was being that way on purpose, that it didn't have to hurt and shame."

She hurried on out of modesty. "I won't go into all the details, but things were worse than ever for me. The gossip was malicious; the jokes were cruel. Even one newspaper carried a so-called fictitious story about a Black Widow who mated and slew after she got what she wanted. Earl was harassing me again. The authorities were keeping a close eye on me." She revealed her pregnancy, miscarriage, and her vile treatment by Craig's brother. "When Paul found out I was carrying his brother's child, he provided support for a while, but after I lost the baby, he was as bad as Craig had ever been. Paul accused me of getting rid of the child and accused me of stalking him as my next prey. He told lies that had people hating me even more than before." She explained how she couldn't find a job, and how Lula Mae had helped her. She told him how alone, frightened, humiliated, ostracized, and almost penniless she was.

"Phillip was Craig's shipper, so that's how we met," she continued. "We became friends. Phillip perceived how terrible Craig was, so he only pretended to be Craig's friend to be near me; he told me that later. But he was out of town during my worst time after Craig's death, the investigation, and my miscarriage. When he returned and discovered what had happened to me, he was furious. He hired me to work for him, and he eventually proposed. I couldn't marry again so soon and make another mistake. I knew the rumors would chew at me and Phillip. He was too kind to be treated as I was. By then, I was wary of most men. I was resentful of all my troubles. But Phillip was so good and persuasive that I agreed to marry him a year after Craig died. I just wanted my life to be peaceful and safe and honorable again." She took a deep breath to soothe her raw nerves.

"I loved and respected Phillip, but I wasn't in love with him. In most ways he was like a brother to me. We did have a real marriage, but only a few times. He knew how I felt about sex and why, so he didn't press the matter. He hoped in time I would come to love him and be a real wife to him. I hoped the same thing, but it never happened. When he died so suddenly, I knew what would follow; the law would investigate me again, and more feverishly than ever. I knew his death would suggest poisoning, as William's had. If it was cholera, I needed to bury him fast and sterilize everything. If it wasn't, I didn't know who had murdered him. He even implied on his deathbed that I would be blamed."

Those words brought Dan to even greater alert and attention.

"All those deaths are strange," Rachel admitted, "but I'm not responsible. Every trap I got myself into, I fell into a worse one by trying to escape it in the wrong way. I never want to be incriminated again. When I get my life straightened out, I want to make a fresh start far away from here. I know William and Phillip loved me, but Craig only wanted to use me. Phillip gave me back my courage, strength, and pride; but I panicked when he left me so unexpectedly and mysteriously."

She looked at Dan. "Maybe I'm bad luck for men. Maybe I'm doomed to never have a mate or . . . I know I won't be in a hurry to risk another man's life to prove I'm not cursed by an evil force. That might sound crazy, but I have three reasons to convince me I really am jinxed. Earl Starger wants to spite me for humiliating him with William and for spurning his wicked advances. He wants me back home so he can punish me and fondle me again. And there's Camellia Jones; she had her eyes on Craig first, then on Phillip; she hated me for winning both, so she fans the gossip. I wish she *had* won Craig; he was evil beneath that

267

boyish charm. But they aren't the only ones who've hurt me. People call me a Black Widow behind my back, and sometimes to my face, the same ones who were nice when my husbands were around."

When she halted, Dan asserted, "Even nice people can't help but be curious and talkative. You must admit, it's . . . unusual to lose three young and healthy husbands in such a short span, and under what appears mysterious circumstances. It's bound to create curiosity and suspicion when such a young and beautiful woman is involved, especially one who inherited a lot of money. Considering your past troubles, Rachel, it wasn't wise to bury Phillip in secret."

"I had to," she said. "Gossip and another investigation aren't the only reasons why I did it. Something terrible is going on; Phillip was in big trouble. Maybe he was hoping you could help him when you arrived; maybe that's what he was mumbling about when he said, 'He's coming soon; he'll help me.' That's why I had to rush to Athens to see Harry."

In view of his arms-contract story, he couldn't admit that Phillip hadn't known if he was alive and on the way, so he couldn't have been referring to him. "You just implied he was in trouble and danger. From whom? About what?"

"He refused to worry me about it. After Harry's visit, Phillip got drunk, really drunk, and talked crazy." She repeated the story she told the investigators. "When I checked on him, I thought he was still drunk; several empty bottles were lying on the table nearby. He started babbling in half-sentences; nothing made sense and he used no names, except Harry's. When he died I was numb, and I panicked. I had to see what I could learn about his warnings to me before I subjected myself to a lengthy investigation and possibly prison. I couldn't allow any needed facts to be destroyed while I was being questioned and harassed. When you appeared, I didn't know who or what you were—friend or foe. Until I was convinced it was friend, I couldn't tell you the truth. That story I told you about why I was taking the trip was a ruse to mislead you. I had to come up with a logical motive for what I was doing. It also seemed the only way to pull clues out of his partners. I can't solve anything until I discover what's going on. I never expected anything to happen between us; that took me completely by surprise. I wanted to trust you so much, but I knew it would complicate matters until I could be honest."

"It caught me by surprise, too," Dan murmured. "But go on."

"Phillip was scared, Dan, very scared and worried. He wasn't himself for the last few months." She related her husband's last mumblings. "He said I would be killed if I didn't honor some deal or return the money. I didn't know about the deal, and I don't know where the money is hidden. I've searched everywhere, but I can't find anything, money or facts. That's why I didn't extend my hospitality when you arrived; I had to search the house and grounds. That's what I was doing in his office in town, but I found nothing there. Where could he hide so much money? If he received that advance George and Harry mentioned, it would be around five hundred thousand dollars. Why wouldn't he tell me where it was, if not returning it to its owner could get me killed or blamed for theft? I know Harry is somehow involved."

Dan couldn't help but wonder how much the money meant to Rachel, as it offered her a means to get out of her trap and out of the state. Did she know about Phillip's letters and know his identity and wonder if Phillip had told him where the money was hidden? Rachel wasn't his only suspect anymore; still, he mustn't trust her too soon or too far, and he mustn't expose his identity and motive until later. "Repeat what Phillip said before he died. Maybe there is a clue hidden there."

Rachel complied, then asked, "Do they mean anything to you? Do you see why I was distrustful of a stranger who mentioned an arms deal?"

"I understand." Heaven help him if she was a superb actress and these were all lies to dupe him into helping her, but it didn't sound that way.

"With my past, I also searched the house to make sure nothing was there to incriminate me," Rachel confided. "I feared that if Harry or the unknown client did something to Phillip to cause his death, evidence might have been placed inside to frame me. With Phillip and me out of the way, that would leave Harry—and George—to earn a big profit from this curious deal. Maybe someone poisoned Phillip; cholera does have the same symptoms as poisoning. Maybe someone figured that with Phillip dead and me inheriting his share of the companies, a woman could be terrified into carrying out their bargain. You heard George and Harry say Phillip tried to back out of the contract, and he told me that on his deathbed. Maybe that's why somebody had to get rid of him. That's what my trip and all the bantering were about; we were all trying to see what and how much we all knew. It's such a hazardous mystery, Dan. I don't know what to think or whom to trust."

She sighed heavily. "I'm going to search the shipping office again tomorrow. I have Phillip's keys, and Milton never works on Sundays. With luck, which I've always been low on, I'll find a name and destination to enlighten me about this deal. Maybe I overlooked something last time. Don't you see, Dan; I had to find clues before I exposed his death?"

Dan nodded. "How do you think the law learned about it? Isn't it odd they pounced on you today, as if they knew your movements?"

"I surmised the same thing, and it scared me. I

know my servants are loyal, so I trust them. Maybe Earl is having me watched, saw what I did, and he exposed me. Maybe Phillip's unhappy client is spying on me, killed Phillip, and alerted the law to have me blamed, or to get it into the open so I'd inherit the money and complete the deal. Or maybe Harry knew Phillip was dead, guessed what I'd done, and he sent that anonymous message to get me into trouble and out of his hair. I'm sorry, but I even suspected that maybe I had misjudged you and you did it."

That last statement didn't shock him. "I didn't know he was dead, so I couldn't put the authorities on to you," he alleged. "Believe that, Rachel. As for Harry, he seemed genuinely surprised to see you there and to hear Phillip was away on secret business. He was worried and angry."

"I know, but I don't know why. The more I learn the bigger this mystery gets."

Dan changed the subject for a moment. "One question, Rachel; you said you didn't love Phillip, correct?"

She hoped the reason for his concern in that area was his feelings for her. "That's true, not as a wife should. That's why I could . . . do what I did with you. It wasn't adultery, Dan; he was dead and I was a widow. I'm sorry you didn't know so you wouldn't chastise yourself about his betrayal."

Dan didn't know if he should be happy, disappointed, or suspicious that she hadn't loved his brother. He had to get to the bottom of the truth, no matter how deep and rotten the barrel that held it. He wanted to trust her, but he couldn't drop his guard, not yet. "Don't worry, Rachel," he comforted. "I won't let anyone harm you. Phillip was my friend; he'd expect me to help and protect his widow. I'm sorry I arrived too late to save his life, even if I intended to steal something precious from him. We'll solve this mystery together and punish whoever's to blame."

Rachel was captivated by Dan and his words. She yearned to have his help and love. "Are you sure? It could be dangerous and deadly. It might even tarnish both our images of Phillip if he was involved in something illegal. If he was, it could either have been by coercion or by choice. He warned me not to go to the law. I wouldn't have anyway, because they'd never believe me. You saw how they acted earlier, so you know they would think I was daft or covering myself if I told them I thought Phillip was murdered by an enemy. And, if I mentioned this mysterious, maybe illegal, deal and the hidden money, they'd think I was involved in that crime, or the money was my motive for doing away with another husband."

"I think you handled matters in the best and only feasible way."

"Thank you, Dan. I need to tell you more about those incidents during our trip."

Afterward, she said, "You can see why I couldn't tell you everything at those times. I still don't know if those two matters are the work of the same person. It scares me to know somebody can forge my script; it could be used for an incriminating note."

"Or for a false confession," Dan ventured. "You've been shot at and threatened. If you were killed and a note left behind in your handwriting, everyone would think it was suicide from a guilty conscience."

"Don't even hint at such a horrible event," Rachel said, then abruptly changed the subject. "Another thing: when we were at the arms company, I noticed something I'm sure is illegal, and I don't see how Phillip couldn't have been aware of it." She explained about the patents on the weapons she had seen the men making and why she'd said nothing about it. "That isn't all: the law seemed intrigued by your presence and corroboration. I don't want to endanger your life by helping me. The authorities might think you aided me in murdering Phillip so we could be together."

"We'll have to be careful how we behave toward each other. If we appear too intimate this soon after his death, it won't look good for either of us. You keep that derringer close and stay alert, woman. Lock your doors and windows, and watch out for strangers. If someone killed Phillip and there's that much money hidden around here, you could be in peril."

"But I searched every inch of the house and grounds nearby."

"It could be buried in the woods, Rachel, or near any one of these trees. It might never be found."

"But I'll be held responsible! No one will believe I don't have it."

"For now, love, all we can do is search the firm's office tomorrow, then wait for that mysterious client to lay claim to his order."

"But I couldn't find anything in Phillip's desk or the safe," she pointed out in dismay, "and Milton's was locked."

"Don't worry, I can get into most locks." He might as well confess that talent today, as she'd surmise it later and perhaps doubt him again. "That's how I got into the office last time when you were there; I wanted to see you again, but I figured you wouldn't answer the door."

"So, I didn't forget to lock it?" She eyed him with confusion.

"Nope. I thought about you for two nights and all of Saturday and Sunday morning. When I saw you go into the office, I had to see you again."

"You come to town to do business with an old and dear friend; you hear horrible gossip about his wife; you find him mysteriously gone when he's supposed to be awaiting your arrival; I invite you along on a

273

private trip—so you decided you needed to study me closely?"

"I told myself I only wanted to get acquainted with the wife of my old friend, a woman who exuded mystery. The truth is, I realized later I was fascinated by you. I never intended to have these feelings for you or to indulge in glorious lovemaking with you; blame yourself for being irresistible."

Rachel returned his provocative smile. "That was sneaky. You scared me silly when you walked in that day while I was searching the office and safe."

"I can understand why. Sorry, love."

His blue gaze was tender and enticing, her heart fluttered. "When I said what I had to confess could change your feelings for me, this is what I meant. Does it, Dan? Do you hate me and mistrust me now?"

"No, Rachel. When it comes to your fourth and last husband, you'll promise me forever, won't you?"

She gaped at him. He was . . . proposing! How could a carefree, adventurous bachelor and avowed seaman love her so much this fast? His old and dear friend was barely cold in his grave and she was being investigated for Phillip's supposed murder; but Dan was wooing her and proposing marriage to the deceitful, recent widow within a few yards of his friend's final resting place! Daniel Slade did not strike her as being an impulsive person. Perhaps it was only his way of telling her his feelings were serious, but he didn't expect an affirmative reply today or ever. Her heart could not help but hope and her body warm, but she fretted, "What if I'm bad luck, Dan? I couldn't bear for you to die. I couldn't say yes until I'm convinced I'm not cursed by fate."

"Give me time, woman, and I'll prove you aren't a murderess or a jinx," he said in a commanding tone. "I'll stake my life on it."

"With my past, that's exactly what you'd be doing.

Don't rush this, Dan. There's so much to resolve, and we must protect ourselves from gossip."

"As long as I know you love me and want me and you'll eventually consider my proposal, I'll wait for you and I'll help you with this mystery."

Joy and relief flooded her. She prayed this wasn't too good to be true. "I do want you, Captain Daniel Slade. When it's safe, we'll become lovers until we're both convinced we want a long future together."

Dan got to his feet, having noticed she hadn't confessed love in her wary and uncertain state. "It's time for me to leave before I lose my head and seize you right here and now. Remember, love, spies can be watching you at any time. Don't do anything risky or foolish. I'll meet you at the door to Phillip's office at ten tomorrow."

"I wish you didn't have to go," she mellowed enough to admit, "but it's best for both of us. Good-bye, Dan, until morning."

"I love you, woman, so take care of yourself while we're apart." He walked to his horse, mounted, waved, and rode for town and Luke.

When Rachel went into the house, Lula Mae rushed to her side to make sure she was all right. "I was 'bout to bring you 'freshments, but I thought you didn't want to be bothered whilst you talked."

Rachel had seen the housekeeper gazing out one of the windows several times. She smiled and said, "I'm fine. There's nothing the law can do to me, because I'm not guilty. But I am thirsty and hungry. Lordy, I'm glad that's over with; I was dreading that chore Monday."

"Why did he stay so long, Miss Rachel?" Lula Mae asked. "Who is that man? Why did he lies for you?"

"He's an old friend of Phillip's; he came to do business with him. I took him to Augusta and Athens with me, so he could place orders with both companies. It looked so bad for me that he wanted to protect me as a last favor to Phillip. I didn't tell you he was going because I didn't want you to worry over me traveling with a handsome man at a perilous time like this."

The woman frowned and chided, "That ain't like you, Miss Rachel, to lies to Lula Mae."

"I didn't lie, my friend," Rachel corrected. "I only kept a secret."

Lula Mae's frown deepened and her tone was stern. "Secrets been gitting you into trouble for years. What if the law finds out he lied?"

"They won't, unless you or Burke tell them. I can trust him."

"You don't know the man! He could be tricking you to get you."

Rachel was dismayed by the woman's unusual behavior. "We're friends, Lula Mae; he's going to help me solve some business problems. I'll be careful how I behave around him; I promise."

"Is there a reason to be careful?"

For the first time, Rachel did not like the woman's tone and boldness. Yet she tried to remain calm and polite, as she thought Lula Mae was probably just upset and worried. "Of course; the law will probably spy on me for a while. I wouldn't want them misunderstanding our friendship or putting Dan into trouble. I need to ask you one question; did you see anyone hanging around here while I was gone? I can't figure out how the law learned about Phillip."

"I ain't seen nobody around here. You know it wasn't Lula Mae or Burke who tawked. Mighty strange goings on, if you aks me."

"I agree, but let's not worry too much about it. With Phillip's death in the open, I can get on with taking care of his affairs."

"You gonna stay here?"

"I haven't decided; there hasn't been time to think ahead that far. I'll let you know when I do; I promise." Rachel couldn't tell the housekeeper about her love for the sea captain or her hopes of marrying him one day. "Whatever happens, Lula Mae, I'll take care of you, as you've always taken care of me. You'll never be poor again. Even if they haul me off to prison, I'll see that you're provided for first."

"I love you, Miss Rachel, like you was my own child."

"I know, Lula Mae, and I'm grateful to have you."

"When I said I didn't see nobody whilst you was gawn, I didn't means nothing happened. I don't wants to scare you, but somebody searched the house whilst I was at church Sunday. Nothing was stolen, not even the money in the cashbox. Ain't that strange as can be?"

"Thank God the culprit didn't leave anything here to incriminate me today! We'll keep our eyes open wide for more mischief."

After the woman left for the kitchen, Rachel went to her room and unwrapped the painting she had purchased in Athens. She exchanged it with the one hanging over her bedroom mantel. She stepped back, admired it, and envisioned Dan in that scene. He was everything she wanted and needed in a man, in a husband. He wasn't stubborn; he bent when necessary. He was understanding and forgiving. He didn't dwell on injured masculine pride. He was caring, tender, and gentle; yet he was strong and confident. Love, she concluded, was glorious; and lovemaking with the right man was sheer rapture. Whatever it took, she would not permit Dan to be harmed in any way or by any one because of her, not even by the cruel fate that might have cursed her.

Rachel answered the knock at the front door, as Lula Mae had retired for the night. She discovered a knife was used to pinion a note to the jamb. She freed the paper and read it. She stared into the darkness, but saw and heard nothing to indicate the villain was lurking there. She locked the door, relieved only a threatening note had been awaiting her this time.

As soon as the door to the shipping firm's office was locked, Dan pulled Rachel into his arms and kissed her. At first it was slow and sweet; then, urgent and swift. His mouth claimed hers many times between treks over her face and nibbles at her lips.

Rachel returned the ardent kisses and clung to him. Once more those flames of desire danced within her body and tingles raced over her flesh. Her hunger for him was so intense that she was tempted to brazenly sink to the floor and make wild and wonderful love to him.

Dan had to struggle against that same temptation and to master the emotions she unleashed within him. He groaned against her mouth. "Stars above, I want you so much, Rachel McCandless. You've woven a spell over me."

She hugged him tightly and replied, "I want you, too, Dan. I ache all over to have you again. I never knew what I was missing until you taught me what lovemaking is. Now, I think or dream about you almost all the time. Will it always be this special way between us?"

"Yes, I know it will. I wish I could take you here and now, but that's too dangerous, even with Luke standing guard to sound a warning to me."

Rachel looked up into his smoldering gaze. "He is?"

"I asked him to see if anybody followed either or both of us. If anyone approaches, he'll whistle a message. We can't be found locked in each other's arms if a visitor showed up unexpectedly. They'd never believe our story. It's hard, woman, but we have to resist those urges today. Soon, we can have each other any time we want."

"Lordy, that sounds wonderful. I crave you so much, Daniel Slade."

"As much as I crave you, my delicious siren?" he teased.

"My heart is so full of yearning, I fear it will burst any moment. I feel like a wild animal who wants to claw off your garments and devour you. I can't be blamed for this new wantoness; you're responsible."

"You don't know how happy and proud that makes me to be the first man to awaken your passions."

"Does it bother you there were two others before you, one your best friend?" she had to ask.

"I wish I were the first and only man; but, in a true sense, I am. No man has received your passionate response except me."

"You are the first and will be the only man I surrender to that way."

"Does that mean you'll make that special promise to me?"

She playfully nibbled his chin to conceal her reaction to the implied proposal this time, as she had expected him to drop that stirring idea for a while. As if she misunderstood, she murmured, "Yes, I shall sail away to paradise in your arms whenever you desire me. But don't ask me to honor my word to become your lover until this mystery is over."

"What if you can't solve this puzzle or things get too perilous and you have to give up everything here to steal away with a lowly sea captain? I have money, love, but not the wealth you're accustomed to. I don't have a home, except for my ship. Frankly, I don't have much to offer you but myself."

She embraced him and, knowing he needed reassurance, vowed that was all she wanted and needed. "The only time I worried about money," she said, "was when I was near poverty and people wouldn't allow me to earn my living. If I found that hidden money, I would return it to its owner and be done with this mystery. He could work out his deal with Harry and George and not involve me. But I was Phillip's wife and only heir. Is it right to throw away everything he worked for and owned when I'm not guilty of anything?"

"If you had to lose it all to have me, Rachel, would you?"

"Are you asking me to forget everything and flee with you? Even if it makes me appear guilty of murder and theft? Even if it causes something to surface that will blacken Phillip's name without me here to protect it? Just let George, Milton, and that wicked Harry take control of Phillip's shares? Is that what I must do to prove my desire for you is real? To prove wealth means nothing to me by tossing it all away? In fact, I intend to divide the plantation between Lula Mae and Burke for their loyalty and friendship."

He surmised she was testing him about marrying her for her wealth as Craig Newman had done. "Have you already promised it to them?"

"For helping me to conceal a crime? Is that what you mean?"

"How could you even ask me such a thing?"

"The same way you asked me such curious questions. At times we seem to know each other so well; at others, not at all."

"What I meant was, if this deal is dangerous and illegal and unsolvable, and you get drawn into trouble with the law over it or over Phillip's death, would you escape with me to avoid prison and separation? Even if you'd lose everything by not staying to fight a battle you might win?"

"If it ever looks that bad and threatening, yes, I will. But you have to understand that for years I've lived under a cloud of doubt and suspicions and gossip. I want my name cleared, my honor and pride restored. I want people to learn they were wrong, cruel, and unjust. I don't care if I can never return here; it's only been pain for me anyway. I just don't want people saying they were right about me all along. I don't care what they say about Craig Newman, but I don't want them joking about William and Phillip being fools in marrying a deadly criminal like me. They were good men, Dan; I don't want their memories stained because of me."

He smiled and hugged her. "You're quite a marvelous woman. You're much stronger and braver than you realize. You'll get through this with me at your side. It's past time the truth about you came to light; I promise to help you prove it to everyone. I guess I got crazy for a minute. Every time I think about something taking you away from me, I panic."

"You?"

"Why not? I've never been in this situation before. I'm learning from scratch, just like you are. Now that I've found the woman I've waited for, I won't take any risk of losing her."

She caressed his clean-shaven jawline. "You've already won my heart, body, and soul. What more do you want?"

"You beside me every waking and sleeping moment."

"Won't you tire of me if I'm like a chain around your neck?"

"Never, my love. I'll hang a pretty ornament on you, right here," he said, lifting her left hand to motion to her third finger. His gaze settled on the golden wedding band his brother had given her; the realities of Phillip's loss and his motive for beginning this romance surfaced to haunt him.

Rachel noticed how her love's smile faded. "Should I take it off, or wait a while? I am a widow, and it's probably known publicly by now."

Dan stared at the ring as he envisioned his brother placing it there with love and trust for this woman consuming him. Was Phillip dead because he tried, any way necessary, to earn more wealth to lavish on this beauty? Phillip had never been adventurous, never overly brave. His brother had always feared the consequences of mistakes and the humiliation of their exposure. Breaking the law and stealing from clients wasn't like Phillip. What had changed him? Or was it, *who* had changed him? Rachel?

"Dan? What's wrong?" she asked in concern and alarm.

"Sorry, Rachel, but I was thinking about Phillip. Everything's happened so fast and I've only been thinking about you, about us. It just struck me that he's dead, gone forever."

If Rachel had any lingering doubts about Dan and his claims, they vanished as she witnessed the grief and sadness in his troubled blue gaze. "You're right, Dan, but I believe we've intentionally ignored his loss to keep from suffering over it. We can't bring him back. We haven't betrayed his love and trust by surrendering to our feelings for each other. All we can do for our friend Phillip is to make sure his name isn't blackened. If there is a crime and a reckless mistake involved, I hope we can resolve it without a scandal to stain his memory. I did love him and care about him."

Dan fused his gaze with hers. "I know you did, Rachel. I suppose it didn't seem real because we've been separated for so long and I didn't see him die. Maybe I kept thinking your ruse about his trip was real and he would return home any day now. Seeing that ring brought him to life."

Rachel understood his meaning. She remained silent while he dealt with his anguish and loss and quelled his guilt over her.

Soon Dan smiled wryly and suggested, "Let's get busy before church is over and Milton decides to make a visit here. If he's in on something strange with Harry, he could be on alert."

"Before we get started, I need to show you the warning I received last night." Rachel took the note from her bag and read it to him. "It says, 'Do not double cross me, Señor McCandless, or your wife is dead. If you think you can protect her from us, ask her how many times we have threatened her and been close enough to keep our word. There is no place you can hide her we cannot find her and slay her. Do as you agreed and she is safe.' It was pinned to my door with this." She held out the knife to him.

Dan examined the weapon. "It's the kind anyone can buy almost anywhere, so no clue there. You didn't see or hear anyone?"

"No, thank goodness. But this tells us one important fact: the client doesn't know Phillip is dead, so he couldn't have murdered him."

"Don't be misled, Rachel. The message could be for you and was only meant to appear it's to Phillip so you won't think he harmed him. The timing is suspicious, as if Phillip's heir needed to be warned before the news of his demise was announced . . . Let's talk about it later; we have to finish here before church is over and Baldwin's on the streets."

Dan jimmied the lock on the man's desk without damaging it. Rachel pulled out a record book, opened it, and scanned the pages.

"Look at this, Dan!" she shrieked in excitement. "A notation about a cargo ship reserved on May fourteenth to sail to Haiti. Isn't that close to Cuba?"

"About forty-eight miles away, within sight from a mountain or crow's nest on a ship. You mentioned Cuba yesterday. Who do you know there?"

"No one. At least, I don't think I know anyone. These two sets of initials mean nothing to me. C. T. and J.C.," she murmured. "This is Milton's handwriting, so he isn't totally in the dark."

She reasoned aloud to stimulate Dan's astute thoughts. "Harry said Milton denied knowing who the client is, but that could have come from loyalty to Phillip by honoring Phillip's request to hold silent. I wonder if Milton's been told Phillip is dead. The authorities said they looked for a doctor who might have been summoned to tend Phillip, so they questioned others before confronting me. They must know I told Milton that Phillip was up North on business. They might even know I deluded his other partners, and even know where I was. Maybe they didn't tell me because they hoped to entrap me. I'll bet I shocked them when I told the truth. They can't prove you lied to help me, so they're bogged down with three witnesses in my favor. I wish I knew which of his partners is lying. Since only initials are listed, maybe Phillip was the only one who knew the details of this deal. I wonder if Milton would reveal anything if I questioned him. With Phillip dead, I am his partner, so why withhold facts? If Milton's involved in this wild scheme and it's trouble, probably not."

Dan was intrigued. "Tell me again what Phillip said about Cuba."

"I don't know what it all refers to."

"Then repeat every word you heard, Rachel."

She obeyed his request as best she could: "Your life, everything in danger . . . . Enemies, get to you anywhere . . . . Stop at nothing . . . to get what they want . . . . Guns and ammunition . . . . Must return the money . . . . Sell anything to repay them . . . . Only way to stay alive and safe . . . . Need guns badly . . . . War . . . . Freedom . . . . He'll come soon and help me . . . . Don't double cross Harry and the— Must honor the deal . . . . All those warnings came . . . . Tried to stop deal . . . . Killing me . . . . got the money hidden . . . . You'll be blamed . . . . Can't go to the law . . . . Go see him in Cuba . . . . He'll help . . . . He'll stop them . . . . Only hope . . . . Sorry got you into this mess . . . ."

Dan scowled as he studied the words for clues and facts. Perhaps Phillip *had been* referring to him as the first helper! It was fortunate his brother hadn't called out his name during delirium. Or had he? No, he didn't believe she knew his true relationship to Phillip.

"I can see why those words frightened you, Rachel, for they hold definite warnings. In your place, I would have taken the same course of action. It surely sounds as if Phillip took their advance and hid it. That would match the hints those two partners gave us. I wish I knew who he was talking about in Cuba; I don't recall any friends or business associates there. If a treacherous or greedy friend got him into this deal, he wouldn't have suspected anything was wrong; but something happened to change his mind. Until we get a real clue about the final destination, it wouldn't do any good to sail there; it's a big island with too many people. We couldn't go around asking who ordered arms and ammunition for a rebellion."

"What do you mean?"

"Cuban Rebels have been fighting for their independence from Spain since '68," Dan related. "A purchase of that size and price could only be to fight a war for freedom: that's what Phillip's clues imply. The American position is one of sympathy but noninterference. Of course, we almost got drawn into the conflict two years ago when Spain captured the *Virginius* and executed fifty-three sailors. She was a gun-running ship, Cuban owned, but some of the crew members were Americans and she flew the American flag. Trouble was averted when King Alfonso XII wisely compensated the families involved—if you can pay for lives you've taken! From what I've heard, horrible atrocities are going on there, so Spain isn't endearing herself to us. We already have trouble with her in other locations: Puerto Rico, Guam, and the Philippines. Those are major shipping routes that have to be protected. The rebel leaders are Antonio Maceo and Carlos Manuel de Céspedes; so you can see, those initials don't match these in the book."

Rachel was alarmed. "If one gun-running ship was captured and sailors slain, that means it is dangerous and deadly to supply arms. It also means our government is trying to remain neutral. If we interfere by providing arms, or they had, it means trouble with the authorities—trouble I don't need. Selling weapons to rebels is risky, and must be illegal."

"And profitable, very profitable, Rachel. Did Phillip need money?"

"Not that I knew of, unless it had to do with a gambling debt. The news that he was a gambler came as a shock to me, if it's true. Both men may be lying for a reason."

Dan liked the way Rachel always seemed to give his brother the benefit of doubt and to protect Phillip's image when possible. "I hope they're wrong."

"Now that my husband's death is exposed, I can check his will, bank account, and all records. I'll start on that tomorrow. And I'll speak with Milton, too. I bet he hates the reality of us being partners, or just being in business with a female; so will Harry and maybe George. Tell me, Dan, how do you know so much about Cuba?"

He chuckled and scolded in a playful tone, "Suspicions about me returning already, woman. Shame on you. I'm a sea captain who delivers cargoes around the world. If I don't keep up with the trouble spots, I could get myself and my crew killed and my ship sunk or confiscated."

"I understand, and shame on you for thinking I didn't," she chided. "I told you about those incidents Phillip considered warnings; from Harry's words about the backdown; the timing matches for that to be true. Those were violent crimes I want solved. Do you think Phillip meant they were killing him, or his guilt or illness was killing him?"

"Either or both, or neither. Maybe it was the fever talking."

"Not with cholera."

"I haven't seen it up close; what does it do?"

She hated to relate how his friend had died. "Vomiting, diarrhea, cramps, fast and heavy drying up of the body, cold and withered skin, drawn face, faint pulse, and enormous thirst. It's infectious, painful, and swift. It usually is spread through contaminated water or food. That's why Burke thought Phillip caught it from drinking that filthy-black river water. I'm certain it wasn't that, or others would have contracted it."

"How does that imitate a poisoning?"

"Arsenic has the same symptoms."

"What was that about almonds that you mentioned concerning William's death?"

"Strychnine can look like a heart attack if the right amount is used. The victim sometimes grabs his chest and has a grimace of agony on his face that freezes there if death is rapid."

Dan pushed aside how his brother had spent his last day on earth, in agony and alone. His heart pumped turbulently with dread at Rachel's revelations, her vast knowledge of such matters. Slips? *Surely not.* "That's gory, but fascinating. How did you come by such learning, woman?"

Chapter 13

Rachel wondered if Dan was trying to sound casual but was really tense. It was best to be honest. "Some from the plantation, from poisons used to kill rodent and weeds. Some from Craig, about chemicals used in the textile and milling processes. And some from doctors during the investigations of me. Does it make you nervous to discover I know so much about those things?"

"Don't be foolish," Dan scolded. "You said Phillip might have been poisoned; I wanted to know how you came to that speculation. It's evident Craig didn't think you were capable of murder or he wouldn't have told you such things. Did you have other suitors between your husbands?"

That took her by surprise. "That's a strange question."

"From a jealous lover?" he teased. "There isn't anyone around who's going to battle me over you now that you're free again, is there?"

"No. The only men who approached me were making lewd advances. They wanted to bed me but not risk becoming one of my victims. Most of them shied away in terror of me putting an evil spell on them."

"Ah, fear of the Sea Witch stealing their souls," he jested.

"Can you be so sure of me this soon, Dan? You've

MORE PASSION AND ADVENTURE AWAIT... YOUR TRIP TO A BIG ADVENTUROUS WORLD BEGINS WHEN YOU ACCEPT YOUR FIRST 4 NOVELS ABSOLUTELY *FREE*
(AN $18.00 VALUE)

Accept your Free gift and start to experience more of the passion and adventure you like in a historical romance novel. Each Zebra novel is filled with proud men, spirited women and tempestuous love that you'll remember long after you turn the last page.

Zebra Historical Romances are the finest novels of their kind. They are written by authors who really know how to weave tales of romance and adventure in the historical settings you love. You'll feel like you've actually gone back in time with the thrilling stories that each Zebra novel offers.

GET YOUR FREE GIFT WITH THE START OF YOUR HOME SUBSCRIPTION

Our readers tell us that these books sell out very fast in book stores and often they miss the newest titles. So Zebra has made arrangements for you to receive the four newest novels published each month.

You'll be guaranteed that you'll never miss a title, and home delivery is so convenient. And to show you just how easy it is to get Zebra Historical Romances, we'll send you your first 4 books absolutely FREE! Our gift to you just for trying our home subscription service.

BIG SAVINGS AND FREE HOME DELIVERY

Each month, you'll receive the four newest titles as soon as they are published. You'll probably receive them even before the bookstores do. What's more, you may preview these exciting novels free for 10 days. If you like them as much as we think you will, just pay the low preferred subscriber's price of just $3.75 each. *You'll save $3.00 each month off the publisher's price.* AND, your savings are even greater because there are never any shipping, handling or other hidden charges—FREE Home Delivery. Of course you can return any shipment within 10 days for full credit, no questions asked. There is no minimum number of books you must buy.

heard the rumors and you've witnessed what the law thinks of me. You know I buried Phillip in secret, and you only have my word for why I did it. I could be lying about everything. How can you trust me?"

"The same way you can trust me, Rachel—on blind faith and feelings."

Should she confess that her heart coaxed her to accept him swiftly and totally, but her wary mind cautioned her to go slowly and to hold back from committing herself fully? She wanted to follow her heart, but her bad experiences with men warned her to listen to her keen mind. "I suppose I'm just anxious about how rapidly and unexpectedly we got so close. I worry about making another mistake with a man. I have to be certain it's you I need, not just a man to protect me when I'm so vulnerable and afraid."

"After what you've suffered, I can't blame you for having doubts and worries about all men. Complete faith and love will come, Rachel, if you don't fight it out of fear I'm like all the others who've hurt and used you."

"You aren't like any man I've ever known. Maybe that scares me more. Your power frightens me sometimes. You, Daniel Slade, can hurt me more than anyone has if you aren't being honest and sincere."

"The same is true of you, my enchanting siren. No woman has been this close and special to me. I want you so much that, even if I learned you were guilty of being a Black Widow, I would still love you and want you; I would believe the power of our love is strong enough to break that curse on you. I never thought a woman would get to me as you have. You're right; it *is* scary. It will take adjusting on both our sides. We won't rush it, love. Let me finish checking this book and locking Baldwin's desk, then we must leave."

As Dan read and turned pages, Rachel observed him. She told herself she shouldn't be so skittish and leery. They cared about each other and about what happened to each other. They were being helpmates to each other. They shared most of the same goals, dreams, and hopes. Even when mistrustful, neither of them was childish, petty, vengeful, or reckless. Weren't those qualities and traits of true love?

"We're all finished. Let's leave while it's still safe."

"What now?" Rachel queried.

"You handle your normal business with the banker and lawyer. See what response you get from Harry and George from your telegrams to them tomorrow. See how everyone reacts to this news. Then all we can do is wait for May fourteenth to see who comes and what's in store."

"What about us, Dan? We can't risk seeing each other at home or in town, not with an investigation of me in progress."

"We're friends and business acquaintances, so that will cover the visits."

"That isn't what I meant," she murmured, her cheeks flushing.

Dan pulled her into his embrace and kissed her. "Don't fret, love; we'll be together soon; I promise. But for now, we must get out of here; it's late. We'll meet for lunch tomorrow, in public to prevent suspicions, in the cafe down the street at one. You can tell me all you've learned."

They kissed a final time, checked the office for slips, and departed.

Again, Rachel was shot at on her way home. Before she could dash for cover, she decided to see if it was only a scare tactic. She halted and glared in that direction. As suspected and hoped, no second bullet or enemy approached her position. Assured somebody wanted her terrified but not dead, courage and daring filled her. "Stop threatening me or the deal is off!" she shouted. "Be nice and everything will be fine!" Those words provoked no response, so she rode for Moss Haven.

Early Monday morning, the two police investigators arrived at Rachel's home. They told her they had come to take down affidavits about Phillip's death and secret burial. Rachel, Lula Mae, and Burke were placed in different rooms with closed doors. Rachel guessed it was to prevent them from overhearing each other and was done without warning in hopes of ensnaring them in a lie. She knew the aggressive men would compare their words with hopes of discovering inconsistencies.

One man took down her explanation in detail, while another did the same with Lula Mae and Burke. She presumed they would take down Dan's statement, too. She prayed that after telling him everything he wouldn't make a mistake and get all of them into trouble.

"Why did you lie to Mr. Baldwin, Mrs. McCandless?" the surly man asked Rachel. "That point confuses me."

"It was to gain time to carry out important business details. If I had told them Phillip was dead, they would have panicked and we couldn't have completed our business. As long as they believed I was acting on Phillip's behalf, they cooperated. I'm sure you realize that men do not like doing business with a female, not even a wife. I deceived Milton Baldwin until I could finish in Athens and Augusta, then meet with him in person to take Phillip's place in their firm. It wasn't wise or kind to leave him a note or drop that shocking news in his lap, then take off for several weeks. I didn't want to leave him worrying over how his partner's death would affect him and their firm. I needed to be present with plenty of time for discussion. Besides, I didn't think I should tell them such news before I told the law."

"What business could be that important?"

"This is a confidential report and paper, is it not?"

"Of course, ma'am."

This time she had to lie. "That's good, because Phillip's motive could create problems and ill will if his partners learned why I truly went to see them. Phillip told me there was a big problem with a very large deal he had worked out with a client, a deal that is crucial to the survival of those two companies. He suspected that his partners were stalling orders, perhaps even making secret deals and not paying him his total share of the profits. As you recall, I worked for Phillip before I married him; I understand books, orders, inventories, and such. Phillip wanted me to get the facts about the companies' actions. The trip was planned early Thursday. Before he died on Friday morning, he begged me to rush there to do my snooping before they learned he was dead. He said that if they panicked, they might lie and cover the truth. The crux of the matter is, he thought he was being cheated. He wanted me to catch them by surprise with an unexpected visit before they could destroy evidence of their guilt, so I pretended Phillip was away on unrelated business and I was on holiday."

"Did you obtain the facts you needed?"

"Not really. Neither man would let me study the company's books without Phillip being present or sending a letter of authorization. I'm afraid neither my husband nor I thought of that angle. I plan to telegraph them today about his demise. Now they won't have any excuse to keep me from the books; after all, I am their partner. Will there be a problem with me taking another short business trip soon? I assure you I shall return home."

"After I examine your statement and the affidavits

of the three witnesses, I'll inform you if you can leave town," he replied.

"Tell me, sir, how and when did your office get this tip?"

"A letter was slipped under our door last Thursday morning."

Rachel realized that was when she and Dan were leaving Athens. Who had known her schedule? Dan, her servants, Luke Conner, the men in the Athens and Savannah telegraph offices, and possibly an unknown spy. "What did it say? Surely I have a right to be told why an anonymous note influenced you."

"There's no reason not to tell you, ma'am. It said: 'Phillip McCandless has been dead since March 26. His wife killed him. She buried him in secret. She went to Augusta and Athens on March 29 to steal his companies. She will return late April 16. Get that murdering Black Widow this time.' We figured it was simple to learn if Mr. McCandless was alive and the letter was a joke. But with you gone and him claimed gone, we couldn't. We did what little investigating we could during your absence."

"I want to view this letter, sir, to see if I recognize the handwriting."

"That might be helpful, if it were possible. But it vanished Friday night."

Rachel gaped at him. "You mean it was stolen from a police station!"

"I'm afraid so, ma'am." The man appeared embarrassed and annoyed.

"Doesn't that strike you as odd, sir? Who would provide a tip, then steal it? For what reason?"

"To get an investigation underway and to keep from being involved."

"But breaking in and stealing are crimes," she reasoned. "Only a fool would do such things in a police station. Doesn't it make you wonder how this informer got his information and why he altered it into lies?"

"I figured somebody slipped up on you, saw what you were doing, got suspicious, left without being seen, then reported it to us."

"So why accuse me of murder, if all this person saw was a burial? And why follow me to see what I was doing and where I was going?"

"I hate to say it, ma'am, but probably because of your past."

"As there wasn't a crime, sir, it seems to me that someone was trying to get me into trouble for revenge or spite. Did the script look feminine?"

He was intrigued. "Why would you ask that?"

"Perhaps it was a woman who loved and lost one of my husbands."

"That's farfetched, ma'am."

"No more than me being accused as a Black Widow, a murderess."

He scratched his head and flicked nonexistent dust flecks from his jacket.

"You have to admit, ma'am, there were good reasons for our doubts and questions every time. It was printed neatly, but I can't say if a man or woman wrote it. I will tell you that this case isn't closed yet. If we find discrepancies in the statements, we'll need to question all of you again. If any other clues come up, we'll check them out. Chief Anderson hasn't decided about having a doctor examine the body; that's still a possibility."

"Whatever you need to do to clear me, do it swiftly, please."

"I'll try my best to have this case solved very soon. If you have nothing else to say, read this carefully. If it's correct, sign it."

After he left the room, Rachel mused on what she'd learned. Lula Mae and Burke couldn't speak correct English, much less write such a letter; and they'd never betray her. Too, others had known her schedule: Harry and George. The tip proved someone knew when Phillip died and how he was buried. It was strange why the culprit didn't report her deed that day, or on the Saturday or Sunday afterward; the waiting period bewildered her. Why say she was trying to steal his companies? By inheritance, they were hers. Perhaps that part of the note was meant to mislead her and the law.

Rachel didn't want to speculate on Daniel Slade, but . . . Having heard the rumors about her on Thursday, had Dan arrived here Friday and witnessed her behavior, assumed she had slain his old and dear friend, then set out to entrap her? She reflected on their many days and one passionate night together. Had knowing Phillip was dead been the reason why he could seduce his old friend's wife—no fear of betrayal? No, she concluded, if Dan believed she murdered Phillip, he would handle the revenge himself, after he was certain she was guilty.

Later, in Savannah, Rachel entered the telegraph office and sent messages to Harry and George: "Sad news. Phillip died. Gave no client name. Cannot find money. Will await client arrival May fourteen. Need facts on deal before honor. Rachel McCandless." *One task out of the way today.*

She went to McCandless & Baldwin Shipping Firm to handle the second. She did not knock, and entered to find Milton at work at his desk.

The green-eyed man glanced up, looked at her a moment, and stood. He smiled and said, "Hello, Rachel. This is a pleasant surprise. Come in and sit down. You won't believe what happened while you were away. The police came to see me Thursday with a foolish story that Phillip is dead."

Rachel watched the man with his black hair and

even features as she responded, "I'm afraid it's true, Milton; Phillip is dead. He came down with cholera and died on the twenty-sixth of last month."

"My God, it's true! Why didn't you tell me sooner?"

To Rachel, he appeared shocked, but seemed to recover quickly. "I'll explain that in a moment. First, what did the officers ask you?"

Milton's quizzical green gaze settled on her face. "They came by and wanted to know where Phillip was. I told them he was away tending to other business; that's what I believed. They asked if he'd acted strange before he left; I said he hadn't. They told me about an anonymous letter claiming Phillip was dead, that you'd killed him and buried him secretly. I said that was mad, that you and Phillip love each other and are very happy. They wanted to know who he used as a doctor. I told them, and they left."

"Did you send that news to Harry or George on Thursday? Or later?"

"Certainly not! I thought it was nothing but a cruel joke."

"Did the police speak with you again Saturday after they saw me?"

"No, they couldn't: I was off fishing with friends. I haven't received any messages or visits since Thursday. What's going on, Rachel?"

She hurried on with questions she needed to learn the answers to. "What do you know about this big arms and ammunition deal with the other two companies, the one you're shipping out on May fourteenth?"

He hesitated a minute. "Nothing much, except the date and two men's initials. For some curious reason, Phillip wouldn't discuss it with me. I assumed it was a private deal. What's going on, Rachel?" he asked again.

Once more she ignored his query to continue her

line of questions. "You have no idea about the names that go with those initials?"

"No. Why? And why does Harry want to know about the deal, too? He and Phillip are—*were*—partners. Why wouldn't he be informed? He telegraphed me to ask the destination of the delivery ship. All Phillip told me was to write down Haiti. Is there, *was* there a problem between them?"

She tried to be clever to delude him, to use clues to extract other ones. "I'm not sure yet. That's why I had to rush off to Augusta and Athens. Before Phillip died, he mentioned a mystery and asked me to check it out immediately. After he died I rushed off to carry out his last wish before this news was exposed. I'm sorry I had to deceive you for a short time, Milton, but I didn't want you dropping a hint to his other partners; and I wanted to wait until we could sit down and talk in person. Do you understand?" She put on her most innocent look.

The thirty-two-year old man murmured, "I suppose so . . . What do you want to do about your share of the firm?"

She noticed he changed the subject to a selfish topic. "I'd like to go over the books with you first, then decide."

"Certainly, Partner. We can do that right now, if you have time."

"The sooner, the better. Thank you, Milton." She observed him as he pulled Phillip's chair over to his desk, unlocked a drawer, and withdrew a ledger. He opened it and located the section he wanted. He didn't seem too grieved over her husband's death, and that troubled Rachel. Neither did he appear distressed to have her as his new partner, if he'd given that much thought yet. He looked up and smiled at her.

"If you'll have a seat next to me, we'll begin. It won't take long."

Milton was right, it didn't. "As you can see, we're

in deep debt," he remarked as he finished his explanation. "Current shipments are just barely keeping us afloat by covering current expenses; not much left over to pay rear bills. Those attacks recently cost us plenty to settle them. Phillip, you now, and I are fortunate we both have other investments for support."

Rachel eyed the ledger. It didn't look altered, as it would if he'd been warned to do so before she viewed it. But how did she know there wasn't another book for other ships and cargoes? Should she believe this was the whole stormy picture? Did she have any reason to distrust Milton Baldwin?

"I'm looking forward to the large payment for delivering that cargo on the fourteenth," he said. "I assume it will proceed. We—you and I—surely need it. There's just too much competition these days to make this business profitable anymore. I've been seeking new clients and trying to recover old ones we've lost to cheaper prices; so far, it doesn't look promising. We sold off two ships last month to cut expenses; keeping so many idle in port was draining us of needed money. If something good doesn't happen soon, selling everything won't even get us in the clear or leave us with much—if any—profit. If Phillip hasn't already told you how terrible matters have gotten, I'm sorry you're having to hear it from me today."

"So am I, Milton, and I was in the dark. It doesn't look good."

He shook his head. "No, I'm afraid it doesn't. If I locate a buyer, are you interested in selling out before we sink?"

"I suppose so. But we'll discuss that possibility later. I do have to leave; I have several other appointments today. Thank you again, Milton."

"If you need any help or advice, Rachel; you know where to find me."

She feigned a smile. "That's very kind of you. Good-bye."

As she walked to the cafe where she was scheduled to meet Dan, Rachel fumed. *Why offer friendship now when you and your wife haven't socialized with me in the past unless it was necessary! Your partner and supposed friend is dead, and you didn't seem to care much. Why?*

Dan was waiting for her. She put on a cheerful smile and joined him.

"Good morning, love," he whispered. "How are things going?"

"Not good at all today. The—" She halted when the waiter arrived to take their orders, then left. "The law showed up very early to take our statements. Have they seen you yet?"

"Early this morning, but a nicer officer this time. I made certain my story will match yours. Lula Mae and Burke knew to say I was present?"

"Yes, I explained things to them after your departure Saturday. That's the only lie they had to tell. Have you noticed any shadow following you?"

"No, and you aren't being followed, either. Luke's across the street near a tree. He just gave me the clear signal. You look upset."

Rachel related her meeting with Milton Baldwin. "It seems all three of Phillip's companies are in almost desperate need of money. That gives more and more of a reason why he would accept a mysterious deal like this."

"Are you in financial trouble, love?"

"Certainly not. I'm seeing the banker, insurance broker, and lawyer after we eat. The companies need money, but I don't think they're broke. I have the plantation and earnings from sharecropping. I'll be fine."

"If you need anything, please tell me."

She tried not to stare at his handsome face. "Stop worrying."

"I will worry until we can risk another meeting on Thursday and you tell me all is fine. I wish you didn't have to do this alone."

"I can manage it, honestly." She told Dan about her home being searched during their absence and about being shot at again. "Whoever it is isn't trying to kill me, just terrify me. Frankly, it's making me more angry and defiant than afraid. We'll finish this later; here comes our food."

Rachel received astonishing news at the bank: their account was almost empty, barely enough there to pay one month's expenses! And that was if she managed it carefully. She had only a little cash at home in her household money box. She stared at the large withdrawals almost every month and wondered where that money had gone. She fretted it had been lost due to Phillip's gambling. Almost penniless . . . That fact evoked horrible reminders of her days near poverty after Craig's death. She left the bank in a state of dismay and confusion, and nibblings of anger.

Her visit with the insurance broker was worse. Phillip had canceled his insurance in February! The man said it was because he couldn't afford to continue it. He said it was a shame it was dropped so close to when it was needed, but Rachel did not detect a wicked implication in his words or manner. The man was polite and sympathetic.

As she walked toward the lawyer's office with a heavy heart, Rachel imagined what people and the law would think if they learned about the cancellation of the insurance: that Phillip had feared for his life and had done it so his murderess couldn't inherit his wealth after she did away with him. She dreaded the new gossip which was sure to come soon and felt her resentment and anger increase.

The lawyer did give her a little good news: she was Phillip's sole heir to his shares of three businesses and the plantation. Yet, the man revealed that her husband had seen him on the street on March twenty-fourth and he had asked for an appointment on the twenty-ninth "to discuss a serious legal problem," but, of course, hadn't kept it. Rachel told him that she didn't know what the meeting would have covered, but she suspected it was to obtain advice about the illegal deal. She was glad he didn't hint at her husband's intention to change his will to exclude a woman he feared.

The lawyer informed her that Phillip had mentioned he might want to sell his two out-of-town partnerships, as they weren't profitable anymore. Nor did he like having businesses so far away. He told her Phillip had hinted at putting the sale money into the shipping firm to get it back on solid ground. The man studied the file to make sure he had covered everything.

In view of the big deal, she mused, how could Phillip think or say the two companies weren't making money? Unless he intended to break that mysterious contract . . . Or to take his profit first, then sell? Had Harry or George—or both men—known of Phillip's plans to break up their partnerships? Would they do *anything* to prevent losing a needed investor? Or perhaps Phillip had planned to sell out only because he needed cash. It was odd her husband hadn't mentioned such things to her.

Rachel thanked the lawyer for his assistance and left. She stood outside his office for a time, thinking and planning her next step. She had no insurance, and virtually no money in the bank. She wouldn't receive support from sharecropper earnings until fall, five months away, if no disaster occurred to destroy the crops. With the three companies in trouble, so was she. Milton had exposed that about the firm; and George and Harry had implied it about the arms and ammunition companies. If that mysterious deal fell through, all those holdings could collapse.

These revelations had to explain why Phillip was so desperate to make money any way necessary. Phillip would never want to lose his masculine pride and be humiliated by financial devastation. He could have used that advance to gamble with, hoping to earn enough winnings to rescue himself, then back out of the hazardous deal with a polite refusal, rich from using their money as a stake. If he had been so foolish and couldn't face ruin, humiliation, and perils, would he take his life to avoid them? Rachel couldn't answer that distressing question and didn't want to think about it.

She asked herself if the other partners could be just as desperate to save their reputations. It was possible that Harry had exploited Phillip's weakness and plight to coerce him into restarting that order. Both had warned that without the advance, the deal couldn't go through, even if it were legal. Rachel trembled in dread. Even if she sold Moss Haven and all three partnerships, she could not collect enough to replace five hundred thousand dollars if she were forced to be responsible for its loss. If she knew the deal was legal, she would have asked the lawyer about that angle. But she was in enough trouble without taking more risks. She had inherited Phillip's section of the assets but probably his shares of the companies' debts, too. She wondered if Dan's orders and payments would make any difference with the companies' finances. She hoped so.

Rachel knew she had to learn where she stood. She returned to the telegraph office and sent Harry and George a second message: "Am your partner now. Please send financial report fast. Will check company books soon. Advise when ready and convenient. Rachel McCandless."

As Rachel waited for Burke Wells to pick her up in the carriage at the agreed time and location, she was lost in thought over her troubles. She had been married three times to wealthy men, but had virtually no inheritance. She had been a fairly good wife and done nothing wrong, but she was believed to have murdered all her husbands and the son of one of them. Surely she was cursed by wicked fate! She yearned for Dan's strong arms to give her courage and comfort.

She was tempted to go to his hotel and to fall into his arms, to entice him to take her away from all these troubles. But she couldn't. That would make both of them appear guilty of murdering Phillip to be together. They would never make it out of port on his ship before the law tossed them into jail. Besides, she had to stay here and fight these cruelties against her, to put an end to the evil spell on her, to be free to marry Dan without risking his survival.

Burke arrived and she got into the carriage. They rode home in near silence as the manager comprehended she had worries on her mind.

"Burke, I need to speak with you and Lula Mae about something important," she told him as she stepped down from the carriage. "Please come into the house after you put away the horses."

When the three gathered in the kitchen, Rachel said, "I want to thank both of you for doing so well with the authorities. I hated to ask you to tell that one little lie, but without Captain Slade's help, I doubt those hateful men would have believed us. They probably would have carted me off to jail, even with no evidence I'd done something wrong."

"We done just like you said, Miz Rachel. Gawd won't go ablamin' us for he'pin' you. Ain't no call fur dem poleece to be botherin' you. Dey'll be pow'ful sorry dey messed wif us if dey do. De worst is over."

She took a deep breath, then murmured, "I wish it was, Burke, but I received bad news in town today." She lightly skimmed the story of her financial condition. It wasn't necessary for her servants to know the private details, only that rough times on the plantation were ahead. "For a while, until I get matters settled, we'll need to be careful with spending."

"You cain't be saying you're bound to lose all your stuff, Miss Rachel?"

She looked at the shocked housekeeper. "No, Lula Mae, but probably some of it. That business I hurried out of town to tend is crucial for keeping those companies alive. There's a problem with a big order; if it fails, we'll all be hurt. But everybody is working hard to make sure it succeeds. Mr. Baldwin is looking for a buyer for the shipping firm here. I've agreed to sell out if he does. But I don't think either of us will have much money left after the firm's bills are paid. We just have to wait until the crops come in and pray nothing happens to them."

"Ah inspect dem ever' week, Miz Rachel. Dey's doin' fine. It looks to be a big year. Don' you go aworryin'. Gawd looks after His children. Ah'll keeps dem sharecroppers workin' hard."

Rachel's heart warmed. "Thank you, Burke."

"No needs to worry 'bout eating, Miss Rachel," said Lula Mae. "The smokehouse and pantry holds a gracious plenty. It won't be a long spell afore the garden comes in. Unless the cow goes dry, she gives a bounty of milk and butter. I'll tends the garden every morning to make her give us all she can. Nothing'll go to waste; I'll can all we don't eat whilst it's fresh. I won't buy nothing at the market we don't has to have."

Rachel sent her an affectionate smile. The woman always came through for her during the worst of times. "Thank you, Lula Mae. I knew I could depend on you two for help and understanding. Nobody has more loyal workers than I do. I love you both."

"I bet yo're plum worn out, you pore girl. You need a hot supper, a long bath, a sip of whiskey, and a good night's rest. I'll tend it for you."

"You're right, Lula Mae; thank you. I plan to go back into town Wednesday, Burke. I'm going to try to borrow money from the bank against the crops. If they'll let me have a loan, it will solve our troubles for a while."

"Ah'll be ready when you wants to go attendin' to dat bisness."

"Lula Mae, would you like to ride along with us and do any shopping? It will give you a chance for a nice diversion."

"I mite could go, Miss Rachel; that sounds most wonderful to me."

"Then, you'll come along. We'll leave around ten o'clock Wednesday."

Tuesday, Phillip McCandless's obituary appeared in local newspapers. Rachel read it quickly, then, again, slowly. Nothing was mentioned about cause of death. Nor was there a hint about the investigation she was enduring, but she was certain anyone seeing it would assume one was in progress, also as usual. She prayed no aggressive and rude reporter, like that Harold Seymour in Augusta, would come to plead for an interview. She told Lula Mae if that happened, not to let him inside the house and to say she wasn't available.

Lula Mae Morris and Burke Wells had on protective airs today, and she was grateful for their love and concern.

Rachel realized with sadness that she could not purchase a headstone for Phillip's grave until her finances improved. Burke said he would make one she could letter herself until she could afford a proper one. He left the house to tend that chore promptly. He also told her he would make a mound over the grave and pretty up the area since the site no longer had to remain a secret. That pleased and relieved her.

During the day, Lula Mae helped Rachel remove Phillip's clothes from their bedroom. They hauled them to the washshed for Burke to go through first for his selections, then the two workers. If anything was left, Burke was to give them to less fortunate and hardworking sharecroppers on her land. Items of value, such as his watch and a diamond stickpin, she placed in her household money box and would decide later what to do with them.

As Rachel slipped off her gold wedding band to put it away, she pondered a curious point: there was nothing—in their bedroom, the attic, the rest of the house, and the outbuildings—of Phillip's personal effects to enlighten her about his past. She found no picture, letter, memento, or anything from the days between his birth and his arrival in Savannah. It was almost as if he hadn't existed before coming here to live! Or had he, in a moment of anguish and turmoil, destroyed all reminders?

If not, perhaps he had them stored in a trunk somewhere, such as in the office storeroom or the warehouse downtown. She must ask Milton. It would be nice, and perhaps enlightening, to see some keepsakes of his past.

It was near one o'clock in the morning when Rachel was awakened by loud noises. She jerked up in bed and listened. It sounded like rocks slamming against the house! The commotion ceased before she could reach the front window and look outside. Her gaze searched the yard and nearby area for movement, but she saw nothing. Her heart pounded, but she couldn't cower there in terror. She retrieved her derringer and crept downstairs. She knew the windows and doors were locked on the first floor as Dan had cautioned her. She sneaked to a window and scanned the area once more, but everything appeared normal. She slipped to the front door, leaned her ear against it, and listened. She heard nothing but crickets and frogs.

Rachel took in a deep breath, then released it. Her lagging courage resummoned, she placed her hand on the knob and eased the door open as silently as the oiled hinges would allow. She peeked into the yard. The waxing moon would be full in three nights and light was plentiful. Her gaze lowered to the porch, which was littered with rocks. The odor of fresh paint filled her nostrils and her alarmed gaze saw the reason for it: ugly names and hateful messages were scrawled in black paint on the porch floor and on the house front and door.

"Damn you, you coward!" she yelled into the shadows at a distance, in case the culprit or culprits were still lurking there.

Lula Mae came running around the house, shouting her mistress's name to avoid getting shot by accident. She was carrying a shotgun and a lantern. "Miss Ra—" The woman fell silent as she gaped at the awful sight and her pale-faced mistress. She propped the weapon against a post, rushed to Rachel, and embraced the trembling and tearful female. "Lord have no mercy on them bastards! Kill them all for doing this most awfullest thing! You all right, Miss Rachel? They didn't hurt you, did they? Speak to Lula Mae! You hurt some place?"

Rachel gathered her wits and control. "I'm unharmed, Lula Mae. They were gone when I came downstairs, or they're hiding out there in the darkness to witness the effect of their cruel mischief. The rocks awoke me. Look what they painted on my home!" she cried in distress.

In a mixture of moon- and lanternlight, both gazes read the words scrawled in black paint: KILLER, BLACK WIDOW, WHORE, and GET OUT.

"It's starting all over again, Lula Mae," she murmured. "How can they be so cruel? How can they judge me guilty and evil without proof? Will I never receive the benefit of doubt? Will this damned curse never end?"

Lula Mae patted her shoulder and coaxed, "Comes insides, Miss Rachel. I'll fix you some warm milk to calm yore jitters. Those bastards won't come sneaking back to do more hurt tonight. We'll pick up them rocks and paints over that mess tomorrow. Don't go aworrying 'bout it tonight. Burke's home's too far away, so he cain't hear what happened. We might aks him to sleeps in the barn or carriage house for a spell."

"I'll be fine, Lula Mae. And don't go to any trouble with firing the stove and preparing hot milk this late. I'll take a sip of brandy. From now on, we'll keep our guns loaded and ready to use if those villains try this again."

"If they do, Miss Rachel, we'll shoot ever blamed one of them! It's bound to be bad awful for a spell. I'll have Burke hangs lanterns on the porch so we can see their wicked faces when we shoot them. The law won't do nothing to stop them, but we will."

"You're right; it's useless to report this incident to them. They don't care what happens to me. You get back to bed, and so will I. There's nothing we can do tonight."

"You want me to stays in the house with you?"

"That isn't necessary. I'll lock the doors and keep my gun nearby." Rachel didn't want to set a pattern for the housekeeper being underfoot at night, especially if Dan . . . Her love, she wanted and needed him. She wished he were here. It would be a while before that was safe; and without a doubt, things would get much worse before that glorious day.

Wednesday morning, Rachel and Burke left for town. Lula Mae insisted on staying at Moss Haven to guard the house against another attack. As the two departed, the housekeeper went to work on the damage.

Rachel sat waiting for Burke to return from his errands, as the meeting at the bank had not taken as long as expected. The man's rejection of her loan came fast and easy for him, or so it appeared to her. He claimed that with the companies in such bad shape and with the uncertainty of the crops, she didn't have adequate collateral for a loan. The last reason was because she refused to put up Moss Haven to back a loan. She couldn't allow anything to take her home away from her, as failure of repayment would do. She wouldn't take that risk until it became absolutely necessary. One hope remained: she had jewelry she could sell, gifts from Phillip.

Excluding her servants and her secret lover she was on her own now. Things appeared grim, hopeless, and perilous, but she was resolved not to be defeated. In three weeks and two days, she would discover if that big contract was legal and if the client would be understanding about the lost advance. If those two things came true and the investigation halted, all of her troubles would be over and she could have a future with Dan.

A terrible reality struck home: no, she wouldn't have an answer on May fourteenth! Phillip was supposed to sail with the cargo that day. It would take a while for the client to realize it was overdue, then more time for him to come and investigate why.

She couldn't understand why she hadn't heard

from Harry and George by now; that made her anxious. If something good didn't happen soon, she would be at the end of her money by the last day of May. Would Dan think she had known of her troubles all along and had set out to entrap him for her survival? Would he—

Rachel's heart suddenly thudded and her gaze widened in disbelief and alarm. To avoid being noticed by passing people who might gape at her, she was sitting sideways on the end of a bench that faced the river and was located in a garden area between Bay Street and Factor's Row; she was almost concealed behind a cluster of large and flowering azaleas. As she glanced toward the street to check for Burke's approach, she saw Captain Daniel Slade strolling down the other side of the street with Miss Camellia Jones on his arm!

Rachel leaned out of sight, but peered through the bush limbs to watch them. They were laughing and chatting as if old and close friends! Fury and suspicions flooded her mind. She wondered if that wealthy witch had hired Dan to ensnare and destroy her for revenge. Phillip's past relationship with the flaming redhead would explain how Dan had known about her husband, and the cunning male could have fabricated the rest of his tale.

Anguish knifed Rachel's heart, and anger ruled her mind. She could imagine Camellia's laughter and taunts when the hateful witch exposed their ruse: for once, the "Black Widow" had fallen under a predator's spell.

Rachel was relieved when they rounded the corner at Abercorn and were gone from her sight. Desperate to get home, her gaze searched the street for Burke's return. She saw him coming, and rushed to meet him. She scrambled into the carriage and urged him to leave fast.

As he flicked the reins, Burke asked, "Mo trouble, Miz Rachel?"

"The banker said no to my request for a loan, but don't worry. I have another plan in mind. We aren't whipped yet, Burke, and we won't be."

"Dat's de spirit, Miz Rachel," he complimented with a grin.

"Stop at the police office," she suddenly ordered as they neared it.

"What you be wantin' in there?"

"I'll only be a moment," she said, hopped down, and went inside. She had to learn if Dan had betrayed her in his affidavit. She could use a request to leave town on business as the motive for her visit.

The meeting didn't take long, as the investigator told her everything was fine so far with the case, which wouldn't be closed for a while longer. It was all right if she needed to take another business trip, he said. This time she smiled and thanked him before they parted company. She didn't mention the vandalism at her home last night, and she wouldn't do so unless it became threatening to their safety.

"Home now," Rachel instructed Burke when she was again seated in the carriage.

"Ah seen Mr. Bal'win like you said, Miz Rachel. He said nary a trunk of Mr. Phillip's was 'round that he knowed about."

She was disappointed, but said, "That's good, Burke. I appreciate you tending that chore for me."

Rachel still thought it was odd for Phillip's personal effects to be missing, but there wasn't anything further she could do about that riddle.

When they reached the plantation, Lula Mae had discarded the rocks and covered the horrible black words with slate-blue paint. Rachel gave the weary housekeeper and manager the news, both bad and good. She thanked them and told Burke it wasn't necessary for him to sleep near the house as a guard. Exhausted in mind and body, she went upstairs.

Rachel entered the water closet to freshen up for dinner, though her appetite was missing and eating was only to appease her housekeeper. She barely suppressed a scream as her alarmed gaze watched a venomous spider struggle futilely to escape the slick-sided basin. She lifted a note from beside the spider's prison: *"Marry me this time, my beautiful Black Widow. If you keep seeing that sea captain, I'll fill his bed with hundreds of these poisonous beauties. No man will ever have you except me."*

Marry who? She thought, her anger rising. *You never reveal yourself. You didn't respond to the flower signal. Why not?* She realized this note was cold and threatening and was written in her script, as the first one. It was as if the same person hadn't written the second and romantic note! If not, who and why? Dan . . .

Rachel realized she mustn't tell Lula Mae and frighten the woman. Her friend, who had done her work today with a shotgun nearby, would be distressed to learn a culprit had sneaked in the back door to terrorize her mistress in her own home.

Thursday morning, a response was delivered to Rachel from George Leathers. Her Augusta partner began by saying he had sent a letter rather than a telegram to keep what he had to say private. He was shocked by Phillip's death and conveyed his sympathies. Rachel knew he would be dismayed and angered by her recent ruse after he learned the actual date Phillip had died. She would handle that explanation when she saw him tomorrow, as she intended to take the train to see both partners in person. George related that the Augusta company was near bankruptcy. With that advance lost, he didn't know if he should ship the order and risk the client canceling it or demanding part of it for the payment taken. He advised that as soon as the contracts were filled, the company should be either closed down or sold, according to which action could be best. After their debts were settled, he anticipated a loss.

George wrote that he planned to retire and live off other investments. He apologized that she would get little or nothing from the sale. Without the profit from that big deal, the outlook was bleak. He enclosed a report to verify what he had said and he added that he had deceived her about the books being gone because he didn't think Phillip would have wanted her to know how terrible things were with the company, as his partner was well informed about the conditions.

The news upset Rachel, but it wasn't unexpected. It was nearing time to handle another nasty facet in her life, and she dreaded it.

Rachel put on her most flattering dress and groomed her dark-brown hair. She must look her best when Dan called this afternoon as scheduled. She wanted the treacherous beguiler to see what he was losing, to yearn to make love to her again. She wouldn't let on she knew about his relationship with Camellia Jones, as that would expose a deceit. She would drop him as a hot iron. She would not allow him to see how much and how deeply he had hurt her. From this day forward, she must never trust another man! Lula Mae was right; most of them only wanted to use a woman!

Just then the housekeeper knocked on her bedroom door. "Cumpny, Miss Rachel," she said nervously. "He's in the parler. I'll be in the kitchen if you need me. I got food on the stove needs watching."

"That's fine, Lula Mae. Tell him I'll be down shortly. Don't serve any refreshments. He won't be staying long." After the housekeeper left, Rachel checked her image in the mirror. Pleased with her appearance but broken-hearted, she went with lagging courage to face her traitorous lover to reject him.

As she entered the formal parlor, Rachel gaped at the man lazing on the sofa. Her body went cold and rigid. He smiled and rose to greet her. This was not the confrontation she had expected. "How dare you come here! Get out of my home, Earl Starger!"

Chapter 14

"Calm down, girl. I read about Phillip McCandless's death in the newspaper. I had to come see if you were all right. Do you need anything?"

Rachel gaped at the forty-one-year-old man who was attired in immaculate and fashionable clothes. "What do you care!"

"Don't you think it's past time to forget our little misunderstanding?"

Her wide gaze enlarged even more in outrage. "Misunderstanding! You beast, you attacked me."

"If I got too friendly trying to earn your affection and acceptance, I'm sorry. If you hadn't jerked away from my fatherly hug, your shirt wouldn't have gotten ripped. I was only trying to calm you down and silence you before others heard the commotion and misunderstood, as William did. I didn't mean to scare you or hurt you, Rachel. I would never do that."

She glared at the hazel-eyed man whose unruly brown hair usually looked as if it were wind-tousled, but today was combed neatly. His long and thin features had an aristocratic appearance, but the man actually had no genteel blood or feelings. "You're a liar! I hate you, Earl Starger."

The visitor sank to the sofa as if weary. "I'm sorry you feel that way, girl, because you're wrong. Your mother has cried every week since you left home and got into so much trouble. How can you be so cruel to her? Come visit her, Rachel. I swear, I won't hug you or peck your check, or even touch your arm while passing in the hall. You have my word of honor."

Rachel remained standing near the entrance to the room, her body rigid and her cheeks flushed with strong emotion. "You have no honor! You tricked Mama into marriage with pretty lies and devious charms. You weren't rich. You only had enough money to pay off our taxes and debts."

"I never claimed to be rich, girl. If you hate me because I wasn't, that isn't my fault. I did save the plantation for you and your family."

"Saved it for us? That's a joke!" She stared at the reason she had been driven from her home and why her last thirty-one months had been like a sojourn in Hades. No matter how much Earl tried to mask the aura of evil, danger, and lechery around him, she saw and felt it. He could be charming and could fool others easily, but not her. His faded hazel eyes were cloaked in concealment now, but she had seen that gaze filled with a wild and intimidating glint. "I'm supposed to believe you randomly chose a beautiful widow with a prosperous plantation in trouble to invest your life savings in," Rachel fumed, "but fell in love with her immediately and married her two months later. You came to our home with a plot to bewitch and entrap Mama, and you'll never convince me any differently. You're a greedy and deceitful carpetbagger! You came to get rich off White Cloud and to take advantage of our troubles. You practically imprisoned me and Mama on the plantation while you played the wealthy and respected planter in town with your Yankee friends. You're the reason my brother Randall is dead, and the cause for Richard and Rosemary leaving home. If Papa and Robert were alive, they'd kill you for what you've done to us."

Earl exhaled loudly as if frustrated. "The war is over, girl; there isn't any North and South anymore, only the Union, the United States. Throw away your hated and bitterness or it will destroy you. Your mother loves me, and I love her."

"Love? You don't know what love is."

Without raising his voice, Earl countered, "And you do? Did you love William Barlow or Craig Newman or Phillip McCandless when you married them? Or even by the time you buried them? No, you only wanted riches and a means of escape. You can't find happiness that way, girl. Come home for a visit, get your head cleared, and let me prove you're mistaken about me. You can leave any time you want and return home."

"You can't dupe me, you evil snake. One day Mama will see the ugly truth about you. Then your hold on her will be broken. And that day can't come soon enough to please me."

Earl stood and came toward her. He halted his approach when she took a few steps backward as if to flee the room. "She isn't my captive, girl. If she didn't love me and trust me, she could end our marriage."

Rachel sent forth cold laughter. "Mama would never create such a scandal, and you know it. She'd endure her predicament to the end before humiliating herself and staining the family name by allowing anyone to learn what a fool she'd made of herself by marrying you."

"The only scandals our families have known and suffered are because of *your* mistakes, Rachel. Don't make any more. Get your life changed and your mind unclouded."

The only black cloud I see is in your eyes! Rachel thought. "With your help?" she sneered sarcastically.

"I'll do whatever I can to repair the damage you've done to yourself. Maybe you can't be blamed for being confused back then, not after what the war did

317

to your family and home. You've had plenty of time and numerous opportunities to experience life to know my actions were innocent, only affectionate."

"Are you mad? What I've done to myself! I'm not guilty of any of those accusations. If I were, I'd be in prison or hanged. Or if I were capable of murdering someone, you would be my first and only victim."

"How can you despise me so much, Rachel? It's eating you alive. Your hatred keeps forcing you to make bad decisions. Can you get out of trouble a third—no, a fourth—time? You can't keep on like this and survive, girl."

She attempted to trick him into making a slip. "Why, because you'll kill me next time instead of murdering my husband to force me back home into your evil clutches? Or you'll make certain there is convincing evidence left behind to insinuate I'm to blame, so I'll be jailed?"

"Rachel Anne Fleming!" Earl cried, "Do you hear what you're ranting? Have you lost your mind for certain, girl? There are good doctors up North who can help you with your illness. Let me hire one of them to—"

"You bastard! I'm not insane, or evil, or cursed, or duped, Earl Starger! You're the one who needs his head doctored and cured. They have ugly names for men with your vile weakness and wicked behavior."

Earl shook his head. "If I didn't know how ill-minded and scared you are, I would be angry; and I wouldn't offer to help you. But I know you're sick and need help; so does your mother."

"I don't want or need any help from you. I would rather die than to lower myself that much."

"If you don't get your life changed, the authorities will take care of that ridiculous threat for you."

"Another veiled threat, my despicable stepfather?"

"I haven't threatened you today, or any other day, girl. You take every word I say and twist it. You're determined to paint me black with evil. What can I say or do to prove it isn't true?"

You act as if you're playing to an ignorant audience, not to someone who knows you and can't be fooled by your evil talents! Rachel fumed silently. "You've harassed me for years, ever since we met."

"How can love and concern be harassments?"

"Don't try to confuse me with your words, you beast," she scolded in a frosty tone. "We have nothing to say to each other, and we never will. Get out of my home and off of my property. Don't ever come back."

"What shall I tell your mother?"

"She knows where I live, if she cares about me and wants to see me."

"She can't travel, Rachel. She's been ill, very ill. I think she's heartsick over you and the other children deserting her and ignoring her."

Worry and alarm flooded Rachel. "Has she seen a doctor?" she asked. "How bad is it? Or is this another clever and cruel trick to fool me? To entice me home?"

"I took Catherine to see a doctor in Waynesboro on the twenty-sixth of last month and again last Thursday. He examined her and gave her two tonics. If she's not better by the sixth of May, I'm to take her to him again. I think seeing you would improve her health. That's why I risked your wrath and hatred today. If you refuse to come visit her, at least write her a letter."

"So you can steal it, read it, and hopefully learn all my secrets?"

"Rachel, Rachel, don't be so heartless and foolish. Even if what you claim was true, how could I endanger you with your mother and servants present? Bring along your own servants for the protection you think you need from me. Hellfire, carry a gun in your pocket if it makes you feel safer! I'm only concerned with your mother's health."

Rachel didn't believe him or trust him, but she

sensed something serious was afoot. "I'll think about both of your requests. Now, leave," she ordered him. She had to write, had to learn if Earl was away with her mother on those two dates. If it was the truth, Earl was out of the picture as a villain. If not . . .

"All right, girl, if that's the way you want it."

"It is, for now. Good-bye, Earl," she stated in a stern tone.

"Good-bye, Rachel; I hope you come to your senses soon."

As he reached the door, Rachel said, "Oh, yes, and you can stop sending me those crazy notes, stop following me, stop searching my room wherever I go, and stop shooting at me. Your threats and attacks don't frighten me."

Earl stared at her as if bewildered, then exhaled and shook his head in pity and frustration. "If anyone is harassing you, Rachel, it isn't me. Hire a detective to watch me so you can get that wild idea out of your head. They're only delusions, girl, imaginings of an ill mind. Get help before it's too late. But if they did happen, you best hire someone fast to protect you."

She had hoped to catch Earl by surprise and evoke a slip, but it hadn't worked. In fact, he looked sympathetic, as if he really thought she was mad.

Lula Mae knocked at Rachel's bedroom door once again. "More cumpny, Miss Rachel," the housekeeper announced to her agitated mistress. "That sea captain."

The young widow's chilly gaze met Lula Mae's worried one. She surprised the woman by ordering in a whisper that couldn't be overheard downstairs, "Don't serve any refreshments this time, either, Lula Mae, because he won't be staying long. I'll get rid of him as fast as possible, this time for good, I hope. I wish he didn't have to remain in port so long until his

320

orders arrive from Athens and Augusta. He's becoming *too* friendly, and I don't like it. I'm tired of men trying to charm me and use me. I won't be sweet and polite today, so maybe he'll stop calling on me."

"Yessum, Miss Rachel; I'll do that for you."

She checked her appearance again in the mirror. Her cheeks were still a mite flushed from her quarrel with her stepfather, but her lingering anger should help her through this necessary episode.

The unsuspecting man stood and smiled, but Rachel frowned. His gaze altered to one of confusion. "I wanted to send you a message, Captain Slade, but things have been too hectic today," she said in a formal manner. "I wanted to suggest you don't come to visit this afternoon, or ever again. I've given our relationship a great deal of study and concluded it won't work. It isn't wise for us to see each other again."

Dan was shocked and baffled. She looked and sounded so cold, not frightened or angry. He probed for a reason. "Our relationship has gotten too close and deep for mistrust. Is this withdrawal from me because you're scared of your deep emotions for me?" he surmised.

"I like you as a friend, Dan, and I enjoyed making love with you, but you've become too serious and demanding too fast to suit me. I've recently buried my husband, so I'm not ready for love and marriage again."

"What?" he murmured in disbelief.

Rachel had practiced this difficult scene many times inside her head, so she seemed to play it now by rote. "I appreciate what you did for me with the authorities, but that's all settled now. I must continue with my life and settle pressing business matters. I can't be distracted by a futile relationship with you. Please don't be angry and spiteful by going to the police and telling them you lied. That would get you into deep trouble with the law and place me in a terrible position. I would be forced to claim you tried to seduce me and, when that didn't work, you became vindictive and want to get me into trouble now by changing your story. You did sign a sworn statement," she reminded in a sweet voice. "Let's part as friends, all right?"

Dan shook his head as if to awaken himself from a bad dream. "What in stars are you talking about, woman?"

Rachel faked her most innocent look and tone. "I'm trying to reject you with kindness. I don't love you or want you, Captain Slade. I'm sorry if I gave you that false impression while I was under such pressure. I'll admit I was wrong to surrender to you and wrong to let you believe we had a future together. It happened because I was too distraught and grieved to think clearly. We had fun together. We liked each other. We spent a passionate night together. But that's all. And just to clear your conscience, I didn't kill Phillip or any of my other husbands, so I wasn't using you as a needed witness. However, you did provide me with one when things looked bleak that day, so I'm grateful. As you'll recall, I did not ask you to lie or to help me. That was your idea."

"What's happened, Rachel? This is crazy, wrong, a damn lie!"

"No, Captain Slade, it isn't; and I'm sorry if I hurt you. All I can say in my defense is that you caught me at a weak moment and I behaved foolishly. Please don't call on me again. It was brief and fiery, but it's over."

Tormented and bewildered, Dan accused, "Why, so you can find a richer and more respected man as victim number four?"

Although he was a cruel traitor, it cut her heart to chide, "Don't behave like a boy who's lost his first love. I don't intend to have a number four. As I told you, my luck with husbands isn't good."

"You don't need another rich husband because you found that advance?"

Rachel frowned and exhaled loudly to expose her annoyance. "No, Dan, I haven't. In fact, I won't inherit very much from Phillip at all. That isn't the point. Men are trouble for me. I don't plan to have another one in my life, except for maybe a brief night of passion."

Dan stared into her muted gaze, but today he lacked the power to penetrate it. "This isn't my Rachel McCandless talking."

"I warned you several times that you didn't know the real me."

"If this is a taste of the real you, then you're right."

"Please, Dan," she urged in a guileful tone, "don't make me hurt you. End this with dignity and pride. You had what no other man has had from me; can't you be satisfied with that knowledge and gift?"

"No, Rachel, I can't. I love you and I want you. Damn it," he pleaded, "you love me and want me, too! Why are you doing this to us?"

Rachel presumed he was only cajoling to preserve his cruel ruse. "What I'm doing is trying to keep you from falling any deeper into this futile pit you've dug for yourself. I like you and enjoyed you, but that's all; I swear it. Please let me help you out of it with kindness."

Dan knew something terrible was wrong, but he couldn't surmise what it was. It wouldn't do to press her today; she looked firmly resolved to end their love affair. Yet he perceived love, anguish, and deceit in her. He had to find out whatever had inspired those emotions before he pressed her for more answers, for the whole truth. "All right, Rachel, I'll back off for now. But I'm warning you, I won't give up on us until you prove I'm wrong. When you come to your senses and get rid of these doubts and fears, you know where to find me until May twenty-fourth. If you haven't cleared your head and gotten courage by then, I'll be gone, and so will your first chance at real love and happiness. If you need me for anything, I'll be available."

Rachel could not conceal her astonishment at his words and behavior. It was a struggle to regain her poise and wits. "Thank you, Dan."

"Thank you, Dan?" he echoed, his tone and gaze sad. "That's all you have to say after what's happened between us?"

"You won't believe this, but I truly wish it could be different."

For the first time, Dan felt she was being honest with him. For the first time since she'd entered the room, her eyes were like liquid honey, not like a frozen grayish olive green. "So do I, Rachel, so do I." Without another word or a farewell, he left the room, mounted, and galloped away.

Rachel watched his hasty departure from the parlor window. Her heart ached. Her body was exhausted. Her love for him raged at her spiteful conduct, but her mind congratulated her for her convincing act.

I love you, Daniel Slade. Why couldn't you have been different from the others? If you weren't a fraud, I would have given myself fully and forever to you.

"Is he gawn?" the housekeeper asked from behind her.

Rachel sighed heavily, "Yes, Lula Mae, and for good."

"Why be so sad, Miss Rachel?"

"It was harder than I imagined, my friend. He is in love with me."

"Does that makes you weak and sorry?"

"Sorry for him, yes; but weaken toward him, no. I did what I know is best for me. That's what I have to think about these days—me and my two best friends, you and Burke. You are my family. I don't need others."

"Do you want something special to make you feels better?"

"A long and hot bath, a glass of sherry, and a delicious supper," she responded with gaiety she didn't feel. She needed to clear her head before writing to her mother tonight.

"That's my Miss Rachel, stronger than any man."

God help me if I made a terrible mistake today, Rachel fretted after the housekeeper left to take care of her requests.

"She did what?" Luke Conner asked. "Did I hear right?"

"You did, my friend. Now, what we have to find out is why."

"You honestly believe she loves you?"

"Without a doubt, Luke, without a doubt."

"Then why did she do this?"

"That's what I intend to learn."

"You know I'll help any way I can. But what if you've been wrong about her all along? What if she is a Black Widow? What if she was only using you as a witness? And what if she has located the money?"

Dan was confident as he said, "There's no way she was pretending in those areas, Luke. What we have to do is trace her steps for the last few days since I saw her. Somewhere along that path is the clue to why she changed and what's troubling her."

"You don't think she found something that revealed your identity and she assumes you're betraying her?"

"I don't think that's the problem. Phillip packed up all his memories and left them in that trunk in Charleston with our family lawyer. I have it stored on the ship. I doubt my brother brought anything along on his move. Phillip remembered how many scrapes I got him out of years ago. He always believed I was the stronger, smarter, and braver of us two. He hoped I was still alive somewhere, would get his cry for help, and would show up by some miracle to get him out of his bind. That's why he left that letter with our family lawyer; that's why he hired a private detective to search for me. It must have cost him plenty, but he didn't give up. I can't give up, either. I have to save Rachel; that's what he really wanted from me. He knew he was too far gone for rescue, but he loved her enough to want me to save her from harm. Somehow he got entangled in gambling and saw this illegal deal as his way out, but he panicked when he realized what it could cost him. By then it was too late; he'd probably lost the advance staking himself to one last big score."

"You don't think he killed himself?" Luke asked in dread.

"No, I think somebody else did it for him, somebody who either needed or wanted him out of the way, or out of Rachel's life."

"That Jones vixen?"

"I don't think so. When I saw her the other day, she did all she could to blacken Rachel's name, but I doubt she's a murderess. Camellia is too smart to risk losing everything on revenge. I was going to tell Rachel about my ruse with that little minx, but I never got the chance."

Luke grinned and his light-blue eyes sparkled. "So, we track her moves for the last three days and discover what frightened her."

"That's the plan, my friend. I've gone over everything from every angle, Luke, and I've faced the truth: I love her, I want her, and I need her. I don't believe Rachel McCandless is capable of murder. I believe her only involvement in this arms mystery is the mess Phillip left her in. Something in the last few days has shaken her faith in me, but I'll win it back. Either that or she's running scared of risking my life on her jinx theory. I could be blinded by love and desire, but I won't accept that until I'm given positive proof she's a criminal. She's mine, Luke. I've never loved or wanted a woman like this before. I won't lose her to fate, to an enemy, or to her mistaken fears."

"After you free her from the past, then what?"

The captain grinned. "I'm going to marry her and sail away with her."

"If I know you, there'll be no stopping you until you succeed. I'm checking on your other suspicions. We'll get answers soon."

At Moss Haven, Rachel was too distraught and angry to care if it was dark and dangerous outside or if a stealthy culprit was observing her action. Besides, with the loaded derringer in her pocket, she wished the despicable snake would approach her for retribution. She replaced Phillip's marker that had been yanked from its location and thrown onto the front porch. She used her bare foot to pack dirt around the wooden stake that was lettered with his name, then the distressed widow gazed at her third husband's resting place and wanted to weep to release her tension, but she mustn't weaken. She returned to the house and went to bed; she needed rest for the events that loomed before her during the next few days.

When Rachel arrived in Augusta on Friday afternoon, she hurried to the ammunition company to see George Leathers before he left his office. She told the carriage driver to deliver her baggage to the Planter's Hotel and to inform them she would be there soon to register for the night. She paid him for his assistance, and he drove away.

Rachel entered the office to find the gray-haired man sitting behind his desk and reading the local newspaper. He stood quickly when she arrived, but looked hesitant and apprehensive.

"After what's happened," George began, "I shouldn't be surprised to see you here today, but I am. Your local paper sent Phillip's obituary to mine, so I saw the date listed. It was a shock, Rachel. What were you doing here having a good time when Phillip was already dead? Why didn't you tell me? You deceived me. I don't understand."

Rachel knew she looked tense. "Please sit down, George," she said, "and listen to my explanation. It was hard to pretend I was on a holiday and to dupe you, but I had a good reason. Before Phillip died, he told me he had qualms about the big deal; and that's why he backed out of it. Incidents occurred to intimidate him into restating it." She revealed the ones that had happened in February. "Phillip never received a verbal threat that I know of, but he was certain either the client or Harry—or both—was behind them."

His brown eyes widened. "Harry? What are you saying?"

She put her new plan into motion. "You must hold everything I tell you in confidence. Can you do that for me and Phillip?"

George nodded.

She took a deep breath and divulged, "Harry was pressuring Phillip about this deal. Both companies need money badly, so Phillip was going to honor the bargain. Something happened, I don't know what, to convince my husband it might not have been legal. It might have something to do with supplying arms and ammunition for a Cuban rebellion." She halted again to relate what Dan had told her about that possibility. "He didn't have time to expose everything before he died from cholera. He warned me this client and Harry could be dangerous, not to trust them. But he also advised me to honor his part of the deal. He knew he was dying and told me to check out both company's books before I told anyone he was dead. He didn't have time to explain why that was important. I thought I could learn something from you and Harry if I withheld the truth. This might sound ridiculous, but I think Phillip might have been murdered."

George appeared baffled. "But you said he died of cholera."

"That's what the symptoms implied and what I told the authorities. I didn't think it was wise or safe to mention my suspicion of murder or an illegal deal that could get us all into trouble. Besides, I had no facts to go on at that time, and only have a few gathered now, but no real evidence."

George stroked his mustache as he questioned, "Phillip actually suspected Harry of being deceitful and dangerous?"

"Yes, he warned me not to double cross Harry, whatever that means." She repeated a few of Phillip's mumblings and related some of the threats against her to give George a small but clear picture of her dilemma. "Do you see why I was so alarmed and frightened, why I had to fake a holiday and dupe you? I'm sorry, George, because I don't think you're involved in this mystery. I have to confide in you, but I can't do the same with Harry, not yet. I'm going to visit him tomorrow and see what I can learn. I can't reveal to him all I've told you, so I'll tell you what to say to him if he contacts you. Will you help me? If this deal is legal and it was nothing more than feverish rantings, we're all fine. But if it's true, we'll have to decide how to handle it. We don't want our reputations and lives placed in jeopardy."

"We certainly can't honor the contract if it's illegal," George said. "I wish Phillip had told me the truth before we stuck our necks out this far financially."

"Phillip needed money badly, George," Rachel thought she should disclose that fact, "and knew both of you do, too. He kept the contract a secret because of his suspicions. He was taking total responsibility for it."

"You mean, he was going to go through with it anyway?"

"Yes. But if anything went wrong, he was going to take full blame. He was the one who made the mistake, so he was hoping to finish the deal and forget about it. He was sorry he got all of us into this mess. He wanted me to carry it out, but he left me with too few clues and facts to do that. To be honest, George, Phillip left me in terrible financial condition. All three companies are hurting for money. I hope we can honor this contract."

"I'm sorry to hear that. Of course I'll help you, Rachel. It sounds like quite a challenge; it'll get the old blood to flowing swiftly."

"There is one big favor I'll need. Please send the order, so I can use it as bait to discover if we can sell it as planned or if we have to back down. If I don't have something to use, I can't get answers from the client when he arrives to check on late delivery. I'll be responsible for the merchandise. If anything happens to it, you can have my share of the company as payment. I'll put that in writing, so you won't worry about me reneging."

"That's generous and gracious of you, Rachel, but your share isn't worth what I have invested in the order. But I'll trust you and do as you request."

She sighed in relief and smiled. "Thank you, George; it will be a big help. Let's both pray the deal can proceed as planned. Didn't Captain Slade's large order help out our finances any?"

"I'm afraid not. I used the money to pay back salaries and to buy supplies to complete that big deal. I still had to borrow money from the bank. But your cousin doesn't have to worry about not getting his purchase."

"That's another thing, George; Daniel Slade isn't my cousin. He's an old and close friend of Phillip's. They grew up together in Charleston. He arrived the morning Phillip died. But it is true he came to do business with Phillip, and his two orders are legitimate. He agreed to pretend to be my cousin and to be on holiday while I took care of private business. But that's something else I don't want Harry told yet. We also thought it would look better if I were traveling with kin, instead of an unattached male."

George shook his head in pity. "You've had a lot to endure and to handle alone, Rachel. I'm sorry. Phillip was a fine man, a good partner. I'll miss him. Was there trouble when you reported his death?"

"The usual investigation, which isn't closed yet." She related what had taken place. "Now do you see why I'm apprehensive and suspicious? And that isn't all. When we were in Athens, Harry had us followed every day and night. Dan trailed our shadow back to Harry's office for his report. I caught Harry in lies several times, but I didn't let on I had. That makes me distrust him even more. To be fair, there may be logical reasons for his strange behavior, but I can't risk exposing what I know."

"I hate to say it, Rachel, but I agree," George said. "Harry's always been a strange man. It may be unfair of me, but I think he's capable of doing such evil things. When he came to see me after his last visit with Phillip, he was abrupt and cold, outright angry. He came close to threatening Phillip if anything went wrong. But it seems stupid on his part to kill Phillip before the deal was finalized. He says he's in the dark about the client's identity and location."

"But that will be simple to discover when the client comes for his order. Maybe Harry assumed I'd be easier to control than Phillip. Have either of them ever mentioned buying licenses to construct patented arms?"

331

That change of topic confused him. "No, why?"

Rachel disclosed her suspicion in that area, and saw George's eyes widen in astonishment. "If Phillip knew, he didn't say anything or halt it. But I prefer to think Harry is the only one involved in that crime. With the arms being shipped so far away, he knows the chance of being exposed is slim. That also gives Harry an excellent reason to go through with the deal; he can't sell patented weapons in the United States. He's already trying to force my hand by saying he won't supply the arms without the advance, but can't get rid of that many weapons anywhere else, and the company will be ruined. I'm still searching for the money; Phillip hid it well."

"What a mystery," George murmured.

"Yes, it is, and we're stuck in the middle of it. I'll keep you informed of everything, by letters sent here for privacy. We won't know much more until the end of May or beginning of June; it'll take that long for the client to realize there's a problem and to come to Savannah to check on it."

"You shouldn't face him alone, Rachel, if he's dangerous."

"Dan will be there," she lied to calm him. "He has to stay until his arms are ready and delivered. He says he'll help me before he sails."

"That's good. I liked him."

"He's a nice and kind man," it pained her to allege, "as you are, George. Please forgive me for duping you, but I had to get to know you better before I was assured I could trust you completely."

"After all you've told me, I quite understand. You're a clever woman, a strong and brave one."

She sent him a warm and honest smile. "Thank you, George. Now, when Harry questions you, as I'm sure he will, I want you to tell him that I duped you, but that I've apologized. I was only trying to discover the condition of the business before I told you of

Phillip's death, as if I feared you'd cheat me out of profits. Tell him you don't think I trust you completely and that you're angry with me for lying. I was also very interested in the big deal, but don't know much about it. I told you I don't have the money, but you aren't certain. Say I told you Phillip became ill fast, lost consciousness, and didn't tell me anything before dying. Tell him I've agreed to go through with the deal, but I want to sell my share of both companies as soon as the deal is completed. Say it all depends on whether or not a new arrangement can be made with the client, since I don't have his advance."

"That will get him furious at you, and suspicious of you."

"That's what I want if I'm going to get any clues out of him. I hope he does threaten me and try to force me to continue the deal; that will tell me how involved and desperate and dangerous he is."

"I'll worry about you, Rachel."

"Thank you, but I'll worry about you, too. Guard yourself well, George. I wouldn't put it past Harry to try to get rid of both of us so he can collect the entire price. I don't believe he's as ignorant about all of this as he claims. Harry's too devious and greedy to trust Phillip this much. Only an honest, trustworthy, and loyal friend and partner like you would let Phillip handle this deal the way he has. I promise you that Harry won't cheat us out of our shares of the profit, if there is one."

"I still hope there is, Rachel, to save us. As I told you I am going to sell out and retire when all my business is finished. What about you?"

"Me, too, George. You can begin work on a sale any time. I'll agree with whatever price and terms you say are fair."

"I'm happy you decided you could trust me and confide in me, because you can, Rachel. I would never betray you, and I'll do all I can to help you."

"I'll be traveling on to Athens in the morning to confront Harry. I should be home by Monday or Tuesday night. After Harry questions you, let me know how he reacted and what he said during your meeting."

"You're certain he'll come to see me?"

"Positive. He'll want to make certain both of us are fooled."

"If Harry is responsible for those incidents and for murdering Phillip, I hope you get the evidence to have him arrested and punished."

"So do I, George." She realized she was still duping George a little, but that couldn't be helped. She couldn't expose every detail to him, not yet. But she did feel as if he were being honest and sincere, and that relieved her. After warning him to be on guard for threats, she bid him farewell.

When Rachel arrived in Athens on Saturday afternoon, her luck wasn't as good as it had been in Augusta. Harrison Clements was away for the weekend, and not expected back until late Sunday night. His wife was with him, or so the housekeeper told her. She left a message she would be at his office first thing Monday morning for a business conference. She assumed Harry had seen Phillip's obituary, too, and was nervous over her deception.

Rachel scowled in annoyance as she found another note on her pillow after having dinner downstairs. She had almost requested for her evening meal to be sent to her room, and wished she had. The daring suitor was on her trail again! She hated being pursued this way and was sorely puzzled by how the man got in and out of her room without her noticing his presence. Didn't that have to mean she didn't know the culprit? Once more her script was used and there were threats against Dan's life if she saw him again. Soon, considering how closely she was spied on, the pursuer would know Daniel Slade was out of her life. She concluded that this matter had nothing to do with the arms deal, so she would ignore it. Until he revealed himself to her, she couldn't spurn him or discover why he used a forgery of her handwriting for his messages.

At six on Sunday afternoon, there was a knock on Rachel's door. She considered not answering it, dreading to initiate a quarrel with Harry in her room. But, she reconsidered, it might only be a bellman with a note saying Harry had returned home, gotten her message, and was ready to confront her in the morning.

Rachel opened the door. Her gaze widened and she inhaled sharply. "What are you doing here?" she gasped. "How did you know where to find me? What do you want, Daniel Slade?"

Dan nudged her backward and pushed the barrier aside. He entered her room, closed the door, and locked it. "We're going to have a serious talk, woman. It's time to clear the air once and for all."

Rachel retreated a few steps and gaped at him. An obstinate gleam filled his dark-blue eyes and his clean-shaven jaw was clenched in resolve. She wasn't prepared for this situation. Her heart hadn't chilled enough against him. Gazing at him seemed to weaken her need to spurn him. "About what? I said all I had to say at home. It's over, Dan; accept that."

"It's only beginning, Rachel McCandless; accept that," he corrected, as he placed a gentle but firm grasp on her upper arms.

She attempted to free her body and gaze, but could accomplish neither. "Don't be stubborn and childish, Dan," she urged. "Or spiteful."

"Those aren't my intentions. I only want to love you and help you. Those are the same things you need from me."

She stared at him. *Don't weaken or be tricked.* "You're wrong. I—"

"You're going to listen to me, woman! I risked my neck to keep you out of prison. I lied to your partners to help you obtain clues. Luke and I checked out your family and servants to see if one of them is framing you. We searched for a jilted or unrequited lover who would kill to free you for himself. We looked for a jealous and spiteful female rival who wants to punish and destroy you. We know you aren't responsible for those crimes. I even courted that repulsive vixen Camellia Jones this week to see if she's to blame for your past troubles. I do everything I can to assist you, but you turn your back on me and close your heart against me. Why? It isn't because you don't want me as much as I want you. What is it then? What happened to make you reject what we both know you want? Are you that wary of all men? Are you that afraid of a permanent love?"

Rachel was overcome with shock and bewilderment. When she retrieved her stolen wits and breath, she inquired, "You've been seeing Camellia to spy on her?"

Dan comprehended he had guessed right, thanks to his and Luke's excellent tracking skills. But all wariness had not left her muted gaze. "Yes, and it was hard, but I did it for you. She hates you and wishes you dead, but I don't think she would murder your husbands to obtain vengeance. She loves herself and all she has too much to risk losing them. It's the same with the others we've been checking on; we haven't found a reason to incriminate any of them. Not yet, but Luke is still working on those angles in case we've missed a clue." Dan saw he had her full attention. "There isn't a spurned sweetheart or lover in your past, not that we could locate," he continued. "You married every man you became involved with. I couldn't find any woman, except that arrogant Camellia, who would want to be spiteful. We couldn't locate any family members who would want or *could* extract revenge, not even your stepfather. True, Craig's brother hated and distrusted you, but he's been living up North a long time. The only way he could be responsible for Phillip's death would be through hiring someone to kill him, and he'd have no motive for the deaths of William and his son. If it's a plot against you, and I firmly believe it is, it began with your first marriage. For a while, I even suspected that Lula Mae had her eye on William, but from what I hear, she doesn't care for any man. Besides, she wasn't around when the first three people died. I was inclined to believe your stepfather was the culprit, but he has alibis for the two days in question." He suddenly changed the subject. "Did you know your mother is ill?" He explained his last question, though she already knew the facts.

Rachel comprehended how much Dan had done for her. "Yes, but how did *you* learn all of this?"

Dan grinned, as he knew she believed him. "Luke and I have our ways. We can be most cunning when a situation demands it. This one does, Rachel. If I don't solve both mysteries, I'll lose you. I warn you, you skittish vixen, I won't give up without a fight."

She tried to suppress a smile of amusement. "How did you find me?"

"Burke likes me and trusts me. He knows how you're suffering and he knows I love you and want to help you."

She looked alarmed. "He gave away my whereabouts?"

"Only to me, Rachel, and for good reason. You can trust him completely." Dan wished he could tell her everything, but he couldn't take that risk now. If she learned he and Phillip were brothers and he had set out to entrap her, it would do more damage or undo the repairs he was making.

He cupped her face between his hands and entreated, "Can't we test these feelings for each other? I won't press you for more than you're willing to give or more than you can share. But give me, give *us,* a real chance. We're so well suited. Can't we at least make a commitment to give our wonderful feelings for each other a try? If you say no, I'll have to get out of your life completely. I can't risk being hurt."

Convince me, Dan. "I told you; I'm probably cursed and jinxed."

He shook his head. "I don't believe that. You have an enemy, have had one for years. We'll find out who it is and why; then this evil will be over."

Persuade me, Dan. "I might not want to marry again."

"I don't want to, but I will settle for you as my lover, if you insist."

Reassure me, Dan. "I might not be able to have children. My pregnancy and miscarriage were hard on my body; vengeful gifts from Craig. The doctor's words weren't promising. You'll want an heir someday."

That took Dan by surprise. Share no children with this special woman? Never have a child of his own? No son to carry on the family name? But, she had said "might." What was more important: having his love and no children, or having children with a woman he didn't love?

Rachel's heart pounded as she watched him contemplate that sad news. *Induce me, Dan.* "You could say it doesn't matter, and it may not at this time in your life, but later it will. You'll make a wonderful father, Dan; you deserve that gift. If we became lovers, it would be painful for both of us to part eventually so you could marry and have a family. The longer

338

and closer we're together, the more difficult it will be for us to end our liaison. If you want me for a while, that shouldn't be too perilous to our emotions. We'd have to be careful and secretive, but I would agree."

"Is that why you discarded me? To spare my feelings?"

Tell him the truth, Rachel. "No. I mean, not totally. I have worried over those things, but I was trying to shut them out of my mind."

"Then what happened between Monday and Thursday?"

"Camellia Jones. I saw you with her on Wednesday."

Dan feigned surprise, then enlightenment. "So that's it. That's all?"

He chuckled and hugged her. He leaned back, gazed into her eyes, and declared happily, "What a relief! You thought I was bedding her?"

Get it all into the open. "That, and more."

"What, love? Tell me, so we can clear up this misunderstanding."

Don't let him think you're silly; explain. Rachel related the doubts and fears that had assailed her when she saw them together.

Dan cuddled her in his arms. "I can understand why you would think such things," he said soothingly, "but it isn't true; I swear it, Rachel, on my name and honor. I love you and want you. I didn't know Camellia until I arranged to meet her to test her."

Trust him! "I hope I'm not being foolish and reckless, but I believe you." She explained her behavior on Thursday and apologized.

Dan said the right thing, "If I were in your predicament, I would have jumped to the same conclusions and behaved the same way. I should have forced you to listen to me, but I was too stunned. I've missed you, woman, and been worried about you. I didn't like you leaving like this all alone."

"It was probably good I did; I learned a few things and put another ruse into motion." She told him about her meeting with George. "You don't think I was wrong to trust him and to entice his help?"

"No. I think it was a good idea, a clever plan."

She explained what she had in mind for Harry Monday morning. "Think it will work?" she asked.

"Sounds splendid to me." His gaze locked with hers.

"There's more, Dan; your life is in danger."

"You aren't cursed, love," he refuted before she clarified.

"I don't mean that." She told him about the notes she had received Wednesday and yesterday that threatened his life. "I can't even use them as evidence because the culprit forged my script. He probably knows you're here now."

Dan caressed her cheek. "Don't worry, love; I'll protect both of us. One day all of this will be over and we can be together as man and wife."

"Why not be together tonight?" she suggested bravely.

"Nothing would please me more, Rachel. Nothing."

Love me, Dan, and never leave me, her bold heart urged. Then her cautious mind only allowed her mouth to say, "Love me, Dan. Now, please."

Just as Dan pulled her into his arms, another knock sounded on her door. "Don't answer it, love, and whoever it is will go away soon."

Rachel glanced at the clock on the mantel and frowned. "I can't. I placed an order for my dinner to be delivered at seven. I'm sure that's who it is," she surmised as the knock became more persistent and a voice called out her name. "Hide under the bed while I take the tray."

Dan complied and Rachel opened the door to a bellman holding a tray. "Just place it on the table," she instructed, eager to have him gone. Flames of desire licked urgently at her body, and she needed to douse them.

Rachel thanked the young man and tipped him. She closed and locked the door following his exit. Dan scrambled from his hiding place and looked at the meal that was sending forth fragrant smells.

Rachel went into his arms, fused her greedy gaze to his, and murmured, "The only thing I'm hungry for at this moment is you, Daniel Slade. Feed me before I perish of starvation."

"Your dinner will get cold. Are you sure?"

"Need you even ask?" she replied, and kissed him ravenously. "Well?" she coaxed as she pulled her lips from his with difficulty.

Chapter 15

That was all the permission and encouragement Daniel Slade McCandless required. He was more than ready to take a second sensuous voyage with her, to find again rapture in her arms and body, and to quench his thirst for her. He knew that fulfillment would last only a short time, but he would bond her to him so tightly tonight that she would be available forever when he wanted and needed her.

Dan unfastened the two clasps on her paletot top. He slipped it off her shoulders and tossed it onto a chair. She turned for him to undo the laces of her pompadour basque. His fingers trailed down her arms as he removed the fancy blouse. He undid the button of her walking skirt, bent, and waited for her to step out of it. He tossed that garment onto the pile he was making on the chair. His hands grasped the tail of her yoked chemise and lifted it over her head. Her full breasts greeted his gaze as she turned to face him. It feasted there a moment before his trembling fingers tried unsuccessfully to unfasten the button on her lace-trimmed knee-length drawers.

Rachel smiled and assisted him. She flung the undergarment away. As Dan squatted to remove her slippers and hose, she didn't feel modest or apprehensive as she stood there naked before the man she loved and desired. In fact, she found it arousing to have him undress her.

When his last task was completed, Dan stood. His eyes roamed her olive skin with admiration and pleasure. "You're exquisite, Rachel. Every inch of you is perfection. Not a flaw on your body."

Rachel hadn't been pregnant long enough for streaks to mark her breasts, stomach, thighs, or buttocks. In a way, she was glad, as this way there were no reminders to Dan that she had carried another man's child within her body. Not that she was happy about not bearing Craig's child, as it would have been *her* child, perhaps her *only* child. But she wouldn't think about that torment tonight. If the doctor was mistaken and she did become pregnant, she would marry Daniel Slade in a moment.

"My turn," she murmured, her gaze like two golden-brown embers that were ready to be ignited by a view of his naked body.

Rachel grinned as Dan held his arms out and enticed, "I'm all yours, woman. Do with me as you wish."

Rachel slid his jacket over his broad shoulders and flung it aside as she tried to control merry giggles. With seductive leisure, she unbuttoned his shirt, then peeled the snug-fitting item away to expose a hard chest with its fuzzy black covering. She placed her fingers on either side of his neck at the collarbone; with a snailish and stimulating pace, she drifted them down his chest, wandering them over his flat nipples, teasing them across the ridges of his rib cage, and halting them at his trim waistline. She squatted to take off his boots, then stood to unfasten his pants, bent again to remove them, with Dan assisting her by lifting one leg at a time. When all of his garments were discarded, her brazen gaze could not resist journeying him from raven-black head to bare feet. She wished there were more light, as no lamp had been lit in her room yet. She had only the lingerings of daylight coming through the two windows to aid her scrutiny. She had never done a study before of the male body, but she relished it with this man she loved. As her palms flattened against his muscled chest and her gaze locked with his, she murmured, "This is perfection, Daniel Slade. You're magnificent. You make me feel so brave and bold. You cast off all my doubts, fears, and restraints. You have made a wanton and greedy woman of me. I have no shame or inhibition with you."

"Isn't that how it should be between true lovers, Rachel?" he asked in a voice made husky from his unleashed emotions.

"I didn't know that fact until I met you, but now I know it's true."

Their unclad bodies pressed together as they kissed. The contact of their flesh enflamed their passions to even higher levels. His teeth nibbled at her neck, her shoulder, her ear. She sighed in contentment. Their fingers traced over naked flesh, noting the textures and contrasts of each. They were eager to unite their bodies and to sate their hungers, but they proceeded with deliberate leisure.

As Dan's fingers caressed her upper body front and back, hers roamed his chest and shoulders. She wriggled when his hand moved along her spine in a tickling manner, then caught her breath as both grasped her buttocks and drew her close against him. Her fingers roved his back and savored the feel of rippling muscles as his body moved to tantalize her. She stroked his arms and enjoyed the sensation of his hair against her palms. She wanted to touch and explore every inch of him.

Dan lifted her and laid her on the bed, not even tossing aside the covers. He wished darkness hadn't stolen the outside light, as his eyes wanted to feed on her tasty skin. He had only the filtered glow of a full moon to view her by. His hands, nose, lips, and ears must be his eyes tonight. His mouth covered hers with a demand that stole his breath.

Rachel inhaled the manly scent of his body, which mingled with an enticing cologne from the islands southeast of America. His mouth tasted minty, delicious, and provocative. His tongue danced with hers in an erotic manner to a silent, seductive beat.

Dan's lips traveled down her slender neck to compelling mounds of sweet flesh. His tongue played with the taut and succulent buds it found there. It circled them over and over, hardening them even more. One hand caressed its way along the path to her triangular forest of dark-brown. The hair in that location was downy soft, and the mist of her arousal dampened it. His fingers caressed her silky valleys as he teethed her nipples lightly.

Pleasure, sweet and tormenting, ensnared Rachel. It began deep within her womanhood, mounted and teased, then sent charges over her entire frame as if tiny lightning bolts striking her flesh from head to foot. She writhed and moaned, her need for him great and urgent. Every inch of her was sensitive and responsive to him. She was so alive and happy with him. She couldn't imagine losing him. Her pleasures increased, but so did her yearning for more; this time, she knew for what.

Dan was thrilled and encouraged by her fiery need and responses. He obtained added pleasure from the delight he was giving her. He eased atop her, parted her thighs, and obeyed her mute summons to possess her fully. The contact was again staggering to his control and impassioned senses.

Dan was enchanted as Rachel's legs curled over his thighs and she matched her movements to his. Her mouth clung to his, as her flesh glued itself to his. She urged him onward with her actions and words. If any lingering doubt that this was the woman for him had existed someplace in Dan's mind or body, it was vanquished forever. He had experienced rapturous lovemaking with other women, but it was different with Rachel, a special feeling that totally consumed his heart, his soul, his whole being.

She felt the same way. If any doubts had lurked within her, they were gone, conquered by the emotions and sensations she was sharing with Daniel Slade. It was a union of more than hungry bodies; it was a fusion of spirits, a forging of their cores. Her senses reeled freely and wildly, compelling her to total abandonment. He was all she needed.

Rachel's unbridled responses and bold actions heightened Dan's desires and coaxed his full possession of her. Her ardor and need inspired him to hold nothing back. Passion's flames engulfed him in a fiery and blazing glow that only she could extinguish. His lips and hands roved her luscious figure and mouth, bringing her to uncontrollable tremors of desire. She uttered feverish moans as she became breathless with need for him. She arched to meet every thrust. Her words and movements provoked him to a swifter pace. Loving him like this was sweet torment. Though she wanted the stimulation to continue, she craved release. "I love you, Dan," she confessed without awareness she had spoken.

The sea captain heard those whispered words and his heart drummed with joy. Yet he knew she wasn't conscious of uttering them. She was ensnared in the throes of love, passion, and overpowering release. He cast his control aside and joined her in an explosion of sultry elation.

Both were damp with perspiration from their exertions. The salty taste of passion touched their tongues as they kissed each other's faces and necks. They relaxed in the languid afterglow of their potent experience, snuggling together to bask in its warmth.

"I told you I would fight for you, woman," Dan

chuckled "but I never realized a battle could be so pleasurable and victorious."

"If this is how you fight, my dashing sea pirate, I'll gladly challenge you every day and night."

"Rachel McCandless, how brazen you've become."

She joined in on his laughter. "You cannot blame me, Sir Pirate. The fault lies with my instructor. He is determined to teach me the skills he knows. Alas, I fear I am most eager and receptive to his tutoring."

"You best take advantage of this class, my lovely and greedy student; there is no guessing when another one can be taken."

Rachel kissed him, then murmured against his mouth, "I am all ears, eyes, hands, and senses tonight, my talented teacher."

"Give me a moment to rest, then I'll make you starve, make you anticipate, then sate you fully."

"So far, you've always kept your word to me. I shan't allow you to break it tonight. Shall I feed you my chilled supper to give you needed strength? I fear I am not properly attired to go downstairs for a hot one."

After a time of kissing and cuddling, Dan got out of bed. To guard their privacy, he drew the drapes before he lighted a lamp. He encircled his manly region with his shirt, then secured the half-covering with a knot near one hip. He checked the dinner tray for anything appetizing.

Rachel donned a loose night robe, secured it with a sash, then joined him. "Let's see," she murmured as she eyed the meal. "Bread, fruit, spring salad, dessert, and cheese appear our best choices. The meat and vegetables are cold and greasy by now. The coffee's cold, too, but we have a glass of water to share. I'll use the spoon and you take the fork."

"I could dress and fetch us a hot meal from downstairs."

"Half of this is fine with me. But if you want something else or need more food than this for nourishment, I will get you another tray."

"This is plenty for me, too. I don't want to exercise later on a full belly."

Her adoring gaze roamed his tousled black hair and twinkling blue eyes. "Daniel Slade, how brazen *you've* become since ensnaring me."

They shared laughter and exchanged smiles.

As they dined off the same dishes and shared the same drinking glass, Dan announced, "It's past time you got to know Luke Conner and my crew, and visit my ship to see how I live. That will help you get to know me better. We'll take care of that matter when we return to Savannah. Unless you're afraid I'll take to sea the moment you're aboard and steal you."

She laughed, but retorted, "You wouldn't do that because you don't want me to appear as if I'm fleeing crimes because I'm guilty and scared. You don't want the authorities chasing me down."

When Dan finished chewing and swallowing a piece of bread and cheese, he refuted, "But you aren't guilty of any crimes, my love."

"The authorities aren't convinced yet; and Harry would make another charge against me—theft of that missing money. He'd think I was escaping with it." She ate a few spoons of canned fruit.

"How could he report lost money from an illegal deal?" Dan queried.

"It isn't illegal," Rachel disclosed, "or so he claims. George told me Phillip got clearance from customs. Harry has the papers in his office. If customs approved the shipment, it might be legal." She took a bite of salad.

"That's a surprise. It puts a hole in our conclusions."

Rachel shrugged. "Maybe, but maybe not. We don't know what Phillip said or did to get those papers. They could even be forged, like my notes."

"You're right. But you can still visit me on the *Merry Wind.*"

"That wouldn't be smart, Dan. We can't risk exposure."

"Bring Lula Mae along."

"That wouldn't help much; she's my loyal servant and friend."

"Bring Milton Baldwin along then. Tell him you want to visit me and see my clipper, but you don't want to inspire any nasty gossip."

Rachel lowered her salad-filled spoon. "That might work, and I'd love to see your world and meet your friends. Perhaps Milton would like to see such a fine and beautiful ship, too. I'll let you know when I make a decision."

"Has anything else happened since I saw you?"

Rachel gave Dan the important news. She told him about her stepfather's visit and about her mother's illness, which Dan had already known. "I wrote Mama a letter before I left home," she revealed. "Her answer will determine my next action."

"No wonder you had the anger and strength to try to break from me."

"I'm truly sorry about that, Dan. I was mistaken and rash. After all that happened last week, I'm surprised I've retained my sanity."

Dan stopped eating to question her words. "What is it, Rachel? Did your meetings go badly?"

She didn't want to reveal her financial condition to him, but Burke might have already told him things were terrible, and she didn't want Dan to think she was keeping secrets from him. Yet she wouldn't paint the entire black picture tonight. "Yes, I'm afraid they did. Phillip recently canceled his insurance, and the news from the bank was depressing. That, atop what I'm learning about the finances of the three companies doesn't look good financially."

Phillip left her near penniless? What had happened

to his wealth? Gambling, a costly search for him his brother, and bad investments? "Do you need money?" Dan asked. "I can give you or loan you what you need until your problems are resolved."

A self-employed sea captain didn't have the amount she required to extricate herself from her dilemmas, and she wouldn't accept it even if he did. "No, thank you. I'll be fine. I have some money at home, and I have future earnings from the sharecroppers. I've told all three partners I will agree to sales when they can work out deals, but only after this problem is solved."

Sell his family's business, even if it was tied up with Baldwin's? "Why not keep the shipping firm for support, in case the crops fail?" he asked.

She ate two spoonsful of salad. "That isn't wise or safe. All of them are in sorry condition. When I inherited Phillip's assets, I also inherited his shares of their debts. I'd rather be free of any future risks of financial ruin."

To make his question sound casual and his mood appear calm, Dan worked on the dessert as he asked, "How will you support yourself?"

She didn't mention the jewelry she planned to sell to tide her over until better luck arrived. She couldn't help wondering why he didn't propose again to get her out of her predicament. Had he decided a mistress would suit his adventurous lifestyle better? "I have land not in use by sharecroppers. I can either farm it or raise cotton or indigo. I do have years of experience and knowledge in that area."

"Will it earn you enough to support yourself?"

"If not, I'll think of something else later. There's no need to waste wits and energy at this time worrying about a problem that's not definite. I have other troubles to concentrate on."

"Such as explaining this sudden trip to the authorities?"

"No, there won't be a problem there. I stopped by to ask permission before I left town; they said it was all right to come. My case file is still open, but they aren't getting anywhere with their investigation against me. They won't either, unless there is faked evidence to frame me."

"I don't like these pranks and threats. Are you locking your windows and doors, and keeping a gun handy?"

"Following orders as you gave them, Captain Sir."

"This isn't a funny situation, woman," he chided with tenderness.

"I know, but I have to keep a sense of humor or cry. Too many times I've allowed a group of hateful and cruel people to push me into bad circumstances; I won't allow that to happen again. I have to believe there are plenty of good and kind people. I merely have to make certain those wicked ones don't provoke trouble for me."

Dan was pleased. "You've had numerous bad experiences, Rachel, but look at the strength, pride, and courage they've given you. I doubt you'll fall into another trap trying to find peace and happiness and respect."

As they finished eating, they made plans for the next day, then returned to bed to once more find bliss in each other.

Rachel lifted her hand and knocked on the door of Harrison Clements' office. She wished Dan were with her, but they had agreed it was best for her to confront Harry alone. She wasn't afraid; she felt strong and determined. Part of that had to do with Dan's love and his faith in her. Part of it was the result of wanting to defeat the flaxen-haired man who opened the door and glared at her.

Harry's ice-blue eyes were like frozen chips. A

351

scowl lined his rugged face and his square jaw was clenched. His body was rigid, as if poised for a physical attack. None of that dissuaded Rachel from her task and she knew she appeared calm and poised.

"Get inside and sit down," he ordered, "so you and I can have a serious talk! What the hell is going on!" he shouted at her as she followed his command.

Rachel took a seat, arranged her skirt, then met his furious gaze—all without changing her pleasant expression and losing her air of self-control.

Harry rounded his desk and dropped into his chair. "Phillip was already dead when you came up here and pranced around town as if everything was normal!" he accused, "I saw his obituary in the *Southern Banner*. What was that sneaky pretense about?"

Rachel focused on his face as she coaxed, "Calm down, Harry, or we won't be able to clear up this matter without ill will."

"Calm down?" he exploded. "What is this scheme of yours?"

"If you'll relax and listen, I'll explain everything. Phillip knew he was dying and instructed me to check the company books before I reported his death; but you refused to let me study them. You have no excuse to deny me access now, *partner*. Why didn't you respond to my telegrams?"

He glared at her. "Because they were stupid, and a bunch of lies!"

"You don't have to get belligerent and hateful, Harry. I was only carrying out Phillip's last request. We didn't know each other well, and I believed it better if you didn't know at the time I was your new partner. But you were too busy to give me much time and attention. George was nicer and more cooperative than you were. However, he is a little annoyed with me at present for duping him, too. I saw him yesterday and tried to smooth things over, but it'll take time."

"You expect us to believe Phillip used his dying breaths to tell you to check on us, but didn't have the time or sense to tell you where he hid the advance? I'm no fool, Rachel, so don't treat me like one! You can't keep that money; it belongs to his two companies. We've both borrowed from banks to invest in this deal of his, so it must be turned over to us or we're all ruined, including you. Is that what you want? Is that what *he* wanted?"

She removed a fabric bag from her wrist and placed it in her lap as she replied, "Of course not. But I don't have the money. That *'stupid'* telegram from me told you that."

"If the two companies bankrupt because of your greed, you'll be hurt, too. As our partner now, our debts are half yours. Turn it over, and I'll forget and forgive you for this little weakness."

"That's kind and generous of you, Harry, but impossible. Phillip was delirious; he didn't reveal its hiding place. But he did mumble about something being illegal and about trying to stop it." She saw him tense in dread of the reference to what Phillip had confessed to her. "Was he referring to this big deal that nobody seems to know about?"

"Don't be absurd! It is legal. One thing I do have is that clearance paper from Savannah customs. It came in the mail, so Phillip did handle that angle, as I insisted before proceeding further, before he died on us."

She faked a look of surprise. "It is legal? Customs will clear it through port? You have a signed paper in your possession?"

"Why does that shock you?"

"It's all been so secretive and mysterious that I assumed . . ." She left those words hanging for effect. "That's why I said I'd have to meet with the client first, to make sure before we honored the bargain and got into trouble. If Phillip wasn't referring to his deal, then to what?"

"How should I know? You were at his side and didn't even understand him. Now that you know it is legal, you can stop refusing us that payment. We both need it badly, and today, Rachel. No—weeks ago."

Rachel pretended to trust Harry and to be honest with him. She had to convince him she wanted this deal, that she was just as frustrated and baffled as he was. "I don't have it, Harry, believe that or not. I would turn it over to you and George if I could find it. As you pointed out, my neck is on that chopping block with you two. I searched the house, grounds, and Phillip's office at the shipping firm, including the safe. I've been to the bank, to our lawyer and our insurance broker. I've questioned Milton. Nothing. I don't know where else it could be hidden. It doesn't make sense. Because of Phillip's mumblings I feared my life was in jeopardy and that the client is dangerous, and I've been getting threats since the day after he died. I was hoping to get answers from you last time, but you claimed you were in the dark. Maybe it was only his illness talking nonsense."

"If that client loses his money and doesn't get his orders, he might well become a threat to you. How would you feel and react if someone stole all that money?"

"Phillip didn't steal it! He hid it for safety. He just died before he could pass it along to his partners or reveal its location to me."

"He had no reason to withhold it."

"Why did he, Harry? Didn't you two trust each other?"

He scowled at her. "I trusted him; that's why I allowed him to keep me in the dark. Obviously he didn't trust me, or he was using the money to stake his gambling weakness."

Rachel put on a look of horror. "Don't even say or

think that, Harry. If it doesn't show up soon, we're all in terrible trouble."

"Just you, Rachel," he refuted. "You're responsible for the missing money. It was in your husband's possession, and you've taken his place."

"How am I to blame? Is there a law to say a wife automatically is responsible? I don't know where else to look, Harry. I'm open to any suggestions you make. If Phillip asked someone to hold it for him, the chance of that person—who is now rich!—coming forward to hand it over to us is nil." She feigned a look of alarm and pretended she wanted to be helpful. "Phillip told me to honor the bargain, but he didn't explain how. I was hoping to get clues from you and George during my last visits, but you both claim ignorance. I didn't even know how much the contract was for until you two told me, and it shocked me to learn it was so large. We must find a way to save it."

"How can we do that, Rachel?"

"Since you don't know the client, you can't tell me if he'll be understanding about our dilemma and be willing to renegotiate. Milton has Haiti recorded as the destination of the cargo, a May fourteenth shipping date, and two sets of initials: C.T. and J.C. But he says he doesn't know more than that about this mystery. That isn't much, if any, help to us. We don't know where to anchor at Haiti or whom to meet there. We have one path still open: the client will come to see me when his order doesn't arrive, and we can go from there. Or there is another possible angle: the men who go with those initials could arrive on or before May fourteenth to escort the cargo to its owner. If so, we'll have contacts to work through to get started on saving this deal." She saw how Harry eyed her differently, as if pondering her honesty and deciding if her speculations had any value.

"Did you tell all of this to George?"

She forced a look of embarrassment. "No, you said

last time he doesn't know anything, even about the dynamite. I didn't want him getting angered and refusing to keep his end of the bargain. We need ammunition to go with our rifles." She lightly glossed over the fabricated story she had asked George to tell Harry. "Was I right to handle him that way?" She saw how he mellowed a smidgen, and that gave her a heady sense of power.

"It was smart and for the best, if we hope to save ourselves."

To check his reaction to another suspicion, Rachel asked, "If this deal fails, Harry, maybe we can find another buyer for those arms. What about the Indian troubles out west? The Army might need ammunition and rifles. We could offer them a deal by taking less profit ourselves. That's better than suffering a loss and risking ruin. Or maybe we can find a foreign market where there's trouble and need. I could ask Dan for suggestions. He's still in port awaiting his two orders. He sails around the world and keeps up with trouble spots to safeguard his ship and crew."

Harry leaned back in his chair. "Those are great ideas, Rachel, but I've already thought of them and checked out every potential customer and location, just in case the worst happened. Companies bigger and more important than ours own and control all of them."

"All of them?" she echoed and looked distressed.

Harry nodded.

"Oh, my, that's terrible. If we can't find the advance or another customer, the only thing left to do is make sure we save any part of this deal we can."

"How can we take a five-hundred-thousand-dollar loss?"

"Surely a third of that would have been profit," she pointed out.

"But that leaves $333,333 to cover. I can't do that."

"Neither can I, Harry." She set out to prove she

was desperate and sincere by exposing some of her predicament, which he might already know about from Phillip or his spy. "I'm almost penniless, so I need this deal to succeed. Phillip didn't leave me any insurance; he canceled it two months ago. All three companies, even if I sold my partnerships, can't earn me much. Phillip's bank account is almost empty, my household cash box is very low. The sharecroppers don't pay off until September, and that's if nothing drastic happens to their crops. All I have to cover an emergency is jewelry I can sell. I can't get rid of Moss Haven and have no home. You must help me save this deal, Harry. Please. You need the profit, too, to save the business."

"The only reason I haven't shut down or sold out is because I was waiting to complete this last deal before doing so. Arms don't make money anymore, Rachel. Phillip was going to get out, too, when this was over. He was damned lucky to find this rich and needy client. I'm already into another business, but I can't take money from it to save a dying company. It's in Atlanta, where I'll be moving when everything here is settled. That's where I was this past weekend, finalizing the terms."

Rachel urged a pitiful look to her face and sound to her voice as she murmured, "What am I going to do?"

"I don't know, Rachel, but I can't be of any help to you. I'm sorry."

Presuming he cared little or nothing for her husband, she fumed, "Damn Phillip for getting us into this bind! I'll bet it's because of his gambling! How could he be so foolish and weak? I never knew he had such a problem or I would have put an end to it. That's the only thing that could have gotten him into this financial disaster he dropped in my lap. I've told Milton and George to sell out, to make the best deals they can. I'll tell you the same. But will you give me time to save our selves before you do it?"

Harry observed her for a moment, then said, "I might as well. The order is almost done. It might be crazy, but I'll complete it with hopes you can use your beauty, wits, and charms to save us."

Rachel interpreted his wanting to continue the preparations as a clue. Perhaps he even concluded she would bring forth the money later if she had no other choice. "Thank you for the flattery and confidence," she said. "I swear I'll do my best. Whatever it requires to solve this mystery and my problems, I'll do it." She knew he didn't comprehend her real meaning, but that was fine.

"Don't go marrying our rich client to win his aid," he joked.

"He may already have a wife," she quipped, as if she'd thought of it.

"If he doesn't, I'm sure he'll be enchanted and tempted by you. He'll try his damnedest to ensnare a rare gem like you as part of his new deal."

"Thank you again . . . may I ask you a question that baffles me? Why did you allow Phillip to handle such a crucial deal in this illogical way?" she rushed on before he could object to her question.

"Because he was a friend and partner, one I trusted. When he said he had to honor somebody's confidence, I believed him. I didn't have any reason at that point not to do so. I don't know if you're aware of it, but Phillip took heavy losses during the '73 Panic and Depression. Maybe that's when he started gambling and ran up heavy debts. Or perhaps it was following those family deaths and scandal. He found this mysterious deal and client, as you called them, and I agreed to help him try to recover his many losses. I suppose I also got greedy and excited about making a big profit, so I allowed myself to get pulled in deeper and deeper."

Rachel didn't believe that claim for an instant.

"Why didn't I ever suspect Phillip had money problems?"

"Men don't usually tell women those things. I also felt partly to blame for his problems getting worse. When he invested in my company, it was doing fine. We had contracts to make weapons for Winchester, Remington, and a few others. But they expanded their businesses and canceled the contracts, just dumped us out in the cold after years of helping them out with expert craftmanship and always honoring our deadlines. They gobbled up all the other available markets, American and foreign. With their names and reputations, it was easy to steal all the customers. A company of this size and with two partners to support can't survive on small or personal contracts. Business keeps slacking off every month."

Rachel heard and witnessed bitterness over those crippling losses, and assumed that was why Harry—and perhaps Phillip—were illegally using those makers' patents for the rebels' arms. Still, she held silent about that suspicion to prevent tipping her hand about her knowledge.

"This could be a dangerous situation, Rachel, not to honor a contract with a rich and probably powerful man, to tell him your husband lost his money either by hiding it or gambling it away. When he arrives, do you think he'll believe you and I know nothing about the money? I doubt it. He's going to be furious. Duped men do crazy things when crossed. You have to find that money or replace it."

She skillfully clenched her hands and licked her lips as if scared and tense. "I've already explained, Harry. I can't. I'm on the brink of poverty. Are you sure he paid Phillip?"

"Phillip told me and George he had."

"Then who would he trust to hold that large amount for him? And why?"

"I have no idea, Rachel. But you can study the

company's books to prove I didn't receive it. As my new partner, they're open to you."

"There is one last point I'd like to mention, if it's true." She noticed how that tone seized his full attention. "The firm's record lists Haiti as the destination for the cargo, but Phillip mumbled something about Cuba, about war and freedom, about needing guns badly. I had forgotten about it until I saw Haiti listed. Dan told me rebels are battling there for independence from Spanish rule. He said a gun-running ship with an American flag and partial crew was attacked and men hanged. Spain had to compensate the families to avoid a conflict with us. Publicly, our country is staying neutral, but perhaps not privately. If the shipment is for Cuban rebels, that could explain why Phillip had to keep it a secret."

"You could be right; it sounds logical."

She felt that Harry knew all she was telling him, but revealing she knew a few things could evoke a slip from him. With cunning, she speculated, "If it is a confidential military operation or assistance, that could be how Phillip got that customs clearance. He's been in shipping all of his life, and he owns partnerships in arms and ammunition companies, so someone he knew or who discovered those things about him must have approached him as the best choice to fill his needs. Maybe he didn't tell Phillip where the order was going and why. Or if he did, Phillip was willing to aid their cause, or make a big profit on it. All you've told me about Phillip explains why he agreed; he was desperate. But it sounds as if something happened to give him doubts; that's why he changed his mind and halted the deal. So, why didn't he return the money? You said he told you he still had it the day before he died. By then he had changed his mind a second time and restarted the contract. The only reason I can guess why is because of several horrible incidents that occurred in February."

After she related them to him, she surmised, "Phillip must have taken them as warnings not to back out; he even mumbled something to that effect during his delirium. I can understand how urgently the rebels need their orders from us . . . but enough to do such evil things to get them? And what will they do to all of us if we don't comply with them or return their money? Damn Phillip for dying before he could tell me everything! Those aren't many clues for us to work with, Harry. What do you make of them?"

"What did he say on his deathbed? Did he call out any names?"

Rachel knew why he was worried. With her most innocent voice and expression, she repeated only the rantings she had used so far to dupe him.

"Will you go through with the deal if it is for rebels?"

"Yes, if there's no trouble. Phillip cleared it through customs, so it must be legal. One thing I will demand from this client is proof of a signed contract between him and Phillip and proof the money was paid to my husband. Evidence first, negotiations second."

"If the deal's confidential, maybe there is no contract or receipt."

Rachel frowned, but concurred, "You could be right, but I will question him on those points. When Milton gave you the destination, did you have any suspicions the shipment was for Cuba?"

"I have to admit that I did, but dismissed it as foolish. I didn't have your knowledge to tell me I was wrong. I don't want any trouble from this matter, Rachel. I wish I weren't involved in it, but I am; *we* are. You'll have to find a way we can honor this deal or find us a safe way out of it. We have to protect our lives, families, friends, and holdings against potential revenge. Let's get it over and done with as soon as possible, so we can both make fresh starts."

361

"What if we discover our client was behind those deadly incidents? What if Phillip did return the money, but they refuse to admit it and try to force us to hand over their purchases?"

"He still had it the day before he died, or he told me he did. He promised to bring it to me the following Monday. When you came here and claimed he was gone for weeks, I was furious and baffled. You don't think he killed himself because he lost it, do you?"

She permitted her expression to show doubt and sadness. "I honestly don't know what to think, Harry. I hope he didn't. No matter, he left us in a tight and perilous bind."

"If those incidents were warnings, that kind of man doesn't play games. If we trick him, he'll have us killed. Nobody twisted Phillip's arm to make this deal, but they'll do more than twist ours to make us stick to the bargain he made. That worries me."

"Me, too. We'll either have our answer in two and a half weeks or a few weeks afterward. Let's pray it's a good one." She sighed heavily. "This discussion has worn me out emotionally and physically. Do you mind if I rest this afternoon and go over the books with you tomorrow?" That would give him time to telegraph George to check out her story and be duped further.

"That's fine with me. How about dinner tonight? My wife is still in Atlanta looking at homes and making new friends. We hope to be moved and settled in by the end of the summer. I apologize for being angry and crude earlier, but I didn't understand the situation."

"That's all right, Harry; it was my fault for deceiving you, but I was so confused and desperate. I'm glad you forgive me. Dinner sounds marvelous, but Dan is with me, so I should bring him along. He's at the hotel or out playing around town. It would be hard to claim it's a private business dinner when we've spent hours on it today." She perceived his annoyance.

"I didn't realize he'd come along again."

Rachel laughed. "He tracked me down last night at the hotel. He was miffed at me for taking off alone. He doesn't realize I don't need a man's protection for such a simple journey. He and his family are old-fashioned; they believe a lady must have an escort wherever she goes."

"That isn't a bad idea with a woman as ravishing and tempting as you, especially in light of those threats you said you've been getting."

She observed that lustful gleam in his eyes again, but she smiled. "Thank you once more, partner. One favor, I don't want to discuss business in front of him tonight, if you don't mind. These matters are personal, just between us, not for my relatives' ears. What are our dinner plans?"

Harry set a time and place, and Rachel agreed. They spoke a few minutes, with him telling her what time to be in his office tomorrow on Tuesday, April twenty-seventh. Then she departed, with the man almost painfully drilling his powerful gaze into her retreating back.

On Friday, Rachel dressed to go into Savannah to meet with a jeweler to see what he would offer her on several of her expensive pieces. As she did her grooming, she reflected on the past few days. The dinner Monday night with Harry and Dan had passed without problems, as had her meeting with Harry the following day. As far as she could detect, the books had not been altered and Harry had been truthful about the company's condition. According to a cable from George yesterday, Harry had gone to see him on Wednesday, and George had carried out Rachel's request to delude him.

She and Dan had spent a passionate, stolen night together in Augusta Wednesday while en route home. Upon her return yesterday, a letter had awaited her from her mother. To Rachel's delight and relief, Catherine Fleming Starger was feeling better and wanted to visit her daughter next weekend. Rachel had sent her mother a prompt plea to do so after Earl had informed her of the older woman's illness. The only part of the letter she found disappointing was her mother's confirmation of her doctor's visits, with Earl as her escort, on the two days in question. That told Rachel her stepfather couldn't be in two distant places at the same time, and Earl Starger would never hire anyone to do his dirty work!

By one o'clock, Rachel was relieved again when Adam Meigs offered and paid her a fair price for the jewelry she sold him. She was to go to Milton's office to entice him to visit Dan's clipper with her this afternoon, but a stunning and malicious episode occurred to prevent those plans.

Chapter 16

"My, oh, my, what do we have here?" a sultry voice with a heavy Southern accent taunted from the doorway. "The merry murderess buying herself new trinkets with her deceased husband's money? Or mayhap trading in gifts for prettier gems with which to ensnare her next victim? If Phillip McCandless had married me instead of recklessly choosing a Black Widow as his mate, he would still be alive and well. Who are you adorning yourself for this time? Who is the fourth victim, Rachel?"

The dark-haired widow turned to confront the tormenting redhead whose striking tresses tumbled down in untamed perfection. Camellia's cattish yellow-green eyes exposed her shallow character, and the woman's sharp claws were unsheathed again today. Before Rachel could leave to prevent an embarrassing scene, the twenty-five-year-old viper created one.

"Only a heartless bitch like you could dump a fine man like Phillip McCandless in an unmarked grave and not give him a decent burial or allow his many friends to say a proper farewell."

Rachel's sherry-colored gaze altered to one with of grayish green as anger consumed her. She glared at the aristocratic beauty with her full, pouty lips and unmarred oval fair-complected face. To her, Camellia's long and slender neck reminded her of a snake's with head held high to strike. Again, the auburn-haired vixen spoke before she herself could, while Rachel eyed the two grinning friends with Camellia who laughed encouragement and nudged each other in amusement.

"Oh, yes," she drawled in a breathy purr, "I know all about your wicked deeds. I have many friends in the police department, more than you have in this entire area. You've entrapped yourself this time. I'm surprised you're still strolling around free, but it won't be for much longer."

Rachel concealed her alarm at those intimidating words and wondered if there was any truth to them. Even if something had come up which she hadn't been questioned about yet, she bluffed with poise, "Well, you're misinformed, and most rude, Miss Jones. Didn't your family and tutors teach you proper manners and good breeding?"

Camellia looked as if she was astounded that Rachel gave any response, as if she'd expected her to burst into tears and run away. "How would you know about good breeding, as you don't possess any? You're a vicious criminal, and you'll get caught and punished this time. Your file is still open, wide open."

Rachel realized her calm and strength vexed the other woman. In a sweet tone she replied, "I won't quarrel with you, *Miss* Jones. You know nothing about me or the real situation, despite tales from your gossipy and mistaken spies. You're the one who's vicious and hungry, eager to devour me out of spite for stealing Craig and Phillip from your grasping clutches."

Camellia's eyes widened and her mouth gaped. "If either or both could speak from their graves or be allowed to choose again, there would be no contest or comparison between us!"

Rachel knew she had touched a raw nerve, and couldn't help but pick at it to silence her foe. "You're absolutely correct; you would suffer two defeats again. A hateful, spoiled, and selfish witch like you could never land a smart fish, no matter how pretty and expensive your baited line was."

Camellia clenched and unclenched her fingers, as if preparing them to attack her despised rival. "How dare you insult me!"

Adam Meigs shifted nervously behind his counter. He wanted to halt the episode, but Camellia Jones was too valuable a customer to offend. He hated being placed in this distressing position.

"The same way you dare to insult and harass me," Rachel retorted. "I've offered you peace and friendship many times, but you persist in being my enemy and tormentor. You create lies about me and fan the flames of unjust rumors. You try to humiliate and hurt me at every turn. Grow up, malicious little girl, and clear your head of such destructive traits; that's the only way any man is going to lean in your direction."

Camellia gasped in outrage. "You arrogant and stupid bitch! I'll—"

Rachel riled her more when she interrupted to chide, "That's what I mean, Camellia. Your quick temper and foolish hatred defeat you every time. I'm not the reason you're still unmarried; *they* are. I didn't steal Craig and Phillip from you, because you didn't own either one. You have beauty, money, and social rank, but some men don't consider those as important enough reasons to marry a childish woman like you. Even if I were guilty, which I am not, you have no reason or right to behave like a—"

"Shut up! Don't you dare call me names or I'll claw your eyes out!"

Rachel noticed the silky hands with long nails that lifted for a moment, flexed a warning, then lowered and tightened into fists. She saw the fiery glint in the woman's gaze. "I see, you can call me whatever nasty

367

names and vile words you wish, but I'm supposed to cower and hold silent in return? I've done that in the past, but no more. I was afraid if I got angry and fought back with people like you, I would do damage to myself even more powerful than those stupid investigations and cruel gossip. I realized I was mistaken. I'm not guilty, so I don't have to behave as if I have something to be ashamed of or to fear. My case file can stay open forever and the authorities won't find any incriminating evidence against me, because there is none, because I didn't harm any of those four people."

"Three dead husbands and a son in three years?" Camellia sneered.

"Strange and unfortunate, but of natural or accidental causes." Rachel roved her gaze over the three people as she vowed, intending to shame the women, "One day, all of you doubters and persecuters will discover I'm blameless. I hope you and others will be adult enough to apologize then."

"Apologize to you? When it snows in July!"

"Stranger things have happened, Camellia; I know from experience."

As if just noticing the pieces of jewelry lying on a cloth on the counter, Camellia snatched up one she recognized, having seen Rachel wear it to a party. Enlightenment flooded her, and she grinned cattily. "I've heard Phillip's companies aren't doing well. I guess this proves it. Having to sell off jewels to eat, my unlucky spider? I'll take them all, Mr. Meigs, every one. You *have* purchased them?" she asked, and Adam nodded.

Rachel fumed at knowing this vixen would have those precious items she'd been forced to part with for survival. She hated the thought of Camellia wearing anything chosen for her by Phillip. She knew the redhead would gloat every time she wore them, as if displaying trophies of victory. "Good-bye. I hope we don't meet again soon, if ever. Mr. Meigs, I—"

Camellia grabbed Rachel's arm to prevent her departure, astonishing everyone in the store. "I haven't finished my say, you—"

Rachel exposed her anger on purpose. "Oh yes you have! You—"

"No I haven't! You forget Captain Daniel Slade as victim number four. I'll see you hanged before he's dead and buried like the others."

Rachel feigned bewilderment. "Whatever are you babbling about?"

Camellia put her flushed face close to Rachel's lovely one. "We both know the answer to the question. Toss this one back into the pond, Rachel. You hook him and harm him and I'll kill you myself, or have it done for me!"

Again, everyone present was shocked by the redhead's icy threat, even though they all assumed she didn't mean it.

"Not that it's any of your business, Miss Jones, but we're good friends; and it will remain that way, no matter how it looks to you and to others like you. It wouldn't shock me to find your pretty nose stuck in my current troubles. If it is, be prepared to have it cut off."

Camellia gaped at Rachel in disbelief. "You're threatening me?"

"You made the threats; mine was a warning. Despite your wealth and prestige, the authorities won't glance the other way if you commit such a crime or pay for it to be done. I'll be certain to mention our meeting today, in detail, to those fine investigators when we speak again. Of course, if you speak with them first, please be sure to explain your meanings clearly to them."

"You'll be sorry if you try to blacken my name, you trollop."

"How so, dear Camellia? Please tell me more about your motives."

One of the woman's friends tugged on her arm and cautioned her to self-control. Camellia scowled, but heeded her advice. "Another time, my cunning Black Widow," she vowed. "Rest assured my eyes and ears will be on you. Make one slip and . . ." She slapped her hands together loudly. "You'll be squashed like a pesky mosquito."

Rachel locked her gaze with Camellia's. "Guilty or innocent, my blood on your hands would give you a thrill, wouldn't it?"

Before she could stop it, the reckless admission leapt from her pouty lips. "You have no idea how much."

Rachel grinned at that slip. "Oh, but I do," she purred. "Take heed, for my ears and eyes are on you, too. Who better than a twice-spurned lover, a jealous and vindictive rival, to frame the object of her despair? Did your 'friends' in Chief Anderson's office disclose that unexpected angle of their case? I doubt it. If I were you, I would watch my words and guard my steps well for a while or you'll be answering as many questions as I am."

Rachel turned to the uneasy jeweler, smiled, and said, "I'm sorry you had to witness such unladylike behavior from both of us, Mr. Meigs. Thank you for your kindness and assistance. Good afternoon."

Rachel's head was held high and her shoulders straight as she left the others gaping after her in stunned silence. She hadn't wanted to conduct herself that way in public, but had been given no choice except to defend herself and to hush Camellia. The bitter confrontation had drained her. Camellia's attention was on her today, so she shouldn't visit Dan on his ship, with or without Milton Baldwin's escort. Nor was she in a mood to see her partner in the shipping firm. Despite how much she yearned to see her love, Rachel had Burke head the carriage homeward where she could relax and think.

"What's going on, Miss Rachel?" Lula Mae asked.

Rachel caught the stern tone and serious expression on the woman's face. She was baffled. "I told you, Lula Mae, I had a terrible quarrel with Camellia Jones in Mr. Meigs's store. That's why I'm so upset."

"I don't means that. I mean with you and *that man.*"

Rachel studied the nosy and bold woman and grasped which two words she stressed. "What do you really mean, Lula Mae?"

"He comes here out of nowhere to sees Mr. Phillip. You sneaks off with him. He lies to the law to keeps you outta trouble. You treats him cold and mean and takes off again. You comes home and you's friends again."

"I explained those reasons to you before. We *are* friends, Lula Mae. I was wrong about him, and wrong to be cruel to him."

" 'Cause he loves you and is helping you? I hope you ain't letting him fools you like Mr. Newman did."

Rachel told herself the woman was controlled by worry and affection for her, but she was nevertheless vexed with Lula. "Dan is nothing like Craig Newman, nothing."

The housekeeper frowned. "No more 'Captain Slade,' is it?"

Rachel hoped the woman would realize soon how much she was provoking her mistress and how difficult it was to master her annoyance and to withhold a stern rebuke. "Is there something wrong with us being friends?"

"I don't trust him."

Calmly, but strongly, Rachel replied, "I do."

"Too much, too soon, I'm afeared. It'll stir up more trouble."

"What reason do you have to dislike and mistrust Dan?"

"In here," the woman said, pointing to her stomach to indicate an instinct. "It tells me, and it ain't never been wrong."

It is this time, Rachel's mind argued. "Don't worry, Lula Mae," her gentle tone advised, "I'm walking slowly and carefully and with my eyes open wide. I won't be hurt or tricked again."

"I got reasons to worry and not believe you, Miss Rachel. I seed them pitchers in your room. I seed hows you two was with each other."

"What pitchers?" she queried, failing to understand the woman's pronunciation of *pictures.*

"Them of you and him on that sneaky trip, them pitchers in your drawer."

Comprehension filled Rachel and angered her. What she'd endured today atop her current troubles and perils caused her to lose control. "You've been looking through my things to check out your crazy suspicion? It's none of your business, Lula Mae!"

The woman took that scolding as an affront. Her shoulders jerked back and her body stiffened as her cheeks flushed. "I was putting away your warsh and seed them. You got so much on you these days, I was trying to do more chores to help you. This ain't no way to thank me or be kind."

Despite that explanation and the woman's hurt feelings, Rachel was miffed. "Why didn't you leave it on my bed as usual?"

"I told you," the simple woman said, "I thawt it would help you. When I seed them pitchers, I was scared. I thawt you was gitting yourself into a fix with him. I don't want you hurt more."

"You mustn't fret." She explained about the party in Augusta and alleged the pictures were George

Leathers' idea, since at that time he believed they were cousins and they would make nice keepsakes. "There's no harm in having them made and in keeping them."

"Could be, if the wrong eyes sees them. Best to git rid of them."

Rachel envisioned burning those heart-stirring souvenirs and shuddered. She tried to soothe the woman's fears with deceit. "I've done nothing wrong with him, so why should I? They're lovely, and I looked my best that night. Besides, worrier, Dan is an old and dear friend of Phillip's, so why would anyone find our behavior offensive or wicked?"

"You forgitting the past," Lula Mae pointed out, "them investigations, the dangers you're in, those loose tongues awagging. It be crazy to look close to a man at this time. You know what mean folks will say; that you done chose number four and were acourting him afore Mr. Phillip was cold and stiff."

She and Dan were being careful to conceal their relationship so it shouldn't create more problems for her. "I'll have to take that risk, Lula Mae; I can't give up all my male friends and acquaintances to prevent more rumors. Gossip will plague me anyway."

"It's them kind of men that's harmed you worst, Miss Rachel. Keep 'em away till this trouble be over," she urged.

"I don't know how long that will be, Lula Mae. I doubt my file has been closed once since it was started years ago. No matter what I say or do, someone will find fault with it. I must live as normally as possible."

"Even if such foolishness gits you hurt?"

"I'll have to be the judge of what's best for me—not you or anyone else. I'm sorry if that sounds mean, but I have to rule my life from now on."

"You ain't never shut the door in my face afore. It's him, ain't it? He's the cause of you acting like this."

Rachel thought the woman sounded jealous and

possessive; her resentment and intrusion were blatantly obvious. To keep peace, she said, "I'm under a heavy strain, Lula Mae. Dan is a big help and comfort. I need that support and strength right now. He isn't pushing himself on me."

"He wants you, Miss Rachel. He's achasing you. Cain't you see that?"

"Even if that were true—"

"He's gonna git you. I jest know it. I can feel it. It scares me."

Rachel was distressed by the woman's uncharacteristic behavior. She asked herself if the housekeeper was addle brained today. Or perhaps Lula Mae was only worried about her mistress losing everything and sending both out on their own again. Maybe the woman was scared she would run off with Dan and leave her to fend for herself.

"All I can say is calm down," Rachel appeased, "and thank you for such love and concern. I'll be fine, Lula Mae; we all will. This should be over soon, and things will be back to normal at Moss Haven."

As she shook her head, strands of Lula Mae's drab brown hair broke free of its confining bun. Her dark-brown eyes dulled with sadness.

"No ma'am, Miss Rachel, not this time, not ever again. I jest knows it. You gonna be hurt real bad this time. Lord have mercy on me; I cain't stops you from doing wrong. What's gonna happen to all of us?"

"Give me love and trust, and a lot of patience and understanding, Lula Mae, and I promise to make things better for us soon. I can't concentrate on solving our problems if we're quarreling. Please help me."

"You wouldn't break your word to me?"

"No, dear friend, never. As long as we've been together and as much as we've shared and endured, you shouldn't even have to ask that."

"You're right, Miss Rachel. I'm ashamed of myself. I'll help you."

"Thank you, Lula Mae. I'll take a long and cool bath in the wash shed. After my trip today, I'm hot and tense and dusty."

"That's jest what you need. I'll git everything fixed. When I'm done, I'll cook you the best supper you've ever had."

Rachel didn't argue with her over preparing the bath. "That's kind of you, dear friend. I'll go get my things and meet you in the wash shed. Remember where I told you I hid the cashbox if you need any for shopping. I don't want anything happening to the last of our money."

"Lord, have mercy on us, it best not."

At seven, Daniel Slade arrived to call on Rachel. He noticed how the protective housekeeper frowned at him when she opened the door. With few words, she guided him into the parlor and went upstairs.

Within minutes, a smiling Rachel entered the room and greeted him. Both were aware of the older woman's presence in the server where she was clearing away dinner dishes and leftover food. Rachel offered Dan refreshments, but he refused. They carried on a casual, genial, and innocent conversation until Lula Mae finished her work and left the house.

"Why didn't you come to visit me today?" Dan asked. "I waited and worried all afternoon. You did say Friday, didn't you?"

Rachel related her confrontation with Camellia Jones in the jewelry shop. "After that, I decided my mood would be better on Monday. I'm sorry you worried. I should have sent you a message, but I assumed you'd realize something had happened to prevent my coming, such as Milton being unavailable."

"That hateful witch," Dan muttered. He wondered what, if Rachel was low on money, she was doing in a jewelry shop? "Why were you there?" he blurted out.

Rachel decided to be honest with him. Dan appeared shocked and dismayed that things were that bad for her.

"Don't worry about the money, Rachel; I'll give you what you need. How much will it take to clear up your problems?"

"None now, but thank you. If things get bad, I'll tell you."

"You shouldn't have to sell your jewelry to support yourself. Are you too proud to accept a gift or a loan from me?"

"Yes," she admitted. "I don't want to depend on you or anyone right now. I must stand strong and tall to take care of myself." While she spoke, Rachel observed Lula Mae lurking near a side window. She was furious, but she didn't let on she had sighted the housekeeper. She tapped her lips with her forefinger to indicate silence to Dan. "Lula Mae at window," she mouthed, then winked at him and grinned as she set out to dupe the woman. "You were a good friend to Phillip, and you've been a good one to me. I appreciate all you've done and are doing to help me through this difficult period. If I need a loan to carry me to better days, I'll come see you. I have to be in town on Monday for business; perhaps we can have lunch and chat longer. I'm afraid I'm very tired tonight, if you don't mind."

Dan caught the clues for a meeting in a few days. He was vexed with Lula Mae for spoiling their visit and intrigued by the woman's stealthy conduct. He kept his voice and expression amiable as he said, "I understand, Rachel. Things like that are exhausting. Lunch Monday sounds enjoyable. Please don't hesitate to send Burke for me if you need anything or there's more trouble here. Why don't you see me out so you can rest?"

"Thank you, Dan," she said as they headed into the hallway. "That's very kind and generous of you."

The moment the walls on either side concealed them from view, they embraced and kissed. Their mouths feasted wildly and swiftly. Both knew the daring woman might come inside if they lingered too long.

"I'll see you Monday on your ship," she whispered.

"I love you, Rachel," he whispered. "You'll love me, too, one day."

"Could any woman resist you very long?" She grinned. "Who could possibly compete with or compare to you, Daniel Slade?"

"No one, I hope."

"Get along with you. I'll explain everything in detail Monday."

He kissed her and hugged her once more. "Good night, love."

She traced her fingers over his enticing mouth. "Good night, Dan."

Rachel opened the door and walked onto the porch with him. After exchanging waves she stood there while he mounted and departed. She went inside, locked the doors, the windows, then doused the lamps and went upstairs. She peered out the water closet window that overlooked the other structure and saw light glowing on the ground outside Lula Mae's quarters behind the kitchen. Rachel decided the woman had hurried to her room while Dan was galloping away toward town.

The widow was curious about why her longtime and loyal housekeeper would spy on her, on them. Was it from loving concern? Or something else? Dan's past speculations about another person being responsible for her misfortunes haunted her mind. If he was right, it had to be someone who had begun their evil work after she wed her first husband.

She asked herself again, as she had years ago, if

Lula Mae had loved and wanted William Barlow. If so, had the unmarried woman felt betrayed when he chose a young and beautiful wife over an older and plain one? Lula Mae had visited them that fateful last day. Lula Mae had detested Craig Newman, and also had visited them on his ill-fated last day. Lula Mae had tried to persuade her not to marry Phillip, had warned her it would end in trouble. During the month before Phillip's death, Lula Mae had acted strangely around him, as if angry with him.

While Rachel was away with Dan, the older woman had their schedule and would have had the opportunity to contact the law. Maybe Lula Mae was smarter than she let on; maybe she could write a legible note like the one quoted to her by the investigator. Maybe the older woman hated all men; she certainly made enough statements to imply that feeling.

William Barlow and his son . . . Craig Newman . . . Phillip McCandless . . . Could an embittered spinster and alleged friend . . .

Don't think such wicked and crazy thoughts! Rachel cautioned herself. *Lula Mae Morris is strange at times, but she couldn't be capable of four murders!*

After receiving that letter from her mother, Rachel knew that Earl Starger had alibis on two crucial occasions. And he would never hire someone to do such crimes for him in the first place. He would do them himself with sadistic delight! It couldn't be her lecherous stepfather.

Camellia Jones? She was mean, but a doubtful suspect.

Craig's brother Paul? Hateful and spiteful, but also a doubtful suspect.

Rachel couldn't think of anyone else with a motive to kill her husbands or a satanic desire to destroy her. That eliminated everyone she knew! It compelled her to return to her wild theory about a jinx or a curse!

Suddenly, a terrible thought entered her mind. The

doctor working on Craig's accident for the authorities had asked her if she ever suffered from blackouts or fainting spells. He had mentioned people doing things and not remembering them, and not being responsible legally for their actions during those times. She had believed then it was a trick to make her confess to escape arrest. Later, Phillip had explained such a mental condition—illness—truly existed.

The past flooded her distraught brain. When William's son died, she had been napping; it had been his scream—hadn't it?—that awakened her. When William died, she had been asleep in another room. When Craig took his fall, she hadn't heard any scream he might have let out because she had fainted while working in the garden beneath a hot sun and assailed by anxieties, and possibly from the strain of being pregnant, which she hadn't known at that time. When Phillip had died, she had been asleep in another room.

Could a person, she fretted in panic, do such horrible things and not realize them? Could one have an evil side that stayed concealed from even the person in question? Could there be a wicked force, another Rachel, living secretly and working insidiously within her? Had Earl's lechery and her hatred of him have birthed another being inside her?

God help me, surely not. That's crazy, impossible. Isn't it? she thought in confusion.

Rachel asked herself how she could make certain, and she couldn't think of an answer. She dared not go to a doctor, which might mean exposure! If her theory was true and she was dangerous and if a Black Widow curse ruled her other nature, her beloved Dan could be . . .

"Stop it, Rachel. There's no way, no way," she murmured, and panicked when she couldn't convince herself with absolute confidence of her sanity and innocence.

On Saturday, Rachel visited the sharecroppers with Burke Wells to assure herself and them that everything was fine. She wore a sedate black dress with long sleeves that became hot and itchy as the sun's heat increased during the first day of May.

After she returned home, she took a long and soothing bath with cool water from the well, then washed her dark-brown hair. She had not slept well the night before, so she was weary and edgy today. As she sat outside to dry her locks while the sun was setting, her mind drifted.

Ever since Rachel had caught Lula Mae spying on her and Dan, the housekeeper had been quieter than usual and very watchful of her mistress. Rachel wondered if she suspected the same awful thing she herself had thought of last night and was trying to protect her by keeping her away from all men, from any likely victim, and from the consequences of being caught. She dared not broach such a subject with Lula Mae, or with anyone.

She hadn't heard from Harrison Clements, George Leathers, or Milton Baldwin again; it was as if everyone was content to let her be a silent partner. Or perhaps they were all only awaiting what might take place in thirteen days, on the dreaded day of May fourteenth. At least nothing threatening had happened again at home or at the firm, so surely that was a good sign.

Her mother was coming for a visit next weekend, and perhaps at long last they could make peace, without Earl around to cause problems.

Dan . . . How she loved, craved, and missed him. She longed to be in his arms, to savor his kisses, to enjoy his caresses. He treated her with such respect and dignity in private as well as in public. They could talk freely and honestly now. But when either needed privacy or silence, the other didn't feel shut out. Their bond was strengthening and growing, but soon he would expect a commitment of marriage and a confession of love. Dare she give them before she was certain she wasn't a danger to him? Her worst fear, she told herself, could not possibly be true. But she knew the only reason she doubted her sanity and innocence was because she couldn't locate another suspect or explain her run of "bad luck."

On Sunday morning, as she'd done with Phillip until his death, Rachel and Lula Mae dressed and attended a small church west of town. She noticed that half of the people were nice, though not overly friendly or receptive. The other half stared at her and frowned as if she had no right to be in God's house because she was an unpunished criminal. The minister welcomed her return and gave his condolences about Phillip's death; he seemed sincerely kind and sympathetic, and she was grateful and relieved.

On the ride home, with Rachel in control of the team pulling the carriage, Lula Mae declared in an angry tone, "We cain't go there no more, Miss Rachel, not with them bunch of hypocrites being mean to you!"

"We can't hurt or deny ourselves to punish them, my friend. And I can't hide at home as if I have something to be ashamed of or to fear."

The woman hadn't argued or responded, and they had reached home in silence. Rachel sensed a change in the housekeeper and in their relationship, one that worried her.

After eating, Rachel worked in the yard on her flowers and bushes. She teased fingers over her gardenias and hoped they would bloom soon so she could place some in her bedroom at night and enjoy their dreamy fragrance. But that heady smell increased as they wilted and died, as if Mother Nature demanded such a sacrifice for their gift to people.

Rachel strolled to where her third husband was buried. She gazed at the homemade marker at one end of the oblong mound of earth. "If someone harmed you, dear Phillip, I will find them and have them punished," she murmured. "I'll solve this mystery. But you really made a mess of things for yourself and me! Wouldn't it be ironic if you're resting near where you buried that infernal money that might bury me if I never find it."

She stared at the grave for a while and mourned the loss of a good friend and rescuer when she had desperately needed one. "Where is it?" she pleaded. "I can't dig up the whole plantation searching for it."

"Searching for what, Miss Rachel?" Lula Mae asked, having heard her last two sentences during her quiet approach.

Rachel jumped and gasped. "You startled me; I didn't hear you." She lied out of necessity. "Phillip took our money out of the bank shortly before he died and hid it somewhere. I don't even know if it was on Moss Haven. I wish I could find it. Then we'd all be fine again."

"Why would he do that?"

"I don't know, my friend. He wasn't himself for a few months before his death. He must have had a good reason. If he hadn't been delirious before he died, he would have told me."

"He acted strange nigh unto the end. He stared at air as if he could see it. He sneaked whiskey. He wasted his food. He spoke mean to me. He even sneaked money from the cashbox. I was plenty worried."

Rachel didn't ask why Lula Mae hadn't told her sooner. "He had business problems on his mind. I'm sure he didn't mean to talk unkindly. But a man can't sneak his own whiskey or steal his own money in his own home."

"I didn't says he stole it. He jest acted on the sly the way he took it."

For gambling? she fretted. "I assumed he'd given it to Burke for supplies or seeds until he could get to the bank to replenish his wallet. I thought he'd forgotten to replace it, and didn't feel I should question him about his own money," she said.

"We wouldn't be bad off if it was still where it should be."

"We're fine now after I sold those jewels."

"Weren't right you had to go and do that!"

Rachel didn't want to argue again today, as such a talk might get out of hand while she was annoyed with the older woman. "Maybe not, but it's past, so let's forget it. Besides, I don't have much need for fancy jewels."

"I cames to aks what you wants me to do with that pitcher you took down in your bedroom to hangs Captain Slade's?"

Rachel was almost provoked to break the promise she'd just made herself not to quarrel with Lula Mae today. "It isn't Dan's; it's mine. *I* saw it; *I* liked it, and *I* bought it," she replied, feeling testy. "You know I never liked those drab flowers in the other picture. It was hanging there when I moved in and I hadn't gotten around to selecting and buying a replacement."

"Why a ship?"

"I do half-own many ships and a shipping firm, Lula Mae, and we live in a port city where we see them when in town. It's lovely, very dramatic and inspiring. Phillip would have loved it, too. If he'd seen it first, it would be hanging downstairs over the parlor mantel. Don't you like it?"

"No ma'am, but I don't care much for pitchers of the ocean. You wants me to git rid of the flowers?"

"Just wrap it and store it in the attic for now. Let Burke help you. I don't want you falling and getting hurt." She ordered the servant to tend the chore because Lula Mae would rebel against her mistress doing that task, and she wanted this conversation and meeting over fast.

"I will, Miss Rachel. You be out here much longer?"

"No, why?"

"Ain't good for you to be fretting and suffering like this. Mr. Phillip shouldna left you so bad off."

Keep control, Rachel. "I'm sure he didn't mean to, Lula Mae."

"Did, all the same. I don't like how you been mistreated for years."

Rachel realized a problem was brewing that must have attention or it would become worse. She dreaded to do what she knew she must. "Lula Mae," she said after taking a deep breath, "I love you and appreciate all you've done for me over the years. I hate to scold or correct you, but lately you've been forgetting I'm your mistress. You've been sharp-tongued and nosing into my private affairs too much for even a close friend. You must stop or it will cause trouble between us." She observed, as with her last reprimand, how the older woman looked shocked and offended.

"Miss Rachel, how can you speaks so to me? Nobody loves you or tends you better than me. Why you wanta hurt me?"

"I don't, Lula Mae. But you've been treating me and correcting me as if I were a child, a misbehaving child. You question me about everything I say and do, and often challenge my actions and decisions. I have to choose my own friends and do what I think is best for all of us. And please don't speak so harshly about Phillip; he was a good man, just a troubled one at the end. I have so many burdens on me right now. Don't make things worse by forcing me to be bossy or mean to you. It hurts me when we don't get along."

"I'm sorry, Miss Rachel; I didn't know I was being so bad."

The woman sounded and looked contrite, so Rachel softened. "Not bad, my friend," she said, "just too protective. I am a grown woman. I can handle people and affairs myself. Right or wrong, they have to be my decisions. All right?"

"Yes, Miss Rachel; I'll behave myself."

Rachel smiled and added, "So will I, Lula Mae. Let's go have our pie and milk now. We won't mention this again."

They walked into the house and server together. Rachel poured the milk into glasses and turned to find Lula Mae staring at her while she toyed with the knife in her grasp.

"Is something wrong?" Rachel asked, then looked down to see blood dripping onto the pie crust and making tiny puddles. "You've cut yourself!" she gasped.

Lula Mae glanced at the injured hand as if she hadn't felt the pain. She frowned and snapped, "Look what I've done! I've ruined the pie!"

"Don't worry about the dessert." She tossed the woman a rag and said, "Wrap it tight to staunch the bleeding while I fetch bandages and medicine." She rushed to the cabinet in the water closet upstairs, gathered what she needed, and returned to tend the injury.

Afterward, Lula Mae stared at her bandaged hand and said, "Thank you. I'll toss out this pie and make another one."

"Don't do that right now. Go lie down and rest. You've worked too hard lately and you're tired. I'll cook supper for us tonight. No arguing."

* * *

Rachel needed to see Dan, but his pictures would have to sate that fierce yearning. She opened the drawer only to find all three gone and a note lying in their place. Again, it warned, in her script, to spurn the sea captain or else he would die . . . Rachel gaped at the last few words, "by your hand as with all the others. If you want him to live, give him up. I'll be the only one safe with you, as you could never murder me."

Someone had done this mischief while they were at church, as the pictures had been there this morning when she dressed. Lula Mae couldn't be responsible for their theft, as Rachel had received the other notes while out of town. Surely she herself hadn't . . .

Rachel dressed with great care Monday to look her best for Dan when she saw him this afternoon. First, she planned to visit Milton Baldwin to check on the firm's business. With good luck, maybe things had improved since their last talk. Maybe he could even make a profit payment to her. Surely he was paying himself a salary, so, as part owner, he should pay her, too. She hoped their conversation was pleasant and productive, as she wanted him to escort her to Dan's clipper to prevent gossip. But even if he didn't, she would go anyway, and let tongues wag if they wanted!

Milton greeted her cordially. He smiled and said, "I was planning to visit you this afternoon, so your timing is perfect. We have an important matter to discuss and settle."

Excitement surged through her. "You've found a buyer for the firm?"

Milton frowned and shook his head. "No, I'm afraid that isn't it. I didn't want to inform you of this problem earlier while you were still grieving. Now that you've had time to get Phillip's insurance and bank account, it *must* be handled." He withdrew a paper from his desk and handed it to her. "Read that agreement. Can you pay off this loan? I need the money, Rachel. Phillip promised he would pay it back by April sixteenth. If he couldn't, as you'll see by the terms, I get his share of the firm. I allowed you a two-week extension to deal with his loss and to get your affairs in order, but I can't hold off any longer. Do you want to buy back this loan paper or turn the firm over to me? It's sixty thousand dollars, and it's past due. Legally the firm is mine by default, but I wouldn't do that to you. Think about it a minute, then tell me your decision."

Chapter 17

Rachel was crushed by the stunning news. Her mind shouted that this couldn't be happening. She wondered how much more defeat she could take. So much money was missing, both from the businesses and their personal resources. Where had it gone? Then a thought struck her. "How can this be true, Milton?" she accused. "I looked at the firm's books, remember? Nothing is—or was—recorded there about such a large loan, about *any* loan."

"It was a private matter between friends, Rachel. Phillip is the one who insisted on using his share of the firm to back it up. I agreed because I couldn't take a personal loss that big. I only loaned him the money because he was desperate and he had that important contract, so I knew he could repay it soon. I hate doing this to you, but I have no choice. Surely you can understand and accept my position. Do you want to repay it or default?"

"I can't repay it! Phillip didn't leave any insurance. Our bank account is wiped clean. Until that big deal is completed, neither Harry nor George could loan me that much, if anything. Those two companies are heavily invested in that mysterious contract, which only Phillip seemed to know about, until May fourteenth. If I sold Moss Haven to come up with the cash and something prevented that deal, I'd lose everything and be penniless. Besides, you told me and the books seem to indicate the firm is going to bankrupt soon, so why waste money I don't have on it?" Nor could she bring herself to ask Daniel Slade for a loan of that size. "I wish you had warned me about this earlier. It comes as a shock."

"I'm sorry, Rachel, but I thought you had enough problems on your mind; and I assumed, once Phillip's affairs were settled, this problem could be handled easily and quietly between us. I don't want to hurt you, but it's a lot of money, my money."

"Why would Phillip set the repayment date before he earned his profit on the deal? How was he planning to get money to get rid of this?" she asked, shaking the paper in her hand.

"I don't know. He chose April sixteenth. Maybe he was going to use part of that advance everyone says he accepted and hid."

"That wasn't his money to spend! This doesn't make sense," she murmured as she studied the signature on the agreement, which looked to be Phillip's. Everyone wanted the missing money, and everyone thought she had it. Were they using tricks on her to get their share? Was this paper authentic and the loan real? If Milton was lying, she couldn't prove it. She would lose one of her three holdings, and was receiving nothing in support from the other two. Instead of an imminent profit from the sale of one firm, it was being snatched away from her needy grasp!

"I'm very sorry to put you in such a vulnerable position, Rachel," Milton said with lowered eyes.

She locked her probing gaze with his unreadable one. "Do you honestly believe this is fair and right? Surely the company's assets—ships, two warehouses, this office, existing contracts, and whatever else—are worth more than sixty thousand dollars. Why couldn't an accountant figure up what I would have to relinquish to settle this amount? I could become a shareholder instead of a partner. I need financial support from this firm until I can sell off my other partnerships. That may take months, and they won't result in much—if any—monetary gain."

"That sounds logical and reasonable, Rachel, but it wouldn't work. The value of things on paper aren't the same as what one can actually get for them. When or if I found a buyer, I could never recover sixty thousand from a sale; we have too many debts to settle. I'd be lucky to make anything off such an action or to find a deal in my favor."

"Can you give me an extension, until the big contract pays off?" She ventured, to see how resolved or insensitive he was. "It's only a few more weeks. What difference would it make, since I can't repay the money now and, by defaulting, it wouldn't help you, either?"

"What if the deal falls through, as all of you seem to think it will?"

"Then I'll honor Phillip's loan agreement immediately."

"I'm sorry, Rachel, but I think that's a waste of time for me."

"You want the firm now, today, is that it?" she challenged.

"I want this distasteful matter settled promptly, yes."

"Why the sudden rush, Milton? What will a month matter?"

"If I have ownership and authority over everything, I can make some tough decisions and take desperate actions to save this firm and myself."

"Why can't you do that anyway?"

"Don't take this the wrong way, please, but I think I can work out my problems better if the name McCandless is taken off the firm. In view of your open investigation and your current partnership . . . I don't want to sound heartless, but your past and current trouble and reputation can damage the firm further. I've already had prospective clients imply you're the reason I can't obtain their business. A few old customers are balking on new shipments until you're exonerated; they don't want their payments to reward a . . . You know what I mean. I'm sorry."

Rachel observed him. From her past treatment by the townfolk, she couldn't call him a liar, but he was out to save himself, no matter how much she hurt. Oddly, she was angered—not saddened or frightened—by the probabilities of new or revived gossip and ostracism.

"Please do this the easy and friendly way, Rachel. I can have my lawyer Frank Henly draw up the proper papers to turn your share over to me, then have you come to his office to sign them before witnesses. If you resist, I'll have to let Frank handle it. I realize this agreement doesn't have witnesses and wasn't written up by a lawyer, but it *is* legal and binding. This *is* Phillip's signature. You don't want that publicity and exposure, and neither of us want to create ill will between us. Legally, we are no longer partners. Help me to make this transition simple."

Rachel wondered who had filled in the due date, and if it was the one agreed upon by Phillip. "I really have no choice, do I?"

"I'm afraid not. I'll have Frank prepare the papers for your signature, and I'll notify you when they're ready to sign. This is difficult for me, too, Rachel, so I'm happy you're settling it so peaceably."

She decided to test his motive and feelings one last time. "If I come up with the sixty thousand, I can buy back the agreement?" she asked.

Milton stared at her and hesitated, but said, "Of course. But it has to be on or before Friday," he amended.

"A week before I'm to be paid for that deal? That isn't fair."

"That's a shipping date, Rachel, not a closing and final payment date. There's no telling how long a voyage and delivery and collection of balance could take. I can't hold off that long."

She pretended to concede. "I just wish you had refused to loan Phillip money, at least that much, when you knew he had a gambling problem."

"Why he desperately needed the money wasn't my business, Rachel. We were friends and partners, so I helped him out of a tight bind."

"And put me in a worse one."

"That wasn't my doing or intent."

"Do what you must, Milton. I'll leave now. Good day."

As she stood outside the firm, Rachel worried over Harry and George having similar agreements that might take away the other two companies. If she lost all partnerships and Moss Haven, she would be in that same state of poverty as after Craig died. What or who had set this evil pattern in motion? How could she stop it? She couldn't turn to Dan as if he were her only escape. She couldn't give herself to him completely until she was on level ground once more.

Rachel was glad she had told Burke Wells to wait for her. She returned to the carriage and she had him take her to Bay Street, where she tipped a sailor to carry a message to Captain Daniel Slade of the *Merry Wind* that was docked below the bluff. She said to tell him something had come up, but not to worry or visit, that she was only changing their appointment to dinner at her home on Wednesday. She lingered there until she saw the man approach Dan's clipper and head up the gangplank, as the vessel with secured sails was visible between two buildings beyond a stone alley.

* * *

At home, Rachel told Lula Mae that Dan was coming to dinner on Wednesday, that her mother was visiting this weekend, and that she had lost the shipping firm. She couldn't decide which or if all revelations astonished the wide-eyed woman, who didn't comment on any of them.

Tuesday morning, Rachel was miffed by an announcement in the newspaper that was delivered by the mail carrier: "McCandless & Baldwin Shipping Firm is now under the sole ownership of Milton Baldwin." It was clear that Phillip's Savannah partner had wasted no time in letting people know he had pushed her out of the firm, so they needn't worry about trading there. He must have turned in this notice before meeting with her in order to meet the newspaper's deadline for publication! "So much for giving me an extension and handling this matter quietly, you sorry . . ." she muttered in anger.

Later, Earl Starger paid her another visit.

"What do you want this time?" she asked in vexation. She didn't know which caught her eye first: the lack of lust and smugness in his hazel gaze, the freshly combed dirty-brown hair, or the deceptively genial smile on his lips that softened his angular features and made him look sincere.

"Calm down, girl. I'm only staying a minute, and I won't even come inside. I wanted to thank you for writing to Catherine. It seemed to make her feel better. I'll be sailing to Boston tomorrow for three weeks, so why don't you visit her? While I'm away, you won't have to fear seeing me."

Mama didn't tell him she's coming to visit! "Is she strong enough to be left alone for three weeks?"

"Yes, and she has plenty of servants around for

help and protection. If I've done things in the past to offend you, Rachel, I'm sorry, and it won't ever happen again. If we can't make peace and become friends, let us have a truce, at least for Catherine's sake. We've conflicted too long and too harshly. Join me in putting the past behind us. You have three weeks of privacy, so please go spend time with her."

Rachel was astonished by his cunning pleas and deceitfully contrite behavior, but she didn't fall for his ruse. Yet she didn't want to endure another bitter quarrel today so she said, "I may go. It sounds like a good idea."

"Do it. You wouldn't want things to end this way between you two."

Her heart pounded as she questioned a subtle threat against her or her ailing mother. "What do you mean?"

"Your experiences since leaving home and Catherine's recent illness should tell you that unexpected deaths do occur. Don't wait too long. I promise I won't do anything to prevent a reunion you both need."

"I'll think seriously about it."

"I hope so. Good-bye, Rachel. Take care of yourself."

She watched his departure with intrigue, and suspicion.

Dan arrived at six-thirty Wednesday evening. Even though they couldn't converse on more than a genial level as Lula Mae served them and they ate, Rachel detected that something was troubling Dan. She noticed it in the way he seemed to force his smile, the unrelaxed way he sat in his chair, and the lack of a usual sparkle in his blue eyes. She didn't think he could be angry over her not visiting him Monday, as she had sent a message and an invitation to dinner tonight. She would question his strange mood after the housekeeper was dismissed and they were alone. And she would make certain the nosy woman did not spy on them again tonight.

Before Lula Mae could serve their dessert and coffee, there was a knock on the back door. Rachel heard the housekeeper talking with a man, so she went to see who had called at this hour and for what reason. It was one of their sharecroppers who said his wife was having a baby and he needed help fast. Rachel observed how reluctant the woman was to leave her alone with Dan, as it wasn't like Lula Mae to refuse to help in a matter in which she was skilled.

"I can finish the serving and cleaning up, Lula Mae. Go along with him; his wife needs you. There's no time to fetch the doctor in town. I'll be fine until your return."

"But you has cumpny, Miss Rachel."

"Don't worry about us. Dan won't be staying long after we finish. I'll even leave the clean-up chores for you, if that will make you feel better about going."

"Jest let me git my things," Lulu Mae conceded with a frown.

After the woman left, Rachel returned to the dining room and explained the emergency situation, then served their dessert and coffee.

Dan was angry Rachel had sold his family's shipping business. He had planned to buy it from Milton and move it back to Charleston, where he wanted to settle down eventually with Rachel. He couldn't do that until after this perilous mystery was solved and he could expose his identity. "I saw something in yesterday's newspaper that surprised me, Rachel," he said. "Why did you sell the firm? I told you I would lend or give you whatever money you need for support. Why didn't you tell me first?"

Rachel didn't know why that matter disturbed him,

but it certainly seemed to. "I didn't sell." She related how she had lost it on Monday.

That news stunned Dan, but it pleased him that she was innocent of his mental charges. "You believed him?"

"Not really, but what could I do? The signature on the agreement was Phillip's. I can't repay the loan, so why cause more trouble for myself fighting a futile battle?"

"Stall signing those relinquishment papers."

She stared at him. "Why? How? For what reason?"

"This secret loan is suspicious. If it were for a few thousand dollars, I'd believe him, but I doubt Baldwin would loan a man with a gambling weakness so much money, even with Phillip's share of the firm as collateral and especially when Baldwin's trying to convince you the firm is near bankrupt. He would try to force you to repay the money before accepting the terms." Dan had decided to hire a detective to check out Baldwin and this curious matter, but he would keep that intention to himself for a while. "If he presses you to sign, tell him to take you to court to prove the agreement is authentic and binding. See how he reacts to that situation."

"He'll be furious, then vindictive."

"That doesn't matter, does it?" Dan reasoned. "I'll be able to help you battle him. We need to get our hands on that paper, even if I have to steal it; that's the only way to see if it's real. Besides, without it, he has only his word he loaned money to my . . . friend."

"But if it is authentic, Dan, that wouldn't be fair or right of me."

"If necessary, I'll give you the sixty thousand dollars to repay him."

"No! The firm is in bad trouble and you'll lose your money."

"I think he's lying and bluffing, Rachel. Give me time to prove it."

Hope and suspense filled her. "How?"

"I'll think of a way after I give it careful study." Something compelled him not to relate his plan to her. He would send for that Charleston detective tomorrow. He would travel by train and could be on this case soon. "Don't sign those papers until we're convinced he's telling you the truth," he advised, then suggested what she should tell Milton.

"Oh, mercy, he'll become an enemy, too. I don't need or want another one. But all right, I'll do as you say, even though it's going to be big trouble."

"Trouble isn't new to you or to me. If we sink, we'll do it fighting."

His plan was cunning. "I'll trust you, Dan, and follow your lead. When you startled me that day I was searching the office safe, I had a stack of papers in my hand, but I put them away without looking at them. The loan agreement could have been there or in Milton's locked desk."

"We searched everything later, remember?"

"You're right! So where was it?"

"Probably didn't exist then."

"I pray that's true, Dan, and we find a way to prove it fast."

"We will. Two good things: your stepfather sailed for Boston this morning, and so did Camellia Jones. I checked on their schedules. Neither is returning for three weeks. At least they'll be out of your hair for a while."

Rachel liked that news. It meant no Earl to intrude on her mother's visit, and no Camellia to run into while flaunting the jewelry she had been forced in to selling.

"I have to leave tomorrow on a short trip," he disclosed, "but I'll be back next Wednesday. My crew is restless, and I've been offered a sweet deal to take a rush cargo to New Orleans. I hate to leave you at this time, Rachel, but we might need the money to finance this deal."

He was leaving! "I can't let you use your earnings to get me out of trouble. It isn't your problem, and there's a possibility of a total loss."

"It *is* my problem, Rachel, because you're involved and in danger."

She warmed and smiled, but she still didn't want him to go. "I wouldn't be if I could find that missing money."

"Why don't we search for it again? Lula Mae will be gone for hours. The timing is perfect. I might think of a place you haven't. Since I'm a man and a man concealed it, I may have a better chance of finding one's hiding spot."

"That sounds good to me. Let's get busy and hurry."

While there was daylight, they searched the outbuildings and around the house's exterior. Dan even took a lantern and examined every area underneath any raised structure. He tried to recall if Phillip had had any favorite hiding spots as a child and he checked those that came to mind.

As the inside of the house was explored, Dan tried to imagine his brother in those locations—the dining room while eating and chatting with Rachel, the cozy combination office and sitting room where he had worked and relaxed, the parlor where he had sat and perhaps entertained, the guest room where he had spent his last hours alive and in terrible pain and alone, the sewing room that had not been given a chance to become a nursery for an heir, and the master bedroom where his brother had slept and had made love to the woman he himself now loved and craved.

As they entered the parlor and sat down to rest, Rachel murmured, "See, nothing. No money and no clues."

"It could be buried anywhere on this large property."

"One strange thing I noticed during my first search; I didn't find any personal effects from Phillip's past, not one. Isn't that odd? It's as if he either destroyed or concealed his past before moving to Savannah."

"He could have left them stored in Charleston to avoid painful memories. I'll check on it for you the next time I'm there."

Rachel walked to an oblong side table. She lifted a decorative box and opened its lid to send forth lovely music. "Phillip gave this to me. Whenever I was sad or scared, he would play it for me as a distraction. Sometimes we would even dance around this room, laughing and talking. Despite all we've learned or suspect, Dan, Phillip was good and kind and special. He was my closest friend. I have to believe he knew what he was doing with this mysterious deal and, if he were alive, he'd know how to straighten out the mess. I'm sorry he died in such physical and mental torment. He didn't deserve that."

Dan was touched and pleased, but it refreshed the sadness and bitterness of his brother's loss. He turned to her and suggested, "Why don't we distract ourselves with a twirl or two, ma'am?"

They danced in silence as they comforted themselves and each other. But when they locked gazes, the close contact and romantic aura became too arousing. They didn't know when Lula Mae might return.

"How about a game of chess?" Rachel asked. "Phillip taught me how to play."

"Sounds perfect, just what we need," he teased and grinned.

Rachel smiled, then closed the music box and put it back in its place. She pulled out the chess board and pieces. She placed them on a small table, and they sat down to test each other's skills.

Soon, their eye and knee contact became too stimulating.

"We're fighting a losing battle, woman," Dan chuckled.

Before she could respond, thunder boomed over the house and caused her to jump and squeal. They were so enthralled with each other, they hadn't heard the distant rumblings or noticed the flashes of lightning that had moved closer and closer over the last hour. A violent storm broke over the area and rapidly sent down a deluge of rain amid noisy roars and brilliant flickers.

"Afraid of storms?" Dan asked.

"No, it just startled me. I'd better close the windows upstairs. Will you check the ones down here?"

Dan shut and locked all windows and doors on the bottom floor. When Rachel returned from doing the same on the one above, he grinned and said, "I doubt Lula Mae can return any time soon, if at all tonight. It's bad outside, and looks to be a long and dangerous storm."

As if taking his words as an invitation to rush into his arms, Rachel replied, "We should wait a little while, in case they left before the storm broke. If she isn't here in twenty minutes . . . Why are you grinning like that? Isn't that what you had in mind?"

Dan stroked her hair, then her cheek as he said in a husky tone, "Only every hour since Augusta and every minute since my arrival today."

"Then we think alike." Her eyes gleamed with anticipation and desire.

"That we do, my bewitching enchantress."

"Why don't you douse all the lamps downstairs, all except those in here? I'll freshen up. Join me in ten minutes, if she isn't back."

"Do you have a slicker I can borrow? I need to put away my horse."

"In the closet by the back door. Lock it after you return."

As she left the parlor, Dan noticed she had gone from twenty to ten minutes before— *Stars above,* his mind fretted. Could he make love to his brother's widow in his brother's house in his brother's bed, the same one where Phillip had—*Yes,* his heart and body replied, and he relaxed.

Dan found the slicker and went to put his mount in the barn, where he unsaddled him and tossed him hay and sweet feed to calm the nervous animal. Inside the back door, he bolted it and removed his wet boots.

Upstairs, Dan found Rachel standing at the end of the hall with the porch door ajar and gazing outside. He came up behind her and slipped his arms around her waist. She signed dreamily and leaned against him. He nestled his cheek against her fragrant hair. Both watched the storm.

The day's heat lessened quickly as breezes grew stronger and cooler. Moss was whipped about as the wind grabbed and shook branches as if trying to viciously rip the limbs from their trunks. Failing to do so, it snatched at their leaves and sent them scurrying across the yard. Spring flowers were yanked around, colorful petals torn off and sent flying to join the severed leaves and broken twigs. Ear-splitting thunderclaps sounded overhead; they shook the house and rattled the windows.

Lightning flickered like glowing fingers slashing into dark clouds to release a torrential rain. More peals of thunder roared and boomed like charges of dynamite going off in rapid sequence. The ground was soaked and visibility was nonexistent. As gusting winds slanted rain and fired it onto the porch, moisture reached Rachel and Dan in the doorway.

"Let's go make a storm of our own," he enticed as he nibbled at her ear and caressed her bosom through her garment.

Rachel turned in his embrace and kissed him as her answer.

Dan lifted her, closed the door with the hand beneath her knees, and carried her into the bedroom. Only a few candles were burning there, and they cast an intimate and romantic glow in the lovely room. Neither thought of who had shared this room and bed in the recent past.

Garments were cast aside as their bodies were stormed by the urgency and power of desires that matched those of nature's deluge. His hands locked around her buttocks and held her tightly against his pleading groin as she sat atop him. Her legs straddled Dan's thighs and her toes dug into the softness of the bed as she removed any remaining space between their straining bodies. Her hands wandered over his sleek body and roved the furry mat covering his chest. She thirsted for this man and she leaned forward to seal their mouths.

They meshed over and over to create a white-hot heat within them. As his hands roamed her naked flesh, his mouth trailed down her throat to taste the sweetness of her skin and to savor her heated response to him. Dan rolled her to her back so his mouth could tease over her torso and drift into the inviting canyon between her breasts. She moaned as his hungry exploration conquered the brown peaks nearby. Her words and movements encouraged him to continue his loving assault and to make it bolder.

Rachel's fingers stroked Dan's back and shoulders, then moved into his silky jet-black hair. He was driving her wild with his stimulation. She tried to do the same with hers.

They made no attempt to delay this heady meal, as they were starved for each other. Desires were unleashed and allowed to race where they willed and at their chosen pace.

Their tongues danced in a frantic and erotic mating

ritual. Their bodies were joined, and they strove for a mutual prize. Thunder vibrated the house; lovemaking shook the bed. Lightning danced on the windows, and passions glowed within them. Joy and feverish need charged through them as powerfully as the storm was attacking the landside. Their pulses throbbed and their hearts pounded as they took and gave of rapture's delight. They desperately needed this unrestrained fusion of bodies and spirits. All that mattered to them was this special moment and their love.

Dan captured Rachel's face between his hands and kissed her greedily. He had an uncontrollable urge to make this woman a part of him.

The heat of their bodies intensified as their exertions increased. They labored until ecstasy was ready to burst within them to carry them beyond reality. When sheer bliss rocked them to their cores, they clung together and drank every drop of their lusty nectar.

After the staggering explosions ceased and calmness came, they remained entwined as they struggled to breathe normally. It was so muggy that their perspiration refused to evaporate and it dampened the sheets. Neither minded, as it was imbued with the erotic scent of sated passions.

"That was wonderful, Rachel. How can it get better every time?" he murmured in amazement and pleasure.

She cuddled against him and smiled to herself. That told her she didn't disappoint him with her skills that she knew increased each time they made love. "I don't know, but I'm glad it does. You're a superb teacher."

They embraced and kissed tenderly, relaxed and happy.

Pressed to his hard body, Rachel wished this were their home and they never had to leave its safety again. She wished no peril confronted them, no danger threatened them, no dark past haunted them. She prayed all of those things could be defeated soon.

Dan wrapped his arms more possessively around her and rested his chin atop her head. A mixture of calm and excitement filled him. Surely it would always be this way between them: stimulating, spontaneous, satisfying, heart-stoppingly wonderful, and tender. What they had found together was more than physical enjoyment. He shifted to fuse their gazes. "You steal my wits and self-control, woman. What am I going to do about this powerful hold over me?"

"Let me keep it, please; and I'll let you keep yours over me. We'll enjoy each other one day at a time. We'll make no promises or demands until our lives are settled. All right?"

Dan cuddled her into his arms once more and didn't respond. He asked himself if he would miss his present lifestyle at sea. Yes, but that was normal. Would he be content to become a landlover with this woman? If he gave up his ship and travels, would that change him or bore him? He didn't think so, not with a fascinating and challenging woman like Rachel at his side day and night. All he had to do was convince her they were matched.

While a sated and serene Rachel slept in his arms, Dan napped in a twilight state and kept an ear on the storm, as he didn't want the too-watchful housekeeper to return and catch them in bed together.

At four on Thursday morning, the strong forces of nature ceased attacking the area. Dan awakened Rachel and told her he was leaving before daylight to avoid Lulu Mae and to set sail. They kissed and embraced, then she accompanied him to the door so she could bolt it after his departure. She saw the lantern go out in the barn and heard him gallop toward town. She smiled in tranquil fatigue. Before returning to bed, she made certain no clues were left behind to expose their passionate night together.

When Lula Mae peeked in on Rachel, she found her mistress sleeping and alone. She sighed in relief and closed the bedroom door, to do her chores quietly in case the storm had kept Rachel awake part of the night.

At dawn, Dan sailed for New Orleans, with a valuable cargo stored below deck. If he hadn't agreed on Monday to accept this job, he wouldn't go, not after learning about Rachel's dilemma with Milton Baldwin. Nothing physically threatening had occurred recently and she and Burke were on guard against trouble, so she should be safe. He needed to get his hands on as much money as possible. Repaying that lost advance might be the only way to protect his love from vengeance and gossip, as no one would believe she didn't have it. She wouldn't be safe until the matter was settled. Whatever it cost him, he wanted to get the perilous situation behind them. Rachel's mother was coming for a visit, and her feared stepfather was far away. Threats had quieted down or ceased, and he would return next Wednesday, two days before the contract deadline. Still, he was uneasy as he took his last glimpse of Savannah for a while.

That afternoon, Milton sent Rachel a message that said the lawyer had the relinquishment paper ready, so would she come to sign it tomorrow at one o'clock in Frank Henley's office?

The deliverer waited while she penned a response: "I have company until Monday so I do not want to spend hours away from them or get in a sad mood. I will come to town next week to handle our business. I saw Tuesday's newspaper so you shouldn't have any problems over my 'trouble and reputation' hurting the firm before our meeting. Work on your old and prospective clients while waiting to see me. Good luck."

The messenger left with her envelope in his grasp, and the first step had been taken as Dan advised. All she could do was pray hard her love was right, or she was in for needless suffering.

Friday at five in the afternoon, Catherine Fleming Starger arrived in a carriage with a servant handling the team and protecting her along the journey from White Cloud, located halfway between Savannah and Augusta.

Rachel hugged her mother, who responded in like manner. Their past troubles and sufferings slipped away during the joyful reunion, as their recent overtures had broken the icy obstacle between them.

"It's been too long, Mama." Rachel said, with dewy eyes. "I've missed you so much. It was foolish of us to stay apart like that. Let's not ever quarrel and ignore each other again. It's been awful without you."

The letter from her daughter had shown Catherine how unfair they were being to each other. She had been closer to Rachel than to any of her children, and she had suffered from the barrier placed between them years ago. "I'm sorry we've both behaved badly, and we won't let it happen again," she vowed, also with misty eyes that exposed her emotions. "Now that we've made an effort to end our separation, we won't allow another to intrude on our new relationship. I should have been more understanding and patient; you were becoming a woman, and that's difficult."

"The war hurt all of us; I suppose we were both fighting changes in our lives. Please forgive me for hurting you and for staying away."

"If you'll forgive me for being blind and selfish. All

I saw was my side, Rachel; I didn't realize you children were so miserable at home. I know Earl can be difficult and bossy at times, but a bachelor has to learn how to become a husband and father. Taking on a widow with four children wasn't easy for him, but I shouldn't have taken his side every time. I'm truly sorry."

"We both made mistakes, Mama, but we won't do so again." Held at arm's length, she studied her mother, who was paler and thinner than when she'd last seen her. Yet, she was still beautiful, with blond hair and green eyes and exquisite features. Until the recent and draining illness, Catherine had appeared to be in her early thirties; now, she looked her age of forty-five, and that saddened the daughter.

"Come inside and rest, Mama; I know you must be exhausted."

As they headed to the porch, Catherine responded, "It was a long and tiring journey, Rachel, but I'm so happy to be here. After receiving your sweet letter, I had to come and make peace between us. My recovery and Earl's trip created perfect timing for it."

"Yes, they did. I'm so glad you came. I've missed you, and I've been worried about you. How are you feeling?"

Catherine smiled. "Much better, almost completely recovered. Of course, I look a fright after being ill and lying abed so long."

"No, you look wonderful—as ravishing as ever . . . She's here, Lula Mae!" Rachel shouted as they entered the house.

The housekeeper hurried from the server. After exchanging pleasantries and telling the servant to put the visitor's baggage upstairs, the woman went to finish dinner preparations, a special meal she had spent hours getting ready. She had told the male servant where to put the horses and where to take quarters for a few days.

"Where's Phillip? Isn't he home from the office yet?"

Rachel stared at her mother. "What?" she murmured in confusion, fearing her mother's mind had been affected by her illness.

Catherine smiled again. "Is he away on business like Earl? I so wanted to see him, too. You are happy this time, aren't you, Rachel?"

"Didn't Earl tell you the news? Haven't you read the newspaper?"

"Tell me what news?"

"Phillip is dead, Mama." When she saw the woman's shock, Rachel related how and when her third husband had died, ostensibly of cholera. "I can't believe Earl didn't tell you; it's been six weeks, and it's been in the newspaper. Earl came to see me twice since that awful day, on April twenty-second and this past Tuesday before he sailed. He didn't know you were coming to visit me, so I didn't mention it. Why is that, Mama?"

Catherine was dismayed by the revelation of her third son-in-law's death. "This comes as such a shock, Rachel. Earl probably didn't want to upset me while I was so ill and then recovering. You two have never gotten along, so I didn't tell him I was coming. I will after my visit here when he returns home in three weeks. Why did he come here? Did you two quarrel as usual?"

Rachel was tempted to confess all, but it would only hurt her mother who would never leave Earl, even if Catherine believed her accusations. They were making peace, so she didn't want to risk another conflict. It was best and kindest, at least for now, to let her mother remain in her safe dreamworld. "He came to make peace, too. We argued the first time, but then we were polite."

"Can you become friends and settle your differences?"

"No, Mama, and I'm sorry. He thinks I'm both crazy and guilty of murdering four people."

"But you said Phillip died of cholera. I don't understand. Surely you aren't in trouble with the authorities again."

Rachel explained about the secret burial, her exposure, and the still-open investigation. Yet she didn't reveal any of her perilous secrets.

"What are they going to do to you?"

Rachel gazed into green eyes filled with love and worry. "Nothing, Mama. I'm innocent, and the case will be closed soon. They have no evidence to arrest me on, because I didn't do anything wrong."

"What's going on in your life, Rachel? A three-time widow at twenty-one . . . Why do these terrible things keep happening to you?"

"I don't know, Mama, but it's been so hard on me."

"Will you be all right, my precious baby?"

"Yes, Mama, fine. I'm stronger and smarter now. Let's not talk about sad things anymore. How are you doing? Earl said you've seen the doctor twice. When? Why?"

"On March twenty-sixth and on April fifteenth. I was tired and weak all the time, but I'm better now. He ordered me to bed rest and gave me a tonic. They cured me, along with your letter. I've missed you so, Rachel. I miss all of my children."

Rachel wondered if she should be so unhappy about her mother confirming Earl's alibis for two important dates: Phillip's death and the police tip. "Have you heard from Rosemary or Richard?"

"No, but I wish the twins would contact me, at least write to say they're safe and happy."

"So do I, Mama. They will one day."

"If I hurt you and deserted you, Rachel, I'm sorry. I don't want anything to ever create another breach between us."

"It won't, Mama; our troubles are over. We'll both promise to write and to visit regularly."

Lula Mae came to tell them dinner was ready to be served. Rachel and her mother went into the dining room to eat and to continue their talk.

To both women's delight, the weekend passed with long and nourishing conversations and relaxing strolls that strengthened and brought a glow to her mother's cheeks. By the time Catherine headed for home on Monday morning, both were at peace with themselves and with their past.

But Rachel had learned something important: her stepfather hadn't been away from home in weeks, except to take Catherine to the doctor twice and on the two days he had visited her at Moss Haven. Rachel knew her mother had told the truth, and it almost disappointed her to mark Earl Starger's name off her suspect list: if nothing more, at least for writing the intimidating love notes. Who was left? Harry, the client, and a yet-unknown prankster.

Tuesday night there was another house-rocking and paint-vandalizing incident. This time, Rachel was certain it wasn't the spiteful work of Earl Starger or Camellia Jones, who were both far away. She assumed it had to be the malicious mischief of someone in town, perhaps young boys. As long as no one tried to harm her and her servants, she would allow them to get such amusement out of their heads and prayed they soon tired of their cruel sport. Once more the black letters were covered with slate-blue paint.

Wednesday, if Dan returned to Savannah, he didn't come to visit her, but another violent storm paid a long call on the area. Rachel stood at the window and observed it as she recalled how she had spent the last one.

Thursday morning, Rachel received a scolding note from Milton for her lack of a visit this week "as promised." It included a strongly worded summons to finish the matter tomorrow at ten o'clock. She dismissed the deliverer, after telling him to report her response would come later in the day.

She sat down to pen her reply: "As commanded, I will be in town tomorrow, but not to sign a relinquishment paper at Mr. Henley's. I will meet you in our office for a serious talk, after I have seen Mr. Henley to check on my legal rights in this strange affair. Until I am convinced that is Phillip's signature and, if so, that the repayment date is correct, leave things as they are. With such terms and so much money involved, I am suspicious of an agreement that had no witnesses and was not handled by a lawyer. I want to learn if I am legally responsible for a personal and unsubstantiated loan before I repay it or default, whichever way I decide to respond later. You appear in a great rush to have me out of the firm before tomorrow's deadline of Phillip's big contract; that arouses my curiosity, just as your insensitive attitude and harsh correspondences arouse my anger to defiance and investigation. If you press me at this time, I will be forced to battle you in court. I am sure this can be resolved soon if we do not challenge each other again. I will see you tomorrow morning."

There, she thought, her refusal and bluff—step two—were done as Dan suggested. She was amazed that, so far, her love had guessed Milton's actions with accuracy. She hoped he was back in port by now to lend her the courage and strength she needed to carry out stunning step three tomorrow. She couldn't

411

imagine how Milton would react to this shocking development when it reached his hands this afternoon. She was eager to learn if Dan also had surmised it correctly.

Later, Lula Mae and Burke went into town for supplies and to deliver her message to Milton. Rachel kept hoping Dan would arrive while the servants were gone so they could talk without concern of being overheard, which was her motive for sending the two servants on errands.

When she heard knocking at the front door, she rushed to respond with a bright smile on her face. She inhaled sharply when her gaze touched on two strangers with dark-brown hair and eyes—Cubans, she decided in panic, a day early for their confrontation and alone with her.

Chapter 18

The first man's gaze roved her from head to foot, but the glint in his dark eyes was appreciative not lecherous. He was tall and had a pleasant expression on his handsome face, but she was tense and scared. She remembered that the attacker with a knife had used a Spanish accent and words. She listened with increased alert and dread.

"Buenas tardes, señorita. I did not mean to startle you. We have come to see Señor McCandless," he said in fluent English, then smiled.

Rachel struggled to regain her stolen poise and wits. At least his voice did not match her past assailant's. "He isn't here," she responded as she glanced at the second man, who appeared to be sullen and menacing. She took an instant dislike to him, and waited anxiously to hear his voice.

"Where can we find him, señorita?" the first man asked, drawing her attention back to him. "Señor McCandless asked us to meet him here today. You have no reason to fear us. We are *amigos.* Friends," he clarified for her.

She realized her apprehensions were apparent. She tried to calm herself and clear her head to meet this challenge, as fear was not a weakness to expose to enemies who would pick at that raw spot.

"You hesitate and seem afraid, señorita. Why?"

"Phillip McCandless is dead. Didn't anyone in town tell you that when you asked for directions to his home?" She noted a mixture of shock and dismay at her disclosure. She couldn't help but release a sigh of relief that the client's cohorts hadn't known that fact, which meant they couldn't have committed that evil deed. At least that much of this situation was good.

"We did not need directions to his *plantación,* señorita. When did this happen? How? Who runs his . . . affairs?"

Rachel was alarmed again. "You've been here before? When?"

"Seven *semanas* . . . weeks ago. Who are you, señorita?"

She didn't know if she should believe him. "Phillip died seven weeks ago on Friday, March twenty-sixth. When did you see him?"

"We visited him on Tuesday of that week." As he repeated his earlier questions, his genial expression and tone vanished.

Rachel decided to play ignorant for a while to glean clues. "He died of cholera. I'm Mrs. McCandless, his widow. How can I help you? What did you want with my husband?"

"Our order, Señora McCandless."

She feigned confusion, but felt he had known from the start who she was. "I beg your pardon?" she said evocatively.

"Are you his *heredera,* his heir?"

She faked greater bewilderment. "Yes, of course. Why?"

"You own his three companies?"

"I inherited half of each one; Phillip had partners in all of them. Why are you asking me such private questions? Why should I answer you?"

"Do you handle Señor McCandless's shares?"

She stared at him, for effect. "Yes," she finally said.

414

"But I shan't tell you more, sir, until you explain what this is about. Who are you?"

"Carlos Torres. This is *mi amigo,* Joaquín Chavous."

Rachel eyed the handsome man, then the churlish one to his right. "I don't recall your names in my husband's books or from his lips. I know nothing of your past visit to our home, which I find strange."

"Señora McCandless was in town that day. He would not speak of us or our visit; our business was *secreto.*"

"Is this a personal or business matter?"

"This is very serious!" the second man snapped at her. "We are no fools!"

Rachel jumped, her eyes wide. She stared at him, but realized his voice discarded him as that suspect with an itchy blade.

"Relax, *amigo,*" Carlos advised his foul-tempered friend. "Forgive Joaquín's mood at your bad news, but our business is important."

"I don't like his rudeness, Mr. Torres, as I know of no reason for it. If you'll explain what kind of business you had with Phillip, perhaps I can help you; or perhaps I can send you to the right person. But if Mr. Chavous persists in behaving so badly, you must leave my home immediately." Rachel knew she couldn't play totally dumb, as too much money was involved for the matter to be dropped, especially by Joaquín Chavous. It was best to fake enlightenment when he clarified and to work on resolving the matter.

"We paid Señor McCandless a lot of money for rifles and bullets. He was to deliver them to us *mañana* for shipment. Can you help us?"

Rachel allowed her expression and response to reveal she might have known about that. "Was it a very large and confidential order? A secret one for ten thousand rifles, many cases of cartridges, and other goods?"

"*Sí*, Señora McCandless. You do know of our bargain?"

"A little, and it isn't good news, I'm afraid."

"What do you mean?" Carlos asked, narrowing his dark gaze.

"Since Phillip died, I've been trying to piece together this puzzle he left behind, but the clues have been confusing and scant. From what I've learned from his partners and from things my husband mumbled on his deathbed, after you gave Phillip the five-hundred-thousand-dollar advance on your contract, he hid it for safekeeping. At least his partners tell me they never received the money. You see, Phillip kept the deal a secret from all of us. I don't know if that was by your order, but it left us in ignorance. We don't even know who the client is, where the shipment is to go, or what your terms included." Rachel saw how the man was staring at her oddly, and she tensed in panic. Yet he didn't interrupt.

"While Phillip was dying, he mumbled something about money and guns, but he was too delirious to make sense. That's the first I knew about your secret deal, which wasn't much. I went to see his partners—here, in Augusta, and in Athens—but they claim they don't know more than that, either. All they know is how much ammunition and dynamite and how many guns you ordered, and that they were to be ready for shipment tomorrow, with the destination recorded as Haiti. Phillip wrote down two sets of initials in his shipping ledger: C. T. and J. C.; so that must be you two. His partners said he accepted the five-hundred-thousand-dollar advance, but he never gave it to them. I've searched everywhere, but I can't find where he hid the money. Is it true? Did you give him a big advance?"

"You lie!" Joaquín shouted at her, his features and tone harsh.

Rachel glared at the belligerent man. "I don't know

416

whose idea it was to keep your bargain a secret, but Phillip died without exposing it to me or to his partners. I have no reason to suspect them of deceiving me. In fact, they're all very upset about this predicament and about losing such a big order. I've tried to unravel this mystery, but how could I with so few clues? I was waiting until the client realized his shipment was late and came to me to resolve matters. I didn't know you were coming to get it. We are talking about the same contract, aren't we?"

"It is the same. But a . . . *predicamento?*" Carlos echoed skeptically, after his hand grasping Joaquin's arm firmly stayed the man's hot retort.

Rachel looked at him as if he must not understand that English word. "Of course, for all of us. You want arms and we need profits. Our companies can't fill your order without payment, and the advance can't be found."

"*Advance?*" Carlos echoed. His gaze locked onto hers in a piercing manner.

"You did pay him an advance, didn't you? Phillip hinted at receiving and hiding one while he was delirious; and his partners told me he had accepted one, but he never turned the money over to them. I told you, I searched for it many times and I can't find it."

"No, Señora Rachel, we paid him no *avance.*" He paused when she gave a loud sigh and smile of relief. He destroyed that happy reaction when he corrected, "We paid him *todo,* everything, *un millón de dólares.*"

"Please tell me that doesn't mean one million dollars," she urged.

"One million American *dólares.* We demand our arms immediately."

Rachel paled and trembled. "One million . . . Phillip had a million dollars of your money, not five hundred thousand?" Dread washed over her.

"*Sí,* Señora Rachel. We paid, so you owe us our

417

guns and bullets. It would be dangerous to keep our *dinero,* our money, and refuse to deliver our arms."

Rachel absorbed three points: he was using her first name now without having been told it, he was threatening her with a surly look and tone, and he never mentioned wanting the money returned. "I don't have your money, sir," she said, "and Phillip's partners won't comply without payment. I'm sorry my husband kept this deal a secret and hid your money, but that isn't my fault, nor that of his partners. Actually, I only have your explanation of the bargain, so I have no way of knowing if you're telling the truth. All of us were kept in the dark, so we're at a disadvantage. It's unfortunate that your payment is missing, but you can't expect us to hand over goods we don't have the resources to pay for. The orders are being made with hopes this deal can be saved with new terms. In fact, the ammunition should arrive soon. But the rifles won't be sent until Harrison Clements gets paid."

Carlos's voice and eyes were hostile as he said, "He has been paid."

"You mean, you gave the money to Phillip and him? But he told me—"

"We paid Señor McCandless; they are partners. Señor Clements is in our deal; he gave his word. It would be unwise for him to betray our trust. You must convince him to . . . comply."

"I've attempted to work it out several times. I tried to get them to agree to lowering our profit if you would accept less arms and cartridges than you ordered. To save this deal, we all have to be understanding and we have to cooperate. So far, he refuses to yield even a little."

"That is your *problema.*"

"Why is it mine? I didn't know about this deal until recently, and then only by chance. If Phillip had died sooner, I wouldn't know anything."

"You are the trusted wife and heir of Señor

McCandless. We know of the rumors about you, señora. Do not try to dupe us and steal our money. That would be foolish and deadly; your bite has less power than ours. The same is true for your partners. All of you are in this bargain. All of you are responsible, and must honor it. If you wish to live, Señora Raquel, to protect your family and holdings, do not betray us. Warn your partners of the recklessness of their decision. I will give you and them *una semana,* one week, until next Friday, to have our cargo loaded for shipment home. It better be good news I hear when next we meet, or all of you will suffer for your treachery, and so will those you love."

Rachel was terrified of his warnings, but she asked, "Why are you threatening me? Is this what you did when my husband backed out of your deal in February? Harry told me Phillip was going to cancel the contract, but changed his mind the day before he became ill and died. Did you commit those vicious crimes to scare him into changing his mind again?" Rachel listed the lethal and destructive incidents before she challenged, "Do you need arms so much you'd do such wicked things to get them? Is that why Phillip backed out, because he realized what kind of men you are?"

Carlos stared at her oddly, then said, "We did not know such things. When we came three times, it was to make our deal, to pay our advance, and to deliver the balance. We came, we did so, and we left. No one here was threatened or harmed by us."

She had an instinct Carlos was telling the truth. "If you didn't try to frighten and coerce Phillip, then who did?" *Harry?* she mused.

"I do not have answers for what I do not know."

With boldness and courage she had to force out, she asked, "Can you prove to me you paid Phillip? Do you have a signed contract or a receipt?"

"You have my word. It is true; you must accept it."

"I'm to accept your word, but you don't have to believe mine?"

"*Sí*, because you do not have much money at stake."

"You, not someone else, brought the money and made the deal?"

"*Sí*. We made no contract for the Spanish spies to find. We trusted your husband. He dared not trick us. The same is true for you."

Rachel tested his wickedness. "What if I go to the authorities and report this misunderstanding and your threats? What if you're arrested?"

Unaffected by her words, he said, "We have *muchos amigos,* Señora Raquel; that would be *estupido* and costly to you and the others. Even if we are murdered, others will take our places. They will not believe you, either."

"But I'm telling the truth!"

"Are you, Señora Raquel? It is *mucho dinero* and the temptation to keep it is great. Resist, or you will not live to spend it."

"That's what his partners think, too; that's why they're refusing to help me resolve your deal. I swear to you, as I've sworn to them, I don't have it and can't find it. If you wish, search for it yourselves."

"*No importa,* the bargain stands and must be honored, or—"

He didn't have to finish or translate for her to grasp his meaning. Still, she tried to bluff him. "What if I disappear so you can't harm me?"

"Will all you own and love disappear for protection from us? Will your family and friends, and companies be safe if you betray us? We know many things about you and the others; we learned before we made our deal with your husband. Your mother's name is Catherine Starger; your *casa* was White Cloud. You do not care if we slay your stepfather. Your servants are Lula Mae and Burke. Many others live and work your lands. Your husband had no family, but he was an *hombre* who cared for others. Many men work for your companies. We know about the other partners, too. If you escape with our money, we will not need to hunt you down to punish you; I promise that others will suffer for your treachery. Is this what you wish, for others to pay for your greed?"

"No, please don't harm any of them because of what you think about me. I don't have your money and I don't know how I can raise it to cover our expenses, but I'll try." She related all she knew and all the two partners claimed they knew about the mystery, but it seemed to have no favorable effect on the two Cubans. "To solve it, I have to know more. Maybe that will give us a clue to where the money is hidden; that's what's holding up the deal. Who is the buyer, the man who sent you to get arms? May I speak with him to try to reach a solution?"

"No. The deal stands as agreed, no changes or refusals."

"When was this deal made? And for what reason? How was it made? If you want me to solve this riddle, you have to fill in some pieces."

"As you wish, Señora Raquel. We met in January and made a bargain. The advance money was paid. The order was to be shipped *mañana*. In February, Señor McCandless insisted on the balance. We brought it to him seven weeks ago. The rebellion grows worse every month. We need those arms *pronto*. We are to escort the shipment to a . . . rendezvous point."

"Where? Why did Phillip record Haiti when Cuba is actually the destination?"

"You do not need that information. It does not change or affect your *problema*. What you do not know, you cannot reveal to spies if captured and questioned. We are at war. Freedom fighters protect their lives and cause and their *amigos.* Never trick or betray desperate *hombres,* Señora Raquel."

She did not refute his last statement, but registered it. "How did you choose Phillip? Maybe the man who got you together is holding the money for him. With his name, I can recover it and settle this quickly and safely."

"Ricardo does not have it; he is in Santiago de Cuba. Our *amigo* told us of weapons and ammunition companies here. We learned your husband owned both, and a shipping firm. He was the perfect choice. We talked and made a deal. We honored our part. Whatever it takes, you and the others will honor his. As a father is responsible for the actions of his child, you and the others are responsible for the actions of Señor McCandless."

It was futile to argue. "Can you give me a little more time to persuade his partners to agree, and time to get the arms here from the other two towns?" she asked. "I'm not trying to dupe you, but I can't work this problem out alone, or quickly. We have to figure out where to get the money to pay for supplies and shipping. We aren't rich people, Mr. Torres, and it's a lot of money."

Carlos studied her muted eyes for a moment, then spoke with his friend in Spanish, but the pugnacious Joaquín seemed to disagree strongly with him. Even so, he told her, *"Una semana,* one week, Señora Raquel. If you fail or if you go to the authorities, we will be forced to . . . persuade you and your *amigos* how unwise and dangerous that is. *Comprende?"*

"I understand. I'll try to do my best to—"

"Do not try, Señora Raquel, *do* it. Many lives depend upon you, here and in my country. We have been taught cruelty by our rulers; we will not hesitate to use it to win our freedom from oppression."

"I'm sorry about your country's sufferings, Mr. Torres, but I'm not to blame for them. I know what

422

war is like, what it is to lose loved ones; I felt those sacrifices many years ago. I know about the battle you've been fighting since '68, and, believe it or not, I hope you win. I wish my country didn't have to remain neutral . . . May I ask one more question?"

"Sí," he replied, and smiled.

"Is this deal legal? If we find a way to honor our part, can we get into serious trouble with the authorities here for selling to you?"

"If that is what frightens and stalls you, there is no American law against it. Your husband had a letter of clearance to ship us the arms."

"His partner told me he has a letter of clearance for customs, but I have to be certain it isn't illegal. If it is, you can threaten me all you want and I won't try to help you get your arms. I have enough troubles of my own without adding another one."

"It is *legal.* But it must be done . . . privately. *Comprende?"*

"Yes. A friend explained your fight for independence to me. He also told me about the ship Spain sank and the American sailors murdered. Can you assure us that won't happen again? I don't want to endanger my crew."

"It will not; you have my word. Answer me a question, Señora Raquel: What other troubles do you have, and will they interfere with our business?"

She knew they might hear the gossip in town, so it was best to try to ward off potential damage. "You said you knew of the rumors about me."

Carlos nodded, and she continued. "They aren't true. But the local authorities are investigating and watching me again. They aren't convinced Phillip died of cholera; they suspect me of killing him. They can't prove it, because I didn't. But that's partly why I couldn't go around asking questions about Phillip's mysterious deal and a lot of missing money; something like that would give them a motive they don't have. *Comprende?*"

"*Sí, señora,* but guilty or not is *no importa* to us, only the arms."

"It matters to me. I didn't kill him, and I don't have your money. If he hadn't died close to bankrupt, I would pay back your money and let his partners finish this deal with you. Right now, I'm in two predicaments, and I want out of both. Phillip left me almost penniless, so I can't repay you; and I can't allow that condition to give a false suspicion that I have your money. His desperate need for money must have been why he made a bargain with you. I didn't know he was facing financial ruin until I tried to straighten out his affairs, and it came as quite a shock. By then, if you care to check out my story, I had already been to see his partners about this mystery and the missing money. I know you'll kill me and destroy what little I have left if I don't help you. I would be a fool or crazy to want your money badly enough to steal it. I'm neither insane nor an idiot."

"That is *bueno,* Señora Raquel, as I would hate to burn down such a lovely *casa* as this and to kill such a beautiful woman."

"You would do that even though I'm blameless in all of this?"

Carlos glued his intentionally frigid gaze to her pleading one. "*Sí,* but it would pain me." He smiled as he coaxed, "Do not make me suffer for your foolishness and greed."

Rachel glared at him with a clenched jaw as she scoffed, "You don't believe a word of explanation I've given you!"

"It is *no importa* if I do or do not. My order is to return with our arms. If I cannot, those who stop me must die. I will do my duty."

She had no doubt he would do as he vowed. "It isn't fair to hold us responsible for a million dollars

424

we never received. We can't handle a loss that big. You're expecting us to pay for your arms out of our pockets when they're near empty and when we don't even have proof you paid Phillip. Why can't you help us resolve this matter so none of us will get hurt?"

"It is not our *problema, Señora* Rachel, but we will solve it."

In an insulting tone, she replied, "I'm sure you will. Where can I reach you when I have news?"

Carlos gave her a lopsided grin. "We will reach you next Friday. If you try to trap or kill us, the *amigos* who take our places will not be as kind and generous as Carlos Torres is being today. When I next lay eyes on this beautiful face, . . ." he began as he caressed her anger-flushed cheek.

Rachel halted his flattering words as she slapped away his disturbing hand and glared at him. She panted, "Don't you ever touch me!"

"Ah, a woman with fire, spirit, and courage. She would make a fine *compatriota,* would she not, Joaquín?" The bellicose man grunted and frowned. Carlos finished his interrupted statement, "When I next lay eyes on your beautiful face, *Señora* Raquel, have good news for me."

She glared at him more forcefully and icily. "I hope I have good news for both of us. I want this offensive matter settled fast and for good."

Carlos chuckled in amusement and admiration. "You are smart, so I do not doubt your success. *Adiós,* flame of my heart."

Rachel watched the two Cuban rebels gallop away as if born and reared in their saddles. She sank against the porch wall, closed her eyes, and exhaled loudly to release her tension. Afterward, she felt limp and shaky. She didn't know how she had gotten through the terrifying situation. She had no doubt those men were lethal. If only Dan were here . . .

Why isn't he? her troubled mind asked. He had left

her vulnerable at a terrible moment and he hadn't returned yesterday as promised. That had forced her to confront two dangerous enemies alone.

Old fears and doubts about him resurfaced to torment her. His absence today was convenient for her to be terrorized by those rebels. Was he one of them? The unknown client? Had his romantic pursuit and assistance been clever ruses to evoke what he believed was the awful truth about her, only an attempt to scare her into handing over the money she claimed she didn't have? Could she be so wrong about her love?

No, Rachel, you've judged a man right this time, she reassured herself. *He loves you and wants you. Something, perhaps bad weather, delayed his return. He'll be back soon and explain. Don't make a crime out of a simple mistake. Trust him. He's the only one who can and will help you.*

But how could even a strong, smart, and brave man like Daniel Slade defeat two dangerous rebels or the many Cubans who could replace them? Trying to save her from them could get him killed, as Carlos threatened, as those recent notes had warned. Yet, she couldn't go to the law for help. They wouldn't understand, or believe her, or help her. They would only think they had more charges to level against her: theft, fraud, gun-running, and probably more. She had no choice but to find a way to complete this deal, to save many lives.

Friday at noon, Rachel was sitting in Milton's office, a tangible strain in the air. She hadn't told her loyal servants about the Cubans' visit and she hadn't seen Daniel Slade yet. But she was determined to handle her troubles as best she could without endangering those she loved.

"I don't understand you, Rachel. What have I done to cause such hatred and spitefulness in you? I'm not

426

to blame for your grim situation, so why punish me as if I am? I thought we agreed to handle this as friends, but I was mistaken. Would you please explain?"

She noted the antagonism in his tone and in his green gaze, but for once she didn't fear it. "I don't hate you, Milton, and I'm not being vengeful or ridiculously stubborn. You told me that day, after you shocked me witless with your news, that you were sorry to take away my share of the firm but you had no choice. Well, I have no choice but to protect myself. You asked me to understand and accept your position; you owe me the same consideration. I have only your word that paper and loan are authentic. As you said, it's a lot of money—mine as well as yours. The whole thing doesn't make sense, especially the repayment date. Neither does your rush to shove me aside. You agreed to a week's extension, then announced your takeover the next day. How did you get that news to the paper so fast? The only way was early that morning before you even saw me. The whole time we were talking, you had no intention of honoring your word to me."

Milton scowled as he admitted, "You're right; I turned in the notice before our meeting. I had to submit it before their deadline. I thought it was impossible for our decision to go any other way, so why waste time? When it did, it was too late to stop release of my announcement."

"Why didn't you warn me about it? You thought I wouldn't see it? And why did you write me that hateful and demanding summons yesterday?"

"Because you broke your promise to come in and sign the paper. I was angry and worried."

"More accurately," Rachel refuted, "you were afraid I would get that contract payment today and not have to default before the deadline you gave me. Is there any way you can prove that loan agreement is genuine?"

"Any court will agree it's Phillip's signature and the terms are binding."

"Will it, Milton? Are you absolutely positive?" To her, he looked nervous when she countered his statement without blinking an eye in fear.

"Did Frank Henley tell you otherwise?"

"I haven't seen him yet. I wanted to speak with you first. Neither of us wants trouble and a scandal at this delicate time."

"That's accurate. What do you suggest is fair?"

She noticed but ignored his sarcastic tone and look. "I've already met with that mysterious client, but the balance won't be paid until delivery of goods," she lied. "Harry's balking on his part. As soon as I convince him to cooperate, the cargo can sail and we'll be paid. After that, you'll be paid."

Wide-eyed he asked, "You still want to remain as my partner?"

"Don't look so horrified. Being a silent and secret partner to protect business and to entice clients suits me fine."

"It doesn't suit me fine, Rachel. It could destroy this firm."

"Are you forgetting who owned the biggest company before you two merged? Forgetting who obtained most of the firm's clients?"

"Phillip never worked any harder than I did! Probably even less!"

Rachel was vexed by his resentment of Phillip. "You've lost another client, Milton. You can cancel the ship for Haiti today. The deal is on delay. But when it's ready, my client wants Captain Daniel Slade of the *Merry Wind* to deliver it. He's offered them a cheaper price and a faster voyage."

Milton jumped to his feet in outrage. "You can't do that to me!" he shouted at her. "I need that contract. Phillip and I had a deal."

With a serene tone, she said, "Show me a signed

contract with my client and I'll tell him he must honor it."

Milton sat down. "I don't have one, and you know it!"

"Do I? It seems there is a lot I wasn't told by you, Harry, George, and even Phillip. I'm weary of secrets that have damaged me emotionally and financially. From now on, I'm fighting back against anyone or anything who tries to hurt me. If you're so confident you can win our dispute, take me to court and prove it." She saw Milton go pale and shaky.

"My God, you're serious! You'd fight this, right or wrong!"

"You're damn right I will!" she replied crudely to prove she was determined. "Push me into another pit and I'll claw myself out fighting."

Milton gaped at her in disbelief and alarm. He jumped up and paced as he reasoned on the matter. Finally he turned to her and said, "To save my firm and to prevent a nasty scandal, if you'll agree to stay a silent and secret partner, I'll grant you another extension. But only until your mystery deal is settled, one way or another. That's as far as I'll go. Agreed?"

Now she gaped at him. He had backed down. Maybe Dan was right about a ruse. Maybe Milton was running scared after being challenged. "I accept," she said to stall for more time to unmask him, as surely Dan knew how. "If you put aside the relinquishment paper for a while, I won't bring the court or Mr. Henley into our dispute."

"This time should I get your promise in writing and witnessed?"

She didn't let him get away with his sarcasm. "If you like. It might be a good idea, so you won't renege on my extension again."

"I was only joking."

Rachel knew his laughter and smile were forced. "I hope so."

"Who is this mysterious client?"

She stood and straightened her skirt. "I can't tell you."

"Why not? One of those secrets you said you despise?"

"No, my client insists on confidentiality. Sorry."

"I see. It doesn't matter to me who he is. Settle this fast, Rachel."

"You can bet I will. Good-bye, Milton. I'll send you news soon."

"I hope so, Rachel, and I hope it's good . . . Oh, yes, a load arrived earlier this morning by train from George Leathers. It's stored in our south warehouse."

"Thank you. I'll tend to it soon. If I were you, Milton, I would put a guard on the order. You don't want anything happening to it while it's in your care, just in case the client decides to use your shipping firm. You do recall those break-ins we had a few months ago. My client wouldn't be happy if anything happened to his ammunition. He doesn't seem to be a man you'd want to cross or disappoint."

"I'll take care of it immediately."

"That's most wise. Besides, another vandalism wouldn't look good to our clients."

"I promise you, it will be safe."

"I'll hold you to your word of honor. Good afternoon, Milton."

Outside the door, she congratulated herself on her success, thanks to Dan's clever suggestions. First, she had to send telegrams to George and Harry to update them. Second, she wanted to ride to Factor's Row to see if Dan's ship could be sighted. She wished she had thought of that sooner, as she was eager for his return. But if he was in port and hadn't seen her yet, she would have to discover why not.

* * *

Rachel stared at the sleek clipper anchored at the end of the docking area, almost concealed from view by numerous other ships. She wondered if it was an intentional action. She was tempted to board the *Merry Wind* to confront Captain Daniel Slade about his curious behavior. She decided to return home to await his imminent visit and needed explanation, whenever it came and whatever it might be.

Chapter 19

Rachel halted to await the rider coming toward her from Moss Haven. As he reined in beside her, she noticed Dan's look of concern.

"Please tell me you didn't get a message and went to meet with that mysterious client alone," he entreated.

"No, I've been to see Milton. Where have you been? You're late."

"A storm held up our sailing and slowed us again during the voyage. I docked a short time ago and rented a horse to come see you. Don't you know how dangerous it is to travel alone? Why didn't you take Burke? For heaven's sake, Rachel, some culprit's been inside and around your house many times; you certainly aren't safe out here by yourself."

"Everybody wants me to carry off this deal, so I'm safe. Those threats are to scare, not injure, me. I was hoping you were in town by now and we could have privacy. Let's get out of sight before someone comes along."

As they led their horses into cover of the dense woods, Dan refuted, "Even from the writer of those love notes? Neither of us believes it's the same villain. For certain he's crazy and dangerous. Don't do anything like this again, woman, or I'll lock you in my cabin to protect you. Understand?"

Rachel grinned in pleasure, caressed his tense face, and coaxed, "I've done fine on my own, so stop worrying so much."

"That's all I've done since I left last week. It was a stupid oversight not to leave one or two of my men here to guard you. I will next time."

Rachel smiled and thanked him. "Your bluff worked with Milton," she told Dan. "He was furious, but he says he'll wait for repayment until after this deal is settled. But he insists on keeping McCandless off the firm's name." She related the shipping partner's motive and her agreement.

"That's all right for a while, but not permanently. It won't be necessary once you're cleared of all accusations and the truth is exposed to everyone." Dan was positive the detective he had hired would unmask Baldwin soon. If the loan agreement was forged, maybe the same deft hand had written those notes to Rachel, which would solve two pressing matters. "Anything else happen while I was gone? Lula Mae said you haven't had any visitors today, so the client isn't wise to trouble with his order yet."

Rachel saved that shocking news until last. She told him about the house being rocked again, about their pictures being stolen and the note left behind during church, and about her mother's visit. Before he could reprimand her again for being out alone after those new incidents, she hurried on to reveal her other news. "I don't know why Earl didn't tell her about Phillip's death, but he must have wanted me to handle that unpleasant task for him. He had no idea she was coming to visit me, but he thinks I might go home during his absence. Mama's doing much better, Dan. But she did tell me Earl hasn't been away from home on those days I've gotten threats. It was obvious she was telling the truth, so he can't be to blame."

"I almost wish he were, so we could resolve part of the trouble."

"I felt the same way," she admitted. "I sent George a telegram to thank him; the ammunition was delivered this morning. Milton's having it guarded in our warehouse. I told George I'm working on new terms with the client. I have to make sure he doesn't get hurt financially helping me."

"I'll have the cases stored aboard my ship for safekeeping. We can't afford for anything to happen to that part of the order."

"That's a splendid idea. Thanks. I telegraphed Harry, too, but I don't expect any help or understanding from him. I told him to send me that clearance letter for customs to see if it holds any clues, and I practically begged him to send along some rifles to appease our client for a while."

"I've already sent Harry the money I made on the New Orleans voyage to buy another hundred rifles and gear. Added to what I've already ordered, it'll come to almost three thousand. If we can find ways to get up to five thousand, that'll cover the half Phillip was paid for. If this deal is legal, we can complete the rest of it and collect the balance."

"I'm afraid not, Dan. Phillip accepted the full million dollars, and our client sent men to pick them up; two Cubans visited me yesterday. I have a one-week reprieve. Besides, it isn't fair for you to buy arms to get us out of this mess; Harry and George are just as involved as I am. I can't let you invest in a deal that has no return profit. If the two companies can't come up with the money or goods, then we have to face the consequences. Harry will let you spend every penny you have getting him out of peril, but I can't. And I doubt the client will settle for five thousand or less arms when he's paid for ten. Don't you see, a million dollars makes renegotiations and reneging impossible? We can't even come up with five hundred thousand worth!"

As Dan held silent and stared at her, Rachel related

434

the scary meeting in detail. "They said they haven't threatened Phillip or me, yet. Dangerous as they seem, I believe them. I bet Harry's behind all the threats, he wants this deal to go through no matter what. He thinks if he scares me badly enough, I'll 'find' that money and turn it over to them."

"Stars above, woman, you could have been killed! I shouldn't have left you alone. I have to sail again Sunday, but two men will remain here to protect you and I'm leaving Luke behind to do some snooping around. It's a bigger offer than the last trip, and we need the money for more guns. Don't argue with me; I'm not doing this to help the companies or your partners. My only concern is for your safety and survival. Crossing rebels is dangerous. Three orders from me should give us enough to bargain with, and we have George's ammo. If you, Harry, and George will cut your profits or cancel them, we may get enough to satisfy . . ." He halted and frowned. "No, not with a million paid. If it was only the advance involved and we could get together half of the order, this trouble could have been settled next week."

Rachel held silent as Dan slipped into deep thought to study the new developments. He was so clever that he might come up with something.

"I still need to go to Charleston, love. I want to see if I can find someone who might be holding the money for Phillip and doesn't know he's dead. I'll check with his old family lawyer and friends."

"That's a clever idea. See if anyone knows where his personal effects are stored. We might find a clue in them."

"I'll check out everything that comes to mind. I'll return in a few days, storm or no storm! You stay inside with doors locked and a gun handy this time. Promise?" He pulled her into his arms and kissed her. He was eager for the day when she became Mrs. Daniel Slade McCandless. "Is it too soon to propose again, woman?"

Rachel was taken by surprise, but kept her wits clear. "Yes. I can't think about another marriage right now. Even if I didn't have all these problems looming over me, I've been a widow for less than two months. Can't you imagine how people would react if I wed again soon?"

"What do we care what they say or think?" Dan quipped.

"I shouldn't and, if I were guilty, I wouldn't; but I'm not and I do. Besides, think of how a swift romance and marriage will appear to the law."

"You're right; I hadn't considered that. I forget we're both still under investigation. Any word from the authorities about your case?"

"None. I don't know if that's good or bad."

"It's a good sign, love. If they had any clues to work on, they would. They just don't want to tell you this soon you've been cleared again." Dan pulled her into his embrace and stroked her silky hair. "I know it's been hard on you, love, but stay strong and brave."

"I will; I have you to make certain I do. Thanks for everything, Dan. You're doing so much to help me and protect me."

He chuckled. "Because I'm selfish. I'm only thinking of myself. I love you and want you. The only way I can have you is to get you free of this mess first. If that costs me money, so what? I can always earn more, but I can't find another Rachel McCandless if I let something happen to you."

The happy woman nestled her cheek to his chest and listened to the steady drumming of his heart. "You're the most wonderful man alive."

Dan grasped her chin and lifted it. He sealed their gazes, then their mouths. Rachel responded, as she needed his comfort and touch. Soon, both were aroused by desires that craved to be sated.

Rachel struggled to regain her self-control. She dragged her lips from his with reluctance. "I'm sorry, Dan, but I can't make love here. I've been shot at twice not far away. Too many forces could be spying on us this very minute. I couldn't relax and . . ."

Dan hugged her tightly and murmured, "I understand, love. I'll escort you home, then get back into town. I want to see if I can locate those Cubans. Maybe I can learn more than you did from them. I'll get my ship loaded tomorrow, then sail at dawn Sunday. I'll see you as soon as I return. Don't forget; I'll have two of my men camped nearby to guard you."

Saturday, Rachel received a response from her telegram to Harry. He said he would send Dan's two orders on schedule, but he still refused to send any arms without payment, regardless of threats to her. The angered woman wondered if he would feel and do the same if he were receiving those threats. If he kept refusing, the hostile rebels might comply!

By Thursday, Rachel was becoming apprehensive. Things had been quiet since last Friday, maybe too quiet, she worried. After all that had happened recently, it was a nice, but suspicious, reprieve. Perhaps no new incidents had taken place because of the two men Dan had left behind, who were camped in the woods near her home.

Late that afternoon, one of them came to the house to tell Rachel his captain was waiting for her at the place they last met. She saddled her horse and galloped to the location in the concealing woods; this time, she tried to make certain she wasn't followed by backtracking, hiding, and other ploys. She slid off the animal's back into Dan's inviting arms.

"Lordy, how I've missed you," she murmured.

"And I've missed you, woman."

They kissed, embraced, and caressed until they were breathless and aroused. Before exchanging news, they had to share passions. Garments were cast aside, and they sank to the leafy earth to make love.

As Dan buttoned his shirt, he said, "I placed a third order with Harry today for another hundred fifty rifles. It's strange, love, but Luke hasn't been able to find a single clue to those rebels. You'd think two Cubans would stand out like gale clouds on a clear day. It's as if they vanished into a fog. Or they're hiding for protection. Luke couldn't even find the ship they came in on. You're the only one who's seen them."

"They certainly weren't figments of my imagination. They're only lying low until tomorrow. What did you learn in Charleston?"

"Nothing, I'm afraid. If Phillip's contact was there, I couldn't find him. I didn't pick up any possessions from anybody while I was there."

"I was hoping and praying you'd return with that money. Where can it be, Dan? You can't hide a million dollars just anywhere."

"I don't know, love; I wish I did. Don't be upset or discouraged."

"I don't like you earning money just to—"

He silenced her with a finger to her lips. "No more talk about that. Besides, we need bait for our trap. I may not have to pass them along. If not, I can sell them elsewhere and recover my investment."

"Keep a few for evidence. If Harry . . . That's it, Dan! I'll blackmail the sorry bastard. If he doesn't hand over those arms, I'll expose him for stealing and using registered patents. He'll have to cooperate."

"Don't go threatening him alone, woman. Desperate men are—"

"I know. *Dangerous*. But I'll finally get that snake. I should have thought of this sooner. I'll telegraph him tomorrow before we meet with the Cubans. This should gain another reprieve for Harry to get the arms here—at least part of them." She hugged and kissed him in her ecstasy. "At last, a good-luck charm. You, Daniel Slade."

Rachel and Dan responded to the message she received about a meeting five miles from the plantation. They reached the location, dismounted, and joined the two men who eyed them with wariness.

Carlos remarked, "You came with protection Señora Raquel, but it is not needed. What news do you bring? When do we sail?"

"There's been—"

"No, señor, she is the only one to speak," Carlos interrupted Dan.

When the blue-eyed American started to argue, Rachel stayed his retort with a gentle grasp on his arm and a smile. "I'll handle everything. This is Captain Daniel Slade of the *Merry Wind;* he's the one who'll deliver your arms when they're finished. We expect part of the order on Monday and the rest a week later. We should be underway by the first of June."

Carlos frowned. "That is not our agreement, Señora Raquel."

"Your verbal contract was with Phillip, Mr. Torres; he's dead and your payment is missing, so I'm doing the best I can to honor his part of the bargain. Either wait while I do, or take whatever action you wish. If you kill me or cause me more trouble, you won't get your *armas* or your *dinero. Comprende?*" she asked in a terse tone.

Carlos's scowled deepened, and he had to calm a riled Joaquín before he responded. "You are the one who does not understand, Señora Raquel. You are not in a position to threaten or to betray us. Do not try to do so."

"I'm not; I was merely giving you good advice for all our sakes."

"Look, she's doing everything she can to comply. She's paid for all she's ordered out of her own pocket, and I've agreed to ship them free as a favor to an old friend. She isn't the problem; her partners are. They're the ones balking. You can't blame them, either; they never got paid."

"How do we know that is true, *capitán?* We do not have our *dinero* or our goods. We will not sail without one or the other."

"Then give me another ten days to comply," Rachel entreated. "What harm can it do? I've tried to come up with money to cover our expenses, but I'm almost broke. All three of Phillip's companies are near bankruptcy, so are worth nothing. The bank refused to grant me a loan. Even if I sell my home, it will take time. What more do you suggest?"

"As I told you before, Señora Raquel, that is not our *problema.*"

"It shouldn't be mine! So give me the extension I need."

"We will think on it and contact you as soon as possible. Do not fail us, or you and others will *sufrir.* Do not *considere* it, *capitán,*" Carlos warned Dan as his fingers curled around the butt of his pistol. "Joaquín is swift and accurate. We have need of your ship and skills, so do not make him slay you. Even so, we have reported to our *lider.* If our next *comunicación* is late or missing, others will come to slay and destroy, not talk as we have done. To kill us will not end the threat to her; it will make it *peor,* worse."

"Don't threaten or scare her again," Dan warned in a frigid tone.

"Ah, so that is the *situación,*" Carlos murmured as he eyed the couple with a knowing grin. "If you wish to save her for yourself, *capitán,* do as we say. You will hear from us soon. *Adiós, amigos.*"

Rachel and Dan watched the two *rebeldes cubanos* depart.

"Damn! I should have had a man watching so he could follow them before they disappear again. We have to find a way out of this trap, love. They'll do what they threatened without remorse or hesitation."

"I know, Dan; that's why I hate for you to be involved. Maybe that telegram to Harry will work in our favor. At least it'll give us enough arms to bargain with. I'd love to see the look on his face when he reads it."

Saturday passed without the anticipated response from Harrison Clements, and Rachel was bewildered. She couldn't believe her blackmail threat didn't panic him into doing as she asked; no, *demanded.* She decided either he must be in Atlanta with his new business and hadn't gotten her shocking message or he was on the way there to challenge her.

Sunday afternoon, Rachel and Dan were strolling outside when two men arrived, the same investigators who had interrogated her after Phillip's death. Rachel tensed as she feared it was about that unresolved matter and the culprit stalking her had found a cunning way to incriminate her after all.

She tried to appear calm. "What can I do for you gentlemen today?"

The officer focused on Rachel. "Chief Anderson asked us to come out and ask you a few questions as a favor to the police chief in Augusta, to save him a trip to Savannah. Do you mind speaking with us, ma'am?"

"Of course not, but I'm confused. What does the Augusta police chief want to know from me?"

"Who murdered George Leathers and why?"

Rachel paled and shuddered. Chillbumps raced over her body. Her heart began to race and she wanted to faint. "George . . . is dead? How? When?"

"Yesterday. Someone blew up the company you two own. He and a worker were killed. One of his men said you were asking suspicious questions recently about explosions and fires. Why was that, ma'am?"

Rachel panicked. "You think I had something to do with his death?"

"Just answer the question, please."

She was tempted to refuse. "Considering the business we're in, they were normal worries, sir. He was giving me and Dan a tour of the factory and mentioned the dangers. I merely asked if we had safety measures and insurance to cover any problems. As a new partner trying to learn the business, why would my concerns seem odd to anyone?"

"When there's never been . . . an accident before, then one happens shortly after your visit and curiosity, it does, ma'am."

"I haven't been there since last month, over three weeks ago. You know when I went; I asked your permission, remember?"

"Yes, I recall our talk. How long have you known Mr. Leathers?"

Don't volunteer more information than he asks for, Rachel; be honest, but brief and careful. "Since I married Phillip."

"How many times have you seen him?"

"Three, with Phillip last Christmas and twice since he died."

"Did you like him?"

"He was a fine gentleman and good partner."

"Do you know if he had any enemies who'd want him dead?"

"How could I? We live too far apart and see little of each other. Our only connection is business. As I told you, I've only seen him a few times. Who would want to kill such a good-natured, kind, and genial man? I can't imagine him having enemies. Are you certain it wasn't an accident? George said gunpowder was volatile, that any impact or spark could set it off."

"No accident, ma'am. Dynamite and gunpowder were used deliberately. If I recall, you were having trouble with your two partners, suspected them of cheating you, and that's why you rushed off to see them before taking time to report your husband's . . . untimely demise."

Rachel remembered the deceit she had used in that conversation. "As I told you that day, on the first visit, neither partner would allow me to check the books without Phillip's permission. When I called on them after they knew of his death, both men permitted me to see all records. I found nothing to arouse my suspicions about any misdealings, and both men accepted my motive for tricking them earlier. I don't know why Phillip mistrusted them, but his fears were groundless."

"Where were you during the last two days?"

"I visited the telegraph office in town Friday; you can confirm that with the operator. I was home yesterday, and have several witnesses to verify my presence. There is no way I could have gotten there and back."

"She was here all day," Dan concurred, having held silent to listen and observe, and to make his presence again less noticeable.

"You were a witness for her last time. Do you stay around much?"

"I've been on trips to Charleston and New Orleans for most of the last two weeks. I returned Tuesday. I saw Rachel on Friday, and two of my men have been camped nearby since last Sunday. You can verify my movements with the port authorities, and you can question my men about hers."

"Why are they staying here?"

"Because somebody has been trying to terrorize her by playing cruel pranks. She's had her home rocked twice, things stolen from inside, been shot at, and had ugly words painted on her front porch."

"Why didn't you report those incidents, ma'am?"

"What good would it do? Even if you believed me, you couldn't help. We never saw the culprit or culprits involved."

"Probably just perverse pranks. They'll stop when things settle down soon."

"They *have* stopped since Dan kindly left his men nearby for protection . . . What other suspects do you have for George's murder?"

"None. Nobody saw a thing. The place is a total loss. I'm afraid you've lost that part of your inheritance. No insurance, either."

"What?"

"No insurance, ma'am. Didn't you know that?"

"George told me it was expensive, but he never said there wasn't any."

"So you were expecting a payoff?"

"How could I, when I didn't know about the destruction until just now? What about Molly Sue, George's wife? How is she?"

"I don't know, but the Augusta chief said Mr. Leathers had private insurance, so she won't be hurt like you are."

"That's not as important as George's death. Is it all right if I go visit her?"

444

"Chief Anderson doesn't want you to leave town at present. He's having a few curious matters checked out."

Rachel tried not to show her anxiety. "What matters?"

"Police business, ma'am."

"You will notify me when I can travel?"

"Yes, ma'am. You two are spending a lot of time together, eh?"

"Is it against the law to see friends and business clients?" Dan asked.

"Ah, yes, I recall; you're waiting for orders. Seems you're out of the Augusta one. Too bad. When will the Athens order come?"

"Tomorrow, if all goes as scheduled."

"Then you'll be sailing? Or staying to replace your loss elsewhere?"

"It arrived Friday, as contracted, if you'd care to verify that, too."

"How convenient for you."

Dan's reply was sharp and frosty. "Yes, it was."

"We'll be seeing you again soon, ma'am."

"I hope not, except to tell me you've found George's murderer and you've closed my other file."

"Mr. Leathers' murder isn't our case, ma'am. But if you think of anything that might be helpful, contact me in town."

Rachel and Dan noticed the officer didn't comment on her case before departing with his friend, who hadn't spoken a single word.

"Do you think the Cubans did it?" she asked in trepidation.

"They know their ammo is safe here, so it could be to scare you and Harry. But it seems crazy for them to move against any of you at this point."

"Should I have revealed that predicament to the police?"

"No, at least not yet; they might not be connected.

Even if they are, we don't have any evidence to provide to help them catch the killer; and we could get ourselves into big trouble unnecessarily. I promise you, if the rebels are to blame, they'll be punished."

"Poor Molly Sue. I'll send her a condolence cable tomorrow. I can't explain to her why I'm not coming to the funeral of my partner, so, unless they told her I'm a suspect, she'll be hurt and confused."

"I doubt it, and she would never believe you harmed him."

"Why do people keep dying around me? I'm such bad luck."

"Calm down, love; this isn't your fault."

"With George dead, will I be responsible for all the company debts?"

"I don't think so. We'll ask your lawyer tomorrow."

"That's all I need, more trouble and debts! Damn, Rachel!" she instantly scolded herself. "What's the matter with you? George is dead; Molly Sue is hurting; and you're worried about yourself!"

"This has been a shock, love, so it's normal not to think sensibly."

"Is it, Dan? Sometimes I think I'm. . . . Let's have a stiff drink to get rid of our tension."

Monday, Dan came to tell Rachel his two orders from Athens arrived by rail: 2,960 rifles with attachments. He had stowed them aboard the *Merry Wind* for safety, and placed guards on duty around the clock.

A telegram was delivered while they chatted. A furious Harrison Clements challenged Rachel to come to his office to examine the licenses he had purchased giving their company permission to use those patented designs on the weapons he was making. He offered to sell her his share of the arms company and vowed he would not stay in business with such an "underhanded and unstable woman." He told her the customs letter was being sent to her, but no weapons at his expense were forthcoming, or were *ever* coming. "Don't ever threaten me again," he ended the communication.

Rachel glanced at Dan and said, "I hope the local authorities don't get hold of this telegram; I can imagine how it could damage me if anything happened to Harry or how it will make him look guiltless if this deal gets nasty and exposed. He may have licenses, but how do we know they're genuine? I'm going to call his bluff like I did Milton's!"

"Be careful with him, love. He's dangerous and unpredictable. As for us, we'd better put a little distance between us for a while. We don't want the law or our enemies guessing the truth about us. I'll see you Friday night, unless something happens and you send for me. I'll leave my men here."

Thursday, a man arrived by train with several papers from Harry. He hadn't halted along the route to sleep, so he wanted to rush his task and leave for a local hotel to collapse.

Rachel eyed the clearance paper for customs and decided it was authentic. She looked over the licenses to use those patented designs for weapons, as the man was ordered to let her examine them and for him to return them to Harry. They, too, appeared legal and in order. To forge handwriting and papers would be a simple task for a trained hand, but making fake seals to use on the two documents would not. It seemed that nothing illegal was involved in the arms deal. She must have been mistaken. If the payment could be found and the deal finalized, she would earn a fat and needed profit and no risks would be taken, but that was a big *if*.

The messenger took the papers she handed to him and left for town.

Rachel opened the remaining letter. She was alarmed by what she read: there had been a fire at the company and one worker had been slain. The damage was minor and wouldn't shut down or slow down business. Harry had posted armed guards for protection, and he knew of George's murder. He begged her to find and deliver the Cubans' money so the contract could be fulfilled before they were murdered! He closed by informing her that Dan's third order would arrive Monday, along with thirty extra rifles from him.

Later, Earl Starger paid her a surprise visit, having returned from Boston. The relaxed and smiling man handed Rachel one of the jewels she had sold to Adam Meigs, which was then purchased by Camellia Jones. "She was on the ship with friends going on holiday. She boasted of how you'd had to sell many pieces for support. It angered me, Rachel, so I talked her into letting me buy this one. I said it was for my wife, but I want you to have it as a peace token, along with this . . ." He placed the brooch and an envelope in her hand before she could withdraw it. "It's only a thousand dollars, but it'll help out until you get your problems settled."

Rachel shook her head and held the items out to him. "I don't want anything from you. I can manage fine on my own."

Earl refused to take back the money and diamond pin. "Consider them gifts from your mother for Christmases missed. Don't be proud and stubborn, Rachel. Taking money from family is less embarrassing than facing financial ruin and public ridicule. If you insist, think of it as a loan and repay it when you can. Don't create another scandal or more hardship for yourself at this difficult time." He changed the subject. "Did you go see Catherine during my absence?"

"No, I invited her to Moss Haven, and she came for a few days. We had a wonderful time, and she's doing much better. Why didn't you tell her you visited me twice? And why didn't she know about Phillip's death?"

"I thought you should tell her the bad news when you saw her. There was no need, in her ill condition, to have her worried over you longer than necessary. I should have told you she didn't know, but I forgot during our last quarrel. Have there been any problems about Phillip's death while I was gone?"

"None, but the case isn't closed yet. When did you dock?"

"Tuesday evening. I had business in town yesterday. I'm heading home after I leave here. Have you seen today's newspaper or heard from your Athens partner?"

"Why?"

"There's an article about trouble there yesterday. I also heard what happened with the Augusta company last week. What's going on, Rachel? Do you need help and protection? Can I hire a guard to watch over you?"

"Why do you ask that?"

"Before I left weeks ago, you mentioned getting threats. I admit I wasn't sure they were genuine, but the attacks on your companies tell me they are. Something's amiss, girl. If you need help or more money, tell me. That's all I have with me today, but I can send more. It won't obligate you to me. I only want to keep you out of more trouble and danger, I don't think Catherine could stand losing another child."

She told herself not to be fooled by his seemingly sincere worry. To prevent a nasty scene, she said, "Thank you for your concern and offer, Earl, but I'm

449

fine. Please keep this news from Mama, if you can. The police should have those crimes solved soon. Besides, I'm perfectly safe; an old friend of Phillip's—Captain Daniel Slade—is in town on business." She watched for a reaction to Dan's identity, but saw none. "He has two of his crewmen protecting me at all times. Whoever was threatening me or playing pranks can't get near me anymore. I wish they would, so they could be unmasked and punished. I reported those incidents to the police, but there isn't anything they can do."

"It's good to know you're safe. You be careful, and I'll tell Catherine you're fine. Good-bye, Rachel. Contact us if you need anything."

"Good-bye, Earl, and thank you."

As a relieved Rachel observed her stepfather's departure, Lula Mae said from behind her, "That's the first time you two ain't fussed lack bitter enemies. What did he want?"

She related the gist of their talk, then handed the housekeeper the money. "Put it in the cashbox. We'll need it next week for bills."

"You took money from him? I cain't believe it. You hate him."

Rachel gave a heavy sigh. "I had no choice. I'll repay it later, even if I have more of a right to White Cloud earnings than that Yankee does."

"You two made peace?"

"Heavens, no. But I wasn't in a mood to quarrel with him. He'll never change, but he didn't harass me as usual, so no harm in being nice and sweet."

The following day was filled with more surprises. Rachel answered the door to find a man who introduced himself as an insurance broker from Macon.

"I came to give you this, ma'am." He handed her a packet of money. "As per Mr. McCandless's orders,

450

if anything happened to him, I was told to deliver this hundred thousand dollars to you in cash. I'm sorry this visit took so long, but I just learned of his demise. If you'll sign this release form, the insurance money is yours and I can get on my way home before the last train leaves."

"I don't understand. I didn't know Phillip had a policy with you."

"He took it out in February and paid the cost through June. Mr. George Leathers had a policy with us, too. When I saw his wife Tuesday, she told me Mr. McCandless had died in March. Your husband's instructions were, in the event of his death to bring your payment in cash."

"This is most unexpected, sir, and greatly needed. Thank you."

After she read and signed the form, the broker left. Rachel stared at the bills in her grasp, wishing it were the missing million dollars. She wanted to keep the money for expenses, but it was more important to buy guns, to save her life and those of others. She hurriedly freshened up, took one of the seamen as a guard, and went to see Dan in town.

"You sure you want to spend this on more weapons?" he asked.

"As you said with your money, our lives are more important. I'll telegraph Harry that the money's on the way; he has guns made and waiting, so he can ship them immediately, before our next meeting with those rebels."

"I'll take it to him myself, so we'll be certain he gets it and obeys. If I don't stop off anywhere and nap on the train, I can be there tomorrow."

Dan sent Luke Conner to Central Station to check on the rail schedule. While his best friend was gone, Rachel told Dan about the letter earlier this week

451

from Harry and about Earl Starger's—pleasant for a change—visit. They discussed how Dan was to handle Harry.

When the first mate returned, he told Dan he had two hours to pack and get aboard, then handed his friend the ticket he had purchased.

"Good, that's gives us time to visit your lawyer, Rachel, to check on your position in the Augusta company. I think, if the company folds, with the books destroyed and George dead, you aren't responsible for its debts. We'll see. I hope so; that will take one worry off your mind. If I were you, I would get rid of my share of that Athens company fast before it leads to trouble. I know that leaves you with only the plantation for support, but don't worry; I'll take care of you. And you might get the shipping firm back if all goes well with our investigation. We'll work on it after this matter is resolved. Luke, I want you to stay near Rachel while I'm gone in case those surly Cubans approach her again."

After Dan left on the train, Luke and Rachel headed for the plantation in her carriage. Along the way, he remarked, "I'm delighted to finally meet the woman who's going to change my life."

"What do you mean?" she asked the brown-haired man who, as Dan had said, always appeared about to burst into a broad grin.

Luke Conner chuckled and his azure gaze mellowed. "You've stolen my best friend's eye and he's determined to settle down with you."

She didn't know what to say, so she hinted, "Settle down with me?"

"He has proposed, hasn't he?"

"Yes, but I haven't accepted. It's too soon."

The first mate's eyes took in her exceptional beauty. "You will. Dan never takes no as an answer to something he wants. I'm going to become the captain of the *Merry Wind* while you two stay home and create a family."

"Family? Dan wants children?"

"What man doesn't? You two will have beautiful babies."

Rachel realized it was time to remind Dan that she might not be fertile. If he was being dreamy-eyed about children, she had to impress upon him the possible truth. If he were not serious about her, Dan wouldn't have mentioned her and a future together to his best friend.

"Did I say something wrong or upsetting, Rachel?"

She smiled at Luke and said, "Of course not. Your remarks just caught me off guard. When a stranger woos a woman, she doesn't always know how serious or honest he's being. I guess this talk means he's both."

"Daniel Slade is the most sincere and trustworthy man I know. I hope you feel the same way about him that he feels about you. I wouldn't want him to get hurt. He's my best friend, my captain, and like a brother to me. You do love him and want to marry him, don't you?"

Rachel glanced at the handsome and genial man. True, he was being bold and nosy, but only out of love and concern for his friend. "I shouldn't be thinking about such things, Luke. Phillip was Dan's good friend and my husband. He's only been dead for two months, the same amount of time I've known Dan. I don't want to rush this attraction between us, and I don't want to risk more gossip about my marrying before Phillip's body is cold. You should advise Dan to slow down and get to know me better before he makes such a serious decision about his future. You know I'm still under investigation; if Dan and I look as if we've gotten too close too fast, the law could suspect us of doing away with Phillip. That might sound crazy and impossible to you, but it isn't when I'm involved. I don't want him hurt in any way."

"I understand, Rachel, but Dan will take care of everything for you."

"You've helped him investigate me and you've met me. Do you think I'm capable of being a Black Widow? Do you think I'm guilty?"

Luke fused his azure gaze to hers. "No, Rachel, I don't."

"Not even in the beginning?"

"I had doubts, but was never totally convinced," he admitted.

"I appreciate your honesty, Luke."

"Relax and let us take care of things for a while. One problem's done; that lawyer is getting you out of trouble and debt in Augusta."

Carlos Torres and Joaquín Chavous were waiting in the barn when they arrived. "Another conquest to protect you, Señora Raquel?"

She glared at the brazen man. "This is Captain Slade's first mate and best *amigo,* Luke Conner. You didn't have to murder George Leathers and destroy our Augusta company to terrorize us. I told you George had already sent his part of the contract; the ammunition is stowed safely aboard Dan's ship. The hold-up is Harrison Clements in Athens, but if you try to harm him again like you did Wednesday, we can't fill your order. Three men are dead, murdered. One company is blown up. Harm another person or set another fire and I'll go to the police and have you arrested. Is that clear?"

"I do not know who is threatening you or why, Señora Raquel, but it is not us. It would be foolish to harm people and places we need to fill our order. Is this another trick to stall or an attempt to betray your word? Monday is the final day to complete our business. If not, *accidentes* will occur and we will be behind them this time."

"Dan is in Athens now picking up part of the order. I have 2,960 rifles aboard his ship. Another 3,040 are arriving Monday. That's six thousand, and the full amount of ammunition. I need more time to get the other four thousand. Or rather, I have to find $127,-000 to pay for them being made."

"Six thousand is not enough, Señora Raquel. We paid for ten. Get the others *pronto*. I will give you until Tuesday, *no más,*" he vowed coldly.

Luke escorted Rachel into town on Monday to meet Dan at the depot. The train arrived on schedule and they greeted each other with smiles.

"How did things go during my absence?" Dan inquired as he perceived a genial aura between his love and first mate.

Rachel glanced at Luke and smiled. "Would you believe your best friend charmed the frown off Lula Mae's face. My spinster housekeeper is most taken with him. If he were older, she would no doubt pursue him."

"How did you manage that magic, my friend? She can't stand me."

Luke sent Dan a lopsided grin and roguish shrug. "I'm irresistible."

"It's because you're a threat to her, Dan," Rachel quipped. "She's afraid you'll steal off to sea with her mistress and put her out of a good job."

"That's my intention, woman, if you ever agree."

"Luke's an excellent chess player. We had a wonderful time getting to know each other. For seamen both of you are superb riders."

"The old change-the-subject ruse, Luke; did you catch how easily and quickly she does it?" Dan teased. "She's leading me on a merry chase."

"I've never been dishonest with you, Daniel Slade, not about that."

"Being dishonest and being direct are two different things, love."

"Can we discuss this at another time and place, sir?"

"See, Luke, I get to her, but she doesn't want to admit it."

"Listen, you two mischievous sailors," Rachel put a halt to the bantering. "We have serious business to tend. What happened? The suspense is chewing away at me," she said.

"I have 3,040 rifles with me. Harry sent thirty extra as promised."

"How generous of him," Rachel scoffed. "I didn't scare him at all."

Dan related his news. "I did my best to persuade him to send the other four thousand and the dynamite, but he wouldn't. I pointed out we had George's ammo and wouldn't have to pay for it; it didn't make a difference. I told him you would sacrifice your share of the profit, and we'd paid for the 5,970 rifles out of our pockets. I even told him what you said about giving up your share of the company if he'd send only half of the remaining weapons. He still said no. He claims he can't write off $127,000."

"But we've spent $207,500 saving our skins!"

"He knows that, love, but it doesn't change his mind. He said the rebels have to take the ammo and six thousand arms and be satisfied. He thinks we've done all we can to straighten out Phillip's mess."

"We?" she echoed with a sneer. "It hasn't cost *him* anything!"

"He says he hasn't made any profit, either. Even sacrificing his profits and yours, the expenses are $334,000 for the full contract. He did agree to give up any profit, but he won't pay for arms out of his personal account and says the company's account is bare."

"He's as responsible as I am. Maybe more so."

"He doesn't see it that way, because Phillip accepted the money and you're Phillip's wife."

"It's because he thinks I have the money and I'll soon weaken!"

"That," Dan concurred, "and the fact he's riled about the trouble last week. He's posted guards at the company and his home for protection. He's nervous, but not budging. He's put the company up for sale, said you had agreed. He has the rest of the weapons ready and waiting, if we'll send the remaining $127,-000. Giving up his profit is as far as he'll go."

"Well, the Cubans will just have to share in the responsibility. I can't come up with any more money. I've done more than my share."

"Let's tell Torres and Chavous we have the order and we're ready to sail." Dan suggested.

"What happens when we anchor and they discover the shortage?" Rachel reasoned. "You planning to dump the cases and flee before it is? They would be so furious about being tricked, they'd send Torres and Chavous back for the rest or for our heads."

"They're only messengers and escorts, love. They don't have the power to make decisions or changes. We need to see their leader and reason with him. Once he learns the whole story, he'll have to work with us to solve the rest."

"You're right, Dan. Besides, we need to discover who Phillip was talking about as our 'only hope.' Somebody must be there who can help us."

Dan decided to let Rachel think she was going along, but it was too dangerous. He would leave her behind at the last minute, along with two of his men for protection. "Let's get these crates loaded on the ship. We'll talk more later. Luke, get things ready tomorrow for sailing Thursday at dawn. Rachel you get packed tomorrow. When we see those rebels in the morning, we'll put our plan into motion . . . I'm starved. Who's for a delicious dinner?"

"Here come the boys with wagons," the first mate said. "I'll take care of these crates, then stay on the ship tonight, if it's all right, Captain. I'll meet you at the hotel at breakfast."

"That's perfect, Luke. Thanks," he said with a grin and a wink. "Well, woman, do you want to join me for dinner, say, the Pirate's House?"

Rachel realized Luke Conner had given them the evening alone for more than sharing a meal and conversation. Dare she risk spending the night in Dan's hotel room? What if they were still being watched?

Chapter 20

As Dan slipped into bed with Rachel, he yearned to embrace and kiss her. Both knew what loomed before them in the next few weeks, especially during the next two days. Even death for one or both could loom on the cloudy horizon. Tonight they would love as if it was their last night on earth. Tonight they would soar toward rapture's heaven on the wings of passion. Later they would worry about the perils confronting them.

Dan lay beside Rachel to hold and caress her. The hotel room was secure, and one lamp cast a soft and dreamy glow on their bodies. For a while, Dan made love to her with his eyes. He stored up exquisite images to carry him through the days of separation ahead, as he would not allow her to sail to the hazardous meeting in the Cuban stronghold. It was possible he wouldn't come out of this alive, and he couldn't risk her life, too. Yet he must do all he could to free her from that threat. His gaze roamed her face and body with tantalizing leisure. He saw a flush of arousal spread over her.

Rachel experienced an odd mixture of tension and relaxation. His gaze was so potent, so enticing, so flattering. Tingles and warmth raced over her. She felt as if she were being teased and pleasured simultaneously. She did nothing to hurry or to slow his thrilling sport.

Dan came forward until his bare chest made contact with hers. His lips ever so lightly brushed over her waiting mouth. His fingers trailed over her face as if mapping it in detail. He pressed kisses to every feature, then rained more down her throat. His mouth halted to bring the brown peaks of her breasts to life with loving moisture and titillating flicks of his tongue.

Rachel groaned as he ignited and fanned her smoldering desires into a raging fire. She savored and craved the way his hands roved her pliant body. As one hand drifted over her stomach, it tightened with anticipation of its continued trek toward her womanhood. She was stirred and tempted and could not keep from pulling his mouth back to hers. She wanted to taste him, to feel him, to surrender totally. Her hands traveled his body as they stroked his tanned flesh and admired its appeal. She closed her eyes to let her unbridled senses absorb everything about Dan and the blissful journey they were beginning.

Dan's loins ached for an urgent fusion of their bodies, but he mastered the urge to move too swiftly. He nuzzled her neck and ear as his nose inhaled her heady fragrance. His fingertips grazed her skin and admired its firm suppleness. He felt as if he had gulped ten bottles of potent whiskey, as she utterly inebriated his senses.

Rachel's fingers wandered into Dan's sable hair, loving the feel of it against her skin. She relished trailing them over his hard chest and sleek torso. With bravery and boldness, her hand worked its way lower and lower, over his taut abdomen, past lean hips, and to his manly region. Her fingers curled around his rigid shaft and stroked the fiery member that instantly responded to her touch. Her mouth melded with his as their tongues danced in fiery abandon.

Dan's lips returned to the rosy-brown nubs on her breasts and blissfully tormented them to increase her hunger for him. He vowed this would be a night she would never forget. His hands kneaded the flesh of her breasts and he gently worked at the buds on them. He felt bathed in wondrous sensation. He was calm yet his body felt as tight as a rope. He felt in control yet was spinning in a whirlpool of unleashed emotions. He grasped her firm buttocks and fondled them before pressing her feminine core snugly against him.

Rachel was captivated and enchanted by Dan. He was aroused to the point of driving within her with swift urgency but was sensitive and caring to her needs and pleasures. She wanted to tell him to enter her to appease his hunger, but she let him decide when the time was perfect. Her thrusting peaks were responsive to his sweet torments. She writhed as his fingers trailed up and down her sides, across her back, along her spine, and finally into her fuzzy brown triangle. The straining bud pulsed and heated at his attention. Her anticipation and desires increased. Soon her head was thrashing on the pillow as his deft finger entered her and dashed aside any lingering control and reality.

Mindless with desire, Rachel's hands moved up and down Dan's back with speed and pressure. They teased over sinewy muscles that rippled with his stirring movements, wandered to his taut buttocks. He had stolen her wits and was driving her wild with a fierce craving for him. Her fingers toyed in the crisp black hair around the root of his manhood. She felt him trailing kisses down her stomach and shifting his position to continue along her thighs, taking him out of her reach. When he brushed kisses over the pulsing spot that only he had pleasured, she stiffened in confusion. She lifted her head and looked at him, questioning the unknown experience and intense sensations he was evoking.

Dan sent her an encouraging smile that told her to relax. His strong and gentle hands stroked the silky inner surface of her thighs, each time just barely making contact with the inflamed area. One finger lovingly massaged the delicate peak as another slipped within her secret haven to create a pattern that matched that of his manhood when it was thrusting within her. The moisture and heat of her paradise told him she was eager and ready to accept and enjoy any pleasure he wished to give her.

Rachel remembered how she had thought that the physical act was either ugly and painful or something to be endured or only for a man's satisfaction. With the right man, though, it was clearly beautiful, magical, enslaving, and inspiring. For her, Daniel Slade was that man, the only man, the one who could entice her total and willing surrender. He could make her starve for his contact, feed her ravenous body until she was thoroughly sated, then leave her craving her next meal of his sensual treats. He reclaimed her strayed attention as he continued his loving assault on her senses. His mouth, tongue, and fingers, gave her pleasures she had not known existed. She squirmed as tension mounted within her. She wanted to relax, but couldn't. She was taut with anticipation of what she instinctively knew would be marvelous. Passion's flames licked at her body and seared it with his brand of ownership.

Dan realized she had reached the point of fiery abandon. He moved atop her, covered her mouth with his, and entered her moistness with a gasp. As if insatiable, she matched his pattern and labored with him. His lips greedily drank from the nectar of her mouth and hardened nipples. She was moaning and clinging to him. Her tongue teased over his lips. Her mouth was insistent upon his, then ardently fastened to his. He noticed how she kept pace with his movements as they worked in unison toward the same goal.

He was coaxed to increase his ardent endeavors to give her supreme satisfaction. As bliss exploded within her, she nibbled at his shoulder and clung tightly to his body.

Dan was charged with energy. He discarded his self-control and scaled the summit to capture passion's peak at her side. His release stole his breath and shook his body. He didn't halt his labors until he was breathless and appeased, as was she.

A golden aftermath of the heady lovemaking settled within them. Both felt limp and fulfilled. Their hearts surged with love and peace. Their spirits were united, as their bodies still were interlocked. They hugged, then parted, to lie close in the intimate setting.

Rachel gazed at Dan. Though his prowess in lovemaking was immeasurable, he was so gentle and giving. She wiped beads of perspiration from his face and smiled into his twinkling blue eyes. Her adoring gaze lingered a moment on the white teeth revealed by his smile. Her fingers traced his strong and handsome features, then wandered into his damp ebony hair. Her gaze locked with his.

Dan knew he was viewing love and trust and contentment in her whiskey-colored depths. He was proud and pleased. He shifted to kiss her and to cuddle her possessively. "You're mine, woman, tonight and forever," he murmured as his teeth nibbled at her ear.

Rachel squirmed and giggled at the tickling sensation. "You are the most magnificent and unique man alive, Daniel Slade. If we did this every night, I could never tire of you or having you like this."

"Good, because I'm a greedy and demanding lover."

"Every time you take me, you give me exquisite pleasure. You're so generous and thoughtful. One day, you'll teach me enough so I can torment you and sate you in these same ways."

"Does that mean you'll agree to keep me around?"

"Except when you're at sea, I want you at my side day and night. I, too, have become greedy and demanding. I'll make you the best mistress you could ever find or train." She waited for his response to those words.

Dan refused to pressure her. He was positive she loved him and wanted him. When everything was resolved, she would marry him, because he wouldn't let her say no. "That's an irresistible offer and a promise, love."

Rachel grasped what his hesitation meant and smiled. "Yes, it is."

"I hate to roust you from this warm and tempting bed, woman, but it will be easier to get you home unseen at this hour than in the morning."

"You're right. I hate to leave, but it's safest for us. I'll get dressed." As she did so, she said, "I'm glad we ate up here instead of in a restaurant."

"It was sneaky of me, slipping you and the food in here."

"It certainly was, my sly hero. Just think . . . in two days, we'll be sailing the tropical seas. I wish . . . Will I see you tomorrow?"

"No, we both have many tasks. I'll see you when you come into town on Wednesday. You'll spend the night here, then board my ship just before sailing time Thursday morning. I don't want you around tomorrow and Wednesday while we're loading supplies and those arms, in case we have problems with customs. If that paper isn't in order and legal, I don't want you getting into more trouble. I won't, because I got it from Phillip and Harry, so I have an excuse for not knowing it was faked."

As she brushed her hair, she watched him in the

mirror as he donned his garments. "You will send word if there's a problem?"

"Yes, but don't worry. I think everything will go fine. You can take care of messages to Harry and Milton late Wednesday. Better still, leave them to be delivered Thursday after we sail. We don't want interference with our departure." *After I'm gone, you won't need to tell them.*

Rachel didn't remind him she wasn't supposed to leave town, but she wasn't going to the police station to ask Chief Anderson's permission! She wanted to be with Dan, to make certain he wasn't blamed and punished for the shortage, and to spend time learning about his lifestyle. That would tell her if he could give up his adventurous existence or she could fit into it.

Rachel talked with her housekeeper as she packed, "I have to take this trip, Lula Mae, to finish that important business hanging over my head. If all goes well, I'll be paid a lot of money and our troubles will be over. When I return, if the police don't shut my file on Phillip's death, I'll have the money to hire a lawyer to force it closed. I want everything settled, so our lives can return to normal. It should take about two weeks. If those investigators come calling again, tell them I had to take care of business and I'll contact them the moment I'm back."

"But they told you not to leave, Miss Rachel. You'll git in trouble."

"Maybe, but I have to take that risk. Settling this deal is the answer to all my problems. Besides, if I'm away, whoever is playing those tricks on me will be thwarted and I'll be safe. This is the only choice I can make at this time. You stay on guard so you won't get hurt while I'm gone."

"I'll be worried silly till you git back. Where you going?"

"I can't tell you; it's a secret, the client's order. This deal is big and important; we can't risk someone forcing the truth from you or anyone."

"I wouldn't tell nobody."

"Not on purpose. Please understand, and I'll explain everything later."

"Wills Captain Slade be guarding you?"

"Yes, and Luke Conner, too. I won't be alone with Dan, so don't worry."

"I won't stop worryin' till you're home again. Why cain't Mr. Clements go?"

"This was Phillip's deal and there are problems with it. I have to go straighten them out and save it. Harry refuses. He's still angry with me about tricking him after Phillip's death. We have the arms company up for sale, but there won't be any profit from it, just debts paid off. That leaves me with the plantation to replace lost earnings from the three companies. I plan to start farming the rest of the land as soon as possible, maybe grow cotton or indigo, to supplement our income from the sharecroppers. I'll have to depend on you and Burke to help out more. We'll probably have to hire more workers, too. That takes money. But we'll do fine. We'll make a real plantation out of Moss Haven. Won't that be—"

Rachel straightened from folding her garments and listened. "Someone is knocking on the door. See if it's the message I'm expecting."

When Lula Mae returned, she handed Rachel a paper that told her it was time to set their daring ruse into motion.

"I have to run an errand nearby. I won't be gone long."

"I'm supposed to go check on Mrs. Willis. I'll goes while you're gone. I'll help you finish packing when we both git back."

"That's perfect, Lula Mae. Burke and the boys are

working outside so the house will be safe from more pranks."

Rachel watched the older woman ride off in one direction in the carriage as she galloped off on horseback in the other. She was surprised, and perhaps a bit intrigued, by how well Lula Mae had taken the news about her impending trip. Perhaps it was a result of her clever disclosures about how they would soon be living. It might be the truth, as she should wait a while before marrying Daniel Slade. It wouldn't be fair to Phillip or good for her stained reputation to disallow a proper mourning period. No matter her final decision, it kept the nosy housekeeper off her back for now.

Rachel reached the location and dismounted. She saw Carlos smile when he noticed she had come alone. She ignored the irascible Joaquín and focused on the raffish leader of the two rebels.

"You no longer fear me, Raquel; you come alone; that is *bueno.*"

"So is my news, Mr. Torres. The ship is being supplied and your crates are being loaded today and tomorrow. Dan wants you to board the *Merry Wind* at five o'clock tomorrow afternoon. We set sail at dawn the next morning. To prevent any trouble at the last minute, the ship will move to the end of the channel and anchor there until departure time. Agreed?"

"You have the arms, ammunitions and explosives?"

"Everything is ready to be delivered. Dan's crew has been on shore leave, so they're being located and called aboard for sailing."

Carlos smiled and complimented, "I knew you would not fail me."

"You have no idea how hard and stressful this has

467

been for me. If that's all for now, I have to get home and finish packing for the voyage."

Carlos showed his surprise. "You are sailing with us?"

"Yes. I want to make certain the cargo I've paid for gets to the right client. If anything goes wrong again, I can't put another one together. This deal is my work and my money, and I'm going to protect it until it reaches your leader's hands. If that missing money is ever found, it's mine. Is that understood?"

"*Sí*, Raquel. You have done well. I hope you find the *dinero*."

"So do I, because I'm penniless. Every cent I could get my hands on went toward paying for this order all of you held me responsible for. The only reason I complied was to live. You don't know how tempted I was to tell all of you to go to the devil. But I knew you would hurt my family and friends."

"It is over; no more threats or dangers. We are *amigos*."

"I hope so. If the Spanish attack us along the way, Dan won't let them board or confiscate his ship. You will guarantee our safety in Cuba? Once the order is delivered, we're free to go unharmed? No tricks or betrayals?"

"No Cuban rebel will harm you, Raquel. You have my word of honor."

"And that of your leader?"

"*Sí, mi lider,* too. After our bargain is met, we part as *amigos*."

"One last question, Mr. Torres: do you swear you're innocent of all the threats and attacks we've received?"

"We have harmed no one in your country, Raquel."

"Good, because I couldn't let you get away with murdering those men."

"You accept my word?" Carlos asked, looking surprised.

"Yes. I don't like your intimidating behavior, but I believe you."

"It takes a smart and brave woman to challenge her enemies."

"First, she has to unmask them. I'll do that when I return home. I'll see you Thursday at dawn. I'm staying at the hotel until sailing time. Don't forget, be at the *Merry Wind* gangplank at five tomorrow. And, Carlos . . .?"

He grinned when she also used his first name. *"Sí,* Raquel?"

"Don't let anything happen to you and your sullen *amigo.* I don't know the rendezvous place or your *lider's* name. After all I've been through, I wouldn't want to be blamed and killed for your losses and a late shipment."

"We will be most alert and careful until *mañana. Adiós,* Raquel."

"Adiós, amigo Carlos," she replied, having decided to try to make friends with him before she faced his leader with the shortage. Knowing all she had done to save this deal, maybe he would speak in her favor.

Wednesday afternoon, Burke Wells dropped Rachel off at the hotel, then delivered her baggage to the clipper. Two seamen stored it in their captain's quarters, as he wasn't there to tell them what else to do with it.

Rachel had written out messages for Milton Baldwin and the police, explaining she was away on vital business and would contact them as soon as she returned in two weeks. She had made out a telegram for Harry, telling him the same, but adding a request to stay ready to fill the rest of the order. She had given

469

them to Burke to deliver and send tomorrow after she sailed.

Luke Conner came by to relate there had been no problem with customs when they inspected and cleared the cargo.

"That's a relief," Rachel said, "because I'm not convinced that permission paper is real. No matter; we used it in good faith and they accepted it."

"Dan will come by for supper and a chat later. The crew is gathered, supplies are laid in, cargo's stowed, and she's ready to sail with the morning tide. I'm going to miss . . . Savannah. I've enjoyed my visit. It's been quite interesting getting to know you and investigate you," he jested, having covered his near slip about Dan's intention to leave her behind in safety.

"We'll have plenty of time on the ship for more talks and chess games. I'm looking forward to tasting Dan's lifestyle and meeting his friends."

"Have no fear; you'll fit in perfectly and easily."

"Thank you, Luke; I needed to hear that."

Rachel answered the knock at her door, eager to see her love, who was early. She gaped at her stepfather and wondered how he knew where to find her. "What do you want, Earl?" she asked, trying to sound polite.

He came inside and she watched him as he finger-combed his wiry hair. "I saw you check in, but I was too busy to speak. Why are you staying here? Is there more trouble at home?"

"I'm only here overnight," Rachel said in annoyance. "This isn't a convenient time to chat; I'm expecting a guest for dinner."

"Captain Daniel Slade?" He scowled when her expression said he was right. "How do I know?" he asked for her. "The gossip is already making its ugly rounds, Rachel. How can you do something so foolish? It's too soon for you to be courted again. Don't you care about another scandal? My Lord, girl, you're still under suspicion for killing Phillip and George Leathers! Don't you realize how this quick romance will look to the police?"

Rachel closed the door to prevent them from being overheard by a guest. "What's wrong with having a male friend?"

"Friend? That isn't what he is, and nobody is fooled, girl."

"It's really none of your or their business. Please leave."

Earl was leaning against the door. He put his hands behind his back and locked it. "We aren't finished yet."

Rachel heard the click and glared at him. "Don't start this again," she warned in a frigid tone. "Get out or I'll scream."

Earl grinned and challenged, "Create more gossip and scandal? Your devoted and worried stepfather comes to offer his protection, comfort, and aid, but you attack him? Who would believe you?"

"Come near me and I'll kill you; or Dan will. He'll be here soon."

"I think not. He's already sailed with the evening tide."

"He's gone?" she murmured, then recalled Luke's near slip.

"That's right. It's just you and me. No servants. No weapons. No refusal. I'm sure that lowly sailor has had you many times, so now it's my turn. You owe me, girl. You teased and tempted me for years. Then you took off with that old man and humiliated me. Your mother doesn't have your fire and spirit; she gave it all to you. Yield to me just this once, Rachel, and I'll leave you alone forever. I'll give you whatever money and help you need."

"You're mad! I wouldn't surrender to you if my life depended on it."

471

"It does. You're penniless and no man will risk marrying you. All of your assets will be lost soon, then you'll be thrown into the street. I'm not asking or demanding you become my mistress; I just want to bed you one time to see what magic you possess to drive men crazy enough to risk their lives marrying a Black Widow. You don't even have to respond."

"My God, you *are* insane! Get out."

Earl pulled a jeweled knife from his pocket. "This little darling can mar your enchanting beauty, girl, or it can put a stop to your evil existence. If you die, no more victims will lose their lives."

Rachel panicked. "You can't murder me and get away with it."

"This pretty baby is a woman's weapon. Either you tried to stab me and fell on it, or you killed yourself in a moment of madness. Everybody knows you have to be either mad or evil to do what you did to innocent men. I would never risk my life marrying a blood-thirsty predator like you. Now, get your clothes off and get on that bed. I'm going to give you some fatherly love and discipline to correct your wicked ways. Do it, now!"

"No. I didn't kill any of them. I'm not insane. I won't bed you."

"You have no choice. Scream, and this knife will end your sadistic criminal life. Whether you realize it or not, girl, you're guilty. Why do you think your mother and I have been worried and afraid all these years? Why do you think she was scared to invite you back home? Because we've both witnessed your mad and dreamy behavior. Be glad we've never told the law about your lunacy. We thought it would stop when you met the right man and fell in love with him. But your hunger for money and your desire to give men pain won't let you. Show gratitude to me for not seeing you hanged."

She was trapped. "You're lying, you miserable and devious snake!"

"Am I? Think back, Rachel. Recall the times you've found things done without remembering doing them. Were you ever awake or sensible when any of your husbands died? You're sick in the head, but can't face it or admit it. Just like you refuse to admit you teased and tormented and encouraged me to fondle you and bed you. As soon as things got hot between us, you'd come around, panic, and accuse me of trying to rape you. Don't you see, girl? You couldn't stand for me to take your father's place so you tried to take me away from your mother. What little good you have inside always stopped you at the last minute. You blame men for the war that killed your father and brother and ruined your life, so you choose one to punish. Until you face the truth and get help, it won't ever stop."

"If I'm so sick in the mind, why are you trying to ravish me?"

"Because you owe me for all those years of painful games. After we finish here, I'll take you back to White Cloud. As soon as I find the best doctor to cure you, I'll send you to him and pay for everything. I won't ever touch you again. You have my word of honor. If you don't believe what I'm telling you, ask Catherine. She knows you're guilty. It's eaten at her for years and finally made *her* ill. The only reason she's getting better is because I've sworn to have you cured, with or without your consent. That's why she left her sickbed to visit you, to see if you could be helped."

"Mama would never believe such absurd lies about me. If she knew what you were really trying to do to me, she would kill you herself."

"After I'm done, tell her. I don't care; she won't believe it, not from her mad and wicked daughter. Enough talk. Strip and lie down."

Rachel was staggered by Earl's words and intention. She couldn't scream for help; either he would kill or disfigure her, or would create an ugly scandal and trouble, preventing her departure . . . Was Dan gone? Why else would Earl be so confident about not being interrupted?

"Get on with it, girl. This is ready for you," he murmured as he rubbed the hard bulge in his pants. "It's been ready for you for years."

"You wrote those notes to me, didn't you? You followed me to Augusta and left them in my room, and in my house. You had someone forge my handwriting so I couldn't show them to anybody. You put that poisonous spider in my basin and that vial of poison in my hotel room."

"No, Rachel. You must have done those things to convince yourself you're innocent. Have the police or a private detective investigate me; that's the only way you'll ever learn I'm not to blame. By damn, I'll even pay the cost to prove who's at fault! I'm tired of you calling me vile names and accusing me of filthy overtures. I'm tired of you treating me like a disease or a fool. The only reason you haven't told your mother about my so-called advances is because deep inside you know I'm not guilty and you'll be exposed for the wicked-minded creature you are."

"You'll never convince me I'm mad, so give it up."

"I don't have to convince you, we both know you are."

"I didn't shoot at myself, write those notes, or make those threats."

"If it wasn't you, check out your seaman when he returns. It could be his method of getting into your bloomers. Come on, girl; you understand my meaning. Scare you into falling into his arms for protection, then he's so overwhelmed by your beauty that he seduces you. And you're so damn grateful that you let him do as he pleases with you."

"That's a crude and spiteful lie, Earl Starger!"

"Rachel, Rachel," he chided. "How can you be so blind and rash?"

"Get out."

"After I get what I came after, what I've looked forward to for years, what you've offered, girl. Then you're going to a doctor up North for treatment. If I don't have you cured, we'll have to expose you to the police. We can't let you murder another man. If we keep quiet, we're as guilty as you are."

"How will it look for my father to sleep with me?" she scoffed.

"I'm not your father, so it won't be incest."

"It would be adultery; you're married to my mother."

"You came after me, girl, not the other way around. Everybody knows you have witch's powers. How can I be blamed for falling under your evil spell for one foolish moment?"

"I am not evil, cursed, jinxed, or guilty. Somebody else killed them."

"Who, Rachel? Only the insidious witch who lives inside you."

"Stop it. I won't listen to any more lies."

"Be thankful I'm saving Captain Slade from your lethal web. You like him, don't you? Just as you liked William and Craig and Phillip. If you snare him, girl, he's dead. Let him escape, and you get help."

"What about you, Earl? Why haven't I murdered you? I despise you."

"Because the evil one inside you knows I know who and what she is. She knows I'll expose her if she tries to murder me, too. She knows who started this game between us, and she wants me. Let her come out and take me. Go into your dreamy state so Rachel won't remember what happens between us tonight. She's the one telling you that you aren't sick so you won't allow a doctor to get rid of her."

Earl stepped closer and taunted her with the jewel-handled knife. Rachel backed away until she reached the wall. A table with a heavy vase was beside her. She waited until Earl stalked her and stood before her. As one of his hands covered her breast, she curled her fingers around the rim, lifted it, and struck him forcefully over the head.

The vase broke, and Earl staggered backward. His hand grabbed his bleeding head. He shook it to clear his dazed condition. He glared at the wide-eyed Rachel and saw the hatred and defiance written on her face. "Damn you, you little witch; you'll be sorry for that. I'll tell all I know about you."

As he came at her again with a blood-glint in his hazel eyes, Rachel used her riding boot to land a near-crippling blow to his groin. Earl collapsed in agony to the floor. Rachel grabbed his feet and used all the strength she could summon to work him out her door. She rolled the disabled man into the hall, relieved no guests were milling about. She closed and locked the door, and leaned against it to recover her breath.

Earl struggled to rise before someone came along and saw his injuries. He decided to slip into the closet across the hall until his strength returned. He was filled with hatred and a desire for revenge. His dark lust for Rachel changed into an evil hunger to see her crushed and punished for her deeds. He swore to himself she would never get away with what she had done.

Rachel jumped and gasped as someone knocked at the door she had swayed against. She feared it was Earl trying to get inside again.

"Rachel, are you there?"

She unlocked the door, yanked a startled Dan inside, bolted the lock, and flung herself into his arms. She was breathing hard and her heart was pounding. She held on to him for comfort and strength.

476

"What's wrong, love?" he questioned in alarm. He tried to put distance between them to look at her, but she clung to him. Dan waited a minute for her to relax her grip, but she didn't. "Rachel, what is it? What happened?" He saw the broken vase and grasped her distress.

"Earl . . ." She finally managed to get out one word.

"He's been here?" She nodded, but didn't look at him. "What did he do to you? If he harmed you, I'll hunt down the bastard and kill him."

Rachel was terrified and confused. If there was only a grain of truth in what Earl had said, how could she tell Dan? How could she plant such seeds in his mind? She mustn't, not until she returned to Savannah, went home, and questioned her mother. "We had a vicious quarrel. I don't want to talk about it tonight. He scares me. I'll be so glad to be away from here tomorrow. I'll deal with him after my return, once and for all. I wish we were sailing tonight. I'm afraid he'll come back. Can I stay on the ship with you tonight?"

Luke had told him about the near-slip he had made earlier. Dan wondered if she had guessed he was planning to leave her behind and this was a ruse to prevent that action. He had been downstairs for a while, delayed by Camellia Jones, and he hadn't seen her stepfather come or go. "That wouldn't be wise, love; somebody might see you. We have to wait until the wee hours of the morning to sneak you aboard."

"Then stay with me here tonight. We'll leave together when it's safe."

"Are you sure you should take this trip? Those Cuban rebels are going to be riled and dangerous when we deliver those arms and ammunition and they realize we've shorted them by thousands. If my ship is stopped and searched, we could get into trouble for gun-running."

"I don't care. I just want to be with you. I want to get away from here. I know the law will come after me about Phillip and George while you're gone. I may be hanged or in prison when you return."

"They don't have any evidence against you, love. Besides, they told you not to leave town until both investigations are over."

"They'll invent some, or that culprit stalking me will."

"You're only upset and not thinking clearly. When I return, you'll marry me. In a few years, when I'm safe and alive, the gossip will cease."

"That isn't funny."

"It wasn't meant to be. It's another proposal. If you don't want to stay in Savannah, you can sail away with me after this problem is solved. I can promise you a life of real adventure."

"Why would you marry me? I said I'd be your mistress. I've been married three times, and all three men are dead under suspicious circumstances. Either I'm bad luck or I have a deadly enemy. I don't want you killed."

"I'm willing to stake my life that you're harmless, woman."

"If you love me and want me, take me with you tonight."

Earl listened to the revealing conversation and knew he had been given his tool to exact revenge. Everything was quiet now, so they must be kissing or heading for the bed. In a rage, he left to fetch the police.

Luke saw the man eavesdrop, then leave hurriedly. He followed Earl Starger until he realized, after hearing him mumble about having the means to "get that evil bitch this time", where the man was headed. Luke rushed back to the hotel and alerted Dan to impending trouble.

"They'll send men to guard the wharf to make certain we don't escape while others come here to arrest us. Everything is ready to sail. Damn!"

"Let Luke hurry to the ship and sail her to Ossabaw Island. You and I can go to Moss Haven, take a boat downriver, and meet him there. We'll tell the desk clerk we're going to dinner and that we're expecting a message, to hold it until we return. That should stall and fool them. If they question anyone at the wharf, no one will have seen us board your ship."

"She's right, Dan. We have to move and move fast. It'll take them a while to hear Starger out, then gather enough men to come after you. Even if everything's in order and legal, it'll take time to sort out this mess. Don't forget, we have two Cuban rebels and arms on board to be found."

Dan knew he couldn't leave her behind in danger. "Let's go."

Rachel and Dan paddled down the Ogeechee River beneath a waning full moon. For the majority of their journey, they moved swiftly on the brackish water. At most places, the black river was wide; at a few, it was narrow. Several times they had to slow their pace to duck their heads to avoid low branches or bowed trees. The twisting route was bounded by impenetrable woods and swamp. Moss-draped cypress and oaks hung over the banks, often with their gnarled roots exposed. Rachel didn't want to think about the dangers that lurked in the water or on the shrouded banks.

"It's so spooky at night," she murmured, shuddering.

To distract her, Dan related his delaying run-in with Camellia, who had flirted and warned him about her predatory rival.

"I wouldn't be surprised if Earl convinced her to stall you while we quarreled. They both hate me, and they're friends."

"She wants me, and he wants you. Is that right?"

"Yes, but neither will win their goals. Is *that* right?"

"Absolutely correct, love."

"I'm relieved we got away without being seen and stopped. The law is probably still waiting for us to return from dinner. I'm glad Burke and Lula Mae didn't see us take this canoe. I hate for them to have to lie for me again. We're twenty miles or more from town, so we should be safe."

Dan noticed her nervous chatter. "This was a clever idea, woman; I'm happy you thought of it in your state. Starger really upset you this time."

Rachel stiffened a moment. "Yes, he did. I'll tell you about it another day. I don't even want to think about him, much less talk about him."

At least Dan knew she had told the truth, and he chided himself for having brief doubts about her again. But he knew they weren't out of danger yet. As soon as the authorities realized they had escaped—believing by Earl's report that they had done something wrong—somebody would be sent after them. He prayed they could get undersail before that happened. And he prayed what they were doing wasn't illegal, or they would both be . . .

When they reached the place the Ogeechee dumped into the Atlantic Ocean, they halted at Ossabaw Island to await Luke and the *Merry Wind.* They climbed out of the canoe and sat on the sandy beach beneath the moon.

"I hope Luke got the ship out of the channel and is sailing along the coast toward us. At least we have the evening tide in our favor. He'll have to go slowly this close to shore, and they have about twenty miles farther to travel than we did. He'll send men after us in a boat. We'll leave this canoe here. Try to relax and sleep until I sight them. Lay your head in my lap."

Rachel did as he suggested. She was exhausted from the chores and episodes of the last few days and the trip downriver. The setting was serene and romantic. The air was warm and smelled of salt. A breeze off the water was gentle and steady. The ocean lapped at the shoreline, giving off lulling sounds. Farther out, waves tumbled over each other and created white crests. Moonglow bathed Dan's face. She watched him as he gazed out to sea and witnessed its strong pull on him. Could he give it up for anything or anyone? Once they were away from her troubles and perils, would she want to return to them? To ever leave his side again?

"Are you scared about what we're heading into?"

"Yes and no," she replied with honesty. Was he safe with her? God help them both if Earl Starger hadn't lied to her . . .

Dan toyed with a dark-brown curl and worried. He wondered what Earl Starger held over her head like a silencing weapon. Something terrifying had happened between them, and he wanted to know what it was. *I thought we were past dangerous secrets, my love. What are you hiding from me now? You're mine, Rachel, and I won't let anything or anyone come between us. If I have to kill that bastard to protect you, I will.*

Chapter 21

Rachel stood on the starboard side of the main deck and observed a setting sun that painted an orange-gold shade across the horizon. Nothing was in view except the seemingly endless blue ocean and sky that appeared to touch far beyond them. Savannah and the troubles there were left far behind. The long and lazy days were underway.

She realized Dan had been accurate when he described the *Merry Wind*. She was one hundred ninety feet long, thirty-six feet wide, and five decks deep. Her stern was squared and her stem was gracefully curved. With a keel of solid rock elm, planks of teak, and copper sheathing to prevent barnacles, she was stout and splendid. She could haul eleven hundred tons of cargo, and was faster than a steamer. The sleek three-masted clipper skimmed the water's surface with ease and beauty, riding the waves as a soaring hawk rode air currents. She sliced through swells smoothly, creating no lift and plunge as most other ships did. She did toss an occasional spray, but mostly made a gentle white curl at her bow.

A breeze played through Rachel's long hair and teased mischievously at her skirttail. She closed her eyes and inhaled the fresh sea air. She felt serene yet restless, happy yet somber. Getting underway, settling in for the voyage, and doing routine tasks had taken up the day for Captain Daniel Slade, his first mate, and friendly crew. To keep out of their way as they scurried about and to avoid being an intriguing distraction, she had spent most of it in Dan's cabin, admiring its masculine decor and gazing out the numerous mullioned windows across the stern.

She wanted to tell him about her confrontation with Earl Starger, but she didn't want to use him like a vessel into which she poured her troubles and frustrations. It wasn't fair to overburden him when he was so busy with his ship and crew and was concentrating on the threats before them. She wanted to share everything with him, but hadn't he already taken on more than enough of her problems?

As the wind calmed, so did the flapping and fluttering of the many rows of sail that were wider and loftier than those of past designs. She listened as Dan gave orders; she saw how quickly, genially, and efficiently they were carried out by a crew that clearly respected and admired him. She watched men lower and secure sails for the night; she heard the anchor being released, signaling the end of their first day at sea on June third.

Crew members went in several directions, some to eat, some to relax, some to play games, and some to guard duty. Any who passed near her smiled and spoke, and she did the same in return. She hadn't seen the *cubanos* since boarding at Ossabaw Island following their escape. She knew they were using the only spare cabin, which had compelled her to bunk with Dan in his large and comfortable quarters. Dan had grinned when he told her she could use the bed and he would take a swinging hammock, but both knew that sleeping arrangement wouldn't last long. The crew and Luke Conner probably knew the same thing, but she didn't let it worry her.

As dusk closed in, the water took on a pearly gray-blue cast, as did the heaven above it. She hoped Dan would be finished with his captain's duties soon and would join her. She turned to see him striding across the deck toward her. His midnight hair was wind tousled and he was attired in a billowy white shirt, snug black pants, and shiny ebony knee boots. As he sent her a broad smile, she thought of a roguish pirate of days past when they roved the seas and took whatever captured their roaming eye. He was so handsome that he stole her breath and enflamed her body.

"How did you fare today, my love?" he asked in a husky voice that revealed he was just as aroused by the sight of her as she was of him.

"I think I'll make a good sailor."

"I had no doubts about it," he replied with a lazy grin.

"You weren't exaggerating, Dan, she's beautiful and swift."

"Haven't you realized by now that I never choose anything that isn't?"

Rachel smiled. "Thank you for the flattery," she said.

"I never flatter, woman; I speak the truth. I'm glad you stayed below for most of the day so I could concentrate on my work. Watching you here for the last hour has been a terrible strain on me. Several times I was tempted to seize you and carry you to my cabin."

"What would your crew think of a captain with such a weakness?"

"After getting a view of you, my enchantress, they wouldn't blame me. In fact, they probably can't understand how I quelled such an urge."

"What did you tell them about me? About my staying with you?"

"They know it's the only place I could put you, under my personal guard. I told them the truth, that you're to become my wife when we return."

"Dan! You know that's too soon for a recent

widow to remarry. But let's discuss that matter at a later date."

"Always putting off the most important decision of our lives," he teased. "How can you keep tormenting me, woman?"

"I'm not. You know what choice I'll eventually make."

"*Eventually,* that's a naughty word."

"You are very demanding and persistent, Captain Slade."

"Sometimes that's the only way to get what you want."

"Is that how I have to behave to get fed tonight? I'm starving. The sea air creates a big appetite."

"For me or food?" he jested with a sly grin.

Knowing voices carried afar, she leaned closer to whisper, "Both."

"Come along, wench," he murmured, grasping her hand and drawing her toward the stern hatchway that led to his cabin.

Dan seated her at a table that was bolted to the floor. He took the chair opposite hers. "Be glad this is a short voyage and we'll have plenty of fresh food. On long ones, meals can get boring and unappetizing. Buelly cooked up his specialty to impress you: beef and vegetable stew, hot biscuits, fruit cobbler, and a bottle of my best wine."

"What do your men eat?"

"The same thing their captain gets. A well-fed and well-treated crew makes a happy and obedient crew."

"A Slade-made proverb?" she teased as she served her plate.

"It's worked so far. No captain or ship has a better crew than me." Dan knew he was fortunate that all his men, except Luke Conner, only knew him as Daniel Slade, not McCandless, so he didn't have to worry about someone making a slip to Rachel before he could explain that ruse. He told himself he shouldn't

485

be upset with her for keeping a secret with good reason when he was doing the same thing. Soon it wouldn't be necessary. Yet he dreaded making that confession, and discovering her reaction.

As they dined, they chatted about ships, his crew, and foreign places he had visited. They were mellow and happy in their private surroundings. Through portholes and the ceiling they heard footsteps or voices above them as men on duty strolled the deck to watch for other ships risking night travel or for unexpected bad weather. They noticed the gentle rocking of the clipper and heard waves lapping at the copper-sheathed hull.

"How long will our trip take?"

"About five to five and a half days. With good winds, she travels fifteen to twenty knots an hour. Most days we'll continue moving for ten hours. If the wind holds and no problems arise, we should make Cuba by Monday night or early Tuesday. We'll stop at Andros Island to take on fresh water. I know of a sheltered pool where we can share a bath."

"That sounds most tempting. Have you used it before?"

"By myself or with male friends, you jealous wench."

"Good. I would hate to use my claws on a female rival," she said playfully.

When they finished, Dan loaded the dishes and leftovers onto a tray and put it outside his door so they wouldn't be disturbed later by the cook fetching them. He slid a bolt into place and turned to look at Rachel who was standing before the mullioned windows. He watched how slanted shafts of a three-quarter moon played over her dark hair. He doused the two lamps, allowing only a silvery glow in the room. It provided just enough light to make out the interior of his quarters and to silhouette the entrancing woman with her back to him. Dan walked to Rachel and locked his arms around her waist. He rested his cheek against her silky head.

She sighed dreamily and leaned against him, placing her hands over his. "After only one day, I see why you love this life so much. It's so tranquil but exciting. You have plenty to keep you busy, but not too much to prevent relaxation. It must be wonderful and stimulating to sail around the world seeing magnificent sites and having heady adventures. I could catch your contagious love for the sea and sailing."

"I hope you do, woman. It will be more fun with you along." He turned his head to brush a kiss to her temple and tenderly squeezed her.

Rachel's heart was filled with love and joy. His world wasn't scary after all, no grim threat to her and their relationship. She wanted to learn everything about him. She was ready and eager to take a risk on love. For the first time since childhood, she felt blissfully happy and safe. She twisted in his embrace, and her hands grasped his face. Rising on her tiptoes, she sealed her mouth to his. A fierce and urgent craving for him overwhelmed her.

Dan's arms tightened around her. His mouth meshed with hers. One kiss fused into another and another. His lips left hers to tease over her face.

Rachel leaned her head back to allow him to continue a stirring trek down her throat. Her fingers grasped the billowy shirt and worked it free of his pants and belt. She slipped her hands beneath it and caressed his hard chest. They moved over curly hair and honed muscles. They journeyed around his sides and up his back. She flattened her palms on the sleek surface and pressed him closer to her. Hungry to taste his flesh, her mouth trailed kisses over his neck. She heard him groan in arousal, and felt the proof of it between her hips.

When she parted them to discard her blouse and chemise, he quickly yanked off his shirt. They embraced, bringing their bare flesh into contact.

Dan used movements of his furry chest to stimulate her already taut nipples as he kissed her with unleashed passion. As their tongues played a heady mating game, Dan shifted his position to cup one breast and tantalize its peak. Rachel's hand roamed to the hardness in his trousers; through the material, she ran her fingers up and down its length. She heard him groan again, and thrilled to how much he wanted her.

Her bold fingers worked with his belt buckle. When it was conquered, she undid the fasteners of his pants and wriggled the garment below his firm buttocks. She captured and stroked his throbbing manhood. Her loving hand did not calm him; instead it made him more anxious to be within her. She released the sleekness of him only long enough to unbutton and drop her skirt, which she kicked aside. Without removing her pantalets, she spread the slit in the crotch with one hand and guided him toward her moistness with the other.

Dan grasped her seductive intention. He lifted her body, entered her, and held her in place by her buttocks as she rode him in a near frenzy to reach her destination. He was almost dazed by her unrestrained action and feared he couldn't hold back his pleading release for long. He spread kisses over her hair and face as she rocked upon his fiery manhood.

Rachel's legs were locked around Dan's hips. She tightened and relaxed them as she controlled this lovemaking session. The position rubbed and stimulated the bud of her womanhood. Even when she was breathless and fatiguing, she couldn't halt her movements. She was overpowered by the need to have him fast and now. It seemed like forever since she had feasted on his body, even though it had been only a few days. She rode him swift and hard until she was rewarded by an explosive release to her steamy journey. She writhed against his flesh, moaning in ecstasy and kissing him any place she could reach. "I love you, Dan, I love you," she murmured in the throes of passionate bliss, followed by noises of feverish abandonment and pleasure.

Dan began to spill his victory into her body, sheer rapture making him feel weak and shaky. As he finished, he walked her to the bed without breaking their tight hold on each other. He thrust a few more times to finish dousing the flaming torch. He was breathing rapidly, but his muscles were no longer tense. He felt limp, sated beyond belief. He withdrew from her and rolled to his side, carrying her along with him. He hugged her tightly. "Stars above, woman, that was wonderful. Absolutely amazing," he said as he exhaled between slightly parted lips. "I love you, Rachel McCandless. You drive me wild."

"I love you, too, Daniel Slade."

When she repeated what she had confessed earlier in mindless passion, Dan shifted to let his gaze pierce the shadows to view her face. It was too dim to see much, and he wished he had left one lantern or a candle burning. He wanted to see her expression as she admitted the truth at last, when he could hear it and she was conscious of what she was saying.

Rachel grasped what he was doing. She rolled to the bedside table. Using the safety matches there, she lit a candle, then returned to lie beside Dan. She locked her gaze to his and said, "I love you. Did you need to see my eyes to know I'm telling the truth?" she teased him and bit him gently.

"I've known it was true a long time, but I wanted to be looking at you when you finally admitted it. This means you'll marry me, right?"

She lightly bit him again. "Weren't you listening when I told you I might not be able to have children? Luke says you want them, and probably soon."

"Might is the magic word, love."

Rachel frowned and rolled to her back. "No, magic is hot fantasy; I'm talking about cold reality. Maybe no children, no heir, ever."

Dan half covered her naked body with his. He stressed, *"Maybe,* Rachel; it isn't a fact. You could be carrying my child this very moment," he ventured and caressed her lower abdomen.

Rachel captured his hand and halted its movement. "And I could never carry your child. Be realistic and honest, Dan. You know it's important to you. Don't fool yourself with wishful hopes. This could be another burden I'll have to bear. I can't let it weigh you down, too."

"Children or no children, I want you to be my wife."

She looked at the ceiling. "Now, but what about later?"

"I'd rather have you without heirs than to have heirs without you."

Her soulful gaze returned to his entreating one. "I'll make you a deal: I'll marry you as soon as I become pregnant. I must prove my fertility before we wed."

Dan tensed in worry. "But what if you're right?"

"If I am, we'll see if that changes our feelings and relationship. Better to test them before we commit than afterward. Right?"

"I don't like making bargains with my future, with my love."

"Think of how much fun you'll have trying to win me," she murmured as she nibbled at his lips and stroked his reviving manhood. "There's only one way to get me pregnant, remember?"

Dan spread kisses over her face and vowed, "If that's the only way to win you, woman, I'll work day and night on my task."

"I'll do all I can to help you succeed," she said, grinning.

Friday afternoon, Rachel stood on the forecastle deck of the clipper and chatted with the handsome *cubano*. She had told Dan of her assumption it was better to make a friend and ally of Carlos Torres than to treat him as an enemy. With reluctance, her lover had agreed. She knew Dan was observing them from the stern near the steering wheel. She tried to act poised and friendly, but she was apprehensive. "Tell me about your country and rebellion," she coaxed with a smile.

Carlos gazed across the ocean. He was unusually amiable as he explained. "She lives in glorious splendor, as you do, Raquel. Part of her is mountainous, but most of her is . . . plains and basins. She is one big island with *muchos niños,* babies. She provides a third of the world's sugar; but also fruit, *café,* and timber. The Central Valley where I am from is important; it is where much of our sugarcane, *café,* cattle, and timber is raised. When we anchor in Bahía de Nipe and go ashore, you will see for yourself how lovely she is."

Rachel leaned forward and propped her forearms on the railing to steady her balance. Although the brilliant sun was at their backs, she squinted from the glare off the water as the *Merry Wind* knifed through the windswept sea. "What about your people? What are they like?"

"Our people are farmers and fishermen, peasants and landowners. Most are *Criollos* whites born there. The rest are *Mestizos,* of Indian and Spanish mix, *Mulatos*—of Negro and Spanish mix, and *Amarillos*—Chinese. Slavery has not been abolished, but trade in flesh was terminated many years ago. *Mejicano* Indians and *Chinos* were . . . indentured to fill that loss. Most are *Católicos;* others—*Africanos*—are Santeria. We arrive before *huracán* season next month, but you get wet *muchos* times; it is our rainy season."

Rachel realized the closer they came to Cuba, the more Carlos Torres drifted toward his native language; yet, she grasped the gist of it.

"You will meet our leader and band of *rebeldes,* rebels. Our war cry is *'No hay nada más importante que la libertad,'* which means, 'Nothing is more important than freedom.' *Pronto,* you will see why we would kill for guns to free our land and people."

"Tell me now so I'll understand when we get there," she urged.

"You thirst to know *muchos* things, Raquel."

"If you were heading to a country where you didn't know the people, language, and customs, wouldn't you be the same way?"

"Sí. Ricardo was *mi maestro,* my teacher."

"If he knows so much about us, why wasn't he sent on this mission?"

"El es la mano derecha de Ramón," he said, shaking his right hand to make his point.

Right-hand man, she mentally translated. "Ramón is your leader?"

Carlos did not answer that question. "Your country is our biggest trade partner. She is our ally, but she fears to challenge the Madre Tierra and its ruler, King Alfonso XII; he is the son of Isabella and has ruled for ten years. The war began long before he came to power; we have battled for independence for eight years. We will continue to fight until we are free *hombres.* They tax us and control us as dogs or burros on ropes. They are *corruptores* and they let us say nothing in the *cortes* and *audiencias."*

When he paused, she asked, "What do those words mean?"

"Parliament and High Courts. They order their *soldados* to be brutal to control and cower us. We asked for *americana* help, but it has not come. El Presidente

492

Grant and war leader *Señor* Belknap resist our pleas for help. Your government does not stop us from getting arms and supplies, but it has not offered or provided them. *Uno día* she will," he said with confidence.

Rachel straightened and faced him. "How did this rebellion start?"

"The eastern provinces banded together under Carlos Manuel de Céspedes, a wealthy planter. When the Orient Province declared independence in October of 1868, the battles began. *El Grito de Yara* was heard across the land: 'The cry of Yara.' Landowners want . . . economic and political freedoms; the farmers and workers want slavery abolished and political freedom for *todo el mundo*. De Céspedes freed every slave who would join the fighting. The Nationalist *lider* is a Black commander named Antonio Maceo. Our band follows his instruction. The soldiers of the government we battle are savage, but you will be safe in our *campo*."

"I hope so, Carlos, and I hope you win your independence."

"You are kind, Raquel, *una mujer valiente y lista*."

At the man's adoring expression, she did not ask him to translate his last few words. He had used the Spanish form of her name many times with a husky tone that worried her. She hoped he didn't think she was flirting with him. Surely Carlos knew she was the captain's woman. As she thought of herself surrounded soon by rugged and earthy rebels in a sultry jungle, she had to struggle not to panic or shudder in dread.

"You worry about something, Raquel."

"It's just the heat. I've been under the hot sun too long. If you'll excuse me, I'll go to my cabin and rest. It's been nice talking with you like this. We'll do it again before we reach your island."

"Con mucho gusto," he responded, grinning at the

493

flush on her cheeks that he did not believe was the result of the tropical sun.

"Good-bye," she said, and left the appealing *cubano* staring after her.

"Hasta luego, llama de mi corazón," he murmured to himself, as the enchanting female truly did ignite a flame in his heart that called for her possession.

A little over three hours after setting sail Saturday morning, Luke Conner came to Dan's cabin. "The Grand Bahama Island is off the port side. It's miles away, but you can see it on the horizon. Care to take a peek?"

"Are those Cubans on deck?"

"Yes. Why? Are you having problems with them?"

Rachel frowned and sighed heavily. "Not exactly, but I think Torres is enamored of me. It might be best to avoid him today. You don't think there'll be trouble in their camp, do you?"

"Yes, but I'm hoping it can be settled quickly with their leader."

"Why don't we just drop the crates and those two and leave?"

"As soon as they opened them and discovered the shortage, with no explanation from us, they'd be after us before sunset. Other lives are at stake."

Rachel recalled the Cuban's threat toward her family and friends, and those toward her partners; so more than her own life was in jeopardy. If she didn't believe that, she wouldn't take this risk. "You're right, Luke. I just don't want Dan, the crew, and this ship endangered because of me."

"You love him deeply, don't you?" he asked in a serious tone.

She noticed that for once he didn't have his perpetual grin teasing across his handsome face. "Yes."

"So why are you afraid to marry him?"

She and Luke had become close friends during the days he had guarded her at Moss Haven and during the last week together. She liked and trusted Dan's first mate. Luke had a sincere air about him. She desperately needed to talk to someone who could understand her predicament and give good advice.

"Why don't we sit down and chat?" he encouraged. "I'm off duty."

Rachel's weary soul and restless heart responded to his kindness and warmth. She took a chair, and Luke pulled the other one around to sit near her. "It's all so confusing and frightening. I'm scared, Luke, scared of something happening to Dan if I marry him. I'm scared I can't have children, and he wants them. He's endangered himself so many times to help and protect me. I could get him killed here or back home. I would die if that happened. I love him and need him so much it panics me."

"Why, Rachel? Don't you realize love is a precious and rare gift?"

"I don't know how much Dan's told you about me or how much you learned while investigating me . . ." she began, giving him a wry smile. "But there's much more involved. I don't know where to begin."

"Tell me the whole story; we have plenty of time. Maybe I can help. Maybe you and Dan are too close to the situation to be objective."

"I don't think anyone can help." Slowly and with anguish, she related her history to him. She paused only a moment before she revealed her deepest fears and Earl Starger's last visit at the hotel. "What if he wasn't lying, Luke? What if I am guilty of all those horrible deeds? What if I . . ."

The brown-haired man grasped her hands in his. With confidence in his azure gaze, he said, "You aren't crazy or guilty, Rachel."

There was anguish in her tone and expression as she refuted, "But—"

"No buts," he gently interrupted, tapping her lips with a forefinger. He wiped away a tear that had escaped her luminous eyes. "No madness and no guilt, woman. Trust me; I know you by now. He was wrong or lying."

"If he wasn't, Dan's life will be in danger."

"You could never harm Dan, just as he could never harm you. Love him and marry him, Rachel; you won't be sorry."

"Are you going to tell him about this talk? He'll wonder what's been keeping you down here so long."

"It isn't my place. You will, when the time is right."

They both stood and Rachel hugged him. "Thank you, Luke. You're a good friend to both of us."

"Any time you need a shoulder to lean on, mine's available."

Hours later, as the sun was setting in glorious splendor, they anchored near Andros Island—the largest of the Bahama chain—to take on fresh water. They would remain there until the morning tide. As Dan had promised, he took her ashore to the concealed pool for a quick bath and stroll.

The island was forested with Caribbean pine and hardwoods called "coppices," and woody vegetation of shrubs and vines. Earlier they had sighted a few fishing and farming villages a few miles upshore, but this area was unpopulated. The climate was perfect.

Rachel and Dan walked across a sandy beach holding hands. He led her into cool greenness that quickly encompassed them. She smelled heady fragrances. The only life they saw was frogs, lizards, birds, and small rodents.

When they reached the sunken pool, Rachel smiled. The turquoise water was shallow; it came from somewhere in the impenetrable forest.

"There's another one not far away; that's where the

men will go to get fresh water for the remainder of our voyage and catch a fast cleaning."

"It's lovely, Dan, so *romántico.*" She glanced at him suggestively.

He caught her sensual hint, shook his head with a grin, and said, "We best hurry; it'll be very dark in here soon. We can't linger."

As evening shadows closed in, they hurriedly bathed and left the cozy location. In his cabin, Rachel revealed her talk with Luke Connor this morning. Dan understood her fears, and told her the same thing Luke had. As if to prove how much he trusted her, he made passionate love to her.

Sunday, Rachel had another talk with Torres. She hoped and prayed it would help save their lives. "There's something I should tell you, Carlos. I don't have the entire order with me."

His dark eyes looked quizzical. "You have tricked me?"

"Not exactly, and please don't be angry. Let me explain. Your payment hasn't been found yet, so I had to come up with the cash to buy these arms and ammunition. Harrison Clements wouldn't let me have any without payment first, but the others are ready. George trusted me to pay him later for the ammunition, and he sent the entire order; it's aboard."

"What good are bullets without rifles, Señora Rachel?"

"I have six thousand. That's all the money I could come up with; I swear it, Carlos." Rachel explained in detail the financial misfortune that had befallen her. "Dan's helped all he could," she finished, "he's shipping the order free, and he paid for most of the arms. I thought this much of the order was better than nothing. The only things that saved me were Dan's generosity and not having to pay George for the ammunition. The company books were destroyed, so there's no record of my debt. I promise to keep searching for your payment. I swear, if I find it, I'll send the rest of your order. More than you ordered, to help your cause and to repay your kindness and patience. That's all I can do."

"It will not please *el lider*. He will not believe you."

"It's the truth. If you weren't threatening my family and friends, I would throw the crates ashore and disappear. No, I would have dumped this problem in yours and Harry's laps. I only came here to reason with your leader. I realized you didn't have the power to change the deal."

"El lider" will not change it. We need those arms, Señora Rachel."

"We're no longer *amigos?* It's back to 'Señora Rachel.' If this will get you into trouble, Carlos, I'm sorry. You did your duty and trusted me."

"You must do your duty, or others will suffer. I will not be the one sent to . . . persuade you and your partner to give us what we bought."

"Please help me explain to your leader," she beseeched. "I've done all I can. Doesn't that count for anything?"

"Only victory matters, and lives in my country and in yours."

Tears welled in her honey-colored eyes and she struggled hard not to cry. She chewed on her upper lip to make the pain distract her from that "feminine weakness." She searched her brain for an escape route. In an emotion-constricted voice, she asked, "Will your leader give me time to sell my home to raise the rest of the money for your arms? That's the only thing I have left worth anything. It'll take time to find a buyer. If I rush a sale, the buyer will know I'm desperate and will offer little. I need a hundred twenty thousand dollars to get the other four thousand rifles and dynamite."

"Why does Señor Clements not help you?"

"Because he thinks I have the money and thinks that when I'm terrified enough, I'll turn it over to him. He says he didn't have anything to do with Phillip's deal, so he isn't using his money to pay for it. He's also furious about the company being set afire and a worker killed. He hired guards for the company and his home to protect them against another attack from you and Joaquín. He claims he isn't afraid of your threats."

"*Aja!* We did not do those things, Raquel. Señor Leathers could not; he was dead. If you did not, he has lied to you. He must honor the deal; he said this in the *documento* I took to *mi lider,* as did Señor Leathers. All three gave their word; they agreed to let Señor McCandless take the dollars and deliver the order. If you have paid for all we carry, Señor Clements is the only *hombre* to make *dinero* on this."

Rachel was vexed. "Why didn't you tell me this before?"

"I did not know you did not know. Señor Clements met with Ricardo on the isle of Bimini the week before your *esposo* died."

So that was why Harry had such a golden tan so early in the year! "I thought Phillip was the only one who knew about the deal."

Carlos shook his dark head. "He said he wished to increase the order and would sell us the next one at a . . . cheaper price. Ramón said we would do so when we get more *dinero americano.*"

"Has Harry been to Cuba? Has he met your leader?"

"No. He contacted Ricardo through de Céspedes. Ramón sent him to the meeting; Joaquín and I were in your country with your *esposo.*"

"So," she reasoned aloud, "Harry learned from Ricardo that Phillip had the entire million dollars. He came to force it out of Phillip, but Phillip must have been angry with him for going to Ramón behind his back. Phillip was already suspicious of Harry cheating him on other orders." To sway him in her favor, she quickly used the ruse she had fabricated at the beginning of this mystery to solve it. "That's why Phillip hid the money and wouldn't give it to Harry and George. He was holding on to it to make certain nothing happened to it. But where did he hide it? I've searched everywhere. My heavens! What if Harry saw where Phillip concealed it when he came to visit the day before Phillip died? What if Harry's had it all along? What if he murdered Phillip? How deeply was George Leathers involved?"

Carlos paid close attention. "He agreed to make and sell us the bullets. He signed the *documento,* but it had no names. If your *esposo* did not tell him about us, he did not know who we are or where the order is going."

"That's good, because I liked and trusted him. I'll bet Harry killed George to keep him silent and to keep from having to pay him. All this time Harry's been behind the threats and attacks to scare me into paying for this order. He's probably planning to kill me when I return so there'll be no witnesses to his involvement." She told Carlos about the notes she'd received in her handwriting. "He's hired someone to forge my script; he'll probably use it to write a suicide note so everyone will think I killed Phillip, took the money, was behind all those other crimes, and then killed myself out of madness and guilt. If his evil plot worked, he would be rich and safe from the law and from your people. But he won't succeed!"

When Carlos remained silent and watchful, Rachel ventured, "If his name is on the contract, he's responsible for supplying arms, too. Force him to give you the rest of them. I've done my part. Besides, you told me there wasn't a written contract. If I had known all of this earlier, I could have solved this perilous mystery sooner. Why did you lie to me, Carlos?"

"There is a paper, but it says *nada* you can use. Ramón buried it to keep it secret. It tells that our order was placed and for how much *dinero*. All *tres hombres* signed it. Your *esposo* signed again when he was given the *dinero*."

"You must convince Ramón to give it to me. I can use it to prove Harry was involved with full knowledge of where the arms were going. Ricardo can give me a signed statement he met with Harry in Bimini."

"*No es posible.* Our deal must remain a secret. It is *urgente.*"

"Without evidence, Harry will get away with all he's done to us!"

"It is for Ramón to decide what is to be done. He will not be pleased at being tricked and betrayed."

"Then help me convince him Harry is the traitorous culprit."

Carlos glued his unreadable gaze to her pleading one. "I can only tell him what you have told me; that does not make it true."

"My name isn't on the agreement, so I'm not responsible."

Carlos pointed out, *"El nombre de su esposo* is, and he had the *dinero*. That is how Ramón will see it. *Qué lástima!*"

"If there's trouble in your camp, convince your leader to punish me, not the others. Let them leave unharmed. Agreed?"

"I can make no *promesas* for Ramón. It is his *decisión.*"

It was nearing dusk on Monday when Bahía de Nipe, their anchoring site, was approached. They had sailed within view of Cuba with her inlets, rugged cliffs, sandy beaches, and islets for hours. The hills and mountains of Sierra de Nipe and Sierra del Cristal loomed before them. The tropical air was balmy, and heady fragrances wafted on its currents. Along the irregular coastline, they had seen cultivated areas near the shore, light-green splotches surrounded by dark jade; the terrain had drifted into woods of valuable exotic timber, fruit trees, feathery palms, and mangrove thickets. It continued into fertile valleys and lush rain forests, Carlos told them.

Where the anchor was lowered at their rendezvous point, there were areas of short or no beachline between the ocean and verdant jungle. The water lapping at the hull was a purply blue, which became turquoise near the coast. The bay where they would land in a small boat was sided on the left and right with rocks, against which waves pounded and sent off white sprays.

"We will camp *aqui,*" Carlos pointed to the beach, "while Joaquín brings my people to get the arms. He will not return until *mañana.* You and Raquel will camp with me; no other *hombres* will leave the ship."

Dan tried to argue in an attempt to leave his love in safety and comfort, but Carlos refused to listen and agree. "She comes with us. *No argumento.*"

As the boat was rowed to shore by Dan and Carlos, threatening gray clouds hovered above the mountainous region. They passed over coral reefs of various shapes, sizes, and colors. Rachel saw fish darting amidst the rugged and beautiful formations, and pointed them out to the others. Dan took a peek, but the two Cuban rebels did not.

The men dragged the boat ashore, and Dan helped Rachel get out. Their shoes sank into soft ecru sand. Carlos spoke with Joaquín in Spanish. The brutish rebel replied at certain points, nodded several times, and departed. He was swallowed almost immediately by the lush greenery.

Twilight closed in as they settled down for the evening. Rachel's gaze roamed the terrain that was a fusion of vivid colors and intoxicating smells. Bougainvillea climbed trees and hillsides to decorate them with red, purple, and white blossoms. Lacy frangipani in many shades added beauty to the setting. Other tropical plants, shrubs, vines, and trees were abundant in a wild array of enchantment. Rachel was eager for dawn's light to let her gaze feast on the alluring landscape, but dreaded what the day would bring.

A hand shook Rachel's shoulder as she slept on her stomach, dark hair concealing her face. She stirred, turned, and looked at its owner. Her gaze widened in disbelief as she discovered the identity of the "only hope" Phillip had mentioned. The American rebel gaped at her in the same manner, scowled in anger, then pressed a finger to his lips for secrecy.

Chapter 22

"You are Señora Phillip McCandless?" he asked loud enough to be heard by others on the beach.

Rachel stared at him as she replied, "His widow; Phillip is dead."

"I am Ricardo," the twenty-three-year-old man said. "I will translate for you. Ramón does not speak *inglés.*"

"You're American," Rachel said evocatively.

"Sí, but I have been many months with my *amigos. Venga,* come."

"May I . . . be excused first?"

The man with shoulder-grazing dark-brown hair and matching eyes turned and asked permission in fluent Spanish to grant her request for privacy. Ricardo faced her again and said, "It is fine, but hurry. Ramón is anxious to discuss the trouble between our sides."

Rachel stood and straightened her skirt. She looked at the roughly clad Cuban rebels, most with lengthy hair and short beards. Dan sat on the ground with his hands tied behind his back; he sent her a smile. Rachel's mind was too dazed to react. On shaky legs, she vanished into concealing trees to recover her wits and poise while she excused herself. She couldn't understand why Phillip had kept such a valuable secret.

Anger and resentment toward her deceased husband resurfaced.

Rachel fingercombed her disheveled hair as she approached the large group of intimidating men who were studying her with keen interest. She wished she were more presentable and clear-headed for this vital meeting. She looked at Carlos, "Did you tell him everything I told you?" she asked him.

"*Sí*, Raquel, but he is *mucho* angry. The *rebelión* does not go well. Spanish soldiers attack and kill our *amigos*. We need the arms, and *pronto*."

She looked at the man Carlos Torres nodded at. He appeared broody and truculent, his eyes as dark as his long and wavy black hair, and they were glacial and piercing. She trembled in dread.

With a deeply lined scowl and gruff voice, the rebel leader spoke to Ricardo, who nodded understanding and focused on Rachel.

"Ramón asks if you *comprende* how *importante* the arms are. He wants to know why you have tricked and betrayed him."

"I haven't, but it's a long story." As she explained the predicament from the beginning, Ricardo observed her and translated. She answered honestly the questions Ramón passed through his American friend and ally. She knew it was safest and wisest for her to be completely honest. When the talk ended, she watched Ramón pace and think. She tried to keep her hungry gaze from feasting on Daniel Slade—or on her brother!

Rachel was filled with a mixture of joy and sadness, of confusion and enlightenment. Richard had grown to over six feet; he was lean and hard and muscular. His olive complexion had been darkened by the tropical sun. He had become more handsome over the six years since she had last seen or heard from him. She wondered if he knew where his twin sister was, as Rosemary had run away a year later. She yearned to

505

hug him, to ask him countless questions, but he had warned her to secrecy of their kinship. To expose it could endanger her brother and further imperil her.

As if he didn't know the beautiful woman, Richard "Ricardo" Fleming ignored his sister. If he had known she was Phillip McCandless's wife, he wouldn't have gotten her enmeshed in this scheme gone sour, a scheme he himself had suggested. How could he get Rachel out of this mess and safely back to Georgia when Ramón wanted to kill her as a threat to the double-crossing Harrison?

The leader came to Richard and talked to him for a while. Rachel got the impression Ramón was asking his trusted friend's opinion of the matter and of her. She waited with rising anxiety until her brother turned to speak.

"Ramón says the *rebelión* is growing in strength and fierceness. He says he must have the rest of the arms so his *hombres* can battle for their lives and freedom. Without them, our cause can be lost. He says you must come to our camp until he decides what to do. You and the *capitán.*"

"Why can't we talk and decide here . . . ? Is he going to kill us?" Rachel asked in alarm. She didn't want to get far from the ship or be trapped in the jungle in unfamiliar surroundings and between opposing forces.

"If the ship is sighted, we cannot be near it. Our *hombres* will unload the crates and hide them nearby. We will return for them later."

"You didn't answer my question. Is he going to kill us?"

"I do not know. *He* does not know yet. Stay calm and quiet."

Rachel caught the subtle warning in his last sentence. She also noticed how her brother concealed his emotions with skill and perfection. She was amazed by how much he had changed. If it came to a choice between her life and his loyalty to the *cubanos,* which would he choose? Considering the odds against them, Richard didn't have a choice.

"You must understand we can not trust a stranger in wartime."

Rachel seized the clue "stranger" that said to continue their ruse. "Your friends were with me when I tried to save this deal. Killing us won't get you the rest of the arms. You'll only be helping Harry get rid of us. If anyone has your money, it's him. I would not lie to you," she vowed, her gaze fused with her brother's.

Without visible reaction, Ricardo told her words to Ramón Ortega.

Carlos chatted with his leader. It was obvious he was arguing on her behalf and just as obvious that he vexed Ramón. He looked at her and said, "I am sorry, Raquel, he will not listen to me. He says I am bewitched by you."

She thanked Carlos for trying. "What now?" she asked.

"Sit while we unload the crates," Richard ordered. "We must hurry before soldiers come and attack. Our lookouts say they are not in this area today, but they might approach undetected by sea."

Rachel joined Dan, but they didn't have time to talk, for her love was released just then to escort the Cubans to his ship to fetch the arms and ammunition.

Richard glanced at her to warn her not to try to escape. *"La junglas* is a dangerous place," he said, "and you will be shot. If you are hungry, eat while we work. That would be wise, as we have a long walk after when we finish."

"Do I have to sit here for hours in the sun or can I move around?"

"As long as you do not run away, do as you please."

"Thank you, Ricardo."

"De nada," he replied, a tiny gleam of a smile in his eyes.

"Vámonos, amigos! Dénse prisa!" Ramon shouted for some of the men to get moving and to hurry with their task.

Rachel walked to the shade of the swaying palms and leaned against one. She watched the small group get into Dan's boat and head for his ship. The others sat on the sand and chatted, occasionally glancing at her. She shielded her eyes against the blazing sun and observed their trip to the *Merry Wind.* She saw her love, her brother, and the rebels climb aboard. Rachel knew Dan had been warned to make no trouble or she would be slain.

Time seemed to move at a snail's pace as two boats went back and forth between the coast and the ship to unload the cargo. The men on the beach worked steadily as they carried the long rifle crates and small cartridge cases into the dense jungle for concealment and later retrieval.

When the task was done, Luke and three seamen were ordered to take the boats to the ship to await Ramón's decision. The first mate looked at his captain with uncertainty and worry. Dan told his best friend to obey. With him and Rachel in the control of the rebels the crew couldn't risk a rescue battle or get enough men ashore in a group to fight one before taking heavy losses. The boats shoved off and returned to the *Merry Wind* to keep eyes alert for possible assistance with a daring escape.

Two Cubans were left behind to make certain Dan's crew didn't follow the others to attempt a foolish rescue. Before they settled down beneath shady palms, the beach and path were brushed clean of telltale tracks.

The trek to the rebel camp began. Cubans walked

in front of and behind the captives, and several took positions beyond and to the rear of the group as lookouts. Ramón Ortega was close to the front of the column on the well-trodden dirt path; Richard journeyed at his side without glancing at his sister. Carlos was assigned to guard Rachel, and Joaquín was farther back with a bound Dan.

The trail ascended into hills and *sierras* of lush vegetation. The terrain was ruggedly beautiful in its striking wildness. They crossed a savannah where cattle grazed on *paraná* grass. They saw coconut, payaba, banana, mango, cieba, palm, ebony, and mangrove, its roots above ground. Carlos told Rachel that most of their soil was fertile and could be cultivated year round. She noticed that bougainvilla and frangipani were abundant in many areas, sending forth a pleasurably intense fragrance.

They skirted *aldeas,* villages, in clearings where ground stolen from the ever-encroaching jungle was cluttered with *chozas*—shacks, huts, and mud-daubed wattles with thatched roofs of grass or palm branches. Carlos whispered the inhabitants were *guajiros,* peasants. The excitingly different landscape was verdant and dense. Vines climbed trees and hillsides, many varieties in splendid bloom. Ferns along the path teased at their legs and shoes. Rays of sunlight filtered through unfamiliar trees with thick foliage that was several shades of green and formed a canopy above them. They used a wooden footbridge at one river, to cross. At another point of the river's winding course, they forded at a shallow spot.

The leader halted them there for a rest and water break. Everyone sat on the ground, but kept silent in the vulnerable location.

Rachel couldn't see Dan because of the many men between them, but knew he hadn't caused his churlish guard any problem. She was glad she was in good physical condition, but the long walk in the tropical climate was tiring. She was also glad she had changed into pants, shirt, and boots to make the trek easier. She watched Ramón Ortega from beneath lowered lashes. His body and expression were taut with suspense and attention. The leader's eyes were in constant motion as they scanned for trouble. She had noticed how brittle and cold they were, and wondered what had made him into such a bellicose man. Perhaps years of fighting had changed him. Ramón couldn't possibly have been this way always, or her brother wouldn't be his friend and ally. Yet, what did she know about the kind of man Richard Fleming was today?

She observed how Richard stayed close to the leader, as if his bodyguard and adviser. She yearned to speak privately with her brother. She wondered at his reactions to their unexpected reunion and her peril, but Carlos halted her speculations, as he helped her to her feet, to continue the trek.

Butterflies and other insects darted among exotic blossoms. Birds were numerous and colorful and noisy, including tiny bee hummers and royal thrushes. Carlos pointed out several brilliantly shaded parrots. She noted the humidity had increased to rain-forest level, sultry, but not oppressive. She had seen small animals—lizards, frogs, spiders, and a rodent Carlos called a *hutía,* which he said was edible. She wondered when they would reach the encampment and how big it was. She knew, from the changing angles of the sun, that they didn't take a direct route to it, so she didn't know how far they were from the coast and the ship. Nor could she guess how to return to them if she and Dan escaped. She had tried to pay attention to their trail for later use, but it was too—

"We rest *aquí,*" Carlos interrupted her thoughts.

A waterfall seemingly burst forth in a rush of white liquid from the dark interior of the jungle and cascaded into a pool of bluish green. Trees, some with long brown pods or exposed roots, cloaked the shoulders of the lovely area. On three sides, tropical flowers and shrubs grew in abundance. Lacy ferns, moss, and lichen in greens and yellows covered banks and rocks of assorted sizes. Sunlight came through an opening in the leafy canopy above the pool, creating a goldish glow. The experienced fighters sat down and sipped from canteens, on alert with rifles across their laps.

"It's beautiful, Carlos. May I wash my face and hands?"

"Sí," he said, and assisted her over rocks to a solid spot near the pool.

Rachel knelt at the edge, wetting the knees of her pants. She cupped her hands, scooped up water, and drank until her thirst was quenched. She used a handkerchief Carlos gave her to refresh her face. "That feels wonderful," she murmured. She wished she were alone with Daniel Slade in this romantic and intimate setting. It would be wonderful and arousing to swim naked and make love here. "How much farther to your camp?"

"One hour," he replied.

"Do you have more men there?"

"Sí, muchos."

"Do you think Ramón is softening any toward us?"

"Do not ask questions I cannot answer, but do not be afraid."

She assumed he was under orders not to reveal anything to her. *"Gracias.* You've been very kind. May I take Dan a drink?" Carlos nodded. Rachel took the canteen he handed to her. She filled it with fresh water and walked to where Dan sat, with Carlos trailing her. She squatted before her love and smiled as she tipped the canteen to his mouth.

Dan's eyes never left her lovely and flushed face while he drank. When he nudged the container with his chin to indicate he was finished, she removed it. He watched her soak a handkerchief and wash perspira-

511

tion from his face. It felt wonderful to his sweaty flesh. He smiled when she fingercombed his tousled ebony hair. "I'm a mess, eh?" he asked, happy to have her near to him.

"Not bad," she replied with a grin. "Do you have to keep his hands tied?" She asked Carlos. "With me in danger, he won't try to escape."

"It is an order from Ramón."

"Will you ask—"

"No, Raquel; it is not wise to anger him more."

"It's all right, Rachel; the rope isn't too uncomfortable."

"I don't like his being helpless in case we run into Spanish soldiers," she told Carlos. "There's a war going on here."

"Just keep a calm head on your shoulders; I'll fine."

She looked at her love. "They have no right to treat us like this."

"Give Ramón time to cool off and think," Dan encouraged. "He has to realize the best thing to do is free us to get the other guns."

"He seems too cold and stubborn to make a truce. He won't trust us."

"What about Phillip's hints?" he reminded. "Will they help?"

Rachel chose her words with care. "I understand, but it won't work. Phillip kept too many secrets, more than we've discovered so far."

Dan perceived a clue in her words, but couldn't grasp its meaning. He wondered if it had to do with the American at Ramón's side. It didn't seem likely, as the two hadn't shown any recognition of each other.

"We must go," Carlos told the couple.

Rachel stood and Dan got to his feet. They exchanged one more smile before they took their places in the human column on the well-worn trail.

t was dusk when they reached the end of their journey, but enough daylight was left to reveal it was a
large camp that spread out into several nature-made
clearings. To the captive couple, it looked as if around
a thousand men and at least fifty women made up the
band. Food was cooking over low campfires whose
smoke didn't seem sufficient to give away their location. The Cuban rebels were busy with evening chores
and activities. The men cleaned weapons of various
kinds, and most wore machetes and knives at their
waists. Some chatted, some gambled, some smoked
cigars, and others rested from scouting treks. There
were a few lean-tos and tents, but most areas had only
sleeping mats of banana or palm branches. Cloth
sacks near those makeshift beds held the men's
possessions. Despite the number of people and work
in progress, the area wasn't noisy.

Rachel and Dan were placed at Ramón Ortega's
campsite. The leader and "Ricardo" sat down to be
served a meal by a lovely beauty with dark, flowing
hair and expressive brown eyes. Her revealing looks
and behavior toward the leader told Dan and Rachel
that she was Ramón's woman.

Rosaria handed the couple metal plates with black
beans, chicken, rice, and fried plantains. She passed
them cups of strong *café cubano*.

The prisoners were ignored as everyone ate, and the
two men talked in Spanish. Rosaria sat near Ramón,
but didn't join the conversation. When they finished,
she gathered the dishes and cups and left to wash
them. One of the returning rebels came and spoke
with *el lider*, who looked as if the news he received
was infuriating. He sent Rachel a fierce scowl that
made her tremble and conclude things weren't going
well for his cause. Tomas kept pointing northward as
he spoke swiftly with excitement.

Richard looked concerned and angered. "I'm going to talk with Ramón," he said to his sister. "Don't try anything foolish or you'll be killed. You're in greater danger from Spanish soldiers than from us, so stay put. This trouble has to be resolved fast and now."

Dan watched the tall and handsome man leave with the rebel leader, then disappear into the forest together. "Do you know who he is?"

Rachel looked at him and nodded. "My brother Richard Fleming."

Dan gaped at her. "But you told me you didn't—"

Pressed for private response time, Rachel interrupted, "I didn't know he was here, and it came as a shock. He signaled me to silence when he woke me this morning. I don't know if he can get us out of this mess, but he'll try; I'm sure of it."

"Is that what you meant about Phillip keeping more secrets?"

"Yes. Carlos said Ricardo suggested the arms deal. They checked all three partners. Harry met with my brother on Bimini Island, remember? Phillip and Harry had to know I'm his sister, and maybe those Cubans did, too."

"Then why did they threaten you, and why are you a prisoner?"

Confused, she speculated, "Richard must not have been told I was Phillip's wife. He looked shocked to see me. Maybe, when the investigations were done, Carlos and Joaquín didn't make the connection or mention revealing names. Maybe they don't know Ricardo's real identity."

"You think that's what Richard is telling Ramón now?"

Rachel glanced in the direction they had gone. "I guess it depends on how close they are. Richard suggested the deal, and the alleged traitor turns out to be his sister! How will that look to Ramón and his band?

514

Maybe exposing our relationship would be more damaging than helpful.

"Any time," she fretted, "he could be a prisoner like us. I don't want him killed just when I find him again. I haven't seen him since '69. There's so much I want to ask him and tell him. I wish we could talk or—"

Rosaria returned and Rachel fell silent, as she didn't know if the sultry woman could speak or understand English. Dan comprehended her caution. Rosaria tended her evening tasks, but occasionally smiled at the couple. Rachel returned her genial overtures, but felt since she was a captive she shouldn't offer to help with camp chores.

The hour grew late. Most of the men and women turned in for the night, but a few stood guard around the slumbering camp. The couple didn't know if an enlightening talk had taken place or if the men had gone on a mission. A sweet-smelling gentle breeze filled the air and cooled them. They heard frogs croaking, crickets chirping, and rebels snoring. Fires had burned to low and smokeless coals. The setting was deceptively peaceful. But somewhere in the dark and steamy jungle dangers abounded.

Rosaria placed a wide sleeping mat nearby and motioned for them to share it, having perceived their closeness to each other. The couple thanked her and lay down. Rachel cuddled close to Dan, drawing from his strength and courage. Soon, exhausted in mind and body, both went to sleep.

At dawn, they were awakened by Richard and brought food by Rosaria. When they finished, her brother and the rebel leader moved closer to talk.

"Can you get the rest of the arms if we free you?" Richard asked.

Rachel nodded. She didn't know how much or if anything her brother had told Ramón about them.

"How long will it take? Our position is fragile."

"A few weeks," Dan responded, "Three at the most. I'll pay for them."

Rachel glanced at her lover in confusion. "How?" she fretted.

"I'll find a way to get the money," he reassured her

"We'll force Harry to hand them over withou more money."

"Let's get this matter settled first, then work or him," Dan suggested.

Rachel looked at her brother and asked, "You'l release us?"

Richard smiled and said, "Today. You must leav before trouble comes. Do not let us down, Rachel; we need those arms and ammunition."

"You convinced Ramón to trust us?"

"Sí, I gave my word to a good friend."

"I won't fail you, Rich— Ricardo."

"Ramón wanted to keep you here as a hostag while Capitán Slade fetched the weapons," he dis closed. "He was going to murder you in a month if h didn't return with them. I persuaded him you spoke the truth and to let you leave. It isn't wise to keep suc a beautiful woman in camp so long."

"I promise you the rest of the weapons will be ir your hands soon, no matter what I have to do to ge them and to protect her."

"We will trust you, Capitán Slade. But do not be tray us again."

"Can we talk alone?" Rachel asked almost hesi tantly.

Richard shook his head and whispered, "It is dan gerous to share the truth with anyone except clos friends."

Rachel grasped his meaning. "When do we leave?" she asked.

"Soon. The longer you stay, the greater the danger of your ship being confiscated and your crew captured. Our men are fetching the hidden weapons as we speak. They will arm many bands to battle our cause."

"I hope you win it. If there's any way possible, we'll send extra arms."

"Gracias, Rachel. Our cause is just, and we will win it; but it will require much time and bloodshed."

"Protect yourselves always. If—"

Tomas and Eduardo raced into the clearing and shouted warnings of an imminent attack by Spanish soldiers. Orders were given and passed along with swiftness and efficiency. The people hurried, but did not panic. The noise of preparations and excited voices were kept at a minimum. Well-trained and experienced rebels grabbed their weapons and possessions to scatter into the encompassing landscape. Only things too heavy or cumbersome to carry were abandoned along with the exposed campsite.

"Capitán Rafael de Cardova approaches. Take these," Richard said as he passed a pistol and machete to Dan. "Keep up and don't lose sight of me," he warned his sister, who appeared alarmed by the approaching peril.

Rachel and Dan followed Richard Fleming and a small band into the jungle. The couple ran as fast as they could, but felt vulnerable in the strange surrounding. Exotic vegetation slapped them in the face and nipped at their arms. Their breathing became labored and swift; their hearts pounded; their lips and throats dried. They didn't know if they would come out of this alive, especially if they became separated from the others.

"Come on!" Richard shouted when Rachel lagged behind with a stitch in her side and Dan slowed to grab her hand and pull her along.

It seemed as if they ran at top speed for two hours,

with enemies blazing guns to their rear and with th
cruel jungle trying to slow their pace with verdant an
tangly obstacles. When shouts of *"Alto!"* were hear
beyond and behind them, they left the dirt path t
prevent being trapped between two forces of the gov
ernment. Several skilled men took turns clearing
passable trail through dense vegetation with slashin
machetes.

Rachel and Dan obediently followed her brothe
and Ramón. Their hearts throbbed in panic and from
their exertions in the humid heat. They didn't notic
their route or the lovely terrain as they mindlessl
moved onward.

They skirted a sugar plantation with cane fields tha
stretched for miles. The thick blades could provid
concealment there if necessary. Workers paid no at
tention to them, as they knew what was taking plac
with their liberators. They moved until darknes
halted them and they stopped to hide and sleep for
few hours. Exhaustion and a lack of privacy pre
vented questions from being asked or answers give
between brother and sister. But Ramón smiled an
spoke to her in Spanish.

"He said not to be afraid," Richard translated. "H
will protect you and get you out of here safely. H
knows the jungle better than the soldiers."

"Gracias, Ramón," she said and smiled, seeing an
other side of the rebel leader, a kind and genial on
she found pleasing. "After we leave here, we won't le
you down; I promise."

Her brother told *el lider* her response. Ramón Or
tega smiled and nodded. He handed Rachel his can
teen, told her to drink, then sleep.

Dan was tense. He didn't know if his ship would b
waiting when—or if—they reached the coast, as h
had ordered Luke to sail if trouble arose.

* * *

t dawn, Richard awakened them. "The others are ping to lead our enemies away from us so I can get pu to the coast and the ship. Stay quiet, not a word; pounds carry far. *Comprende?"*

Rachel and Dan nodded. Ramón and his men eaded to the right, cutting a slightly obvious path to ptice pursuit and deception.

"We have to struggle through and try not to make ur passing and direction noticeable." Richard inructed. He told Dan to take the lead, that he would pver their tracks. "No broken limbs or crushed rns," he cautioned. "Wriggle around any obstacle rithout damaging it. Be ready to flee if I give the ord. Get to the ship and sail. I'll hang behind to pver your retreat and lead them on a merry chase way from you."

"No," Rachel protested. "You'll be captured and illed."

"Do as I say, my sister, or we will all be killed for pothing."

"Why are you doing this? What are you doing ere?"

"There's no time to explain, and the less you know he better for everyone involved. Tell Mama I'm fine nd I'll be home in six to twelve months. I'll explain verything then. A friend of mine will contact you to elp you with the rest of the arms. I told Ramón ou're my sister and to trust you. Don't let me down, Rachel. I love you, my beautiful and brave sister. *Hasta luego.* Now, go, before it's too late to save any f us," he commanded in a stern tone.

With caution and skill, Dan urged her toward the oast, and Richard brought up the rear. Every time hey stole a short breather, Rachel tried to question Richard in whispers, but her brother halted her, adising her to rest and save her energy and to wait for nswers until later.

The desperate trek was arduous and frightening but they succeeded.

When they reached the edge of the forest, Richard glanced at the ship beside Dan's but it didn't worry him. "Don't wait for a boat," he ordered. "Swim for the ship. I can hear the soldiers closing in." He rushed the couple across the beach where deep sand grabbed at their feet. "Go!" he demanded when his sister hesitated. "Take her now, Slade, or she's dead."

"Come with us, Richard," she urged in panic, reaching for his arm.

He eluded her grasp. "No, I'm safe here. Go!" he shouted again. He took a position on one knee a few feet away and began firing at his foes.

Rachel took in the danger. From one direction, Ramón's small group of rebels poured onto the beach to provide cover for the daring escape. From the other, a larger group of Spanish soldiers were in sight. She realized they were in the middle of what appeared to be a fierce battle in the making; the odds were against the rebel side.

"Get her out of here!" Richard demanded, looking worried.

As Dan yanked on Rachel's arm and dragged her into the aquamarine sea, she resisted and yelled, "I love you! Please come with us!"

"My place is here. Keep your promise. Damn it, Rachel, go!"

In that moment of distraction, Richard's vulnerable body was thrown backward as he was shot by government soldiers. Ramón and others reached him first. The rebel leader cradled the American in his arms like an injured child as the Cuban fired shot after shot at the advancing soldiers who dropped to their stomachs to make more difficult targets.

Dan pulled Rachel farther into the crashing waves, refusing to release her hand as she jerked to free it to return to her fallen brother's side. "No, love; we must leave. He risked his life to save yours. There's nothing we can do against such odds and unarmed." He had tossed his borrowed weapons back to Richard to have his hands free for swimming.

"Let me go," she pleaded, but Dan refused.

An excellent and strong swimmer, Daniel headed for the boat rowing toward them. He kept his attention on Luke and on the three men with him who were covering the distance between them with speed and urgency. He heard shooting behind him and the pleas of the woman he was dragging by one arm, but he didn't halt in his intention. He saw another ship anchored near the *Merry Wind,* but didn't want to imagine who was aboard and why they were there, as neither was flying an American or other country's flag. His crew's behavior and a lack of response to the battle ashore told him it couldn't be a Spanish ship.

The boat met them and hauled them inside, then immediately headed back to the clipper. Rachel struggled to see the lethal action on the beach. Dan watched with her as Richard was thrown across Ramón's shoulder and taken away. Neither could guess if he was alive or dead, but he clearly wasn't being left behind to face the persistent Spanish attack. The rebels vanished into the jungle under heavy fire with the soldiers in swift pursuit.

Rachel collapsed into Dan's arms and wept in fear. No one spoke after Dan shook his head to order them to silence. The boat reached the *Merry Wind* and they were taken aboard.

A man with white-blond hair and ice-blue eyes met the fatigued couple, along with armed American sailors. "I'm Peter Garrett," he introduced himself. "A United States special agent. I was ordered to come after you, Captain Slade and Mrs. McCandless."

"Are we under arrest?" Dan asked as he sized up the stranger.

Rachel prevented Peter's reply when she shouted,

"You have to go ashore and rescue my brother. He was shot. We must get him home to a doctor. Please, Dan, you can't let them leave Richard here at the mercy of those Spanish soldiers."

"Your brother is fighting here?"

"Yes. Richard Fleming, an American. He helped us escape. We can't leave him; he's wounded and I doubt they have skilled doctors here to treat him."

"Let's talk in your cabin, Captain Slade; this is a serious matter."

"No, go rescue Richard!"

"We can't, Mrs. McCandless; that's Spanish soil and we're American officers. I'm sure his friends will take care of him. I was watching with my fieldglasses; he took a bullet in the shoulder and they got him away. Look for yourself; the soldiers are back on the beach, watching us. They're not in pursuit." He saw her hug the railing as her gaze studied the shore where only Spanish soldiers were watching them. "We have to sail before they alert their government to our presence; they'll send its ships to destroy ours. We can't be taken prisoner. I'll stay aboard to question you two." Peter Garrett ordered the armed sailors to return to his ship and to follow the *Merry Wind* close, with cannons aimed at her to halt a rash flight.

Dan knew he couldn't battle his country's forces. He put Luke in charge, then guided Rachel and the agent to his quarters. The two ships got undersail within minutes.

Rachel—dirty, sopping, her hair tangled—rushed to the mullioned windows and stared at the receding island where her only remaining brother lay wounded and in peril. She prayed for Richard's survival and safety as tears eased down her flushed and scratched cheeks. She didn't care if the salty liquid stung or how disheveled she looked. Her heart was filled with sadness, fearing his loss was final this time.

"If you have brandy or the like, Captain Slade, she

can use some to calm her down," the blond-haired agent suggested. "So can you. I'm sure what you've experienced has been difficult."

Dan prepared two glasses. He walked to Rachel and pressed one into her hand. "Drink it, love, you need it."

Rachel tossed down the contents in almost one swallow to relieve her tension. As the fiery drink hit her throat, she coughed and struggled to breathe. Her soulful eyes watered even more and sent tears racing down her face.

Dan wiped them away with gentleness and soothed, "That'll make you feel better."

"How can I relax until I know Richard's alive and safe? Why couldn't we try to rescue him?"

"The forces against us were too large, love. I'm sure Ramón and the others will take good care of him."

Rachel faced the man with crystal-blue eyes and pleasant features. "You and your men could have helped! How could you leave an American in such danger? Don't you know or remember what the Spanish did to our sailors aboard the *Virginius* in '73?"

"Yes, but we couldn't interfere and create a nasty incident. America has taken a neutral stand for now. We're American authorities, so we can't risk provoking a war with Spain to save one man's life. Richard Fleming is there by choice, just as you two were. That's what we have to discuss. I was sent to capture you for gun-running and for possible connections to the murders of Phillip McCandless and George Leathers."

Chapter 23

"That's a lie!" Rachel refuted. "We didn't kill anyone."

"If I'm going to help you two get out of this mess, you have to be totally honest with me. Tell me from the beginning, everything about you and what you're doing here. *Everything*," he stressed.

Rachel looked at Dan in trepidation, but he advised, "Do as he says, love. We have no choice."

"But it might blacken Phillip's memory," she argued.

"We can't worry about that. Phillip got himself into this trouble with his eyes open wide. We have to clear ourselves."

"He's right, Mrs. McCandless. The charges and accusations are serious. To save yourselves, you have to be honest with me."

"We didn't kill George Leathers or my husband. You can't have any evidence to the contrary, unless it's forged or planted."

"What about gun-running?" Peter ventured. "Why are you two here?"

"We had a clearance from customs to ship arms."

"I know," Peter replied in a calm tone. "But to Haiti, not Cuba, where there's a rebellion in progress."

"How do you know we didn't drop off our cargo

there before sailing here to visit my brother?" Rachel countered. "It's not far away."

Peter was impressed by her courage and wits. "Carlos Torres and Joaquín Chavous brought you straight here to deliver arms and ammunition to Ramón Ortega, and we all know that to be a fact. What I don't understand is why you're claiming to be Richard Fleming's sister."

"Because I am! I was Rachel Fleming before I married."

"No, you were Rachel Newman; that's what I was told."

"Richard and I were born on White Cloud, our family's cotton plantation in Georgia," Rachel said. "He ran away from home in '69 because of our cruel Yankee carpetbagger stepfather. Our father and older brother were killed during the war. I ran away from home in '72 when I married William Barlow. He died, so I wed Craig Newman. After *he* died, I married Phillip McCandless last August. I haven't seen or heard from Richard in six years. When I learned he was in Cuba, I visited with him. Is that a crime?"

"Your mother's name is?" Peter evoked.

"Catherine Fleming Starger."

"Do you have other brothers and sisters?"

"Rosemary is Richard's twin, but she ran away the year after he did. We have two deceased brothers, Randall and Robert; one died in the war and one drowned after our mother married Earl Starger."

After the genial agent nodded agreement to each fact related, Rachel asked how he knew so much about her and her family.

"I've been on this case since January, so I know everything about it" was his answer.

Baffled, Dan inquired, "If you knew, why didn't you stop it?"

"Because the arms deal was my idea." Peter observed the stunned reactions of both people. "America is publicly neutral and must appear to remain that way, so it gave us the means to supply arms to the rebels without involving the United States openly. I'm the one who found Phillip McCandless and gave the information to Richard; and he passed it on to Ramón Ortega as his idea. Since he was from Georgia, it was logical he knew such people and things." He saw their astonishment increase.

"Why would my brother and the rebels trust you?"

"Because Richard and I are friends and partners. Richard Fleming is a special agent for the American government; he has been for years. He couldn't tell you and risk destroying his cover; we need him in Cuba. She's a major supplier of sugar and other products, so we have to protect our interests. And we also believe in their fight for independence."

"You're telling me my brother is a secret agent for the United States?"

Peter smiled and admitted, "Yes. That's why I had to make certain you were his sister before I revealed anything to you."

Rachel was stunned. "How? When?"

"After Richard left home, he spent some time in Athens, Augusta, and Savannah. He decided to hire onto a ship to seek adventures around the world. During one voyage, he docked in Charleston. From there, he took a sugar ship. He liked that trade and Cuba, so he kept it up; that's how he learned to speak Spanish. We were in the same port one night when several bullies attacked me. Richard saved my life. We got to talking and became friends. I convinced him to become a fellow agent. We've done many missions together. Don't worry about him; he's smart and skilled. When things got hot in Cuba, since he knew the language and the island, he was assigned there fifteen months ago to spy and to protect American interests. He caused trouble with Spanish soldiers to catch the rebels' eye and trust. He joined up with

Ramón Ortega's band and became close friends with him. Their biggest need was arms and ammunition. I found McCandless and passed word and money to him to make the deal. He sent Torres and Chavous to prevent him being recognized or connected to the deal. When problems arose and were reported to him, he alerted me to investigate."

"The million-dollar payment was from you, from our government?"

"Partly from our government, from private businessmen with interests there, and from Cuban landowners who want freedom. After I got the information to Richard, he sent Torres and Chavous to make the deal in January and to pass along the advance. In February, your husband sent a message to Richard that he wanted out of the deal unless the balance was paid. Richard sent the same two men to deliver it on March twenty-third, but he alerted me to trouble. I met with McCandless. When they went to escort the shipment home on May thirteenth, they were told of more problems. They telegraphed their contact in Charleston, who sent a message to Richard on a sugar ship. That's when Torres and Chavous took it upon themselves to do further checking on the partners and their families, to use the information as threats. They sent another message on May twenty-second. Richard received it on the twenty-seventh and alerted me again. I got the news on June second that McCandless was dead, the payments were missing, and his widow and partners were trying to renege on the deal. I reached Savannah on the third, after you'd sailed. The local authorities had sent for government help, because you'd fled the country out of their jurisdiction. Your stepfather reported you two were running guns to Cuban rebels, and the Chief told me you were a suspect in two recent murders and several past ones. He relished telling me your whole story. Naturally I

527

couldn't say I was already involved, so I sailed here to handle things."

Dan probed for clarification, "You found Phillip for them?"

"That's right. When he got nervous in February, I met with him, explained the situation, and convinced him to stay in the deal to help his country. That's when he learned Richard Fleming was our contact, but he didn't tell me his wife was Richard's sister. From my study, I knew you as Rachel Newman. I doubt Torres and Chavous know Ricardo's American name, or mentioned the names of the widow's or her mother in their reports. I knew the rendezvous point, so I came straight here. You were already ashore. All I could do was wait and hope for the best."

Rachel was angered and accused, "If Richard is your friend and partner, why didn't you rescue him?"

"I told you, we can't get publicly involved. Richard and I know the risks we take, and we accept them. He wouldn't want me to destroy this mission. Besides, we couldn't have gotten to him. We don't know where the new camp is located. Right now, the jungle's crawling with soldiers. The best way to protect Richard is to leave his survival to his friends there."

"What about that clearance letter for customs?" Dan asked.

"I was the one who supplied it."

Rachel realized that if the United States Government was at the heart of this matter and the money was lost on gambling, it would explain why Phillip had panicked after losing the advance; that would explain why he had demanded the balance to use to save himself and the deal. It also gave a reason for his moodiness toward the end. "How is Harrison Clements involved, and George Leathers? Did you approach them, too?"

"Only McCandless; he was in charge." Peter Garrett related the facts and his assumptions about every

528

point and person, and they matched Rachel's and Dan's. "Tell me all you know and did," the agent coaxed.

Rachel and Dan complied, then she concluded, "Phillip must have been furious when Harry met with Richard behind his back. I'm sure Harry is responsible for those threats Phillip and I received. He might have the missing money."

"I have an idea how we can find out," Peter hinted, then explained.

"That's clever," Dan complimented the agent when he had finished. "What about us and the rest of the arms? We promised Richard we'd send them in a few weeks. If we fail, the rebels will either doubt him or they'll send Torres and Chavous to harm us."

"I'll take care of that, so forget about it. We have to protect you two and Richard's cover. By the time I finish with Harrison Clements, I hope to have enough to see him hanged for murder and other crimes."

"You probably can add one more," Rachel disclosed, then told him of her suspicions about the patented designs used. "If he forged those intimidating notes to me, he could have forged the licenses, and maybe Milton Baldwin's loan agreement to steal the shipping firm from me also."

Dan explained her meaning as Rachel sipped water to wet her throat, dry from hours of talking.

"We'll know the whole truth soon. Don't worry; I'll have you two exonerated of gun-running after we dock. I don't know what I can do about those other allegations, unless Clements exposes facts about them."

"You believe us?"

Peter smiled and said, "Yes, Rachel, I do. You're a very brave and smart woman. You've handled yourself well in this trying situation." He turned to Dan.

"How did you get enmeshed in all of this, Captain?" he asked.

Dan had no choice except to use his original ruse, which he did. He would tell Peter Garrett the truth later and swear the agent to secrecy until he could tell Rachel everything in private and at the right time. He wanted to wait until all matters were resolved before he confessed his big secret. He didn't want to say or do anything to repulse or hurt his love at this delicate time and when she was so distraught over her brother's fate. He was amazed and pleased by the turn in events and relieved they'd done nothing illegal. Yet, Phillip's initial motives and the money were still missing . . .

As they completed their conversation, Dan realized that Peter obviously had not checked the details of Phillip's deceased family, as the agent hadn't seemed to know the name Daniel Slade. If he had, Peter surely would have queried the similarity.

By the time both ships anchored at Grand Bahama Island for fresh water on Sunday, June thirteenth, Rachel, Dan, and Peter had talked of their plans many times. Peter dismissed the other ship with orders to return to its home port while he stayed aboard the *Merry Wind* with two of his agents who would help entrap Harrison Clements in a few days.

At a lovely lagoon, Dan and Rachel were given their first real moments of privacy since anchoring at Cuba. She had used Luke's cabin while the three men shared Dan's larger quarters. At last, they were alone. The location was verdant and dense with tropical vegetation, trees, vines, and exotic flora. The setting was sultry and humid. Lacy ferns and feathery palms were stirred to life by a breeze that swept through the area in a rush. Wonderful smells clung almost intimately to the still air left behind. Unfamiliar flowers

530

and blossoms on plants and vines decorated their romantic surroundings with color and beauty. The pool was an aquamarine shade, and most enticing. Their awakened senses took in nature's splendor, then each other.

As they embraced and kissed, she murmured against his lips, "It's been so long since we could touch like this. I've missed you."

"With Peter in on the case, we'll be free of all entanglements soon. Maybe he can help extricate you from those other troubles."

"I don't know how, Dan; they've been hanging over my head for years. If someone else is to blame, how could he find out and prove me innocent?"

He tenderly cuffed her chin. "After he's done with Harry, we'll turn over the notes and papers to him," he told her. "Maybe he has skilled men who can unravel the riddles in them."

Rachel didn't want to build up false hopes. "That would be wonderful. I want to be free and clear of all suspicions."

He gazed into her eyes. "When you are, will you marry me, woman?"

"I haven't proven myself yet," she reminded.

"Well, let's get busy taking care of that right now," he jested.

"Do with me as you will," she sighed seductively. "How could any man resist an offer like that?"

Rachel's lips touched his, brushing them lightly with hers. Dan's arms banded her body and drew it close. It was nearing dusk, so they had little time to stay there. Both were aware of how long it had been since they'd made love with blissful abandon. Their hungers raged, and neither wanted to rush these precious moments, but they knew they must.

They parted to remove their clothes, too much in love and ensnared by passion to be modest. Dan bent forward to kiss the tip of each breast before traveling up her neck to tease her ear, then ravenously devour her parted lips. They kissed and caressed, stroking and stimulating each other. Their tongues moved with skill and eagerness. They were intoxicated and entranced by each other.

The palm of his hand moved over one breast in a circular motion to enflame and tauten it even more than it was, then went to the other to do the same. He used his mouth to sear fiery kisses and burning caresses over her quivering flesh. The sea captain voyaged over her bare shoulder, the hollow of her throat, and the pulse point that told him how aroused she was. His lips tasted and explored her sweet desire and heady surrender. He wanted to stir her to greater heights before he joined their bodies.

Rachel's arms were around him, and her hands drifted up and down his back. She enjoyed the hardness and suppleness of his muscles and skin. Her body tingled and smoldered from his touch. He was tantalizing and pleasuring her from head to toe. She was glad she didn't have to battle her need for him. She had longed for this staggering contact for days.

Dan's body was aflame with need, too, and scorching desire. Every place he touched with hands or lips was responsive. He yearned to bring every inch of her to awareness and blazing life. He was enchanted by the way she gave him free rein over her body and will with such deep love and trust. Her nearness was driving him wild. Her skin was as silky as a satin ribbon, its olive hue glowing healthily. Every part of her called out to him to touch it and adore it. Rapturous sensations assailed him as her hands wandered over his body. When his mouth fastened to hers, she slipped a hand into his hair to hold him there a while longer. He loved her and wanted her to be his forever.

Rachel felt enslaved to the man who had captivated and mastered her emotions, wits, and will. He was so giving, gentle, and caring. With every part of her, she wanted him completely, now and forever. She used her voice, newly acquired skills, and reactions to tell him so.

Dan's fingers roamed across her flat stomach to seek the brown forest and the vital peak that summoned his exploration and craved his attention. He wanted to warm himself in the steamy core. Soon, he had her writhing with unleashed passion, as was he.

Rachel's fingers roved his torso with delight, then trekked lower to stimulate his flaming need to a brighter and higher level. She teased down his sleek sides and captured the prize of love's war that could send her senses spinning beyond reality, beyond resistance or withdrawal. With gentleness, she stroked it and absorbed its warmth. She created more heat and strength. She thrilled to his prowess and response. Intense joy filled her when his body shuddered and she heard a groan of pleasure come from deep within his chest.

Unable to restrain themselves further, they fused their bodies. Dan tried to move with leisure and caution, but Rachel urged him to move swiftly and urgently, as she did. They rode the undulating waves of love's sea, reveling in its dips and crests.

Rachel sensed the strain he was experiencing to give her release first. She arched to meet every thrust, but allowed him to set their pace. She let him know when she reached the precipice. She labored with him as she fell over esctasy's edge, then he quickly pursued her into the swirling depths.

Their mouths meshed when the triumphant moment arrived. They kissed and caressed until every sensation of the glorious moment was extracted. Afterward, they bathed and returned to his ship.

On Tuesday afternoon, they docked in Savannah. Rachel and Dan stayed aboard the *Merry Wind* while

Peter Garrett went to see Police Chief Anderson. The couple waited anxiously until the agent returned.

When he did, Peter grinned and told them they had been cleared of gun-running charges: he had convinced the chief that Earl Starger had misunderstood what he overheard. The ecstatic couple listened as he related, "Anderson's investigator wasn't pleased you'd left town, Rachel, and made quite a fuss about it. I asked to view the evidence against you, and they don't have one piece or even a clue to incriminate you. I pointed out they couldn't arrest you or limit your movements without any to base it on. That investigator said they had intended to exhume McCandless's body to have it examined, but the doctor told them it was too late to accurately determine the cause of death. I made it clear the United States Government would be interested in a case they kept open and a citizen they harassed without a verifiable reason to do so. After our little chat, they understand suspicions and gossip don't count in the legal system."

"You mean they're dropping the charges against me?"

"You never *were* charged, just suspected and investigated. Since they haven't come up with any hard facts by now, they have to let the matter go."

"That's wonderful, Peter. But unless your ruse with Harry works and he's to blame, we might never know who killed Phillip and George."

"Most crimes have a way of being solved eventually," Peter told her.

Rachel was pleased for herself and Dan, but hated to see a killer go unpunished. "I hope so. What do we do now?"

"I'll leave first thing in the morning for Athens. I'll see you two the minute I return. Hope for good news."

"We will," Rachel and Dan replied at the same time, and smiled.

After Peter left for the hotel, Dan and Rachel
etired to his cabin . . .

Peter and his two men left by train on Wednesday
morning. Dan went to pick up a report left at the post
office by the detective he had hired to check on Milton
Baldwin. It told them something very interesting and
helpful, so they went to Milton's office to confront
him.

Milton asked what they were doing there. "The
police are searching for you," he said, noting the odd
way they looked at him. "It was in the newspaper two
weeks ago, something about gun-running and murder."

"I've been cleared of all suspicions, Milton, all of
them," Rachel disclosed. "I'm free. The newspaper
will have to run an apology and retraction."

He appeared surprised and disappointed. "Did you
deliver the cargo?"

"Yes."

"Then you have my money. That's why you're
here?"

"No, but we have something else: proof that agreement is a fake."

Milton's expression altered. "What are you talking
about?"

"Phillip didn't sign that loan agreement; his signature is traced. And the date is in your handwriting,
not his. We have an expert witness who'll testify
against you in court. You've broken the law, Milton."

"You're crazy, Rachel. I haven't broken the law."

"That isn't what the United States special agent
thinks. Dan and I have spoken with him in detail. He
believes you're in deep trouble. I'm not lying or
bluffing, Milton; I'm taking you to court on this matter. And I'll win."

The man panicked. "Wait a minute, you two! That

loan is for real. I'll admit that isn't the paper Phillip signed, but he owed me the money."

"Why don't you explain before we're forced to head to the police station?" Dan suggested. "Unless you prefer to tell your story to them."

"All right!" he shouted. "The loan was from Harry to Phillip, but I purchased it. Phillip borrowed sixty thousand dollars to cover a gambling debt, and he put up his share of the arms company as collateral. After he died, Harry came to me and suggested I buy it so I could use it to force Rachel out of the shipping firm. He thought if she was desperate for money to settle a debt or lose part of her inheritance, she would either have to honor the deal we all needed or she'd expose the fact she had the missing money when she took some from it to pay me. After those tricks she pulled on all of us, none of us trusted her or believed her. Harry had my name and company switched with his, Phillip's signature traced, and I filled in a date I knew you couldn't meet. When you called my bluff, I got scared and didn't want to press too hard and provoke you to examine the agreement too closely."

"That's fraud and forgery, criminal offenses," Dan asserted.

"What difference does it make which partner he owed or which company he would forfeit?" a frightened Milton reasoned. "The loan was real, and overdue. He couldn't pay it off and neither could she."

"That doesn't change what you two did to deceive and defraud her. We'll press charges and you'll go to prison. Unless . . ."

"Unless what?" Milton asked Dan.

The sea captain had already discussed the course of action with Rachel. "You agree to dissolve the partnership and divide the firm into the same shares as when you merged. That's how you can avoid prosecution."

"That isn't fair! I'll be out sixty thousand dollars!"

"And you'll be out of prison. We'll adjust the split to keep you from taking a total loss of the money, which Rachel doesn't have to do in light of how you tricked her. Is it a deal? Oh, yes, McCandless Shipping will be moving back to Charleston, if that influences your decision any."

"How would we work out the details?" Milton asked, cornered.

"I'll spend the next few days here working them out with you. Rachel has agreed to let me handle the matter for her because I know how shipping firms work. We should have everything settled within a week."

Milton thought a few minutes, then said, "We'll do it your way."

Rachel wanted the distressing situation ended, so she was polite. "Thank you, Milton. I want this handled swiftly and secretly. I don't want to hurt or embarrass your family because you made a foolish mistake. Over the years I've learned that gossip and scandals can be painful and humiliating. Don't you think this way will be best for everyone's reputation and business?"

Milton gaped at her in astonishment and gratitude. "I'm sorry, Rachel. Things were so bad, I got greedy and desperate. Harry's scheme sounded good at first. By the time I realized it was crazy and hazardous, I was in too deep to back out, and he wouldn't let me. I was also angry with Phillip for getting us into this trouble. If he'd kept his mind on business and kept away from gambling, this wouldn't have happened to any of us. If I was going to save myself, I had to get the notorious Black Widow out of my company. I know you can't understand how I could behave so recklessly, but I was under such pressure that I didn't think clearly. I'm glad it's finally in the open and can be cleared up. I never wanted to hurt you. I'm sorry."

"So am I, Milton. Sorry this happened. I'll be gone

soon, and we can both be free of the past. I wish you good luck with your new company."

"That's more than kind and generous, Rachel; thank you."

"I'll head home, Dan, while you two begin your work and talk."

The sea captain walked her to the door and said, "I'll see you in a few days. Rest and get things packed for your move. Unless it's an emergency, stay out of town until everything is resolved."

"I'll wait to hear from you." Rachel left with two of Dan's men to protect her along the way and at the plantation until Dan and Peter arrived.

After Rachel explained matters to Lula Mae Morris and Burke Wells, everyone calmed down from the excitement of her return to Moss Haven. "I have half of Phillip's shipping firm back, so it should be earning money again soon. Captain Slade is handling it for me for a while. Isn't it wonderful? My files are closed; no more questions or investigations. Home," she murmured as she allowed her gaze to roam the lovely setting.

"Dat's good news, Miz Rachel. Ah told you to have faith," Burke said.

"I'll help you unpack. I bet you're bone-tired," was Lulu Mae's offer.

"Yes and no; I'm too elated to decide. As we speak, Harry is being investigated for Phillip's and George's murders. If he is found to be the culprit and there's proof, it will all be over at last."

Saturday evening, Peter Garrett arrived at the plantation. Rachel was disappointed that Dan wasn't with the agent, as she hadn't seen or heard from him in days. He had teased about letting her miss and crave him for a while to convince her how much she loved and needed him, but she hadn't taken him seriously. Yet she'd promised to stay home, and obeyed.

"Have you seen Dan?" she asked after they exchanged greetings.

"No, I assumed you'd both be here. Where is he?"

Rachel explained what had taken place with the shipping firm and what Dan was doing in town. "What did you learn from Harry?"

"Wait until you hear my news. My men and I pretended we were working for Ramón and we'd come to kill him over his refusal to send the arms and for stealing our money. We bound and terrified him until he was convinced his life was nearing its miserable end. I don't work that way often, Rachel, but I knew he was guilty and needed persuasion."

"I understand," she said, but wasn't sure she did.

"Harry tried to play the ignorant and innocent pawn in your game. If we hadn't gotten rough, he wouldn't have talked. I told him we have you and Dan captive in Cuba and we'd forced the truth from you two. He finally spilled all he knew before the night was over. He told us he doesn't have the money and how he'd tried to scare it out of you: he ransacked your room and had you spied on in Athens during your first visit there; he had a man threaten you with a knife and had your home searched. He shot at you, but only one time, and had your house rocked and painted. He sent that scary note about the deal, but not those weird love notes. It helped knowing all those things from you so I could question him about each one."

Peter took a breath and continued. "He even confessed to blowing up the ammunition company, but claims he didn't know George and that worker were inside. He knows we know he's lying about that part, and I'll get him to admit it soon. I have him under guard at the hotel in town. My ship's coming late

539

Monday, and I'm taking him with me for more inter-rogation. I convinced him to tell me how he controlled Phillip. He altered the company books to make things look bad so Phillip would sell out to him. When Phillip came up with the arms deal, Phillip's desperate need of cash and the sorry state of his financial affairs gave Harry the means to keep Phillip from backing out. He has an interested buyer for the arms company, but you and his wife will split the profit after he's in prison."

Presently that wasn't her main concern. "What about Phillip's death?"

"We never could get Harry to admit he killed him or has the money. He was petrified, so I'm inclined to believe him. Evidently Phillip did hide the money from everyone, and either he did die of cholera or somebody else killed him."

"What about the guns for Richard and the Cubans?"

"Harry had them ready, so they're on the way there now. He had no choice except to turn them over to us. After he spilled his guts, I told him who we are, and he almost fainted. About those licenses, I have them in my possession, but he's already confessed they're forged. You'll be pleased to learn, that Phillip didn't know anything about that crime."

Rachel was relieved by that. "What you're saying is that my husband hadn't done anything illegal with the arms deal? His only mistake was creating gambling debts that made him desperate for money?"

"That's how it appears to me. He concealed the money to protect it, but that isn't a crime. If he used any of it for gambling, more than his share of the profit, that's a different story. Until or unless we locate it, we'll never know the truth."

"I almost wish I never find it, but we need it to pay bills and salaries for the arms, or to repay bank loans. With George's records burned, I don't know who the

Augusta company owes. Of course, I'll try to pay any indisputable bill. Once we go over the Athens books, I'll make certain all honest debts are paid out of the sale price before Mrs. Clements and I split the profit. It isn't right for innocent people to suffer because George was murdered and Harry was crooked. If the missing money turns up, I'll let you know."

"You're a good woman, Rachel McCandless. Any message for Dan? I'll report my findings to him when I return to town."

She thought a moment, then replied, "Tell him I said hello and I miss him, but I won't disturb his hard work."

The following afternoon, Rachel visited with Dan's men in their camp nearby and brought them cookies and lemonade as a treat. They finished a card game as she approached. While they chatted, Rachel said, "I'm sure you're eager to set sail again soon. Is Turkey an interesting place?"

"Turkey, ma'am? Don't know, ain't never been there."

That took Rachel by surprise. "I must have misunderstood; I thought that was where you'd come from before you docked here."

"No, ma'am; we came from Scotland. Delivered a shipment of wool."

She assumed Dan's arms deal was a secret even from his crew. Or if the man knew about it, he must have been ordered not to mention it to anyone. If a secret, she wondered what excuse her love had given his crew for his trip here. "What made Dan decide to visit Savannah?"

"Don't know, ma'am. When we docked in Charleston in March, Capt'n Slade was in a rush to get here to visit somebody important. He don't talk about his private business."

"Where do you head after you leave Savannah?"

"Mr. Conner said we'd be sailing on Tuesday. Heading for Africa."

Again, she was surprised and intrigued. As the man sat cross-legged and chatted, Rachel viewed the paper lying on his thigh. "What's that?"

"My helper," he replied, then chuckled. "I can't ever remember from one time to the next which hand beats another in poker. Mr. Conner gave me this paper to use when I play. It's getting in bad shape."

"May I see it?"

"Sure, ma'am." He passed the fading page to her.

Rachel didn't care about the list of poker hands in winning order. What she wanted to study was the handwriting she was sure she recognized. "If I can borrow it for a short time, I'll make you a new copy."

"I don't want to trouble you, ma'am."

"No trouble. It's my way of thanking you for being a good protector. Enjoy the snack. I'll return this to you soon."

Rachel went to her room and retrieved a paper she had kept hidden. She lay the two on her bed and studied them. The list handwriting matched the flowing and neat script of the second love note she had received! Luke couldn't have delivered it; he was here. Dan was with her, so he must have. . . . But why would he send such a provocative message, then never admit it?

She paced the floor. No trip to or from Turkey. . . . No private arms deal . . . So why had he placed orders with Harry and George? To protect his cover lie about why he had come to visit Phillip? Again, why? Maybe he had witnessed the burial and suspected her of murdering Phillip. Or maybe he was an agent like Peter, assigned to keep Phillip in tow; when he died, Dan was ordered to stick close to her . . . Whatever the answer, she was thinking too wildly to confront Dan today. It was best to let him come to her and explain; surely that would be soon.

Monday morning, Lula Mae handed Rachel a letter from Harry, one postmarked the day she sailed for Cuba. "It's been opened and resealed," Rachel observed.

"The man who brung it didn't say nothing about that."

"Maybe Harry forgot something and he did it. Strange. Thank you, Lula Mae," she said, dismissing the housekeeper.

When she was alone, she ripped open the envelope and read the shocking letter. In dread, she read it once more:

Rachel
I had Daniel Slade checked out with friends in Charleston. He's lying to both of us, but you'll be the one to suffer. His real, or I should say full, name is Daniel Slade McCandless, known in the past to friends and family as Mac. By some miracle, he's Phillip's missing brother. I don't have to speculate on what his plans are for you, do I, my pretty spider who devoured his brother? He's trying to lure you into his web like you did his brother; then he'll turn on you and murder you before you can kill him, too. What a wicked trap you're in, my ravishing and foolish Rachel. You'd better get away from him while there's still time to escape. Oh, yes, the authorities came to visit me again today. They say they have new evidence against you and will be coming to arrest you soon. If I were you, I'd take that stolen money and get myself hidden.

She wasn't worried about the law, as no doubt that was concerning those charges Peter had destroyed.

Dan was Phillip's brother? Harry wouldn't say something she could check out and disprove. She recalled their talk in Athens about "Mac." He had been telling her about himself! Perhaps Phillip had known Dan was alive and had sent for him, as he murmured on his deathbed. But Dan could be trying to entrap her! Maybe Peter had convinced Dan, as he had Phillip, to go along with the arms deal until it was completed, then work on his personal problem of revenge. If Harry wasn't responsible for those other threats, someone who had the motive and opportunities was. His claims of love and those proposals . . . What better way to expose a Black Widow than to marry her and ensnare her when she tries to kill you?

Cruel fate was making another attempt to hurt and destroy her. The first man she loved and wanted hated her and craved her punishment for something she hadn't done. If he had decided she was innocent and had fallen in love with her, he would have confessed the truth by now. Instead of being with her, he was in town trying to save *his* family's shipping firm, probably with plans to snatch it away from her. Would he actually go so far as to marry her to expose her? If he felt she had gotten away with past murders and might do the same with Phillip's, yes.

She had surrendered her all to him and told him everything about her. She had come to love him and trust him. But she should never have let down her guard with Daniel Slade *McCandless*. Lula Mae had mistrusted him and had warned her to do the same, but she hadn't listened. He had worked on the mystery only to clear his brother's name and to help their country. Should she confront him, or spurn him and leave? Could she let him see how he'd fooled her and hurt her? As with Craig and Paul, Dan would find a way to keep her from inheriting anything from his brother.

*Phillip would hate you for what you're trying to do to
ne,* she thought bitterly.

Edgy, confused, and tormented, Rachel left the
louse for a walk, her heart burdened by the recent
·evelations. She must think and plan.

In town, Dan made an elating and unexpected discov-
·ry. While going over records and bills, one entry
stood out to him. It involved a favorite past hiding
place of Phillip's, but one Rachel had said was impossible. It was obvious she hadn't known about the
·eplacement or she'd have told him.

Peter Garrett arrived shortly after Dan found the
clue. He explained his suspicion to the agent. "If I'm
right, I know where the missing money is hidden. You
have time to go with me before you sail?"

"I surely do," a smiling Peter replied.

Rachel heard voices as she neared the side of the
house: Dan's and Peter's. She sneaked to the corner
and peered toward the front porch. The bottom step
had been demolished. After the facts she'd learned,
she was compelled to observe and listen.

"Here's the missing money, Peter, just like I said,"
Dan remarked as he withdrew a large bag from its
hiding place. He opened it and the two men eyed the
contents, then exchanged grins of success.

Rachel was stunned. Had Dan known all along
where it was hidden?

"There's a letter here to you from Phillip," Peter
said. "And a picture of you two years ago."

So, Rachel fumed, it was true: Daniel Slade
McCandless . . .

"I'll read it later; it's probably personal. I have one
more thing to do here; visit my brother's grave, then
go find Rachel. You've heard the gossip about her

being a lethal predator. After I capture her in the web I've weaved, I'll expose the truth about her to everyone."

"What are you planning to do with her?"

"Just what I told you on the ship and in town."

Peter grasped his meaning, as Dan had related his love and marital intentions and his hopes of proving her innocence in past episodes.

"You want to walk to his grave with me before you leave?"

"Yes." Peter replied. "Maybe I can give you some suggestions about how to solve Phillip's murder and those of the other men."

Rachel waited until they were far from the house. She sneaked to the barn and saddled a horse. She walked him out the back door and across the pasture. She mounted and rode away, needing time to settle down before she faced Dan for an enlightening confrontation on both their sides.

The sinister culprit who had been stalking her for years watched her movements and followed. When he called out and she reined in to speak with him, he brutally punched her in the jaw and knocked her unconscious. With hatred and a hunger for revenge gleaming in his eyes, he held her limp body in place while he rode to a secluded shed on her property. He hauled her inside, bolted the door, and glared down at her. At last Rachel was at his mercy, and he would show none.

Chapter 24

achel awakened, her hands bound behind her with
belt and her jaw smarting from the blow she hadn't
en coming in time to elude it. She lifted her head and
w her sinister stepfather lazing against the only en-
ance, which was shut and bolted. He had her captive
an abandoned storage shed on her property, so he
adn't taken her far, which would be helpful if any-
e realized she was missing and looked for her. The
ed was large and cluttered with old tools and bro-
en crates. Plenty of light came in through holes in the
llapsing roof, but the structure was still sturdy. He
as standing there gloating over his brazen deed,
hile she lay helpless near the rear of the shed. She
idn't know how long she had been unconscious, but
e doubted much time had passed, as he hadn't got-
n antsy and tried to arouse her. She was frightened,
ut tried to look brave and controlled. In an insulting
ne, she asked, "Are you mad? Don't you know this
ill get you into big trouble? A United States special
gent is at my home right now with Daniel Slade.
hey'll come looking for me, and you'll be arrested
or kidnapping and assault. Earl Starger, you untie
e and let me go this instant!"

Unruffled by her anger and warnings, he laughed
nd replied, "I saw you sneak away, girl. I also saw
em find that money all of you have been searching

for. When you don't return from your walk and the
can't find you near the house, they'll take it and go
That's all the agent wants. As for the sea captain, he'
assume you took off to avoid him, so he'll leave, too.

She glared at him. "How do you know about th
money?"

He laughed again and said, "I know everythin
about you, girl; Lula Mae has kept me informed fo
years."

Rachel was shocked and dismayed. "Lula Mae?'

"That's right; she works for me."

It made sense, how he had always seemed to kno
her every move and condition! "What did you pay he
to spy on me and betray me?"

Earl leaned against the door and crossed his arm
over his chest. "Not much; she did it because she love
you and wants to protect you."

"How can that be true when she works for you?'
Rachel refuted.

Earl stroked his elbow as he explained, "Afte
Newman died, I hired a man to pose as a doctor. W
convinced her that you're crazy, and aren't respons
ble for your actions. We told her if she watched ove
you and kept us informed of your condition and be
havior, we wouldn't go to the police. We warned he
how dangerous it would be to you and others if sh
revealed she knew the truth to you, so she kept silen
all this time. We put on such a good act we had he
believing an evil witch lives inside you and migh
jump out and attack anybody around if they learne
she existed. We even told her that evil side would ki
you to protect herself. Lula Mae believes in all tha
stuff about God and the devil; she thinks the devil an
his helpers can work his evil on humans. She cried an
wailed about her sick-minded baby and agreed to d
anything to save you and protect you from his wicke
clutches. She even believes you got rid of Newman'
baby because of how he abused you during your mar

548

iage to him; of course, she hated him, too. That
money she gave you for support so you wouldn't
tarve was from me. I couldn't give you too much or
ou would have become suspicious of where she got
. She believes I love you like a daughter and only
ant what's best for you. I made sure every talk she
verheard between us went in my favor."

So, the woman *had* been spying and eavesdropping,
ut longer than she had realized, and for a much
ifferent reason from the one she had imagined. Yet
he spinster's motive had been a good one. Poor
misused Lula Mae, she fretted. "You tricked her and
ook advantage of her."

"That's right. She's a stupid, gullible, and supersti-
ious woman. You made a mistake trusting her and
onfiding in her. When she learned you'd been asleep
r had fainted when all those men died, it was easy to
make her think you'd been under some evil spell you
ouldn't remember."

"She told you . . . everything about me?"

"Everything. I was supposed to pass it along to the
. . *doctor*. Of course, I already knew everything, and
mentioned those alleged fits you had at home. I told
er how worried and afraid your mother was. Lula
Mae believes I'm a kind and generous and tender-
earted man you've lied about. And that night at the
otel, I almost convinced you of your madness."

Rachel recalled how he had cast brief doubts in her
wn mind about her sanity and guilt, so a simple
woman like Lula Mae might be easy to fool, especially
y a "doctor." "You low-down snake," she sneered.
I hate you. You've never done one kind or good
hing in your life."

Earl straightened and took a spread-legged stance
vith hands akimbo. "Come off it, Rachel. Be glad I
ot rid of those groping men for you."

Fear knotted her stomach and sent tingles of alarm

over her body. "You . . . got rid of them? You mea
. . . you killed them?"

"Of course. Don't look so surprised; surely you ha
suspicions."

"But Mama said you were home when Phillip die
Did you pay—"

"She knows only what I tell her she knows. She wa
too drugged on medicine to realize or remember m
comings and goings. When I'd tell her what date
was, she believed me. She was too drunk on that stu
I got from the real doctor to even be aware of whe
I was or wasn't home. She doesn't know I was gor
during those incidents that plagued you."

Rachel leapt on that clue to get answers while th
insane man was in a boasting and cocky moo
"You're the one who was sending me those note
following me, and threatening me!"

"Yes, and mighty clever of me if I do say so m
self."

"Clever to kill four men in cold blood? How coul
you?"

Earl came over and squatted down beside her as h
revealed, "William's boy was easy; he was sick an
feverish; and you were napping. I knew it wouldn't b
long before he'd be chasing you around the house an
trying to sneak into your bloomers. I couldn't allo
that to happen to my Rachel. I wasn't worried whe
you married Old Willy; everybody knew he couldn
hump a woman anymore. I figured, in time, you'd g
an itch and I'd be around to scratch it for you. Don
you recall how contrite I was? I did everything I coul
to make peace with you."

"You didn't fool me; I saw through your little pr
tenses."

When she tried to sit up, Earl pushed her bac
down. "I know. That's why I had to put you in a har
spot. William's death was easy, too. Since you slept i
separate rooms, I sneaked inside and forced him t

550

drink that poison. I figured it would look like a heart attack, and he was so scared I thought he would have one. Then you'd be free and rich and come to me. When you kept being mean and distant, I helped Canellia fan the flames of gossip about you. I knew that if you were tormented enough by them, you'd run home eventually. But you fooled me; you married that Craig Newman. I should have left you in his trap longer so he could beat some sense into you. But I didn't like anybody doing my job for me or marring my property."

Rachel listened in horror as Earl Starger continued his confession. She didn't know how she was going to get out of this predicament, but she wouldn't let him ravish her without the fiercest struggle she could manage. If she escaped him, who would believe this incredible tale? She had to keep him talking in case Peter and Dan did come looking for her.

Earl's voice and expression were cold and cruel as he said, "I came to see you that morning. Newman was drunk and gave me a hard time. He ordered me to never come to his house again. I saw you faint so it gave me the opportunity to get rid of the bastard. I dragged him up the steps and threw him down, twice for good measure. I figured it would appear an accident. Even if it didn't, they couldn't prove you'd done it. I knew you'd be free again soon and be even richer. I should have killed Paul when he stole everything from you, but that might have been dangerous for both of us."

"Might?" Rachel scoffed. "It was dangerous for me, you beast. I'm lucky I wasn't imprisoned or hanged. How did you kill Phillip?"

"I sneaked inside like I did with William and poisoned him. He was so drunk, he didn't see me in the room. I poured the poison in the whiskey bottles and kept nudging him awake so he'd keep nursing on them. I gave him enough to kill him twice. I knew he'd be gone soon. I returned home, made sure Catherine knew I was there and what the date was, and waited for word to arrive of your new dilemma. When nothing happened, I came to check it out. Lula Mae told me how you'd buried Phillip in secret, even destroyed the whiskey bottles, and were leaving on a trip. She remembered how she'd begged you not to marry Phillip, on mine and the doctor's orders. She figured he was poisoned by you the night before and didn't want you being arrested. You saved us both from trouble when you hid his body for a time to rot away any evidence; that was cunning, girl."

His description repulsed her. "I didn't do it to protect you. I—"

"Oh, I know why you did it, that arms deal and the missing money. I bet I scared you silly when I shot at you that Sunday after Phillip died and sent you those notes. Clever of me to use your handwriting, wasn't it? I've practiced for years on letters and papers you left behind when you ran away. I had a feeling I might need that skill one day. When I left the vial in your hotel room in Augusta, your friend almost caught me. I was hiding under the bed when he and that bellman came to leave flowers. I saw that silly card he wrote. You made me furious, girl, when you started clinging to that sea captain. That's why I tipped off the police to get you into trouble. Of course, that was a mistake at the time, I didn't know about the other trouble you were in and that Slade was only with you on business. But you spent too much time with him and started getting too close. I never overlook anything, girl; even stole back my tip note to the police. And those whiskey bottles you burned and buried, they didn't have poison in them. Did you like the little spider put in your basin?"

"It could have bitten me before I noticed it!"

"You would have deserved it for sleeping with that sailor. I saw those pictures of you two; I know sate

552

looks when I see them. I enjoyed tearing them to pieces and burning them. He'll never have you again."

Rachel realized she was running out of time, as Earl was getting cold and hateful. And there wasn't much, if anything, more to brag about to her. At least she had discovered two important things: she wasn't to blame for any of the deaths and Dan was responsible for only one note to her, one written before their entwining trip and delivered early after their meeting when he doubted her, before he came to know and love her. Surely that was why he hadn't intimidated her further. "I should have guessed the truth when nothing happened while you were away. I thought it was because I had protection from Dan's men, and Mama told me you were home all those times I received threats. Why did you leave and let up on me?"

"I thought you needed a little simmering time. With those other men threatening you, I knew you'd be boiling soon and need my help."

"Is that why you alerted the police after our fight?"

"You provoked me, girl. It was your fault, but you got out of it."

"You tried to attack me!" she charged. "You tried to convince me I was crazy, a murderess. This time you'll be exposed and punished."

"That traitorous sea captain won't protect you. That interesting letter from your partner came while you were gone. I read it when I came to see Lula Mae. I told her to hide it until the right time came to give it to you. I warned her it might entice you to murder him out of revenge. I sneaked to the house this morning and told her to give it to you, to test your reaction. If you became angry and dangerous, we'd send for the doctor, I said."

"What are you planning to do with me?"

Earl trailed his fingers over her flushed cheek. "I'm going to enjoy you to the fullest, hurt you like you've hurt me many times, then kill you. I'll sneak your body away, bury it secretly, and forget you existed. No one will ever suspect me. They'll think you ran away after learning the truth about your lover, how he was betraying you. It's actually amusing you'll end up like Phillip did, in a secret grave. After things settle down, I plan to divorce Catherine and marry the rich and eager Miss Jones."

Rachel tensed. "She's in on this plot, too?"

Earl yanked her hair. "Don't be absurd. I wouldn't tell anybody my secrets. She and I have been just friends for years, but she took a different liking to me on the ship to and from Boston. That was a coincidence, but we've been lovers since our return, so I don't need you anymore. But I can't let you get away with what you did to me. I have to punish you. Once I've sated myself with you and you're dead, I won' think about you again."

Rachel tried a ruse. "Camellia is making a fool o you, Earl. She lost two men to me, so she's taking yo away from my mother for spite."

Earl sent wild laughter into the shed. "That isn' true, girl. After I finish with you, you'll understanc how enslaved to me she is. Maybe not, because won't be gentle and generous with you like I was wit her. Now let's get those clothes cut off and get busy I have to get my alibi—"

The door was kicked in with a loud crash and Dan shouted, "Touch her and you're dead, Starger!"

Earl had instinctively dodged the splintered woo that was sent flying in all directions. He flung dow the jewel-handled knife and drew his pistol. "I'll ki the witch first!" he yelled in frustration and madnes:

A bullet from Peter Garrett's gun struck Earl in th shoulder, as the distance was too far and the dange too imminent for him or Dan to reach her derange stepfather and disable him. The wild man staggere backwards a few steps, but raised his weapon to carr

554

out his objective to murder Rachel. The second bullet made Starger's heart its accurate and lethal target.

Dan picked his way over the debris, lifted the bound Rachel, and carried her into the fresh air and sunlight. Peter followed to make certain she was all right, as Earl Starger was beyond assistance.

As Dan unfastened the belt to free her hands, he asked if she was hurt. "We hated to wait so long, love," he explained, "but Peter wanted his full confession to end this matter once and for all. We didn't know he had a pistol."

She was trembling and dazed. "How did you find me?"

"Burke saw him attack and abduct you. He came after us. We got on your trail fast. Thank God Peter's a swift and skilled tracker. We sneaked up outside just as Starger began confessing his crimes. Peter told me to hold off a rescue until he had his say. This clears you of all suspicions, love."

"I knew he was evil and mean," Rachel sighed, "but not to this extent. He probably made Mama ill just so he could keep her drugged to give him alibis. It's over; it's finally over—the mysterious deal, the suspicious deaths, my dark past."

"Now you can make a fresh start, Rachel."

"That sounds easier than it will actually be, Peter. Thank you for your help."

"Before I sail, I'll file a report with the police chief. Not only will your files be closed, I'll make sure they're destroyed. I'll also make certain the newspapers tell everyone the whole story. People around here will never gossip about you again. Plenty of them will owe you apologies."

"I don't care about that part. I just want everyone to know I'm not guilty. I want my name and reputation cleared."

"I'll see that they are, Rachel; you have my word."

"What about my brother? Will you find a way to check on Richard and let me know how he is?"

"Just as soon as possible, but I'm sure he's fine. He's a good agent."

"Peter," a nervous Dan asked, "will you take Starger's body back to the house? Rachel and I need to have a serious and private talk. There's something important I have to tell her, a long overdue confession."

Peter Garrett knew what Dan meant and his feelings were with the man for what was coming. "I'll head on into town and handle matters there. I'll postpone my sailing until tomorrow and return to the plantation later."

Dan helped the agent load Earl's body on his horse then the man left. As Peter vanished from sight, the apprehensive sea captain returned to Rachel's side. "I don't know how to begin, woman."

Rachel looked at her lover and said, "You're right we need to have a serious talk, Daniel Slade . . . McCandless. Mac! Don't you agree?"

Dan gaped at her in astonishment and dread. "You know?" When she nodded, he asked, "How? When?"

Rachel explained about Harry's letter, then told him about her other discovery. "You've lied and deceived me from the start. Why, Dan?"

"I'm sorry, Rachel, and I'm going to be totally honest with you," he vowed, and was. After he finished his story, he said, "You can believe me and forgive me and we can share a wonderful life together or you can doubt me and reject me, and we'll both be miserable. I love you, Rachel, with all my heart. And to hell with that 'deal' of yours. Even if you can't have children, I love you and I want to marry you. And not to prove you're a killer, either. We both know that isn't true. I've trusted you since before you tried to spurn me the last time. I kept putting off telling you the truth because something always came up to sto

556

me—either perils or doubts you had about me or fear you'd turn against me when you needed me most. The timing always seemed wrong for exposing my secret. If you need time to think, I'll give it to you. Just don't make a hasty decision while you're hurt and angry. What else do I need to explain?"

"How did you know where the missing money was hidden? I saw you two recover it, and I heard what you said." She repeated the words to him.

"This morning I found a notation in the company books about Phillip ordering supplies to repair your front porch steps. When we searched the house and I mentioned that favorite hiding spot of his, you said no work had been done on them recently. But I found a bill indicating work *had* been done. I realized you hadn't known about it, so it was suspicious. I didn't know I was right until Peter and I checked."

"Phillip must have sent me to visit one of the share-cropper families or into town to shop," Rachel speculated, "because I didn't know about it."

"I believe you didn't know, and so does Peter."

"All this time it was right under my feet every time I walked them. If we had looked that night, we wouldn't have had to go through all this trouble."

"It's a blessing in disguise, love," Dan pointed out. 'If we'd found and used the money, we wouldn't have learned the truth about everything. It was difficult and scary, but things worked out for the best."

"I guess you're right," she conceded. "But why did Phillip send for you? He believed you were long dead, didn't he?"

"Yes and no. He did for a long time, but he changed his mind. He hired a detective to track me; that's where part of his savings went. The man found news about a Captain Daniel Slade and sent word to Phillip. My brother hoped and prayed it was me, so he sent a letter to our family lawyer in Charleston. When docked there, he gave it to me." Dan reminded her of the letter's hazy contents he had related earlier. He told her why he had returned home finally to make peace with his father and brother. He told her about the trunk he had picked up with all of Phillip's personal effects and said she was welcome to go through them. He revealed how the misunderstanding about his "death" had occurred.

"The ammunition company and shipping firm weren't doing well, but the arms company was in fine shape. Harry just convinced Phillip it wasn't, to serve his own wicked purposes. When we went to visit the first time, Harry didn't know Phillip was dead, so he was angry and bitter about him being away on that alleged trip and for holding on to the money. He used those early threats to scare Phillip and you. After he learned Phillip was gone, he was sure you had the money, so he became more threatening."

Dan paused, then went on. "Phillip used a lot of money to locate me, and he wasted a lot on gambling. He left a letter with the money to me. He said he was in terrible financial straits and accepted the arms contract to get back on his feet. He said he'd sworn off gambling, but he owed several bets. He did use two hundred thousand of the Cuban's money to try to win big, but he didn't. After he learned the United States Government was involved, he panicked. He didn't have any way to replace the cash he'd lost. He was afraid if he turned the shorted amount over to Harry, the bastard would kill him and keep it, and claim Phillip had lost it all gambling. He hoped I would get his other letter and come help you if anyone caused you trouble. He loved you and trusted you, Rachel. If he had been lucid the morning he died, he would have told you where the money was hidden."

"I'm sure he would have; he was a good and kind man. I'm sorry he got himself entangled in such problems. If he'd confided in me, maybe I could have helped him."

"Maybe some of it was my fault. If he'd known I was alive, maybe he wouldn't have punished himself with guilt and anguish."

"You can't blame yourself for Phillip's weaknesses."

"Just as you can't blame yourself for what Starger did to get you."

"If it hadn't been for his lust over me, they would all be alive."

"It isn't your fault he craved you. He was mad and evil, Rachel."

"But I kept giving him obstacles to remove."

"But you didn't know that."

"I know, but—"

He pressed a forefinger to her lips to halt her from punishing herself for something beyond her control. "No buts, woman. Just as Phillip chose his ill-fated course, so did Earl Starger. I'm sorry I didn't tell you the truth sooner. But there were times when you were reluctant or afraid to tell me things," he reminded. "We've gotten close over the last few months, love, so we can't let this come between us."

"How are things going at the shipping firm?"

That wasn't the response Dan expected or wanted, but he didn't press her. "Fine," he answered "We should have everything straightened out and divided in the next few days. I think Milton Baldwin is basically a decent and honest man. He just got caught up in a desperate ploy to end his troubles. He was aggravated with Phillip for creating problems for them with his gambling and moody behavior at work. When you, as his new partner, came under another dark cloud, things got worse. Harry offered him a way out, and he grabbed it without thinking. You'll have McCandless Shipping back this week. Do you remember enough from working for Phillip to run it?"

"You told Milton it was being moved back to Charleston."

"That was when I thought you'd marry me and move there to live."

"Do you think anyone here would trade with me the Black Widow?"

"Why not? Everyone will know the truth soon."

"Even if they believe the report, they'd be too embarrassed to deal with me. Do as you promised Milton; move your family's company home."

Her words dismayed him, but her tone wasn't accusatory or bitter. "I don't want to take the company from you, love. I don't want to take away anything Phillip left you. He loved you; you're his widow and heir."

"That's because he thought you were dead. He would have left the firm to you if he had known you were alive. I think you should have it."

"Why, Rachel?"

"Because you'll need it to support a wife and hopefully a family."

Dan trembled with anticipation. "Does that mean . . . ."

"That I love you and want to marry you? Yes," she said with a smile.

"You understand and forgive me?"

"Yes, Captain McCandless, if your offer is still open to acceptance."

Dan swept her into his arms and hugged her tightly. "It is, love."

Their gazes met and they kissed, washing away the pain and doubts of their pasts. Their love was too strong and special to allow a mistake to destroy it. Their lips meshed many times until they were breathless.

"We have to stop this, sir. Peter will come looking for us soon."

"Only if you'll agree to marry me this week."

"How about Friday afternoon?" she suggested.

"Why so long?" he asked, putting on a painful but humorous look.

"We have matters to settle first: the firm, telling my mother about Earl, a talk with Lula Mae, and plans for a wedding. I don't care what people say or think, I want this last one to be done right and proper."

"A real wedding, eh?"

"Yes, for once, for a last time, forever."

Two days later, Richard Fleming arrived at Moss Haven. His shoulder was still bandaged and in a sling, but he was fine. He, Rachel, Dan, and Peter spent hours talking about their adventures. Her brother was delighted and relieved to learn Peter had shipped the rest of the arms last week, and they should have reached Ramón today. Richard was returning to Cuba after he was healed, but only for a short time. He had a big surprise for Rachel and their mother: he had located his twin sister.

"I've already sent Rosemary a telegram and told her to come here Thursday. With your good news, my request and arrival are perfect timing."

"Did Dan tell you the other good news?" Peter asked Rachel.

"About me keeping the arms money?" After the agent nodded, she said, "Yes, and that's wonderful. I can use it to settle the companies' debts in Athens and Augusta. I'll repay Dan his investment, then give any left over to Molly Sue Leathers. Harry's wife has the profit coming from the sale of the arms company and has other holdings for support, and Harry's family doesn't have a right to his share after what he did. Molly Sue lost everything except George's insurance, so she deserves his share: George was a good and honest man, and he did his part. Since my husband gambled away his share, it isn't fair for me to take any of what's left after the debts are paid."

"You used your insurance money on the deal and lost your share of the profit, so you're out a big sum of money. Phillip was my brother, so you don't need to repay me. The men who lost their jobs and earnings at the ammunition company need any remaining cash more than I do."

Rachel smiled at him. "That's very kind and generous, Dan. Molly Sue will take care of that part for us. I did receive a cable from that buyer in Athens; the sale for the company and store in town is being handled this week, as soon as those outstanding debts are cleared, which weren't as large as Harry claimed. At least the out-of-town matters will be resolved and I will make a little profit on that sale. Peter, what about problems with that illegal use of the arms' patents?"

"Those faked licenses have been destroyed, and the arms made by them are out of the country. We'll drop that issue. As soon as Harry's tried in court, he'll never get out of prison."

A special dinner was prepared and served by a relieved and happy Lula Mae Morris. The housekeeper, who was moving to Charleston to tend the couple's new home, hummed as she worked. Her frown lines had softened, as had her mood. With a heavy burden lifted off her shoulders, she was a changed woman, and a trustworthy one. She was ashamed of how she had been duped by Earl Starger, but everyone understood how it had happened and forgave her. Never again would she doubt or be disloyal to the mistress she loved as her own child.

Thursday, Catherine Fleming Starger arrived for the wedding of her youngest daughter. She was contrite over her mistakes, but she found it difficult to grieve over the deceitful and wicked man she had married. It would take time to get her life and emotions back under control, but she knew she could do it. As with

Lula Mae, the still beautiful blonde was elated over not being blamed for her past mistakes.

That afternoon, Rosemary Fleming Sims and her husband reached the plantation from their small farm in Macon. She told her sister and mother how she had met her husband and where she had been living for five years in central Georgia. The couple had two children, both boys, who were staying with her husband's sister. She promised to bring them to get to know their grandmother, aunt, and two uncles soon at White Cloud and in Charleston. She said she hadn't contacted them since leaving because she didn't want the mean Earl Starger to know where to find her.

Rachel and her family had a wonderful and tearful reunion, together again in happiness for the first time since the war. They talked for hours, telling each other what had transpired for them over the years.

Later in private, Rosemary confided to Rachel, "I couldn't write or visit Mama because I wanted Earl out of my life forever. He was always pawing at me and I knew it would get worse if I didn't leave home. I was afraid to tell Mama about his wicked behavior because I feared he would hurt her. I saw him once and he threatened to hurt both of you if I ever saw or spoke to you again. I knew you had married and left, too, but I didn't know where to find you. He was vile and dangerous, Rachel; I think he killed Randall, but I don't want Mama to know; it would hurt her too deeply."

"You're right, Rosemary; we can't ever tell her. I suspected the same thing, and we all know now he was capable of murder. Thank God, he's out of our lives. I've missed you so much. I'm happy you're here."

"So am I, little sister. Tomorrow will be a glorious day for us."

* * *

That evening the Fleming family and Dan read the newspaper, and enjoyed the feature story by none other than Harold Seymour about Rachel's incredible experience as an alleged Black Widow. At last she was exonerated of all suspicions and allegations, and her name was cleared. They also noticed an article about a move north by Miss Camellia Jones. That was another secret Rachel wouldn't burden her mother with, Earl's affair and his intention to leave her for the flaming-haired vixen.

Rachel knew the police chief was sending a copy to Craig's brother so Paul would know who had murdered his brother. She was glad he would learn the truth, and hopefully it would make him feel guilty over his past mistreatment of her.

Friday at five o'clock on June twenty-fifth, friends and family gathered in the church outside of Savannah to watch Rachel Fleming Barlow Newman McCandless marry Daniel Slade McCandless, her former brother-in-law. Dan's ship hadn't sailed for Africa, so Luke Conner could be his best man and his faithful and genial crew could attend.

Nor had Peter Garrett sailed, so he, too, could be at the ceremony. Molly Sue Leathers came from Augusta to share in the happy event. Milton Baldwin and his wife were also present. Burke Wells and his wife wouldn't have missed the joyful moment for anything and Lula Mae Morris, as with Catherine, wept tears of happiness. Also present to witness the occasion were lawyer Frank Henley and his wife, jeweler Adam Meigs and his wife, reporter Harold Seymour—who hadn't been invited, but who wanted to write one final story, the happy ending—and most of Rachel's sharecroppers.

The smiling couple stood before the preacher who was ready to begin the ceremony. Rosemary, her matron-of-honor, and the groom's best friend and first mate were positioned on either side of them. Richard had retaken his seat beside his mother after giving away the radiant bride.

"Rachel and Dan, friends and family," the pastor began, "we are gathered here today under the eyes of God and these witnesses to join this couple in holy matrimony." He read several Scriptures relating to marriage and their duties to each other, then asked them to repeat their vows.

In a soft voice, the bride in a lovely pale-blue dress responded, "I, Rachel, take you, Dan, to be my lawful husband, to love and to honor, in sickness and in health, in good times and in bad, for richer or poorer, and until death us do part."

After his instructions, the groom, handsome in a dark-blue suit, responded, "I, Dan, take you, Rachel, to be my lawful wife, to love and to cherish, to support and protect, in sickness and in health, in good times and in bad, for richer or poorer, and until death us do part."

After some words from the preacher, Dan slipped a gold band on her finger and said, "With this ring, I thee wed." He smiled and added, "Forever."

Rachel gazed into his adoring blue eyes and repeated, "Forever."

The pastor placed a hand above and below their clasped ones and said, "By the power given to me by God and this state, I pronounce you man and wife. What God hath joined together, let no man put asunder. I wish you much joy in your blessed union. You may kiss your wife, Captain McCandless."

Dan and Rachel faced each other. For a moment, they exchanged smiles and gazes, then kissed briefly. As they embraced, each whispered, "I love you" into the other's ear.

While they did so, the pastor announced that the

guests would be dismissed to the grounds for a party where they could speak with the happy couple.

When they parted, certain people couldn't wait that long to give their congratulations and affections. Rachel was embraced by her older sister, and Dan was hugged by Luke Connor. Richard, Catherine, Lula Mae, and Burke joined them to do the same.

The newlyweds were guided outside to a location shaded by live oaks with lacy moss and set up with wooden tables and chairs. An assortment of food and sweets had been prepared by Catherine, Rosemary, and Lula Mae. Champagne had been furnished as a gift from Milton Baldwin.

Everyone, particularly the bride and groom, had a wonderful time chatting with friends, eating the delicious fare, and sipping champagne.

With a houseful of family and a ship loaded with crew, Rachel and Dan went to a hotel on the edge of town to be alone. A short time after arriving, the couple was undressed and in bed. They set out to weave golden webs of rapture and enchantment around each other.

"I love you, Rachel McCandless," he murmured and kissed her.

"I love you, Daniel McCandless," she responded before the next one.

Rachel gazed into her love's eyes. Her journey to find and win him had taken almost three years. At last the dark cloud over her had lifted, allowing glorious sunshine to replace it. She was wed to her fourth and last husband, to the only man she had ever loved or desired. The Black Widow gossip and accusations had been laid to rest. Dan had asked her to "promise me forever," and she had. For now, their bright future would be ignored while they concentrated on their present and each other.

Epilogue

Charleston, 1880

"What are you doing, love?" Dan asked as he entered their bedroom.

Rachel glanced up at her handsome husband and smiled. "Catching up on correspondence. The only time it's quiet and calm enough to do so is when the children are napping or after they're put to bed at night. They're a handful of energy and curiosity. They keep me busy."

"You're the one who insisted on proving herself," he jested.

Rachel laughed and teased, "I'm not sure I meant three times in five years, my virile captain. You do want me to have time and stamina for you. I don't know how I would manage if it weren't for Lula Mae. I should tell you to order seaman Zed Tarply to stop courting her before we lose her."

"Did you ever imagine that grumpy spinster turning sweet and soft on men? She and Zed are behaving like youths experiencing their first loves."

"They are, and I'm happy for both of them."

"So am I. Everybody should be as lucky as we are."

As he removed his jacket and put it away, she asked, "Did your meeting go well? You're home early today."

Beaming with pride, he answered, "Yes, it did. I hauled in another big client and account. McCandless

Shipping Firm is very successful and prosperous, woman. I'm glad we moved it back here. Milton's doing well, too. We've worked out a few nice deals together."

"I'm glad we settled our past misunderstanding. You were right; he is a decent man, and we all make mistakes. Is Luke coming for dinner tomorrow night? He docks this evening, doesn't he?"

"Yes. He's enjoying being the captain of the *Merry Wind* and has done a fine job of it these past years. He says she still handles as if new."

"Do you miss being at sea and roaming her decks?"

"I don't have time. Too much business to tend and too busy with my wonderful family. The few trips I make satisfy me . . . Who are you writing?"

She watched him approach with easy strides. Even after years of being with him, he still made her heart flutter wildly and her body flame with desire just by being near. "Mama and Rosemary," she answered, "living and working together at White Cloud is good for all of them. Mama's healthy and happy again. Even with Rosemary and Tom selling their small farm and moving in with her, Mama's become strong and independent. Rosemary needs the help with her children; my heavens, six balls of energy to chase and keep out of trouble!" she murmured, referring to two sets of twins added to the two boys her sister had when she and Dan married.

"Six children are a handful. I'm relieved ours came in ones."

"Me, too," Rachel concurred with a grin. "I bet those children love living on a big plantation and romping all over the place."

"Do you ever miss Moss Haven or Savannah?"

"No. I was wise to sell it to Burke Wells. He hasn't missed a yearly payment yet. He has his sharecroppers bringing in hefty earnings for him."

"That and farming the rest of his land. He's smar

and hardworking. He was pleased to see me when I visited two weeks ago. He wants you and the children to come next time. Have you heard from Richard this week?"

"Today. I plan to write him tomorrow. I did tell you his last letter said Ramón and Rosaria got married?" Dan nodded. "Richard's being sent to South America this time. Something about trouble between Chile, Peru, and Bolivia. His skill with the Spanish language has been helpful for him again."

"Your brother did a superb job in Cuba. The truce won't last long, but at least it's quiet for now after years of fierce battle."

"He said they're calling the rebellion the Ten Years War. Sad, but it began long before '68 and it's still rumbling after '78. It isn't over."

"Richard and Peter expect a big and final war to settle things. Luke hopes it stays quiet, because he's been making runs to and from there."

"How is Peter?" she asked. "Have you heard from him lately?"

"Not in a few months. He's doing fine, still agenting," he teased.

"I doubt he or my brother will ever give it up; they love that exciting and challenging and adventurous life."

"When either or both find a woman like you, like I did, they will."

"Thank you, kind sir, but I'm the lucky one to have found you."

Dan leaned over and nibbled at her neck. Rachel giggled and squirmed. He held out his hand in seductive invitation. She met his gaze, read the enticement, and stood. Their mouths meshed in a heady kiss.

Nothing had changed their desire for each other over the years. They knew how fortunate they were to be so happy and prosperous. Their life and family were fulfilling.

They had moved Phillip's body to the McCandless family plot near Charleston, and all ghosts concerning him and the past had faded and vanished. Only good things seemed to happen to them now.

Following many kisses and caresses, they were breathless and burning with need. "I'll lock the door," Rachel said. "We don't have long, my love. Naptime only last two hours or less, and minutes are wasting."

Rachel turned after bolting the door for privacy. She gazed at the naked man awaiting her on the bed, as he had discarded his garments swiftly in his eagerness. His sable head was propped against the headboard with his back resting against pillows. His bare torso was exposed, but a light sheet concealed his lower half, a teasing ruse. She grinned.

Dan watched his wife walk to the bed and halt beside it to strip. She removed her shoes with mischievous leisure. She unbuttoned her dress and peeled it off her shoulders, then worked it over her hips, wriggling seductively as she did so. With playful tantalizing, she unlaced her chemise and slipped it over her head, exposing full breasts to his merry gaze. She worked her bloomers off and kicked them aside. Her body was still slim, sleek, and taut. Its olive covering was satiny to the touch, and he yearned to trace his fingers over it.

"You're tormenting me, woman," he said with pride and desire.

Rachel seized the sheet and whipped it aside, revealing his splendid form. "We promised we'd never have anything between us, remember?" She lay down beside him. Her dark-brown hair fanned out on the pillow and haloed her face. Her expressive eyes were like golden honey and filled with hunger for him. She raised herself to trail her fingers over his hairy chest, making tiny curls along her path. She felt his heart beating at a swift pace. Her fingers paused at his pulse

570

point to feel it racing with need. She roamed his jaw-line, smoothly shaven and strong. She sent her fingers to journey over his lips and nose. She so enjoyed touching and arousing him.

Dan shifted to send his hands and lips to work on her exquisite body. He wanted to make her senses spin wildly, as she had his. He savored the sensation of her silky skin beneath his fingertips. He roved her in all directions as if mapping a route to paradise. His hands buried themselves in her lush mane and didn't seek freedom for a time as he kissed her deeply.

They embraced and clung together, relishing the intoxicating contact. They explored each other's body with equal and rising passion.

Dan's mouth left hers to travel slowly and purpose-fully down her neck, over her bare shoulders, and around her firm breasts. He brushed his lips ever so lightly at first over each taut peak to allow his hot breathing and warm moisture to tease and enflame the straining bud. He urged his tongue to lavish bliss-ful attention there while he drank sweet nectar. He felt her quiver in anticipation and heard her groan with pleasure. He sent his hands on a sensuous mission to the steamy core of her womanhood. With skill and tenderness, he caressed her moist and satiny flesh there.

Rachel closed her eyes and absorbed the rapturous inducements. She dreamily stroked his muscular back, fondled his tight buttocks, and sought his throbbing hardness. She smiled when he sucked in a loud breath of air and stiffened for a moment as she caressed and stimulated his maleness.

Soon both were consumed by passion's flames. She didn't have to tell him she was ready and eager to have him thrust within her, and he didn't have to be told or urged. He moved atop her and slipped inside her. United, they worked as one to heighten their ravenous appetites and to appease them. They labored with skill and knowledge, as they knew from experience how to please each other and themselves.

"This is wonderful, Dan," she murmured against his mouth.

"Always, my love," he replied and sealed their lips.

They couldn't restrain themselves any longer. They ardently raced toward victory and captured it.

After, as they lay contented and aglow in each other's arms, both shifted their heads at the same time to gaze at the other. They exchanged smiles, then a tender kiss.

"I love you, Rachel, more and more every day."

"I always think I can't love you more or enjoy lovemaking more, but it happens every time. I think I've had the best experience of my life, but the next one is even better than all the others put together. I still feel weak and hot when you look at me or touch me. How I do love you, Dan."

He hugged her possessively as his heart surged with deep emotion. "Destiny, woman; we're matched, perfect for each other. I think I sensed that the first time I looked into this beautiful face and these unusual eyes. You bewitch me, wife, and don't ever break your spell over me."

"I won't, my love. Remember what you demanded and I promised?"

Dan smiled and murmured huskily, "Forever."

"Yes, Captain Daniel Slade McCandless, forever, and you'll get it."

DISCOVER DEANA JAMES!

CATCH A RISING STAR!

ROBIN ST. THOMAS

FORTUNE'S SISTERS (2616, $3.9...)

It was Pia's destiny to be a Hollywood star. She had comple... self-confidence, breathtaking beauty, and the help of her dom... neering mother. But her younger sister Jeanne began to steal th... spotlight meant for Pia, diverting attention away from the rut... lessly ambitious star. When her mother Mathilde started to retu... the advances of dashing director Wes Guest, Pia's jealousy su... faced. Her passion for Guest and desire to be the brightest star... Hollywood pitted Pia against her own family—sister against si... ter, mother against daughter. Pia was determined to be the on... survivor in the arenas of love and fame. But neither Mathilde n... Jeanne would surrender without a fight. . . .

LOVER'S MASQUERADE (2886, $4.5...)

New Orleans. A city of secrets, shrouded in mystery and magi... A city where dreams become obsessions and memories once aga... become reality. A city where even one trip, like a stop on Claud... Gage's book promotion tour, can lead to a perilous fall. For Ne... Orleans is also the home of Armand Dantine, who knows the s... crets that Claudia would conceal and the past she cannot remem... ber. And he will stop at nothing to make her love him, and w... not let her go again . . .

SENSATION (3228, $4.9...)

They'd dreamed of stardom, and their dreams came true. No... they had fame and the power that comes with it. In Hollywoo... in New York, and around the world, the names of Aurora Style... Rachel Allenby, and Pia Decameron commanded immediate a... tention—and lust and envy as well. They were stars, idols on pe... estals. And there was always someone waiting in the wings... bring them crashing down . . .

Available wherever paperbacks are sold, or order direct from t... Publisher. Send cover price plus 50¢ per copy for mailing an... handling to Zebra Books, Dept. 3764, 475 Park Avenue Sout... New York, N.Y. 10016. Residents of New York and Tenness... must include sales tax. DO NOT SEND CASH. For a free Zebr... Pinnacle catalog please write to the above address.